THE ART OF

MEGAN TREVIÑO

@IDWPUBLISHING
IDWPUBLISHING.COM

STANDARD EDITION 979-8-88724-331-3
EXCLUSIVE EDITION 979-8-88724-424-2
29 28 27 26   1 2 3 4

COVER ARTIST:
Barry J. Kelly

COLLECTION EDITOR:
Alonzo Simon

BOOK DESIGN:
Nathan Widick

Special thanks to Mike McMahan and to Risa Kessler, Marian Cordry, Dayton Ward, and John Van Citters of Paramount Global for their invaluable assistance.

For international rights, contact licensing@idwpublishing.com

EU RP (for authorities only)
eucomply OÜ
Pärnu mnt. 139b – 14
11317 Tallinn, Estonia
hello@eucompliancepartner.com
+33757690241

Contracting Partner:
Tara McCrillis, IDW Publishing | EU RP Partner: Marko Novkovic, CEO

LCARS 40274

02-654598

TABLE OF CONTENTS

INTRODUCTION BY MIKE McMAHAN

When I was in my twenties, I was an assistant at a Hollywood TV studio, and I dreamed of writing *Star Trek.* I never thought I could be so lucky, so instead I wrote tweets (for a thing called Twitter), which were imagined episodes from an eighth season of *Star Trek: The Next Generation.*

At the very inception of *Star Trek: Lower Decks*, in my first conversation with Alex Kurtzman, I imagined that the art of this show would be a marriage of styles: The characters had to look comedic while the ships and backgrounds needed to be beautiful and inspirational. In the live-action *Star Trek* shows, the costumes, alien makeup, sets, props, models, and VFX created the illusion of the future, while the actors brought the emotion and the humanity. If our show was going to work, we had to do the same in animation.

The characters (our source of comedy) had to inhabit a futuristic world. The stakes had to feel real, even when Mariner and Boimler were joking around. When Tendi looked out the back window and sighed at the beauty of the nacelles at warp, we had to sigh too.

What I didn't realize was the immense amount of work I was going to be piling onto the show's artists. Because the biggest stylistic element of *Lower Decks* was that it had to LOOK LIKE *STAR TREK.* When Rutherford said he loved the warp core, it had to really look like a warp core. The props all had to be designed to reference earlier props. The ships, costumes, the world all had to feel like *Star Trek*...which meant we had to reference, by hand, every other season and movie that had already aired. Not as an Easter egg hunt, or as hollow nostalgia. To be *Star Trek* we had to follow the rules of *Star Trek* more than any other *Star Trek* that had *Star Trekked* before us...because we were going to be funny. We were going to have a good time, and honor the other shows. We had to love *Star Trek* more than anyone else had ever loved *Star Trek.*

Which is why every episode of *Lower Decks* required new backgrounds and characters. Every episode was very, very hard to make.

But we did it, and it was worth it.

When you watch *Lower Decks,* you get a tiny miracle. If you're new to *Star Trek,* then it's a fun show full of lovable characters in sci-fi situations. If you're a *Star Trek* fan, *Lower Decks* feels like a continuation of all the *Trek* shows before it. The cast makes you laugh, the music makes you feel, but the art is what holds it all together and creates a *Trek* world.

I had no idea, while tweeting, that someday I would get to create a Starfleet ship, and uniforms, and characters you'd want to hang out with in space. We had some old friends stop by, and met some new ones along the way. We created new alien species and dug deeper into cultures that hadn't been on TV in decades. We played with all the elements I love about *Trek* while, sometimes, expanding *Trek* into new areas too.

This is more than an art book. It's a thank-you note to everyone on the *Lower Decks* team who spent years (and a pandemic) building something unexpected, funny, and beautiful. Know that there are thousands of images that didn't make the cut, but this book gives you a good sense of the thought, passion, and talent that went into making an amazing five seasons of *Star Trek.*

Thank you to Barry Kelly, Megan Treviño, Brad Winters, and Nollan Obena for always being at my side, translating my stupid notes, and helping make this show I love. And even bigger thanks to the army of artists, actors, writers, musicians, and everyone who lent their talents to *Lower Decks.*

INTRODUCTION BY BARRY J. KELLY

Five seasons. Fifty episodes. A crossover. Three to four hundred shots per episode—roughly 17,500 shots total. Over a thousand minutes of funny, heartfelt scripts transformed into sci-fi comedy by an incredible team of artists.

That's *Lower Decks.*

This crew was made of damn strong stuff. Through a global pandemic, a network change, and a writers' strike, they still delivered what I think is the best sci-fi comedy of the last decade.

It gives me immense joy that this book gives a glimpse into all the fantastic work that made it to screen—and some that didn't. Some pieces were made just for ourselves, to get the bad ideas out of our heads and make room for the good ones.

Like many *Star Trek* fans, I was skeptical when I first heard about a sitcom-style *Trek.* But that doubt vanished fast as I read the first page of the first script and said, "Oh s***—this works!"

The first time I met Mike McMahan, he walked into our storyboard handout wearing a T-shirt covered in Counselor Trois in different colors. "This is my kinda guy," I thought. I hope that some of his doodles are in this book by the time it comes out because I love them as much as he probably hates them! Ha!

I grew up on the *Star Trek* feature films and *The Next Generation*—my ultimate sci-fi comfort food. A *Lower Decks* script was just as dense as any 44-minute episode of Trek, crammed into a 22-minute animated package: "Fun-size!" I was lucky to be surrounded by artists who cared as deeply as I did about both the story and the art.

I started as an episodic director working alongside my partner Juno Lee. When he had to step away, I became supervising director for the rest of the series. "S.D.," a common role in animation—basically, I was the director for the directors. It's like I'm the crew's lawyer, helping bridge the gap between the writers and the artists so we could compromise and tell the best version of our story. While the episodic directors focus on the specifics of a singular episode, I focus on the entire season as a whole, from pre-production all the way to post delivering the final mix of an episode.

In this book you'll see the vision of our longtime art director, Nollan Obena—whose eye for that "'90s future" aesthetic helped bring the *U.S.S. Cerritos* to life. (His IMDb page is basically a flex, go check it out!) You'll also see the work of character designers like Alex Pelletier and Marisa Livingston, whose design passes brought out the weird, the wild, and the deeply human in all our characters. Many, many other artists will be featured here, character designers, background designers, painters, prop designers, animators, 3D modelers, and compositors. Our producers may have some fun doodles in here as well! Soak it all in and then read through it all over again!

So whether you're a lifelong *Trek* fan, an animation nerd, or just someone who likes looking at cool spaceship art and weird aliens, I hope this book brings you as much joy as we had making the show. Every tribble, every moopsy!, every sarcastic Vulcan salute—someone obsessed over it. *Lower Decks* was made by people who loved *Star Trek* and loved making each other laugh. This book is a thank-you to the crew, and a love letter to the fans who kept at warp speed. Enjoy flipping through it. And as they say on the *Cerritos:*

LOWER DECKS!!!
LOWER DECKS!!!
LOWER DECKS!!!!

CHAPTER 01

LCARS 40274

02-654598

THE LOWER DECKERS

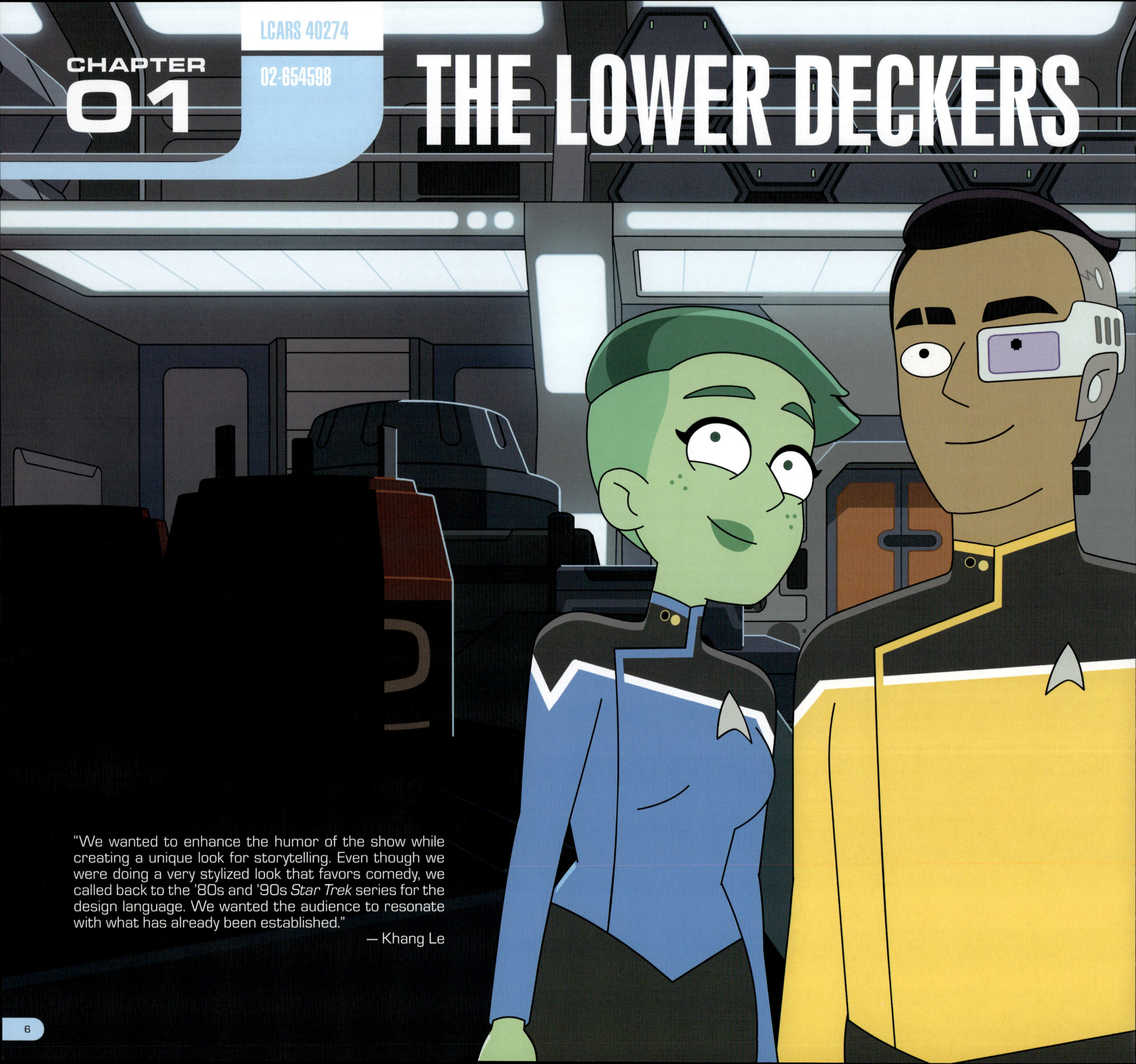

"We wanted to enhance the humor of the show while creating a unique look for storytelling. Even though we were doing a very stylized look that favors comedy, we called back to the '80s and '90s *Star Trek* series for the design language. We wanted the audience to resonate with what has already been established."

— Khang Le

ENSIGN/LIEUTENANT JUNIOR GRADE

BECKETT MARINER

HUMAN

VOICED BY

TAWNY NEWSOME

Mariner is the spiritual lead of the show. We wanted her to be visually somebody who looked distinctly Starfleet from *Star Trek: The Next Generation* (TNG), but also had her sleeves rolled up to have a bit of a Miles O'Brien on *Star Trek: Deep Space Nine* (DS9) vibe; the everyman with her hair in a ponytail. She's the star of the show.

smaller nose + softer jaw + smaller ear + centered hair + smaller mouth + boots
collar easier for animation
smaller eyes
smaller head
redraw

"The process of figuring out the design of Mariner and Boimler was exciting, because I don't really get the chance to do it. As animation director, I usually get the design and that's what I have to work with."

— Alexandre Pelletier

We wanted the uniforms to feel TNG, but not quite. We made the colors brighter, more vibrant, so they stood out as the animated show. We also made them asymmetrical and added the white line on the chest to really say that we're taking place after TNG. Even though it was really tough for animation, we stuck with it, and they look great

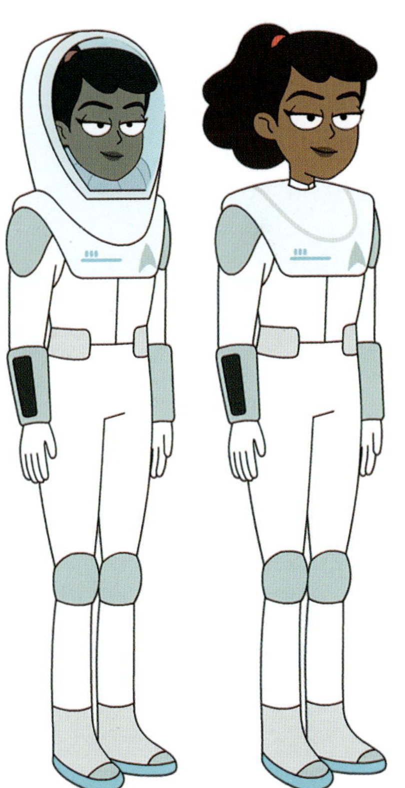

ENSIGN/LIEUTENANT JUNIOR GRADE

BRADWARD BOIMLER

HUMAN

VOICED BY

JACK QUAID

Boimler was supposed to look like every *Star Trek* lead: a competent guy that follows the rules. But we did give him purple hair with a spikey silhouette to make him stand out. He needed to easily read as Boimler in a crowd.

02-654598

LCARS 40274

"This show has a good balance of different colorful personalities, which affect the way they move."

— Alexandre Pelletier

Pupils #1
Pupils #2
Pupils #3
Pupils #4
Pupils #5
Pupils #6
Good for scared expressions
Good medium size
Good for characters on drugs

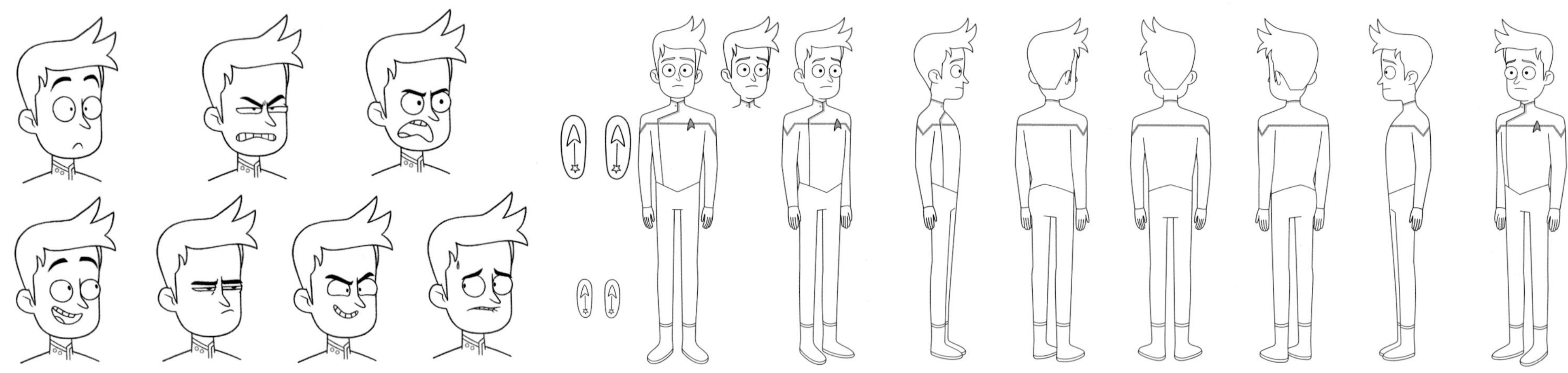

We definitely took inspiration from the "Monster Maroon" uniforms of *Star Trek II: The Wrath of Khan*. We liked that the flap could be opened, which gave the uniforms a more dynamic personality. After the fact, we saw an unused uniform design for *Star Trek Generations* that also had a flap. Mike recalled the TNG toy lineup with this design, but it wasn't in our heads while designing the uniforms for *Lower Decks*. It was kismet. We were cooking with the same ingredients.

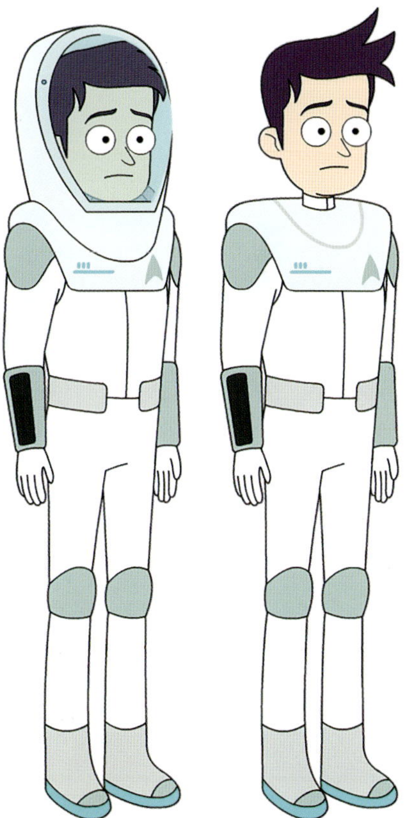

ENSIGN/LIEUTENANT JUNIOR GRADE

D'VANA TENDI

ORION

VOICED BY

NOËL WELLS

Tendi is so excited to be in Starfleet and geeks out on all things science. We didn't want her to look like an over-sexualized Orion like we were used to seeing. So we gave her short hair that reads more as a Starfleet nerd instead of a male-gaze kind of character.

02-654598

LCARS 40274

"I really like drawing Mariner and Tendi. Tendi has a big personality with expressions that we can push. She was always a bit more exaggerated. Mariner is the other aspect of the show, which is more actiony with strong poses. She's fierce. There's an intensity that comes with Mariner that you don't often get in comedies."

— Alexandre Pelletier

my favorite
slightly darker green
slightly darker green
slightly darker green
slightly darker green
1
2
smaller nose
3
smaller nose + less makeup
4
smaller nose + less makeup + smaller eyes + less exaggerated mouth
LIP SHAPE EXPLORATION
LIKE HAIR
NOT THIS HAIR STYLE
LIKE THIS HEAD SHAPE. TRY HAIRSTYLES ON THIS.
LIP COLOR CAN CHANGE TO BE LIGHTER THAN THIS. BUT KEEP THEM SELF-TRACE. NO BLACK OUTLINES.

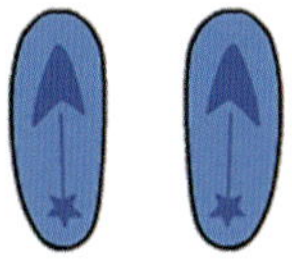

"Personally, when I go on a hike, I like looking at the trail and seeing the shape and pattern my shoes are making. I thought if the crew are going to all these different planets, it would be cool to see their mark. We gave medical white boots because that seemed clean and sterile."

— Antonio Canobbio

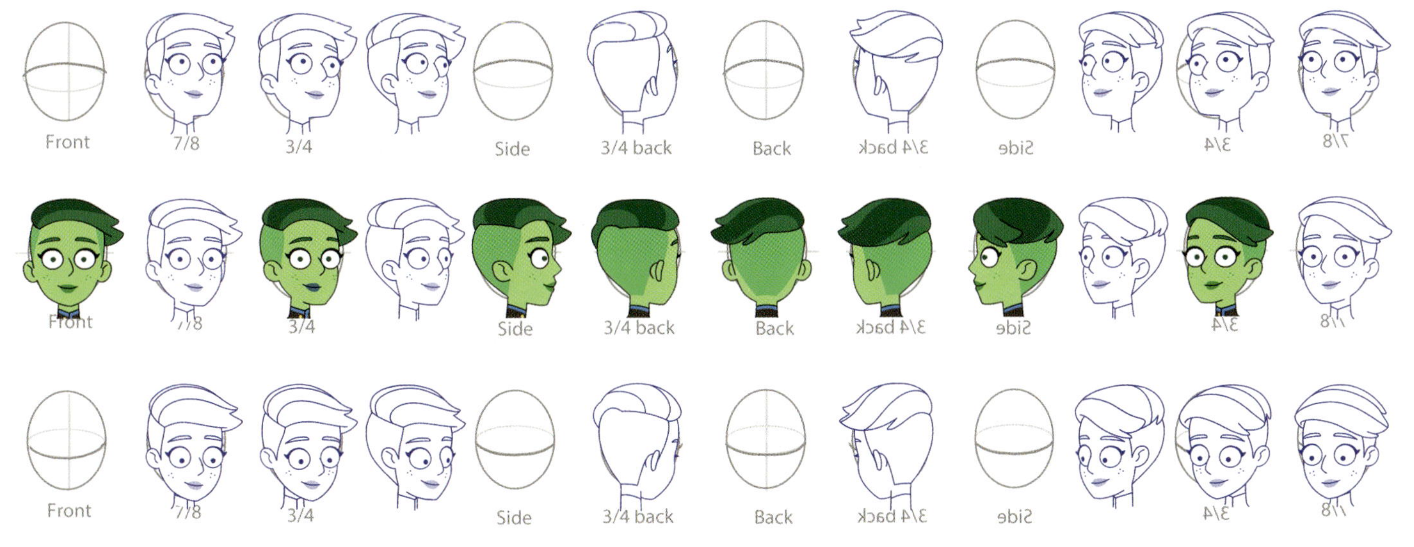

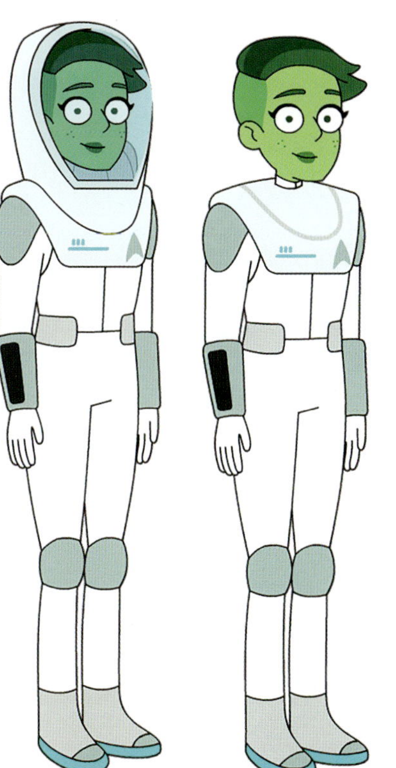

ENSIGN/LIEUTENANT JUNIOR GRADE

SAMANTHAN RUTHERFORD

HUMAN

VOICED BY

EUGENE CORDERO

Rutherford is our Data and our Spock. He's so into technology that he's actually wearing it. But the reality is that it's all still new to him, and he doesn't have it all figured out.

02-654598

LCARS 40274

smoother chin + smaller ear

"We wanted to go with something unique and simplified for design (of the uniforms) to make room for acting."
— Antonio Canobbio

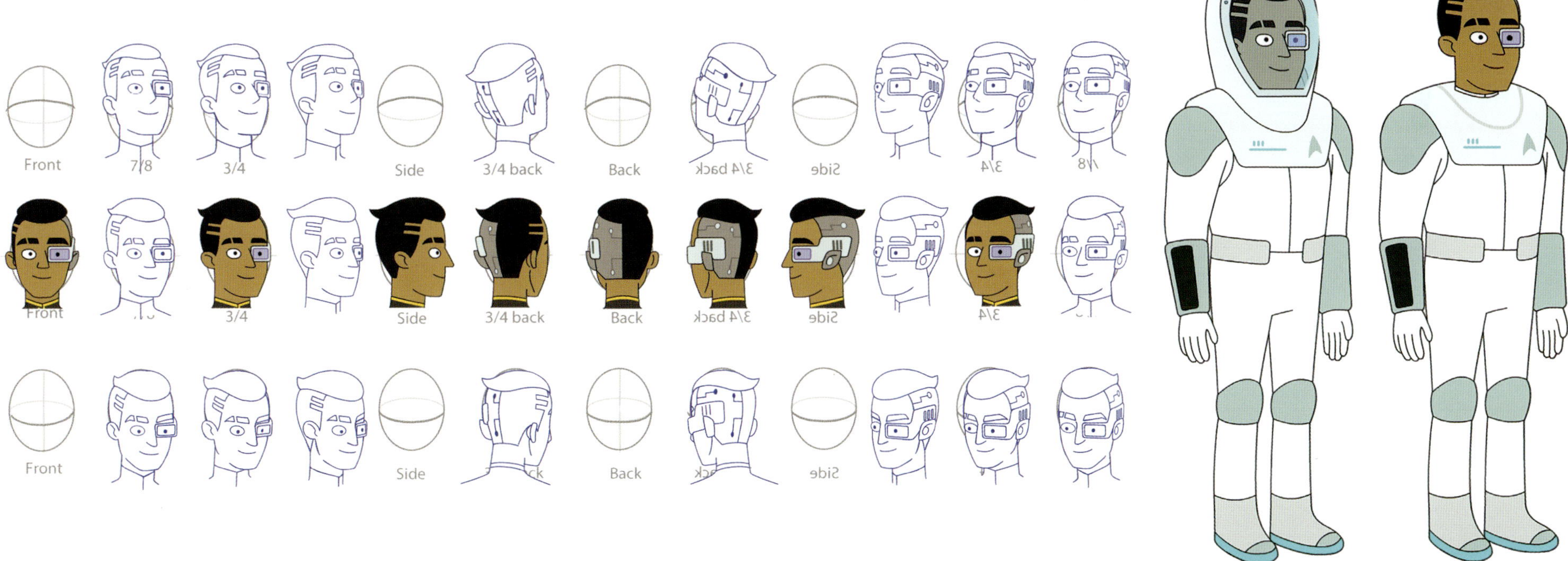

CHAPTER 02

LCARS 40274

02-654598

THE BRIDGE CREW

SYS 8554.1
SCIENCE

CAPTAIN CAROL FREEMAN

HUMAN

The initial idea was that we were going to kill off the bridge crew like inverted "redshirt" characters, but then we kept them alive, mostly.

We needed to design them like they were stars of a show that we weren't watching. Ensigns needed to look up to them. Our fierce Captain Freeman is stern with a streak in her hair.

VOICED BY

DAWNN LEWIS

Front
7/8
3/4
Side
3/4 back
Back
3/4
Side
3/4 back
Back
Front
3/4
Side
3/4 back
Back

COMMANDER JACK RANSOM

HUMAN

VOICED BY
JERRY O'CONNELL

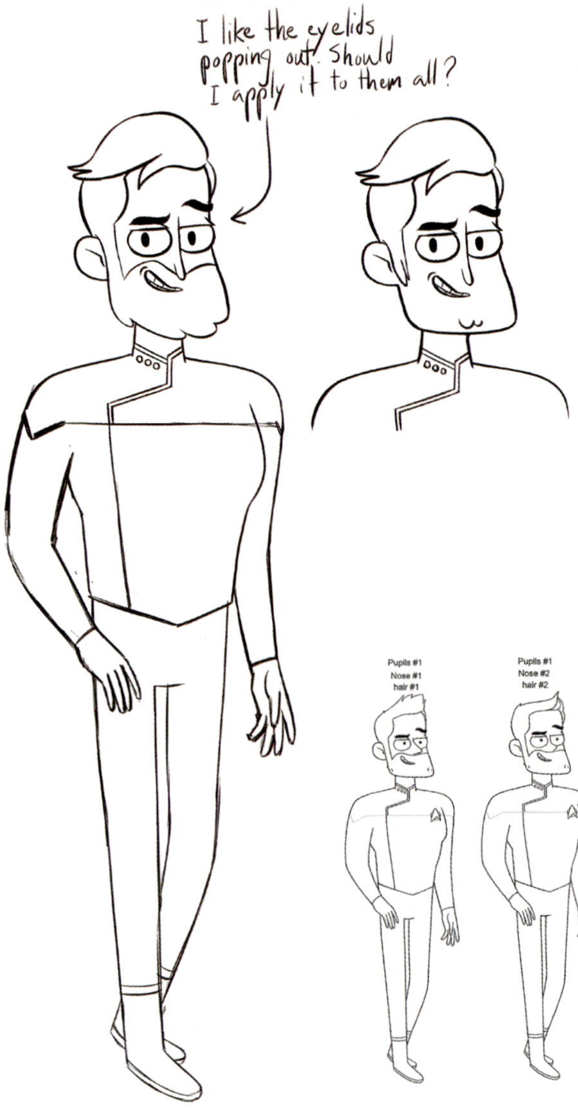

Ransom had to feel like Riker times ten. We often called him California Riker. He's tall, broad shouldered, handsome. We wanted you to feel his commanding energy but also for him to be someone that you could roll your eyes at.

I like the eyelids popping out. Should I apply it to them all?

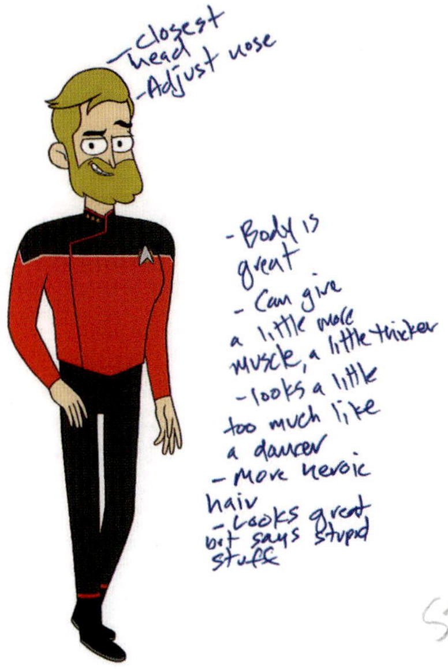

-closest head
-Adjust nose

-Body is great
-Can give a little more muscle, a little thicker
-looks a little too much like a dancer
-More heroic hair
-Looks great but says stupid stuff

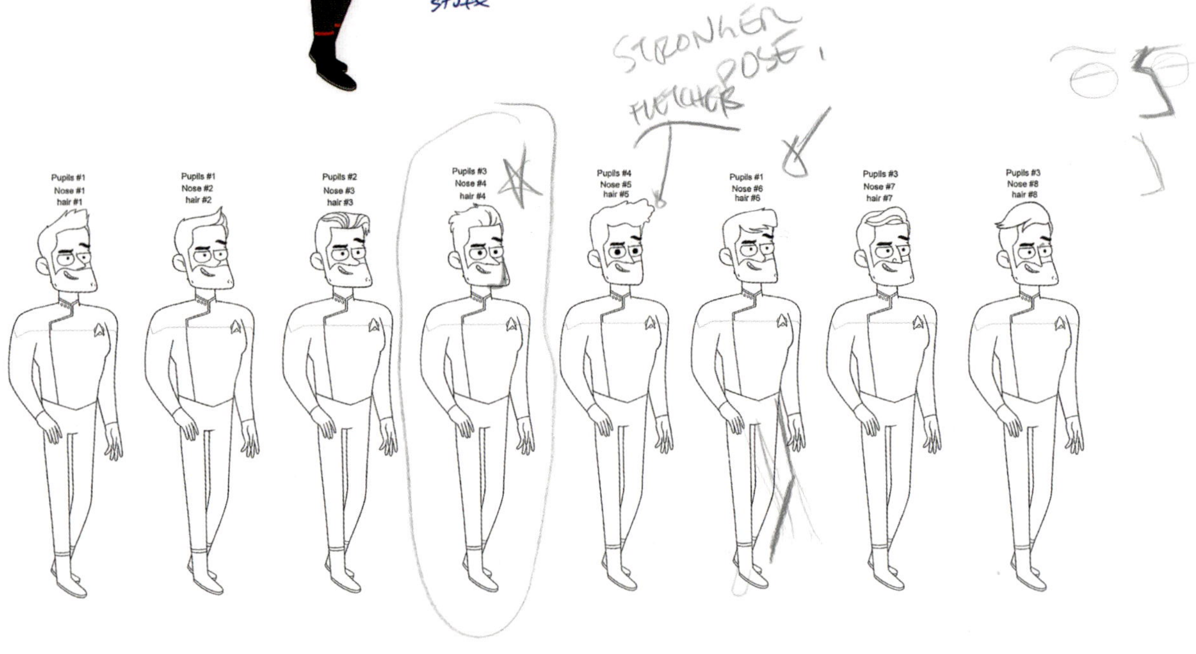

STRONGER POSE!

FLETCHER

Pupils #1 Nose #1 hair #1

Pupils #1 Nose #2 hair #2

Pupils #2 Nose #3 hair #3

Pupils #3 Nose #4 hair #4

Pupils #4 Nose #5 hair #5

Pupils #1 Nose #6 hair #6

Pupils #3 Nose #7 hair #7

Pupils #3 Nose #8 hair #8

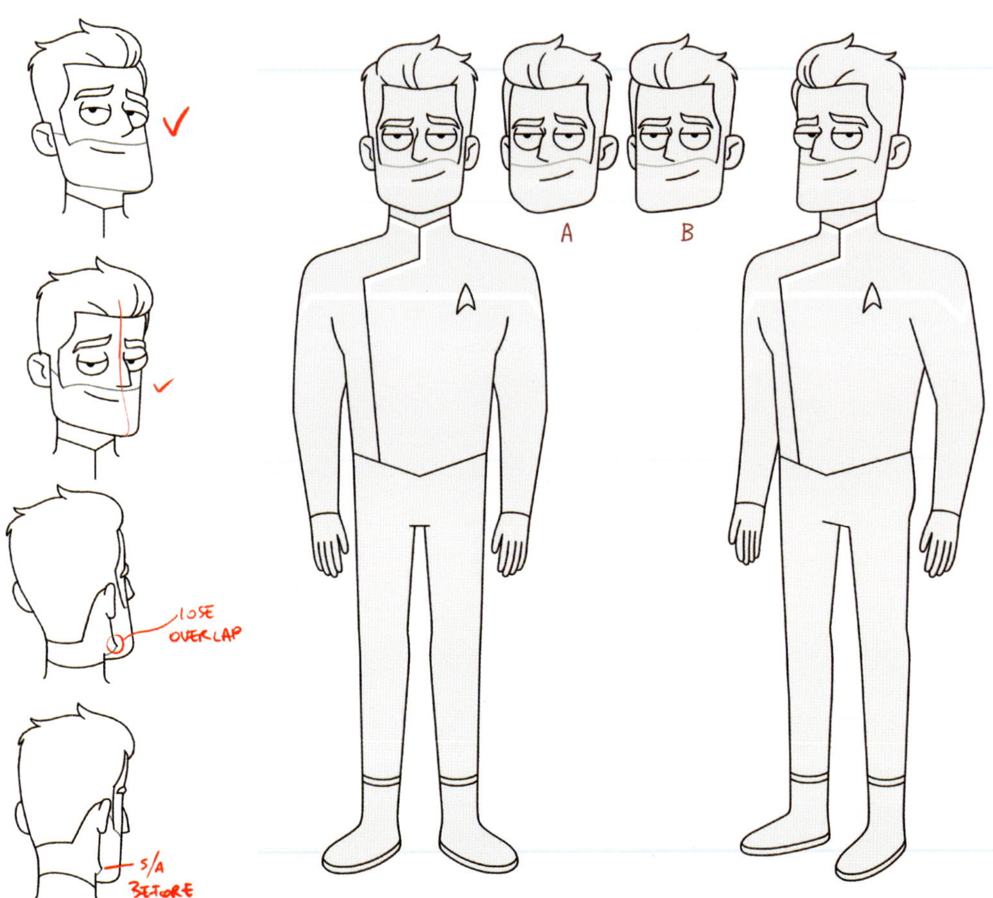

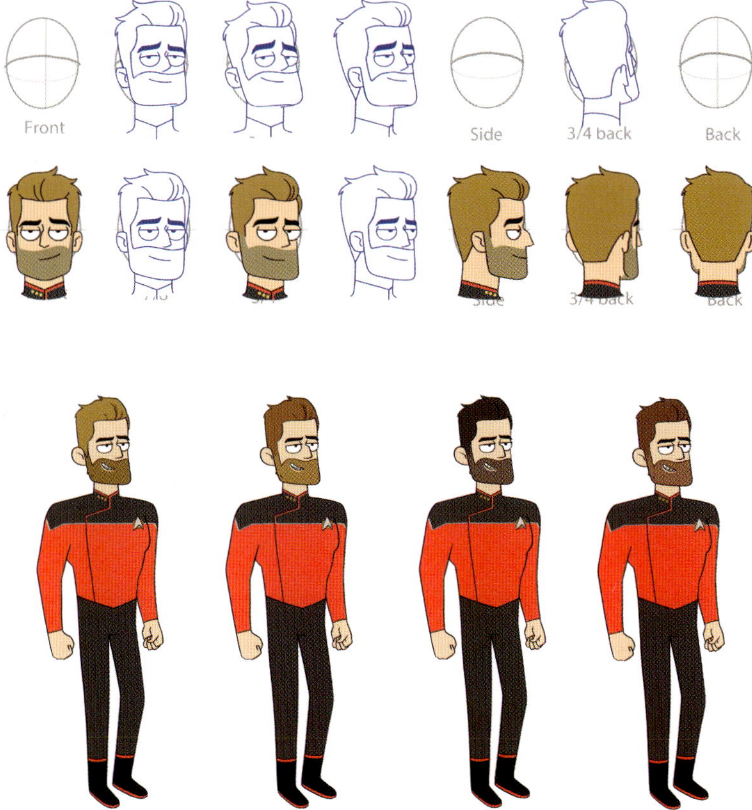

"There were some preexisting rules that we were following like the sideburns had to come to a point."

— Alexandre Pelletier

DOCTOR T'ANA
CAITIAN

VOICED BY
GILLIAN VIGMAN

Doctor T'Ana is a mix between Bones and Doctor Pulaski. She's based on an alien species from *Star Trek: The Animated Series* (TAS) that had a sexy design. However, we made her hunched over and crusty, like a feral alley cat, to match her personality.

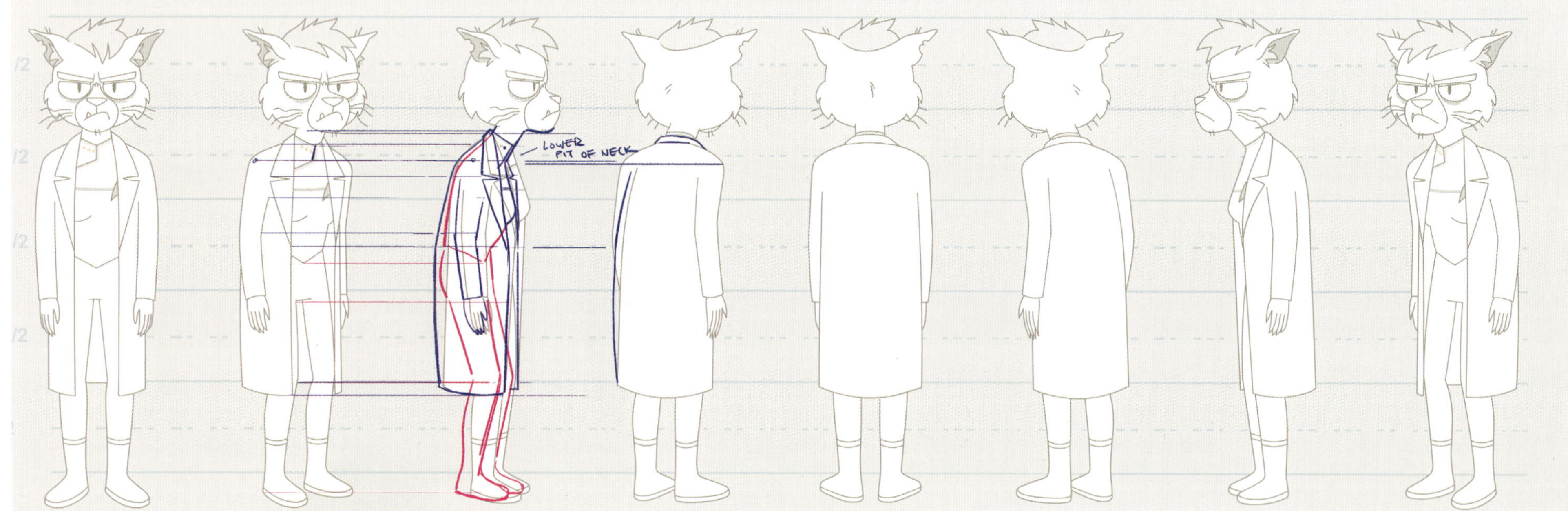

- a little further from where we were.
- Give her cat pupils
- Mess w/ hands, not so pointy
Front
7/8
Side
3/4 back
Back
Front
7/8
3/4
Side
3/4 back
Back
Front
7/8
Side
3/4 back
Back

LIEUTENANT SHAXS BAJORAN

VOICED BY

FRED TATASCIORE

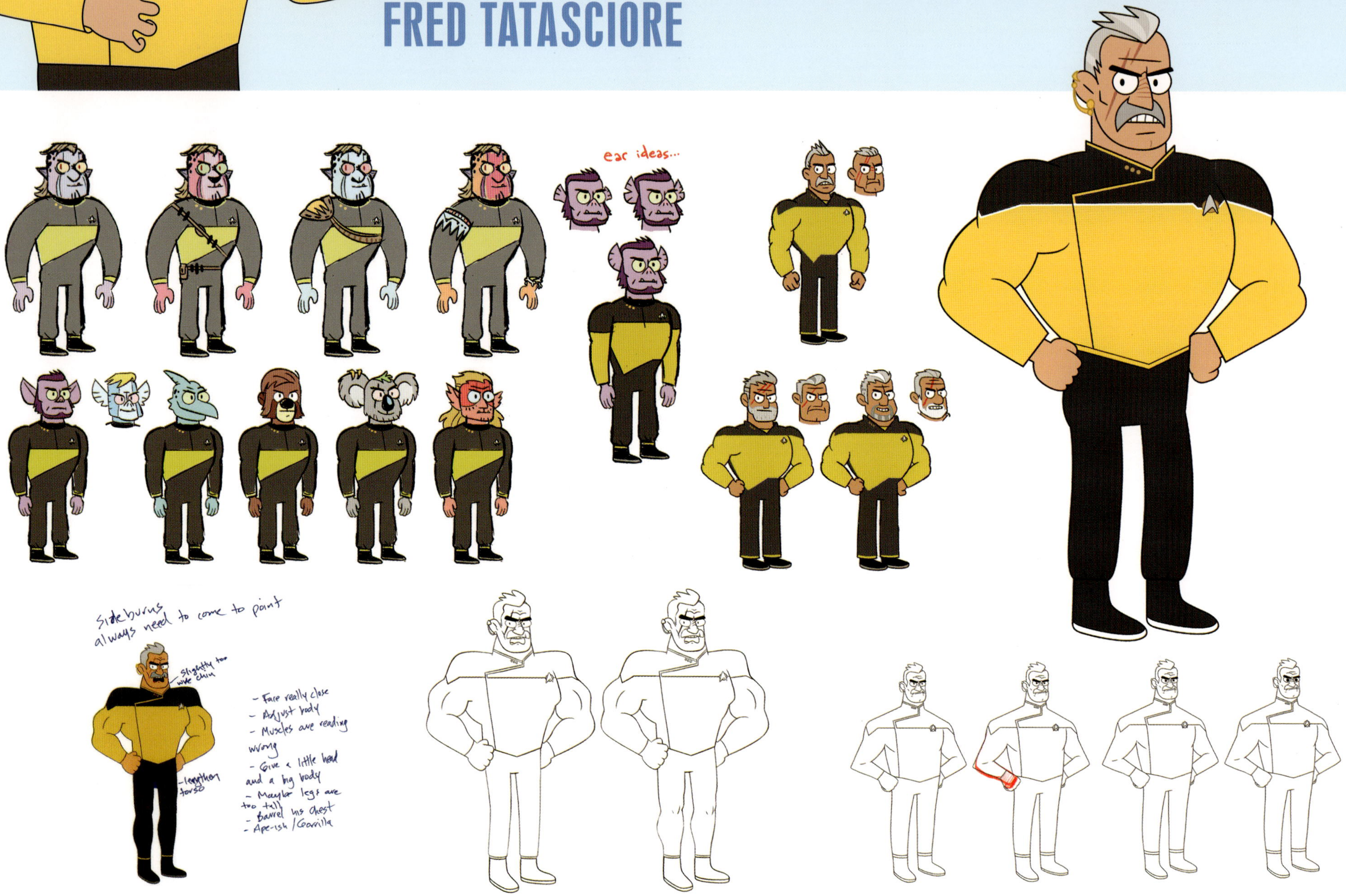

Our head of security is a big alien dude. Bajorans are already tied into a military vibe, so it made sense for Shaxs. His big stature, scarred eye, and gruff voice are also a great juxtaposition to his softer side as Papa Bear.

ear ideas...

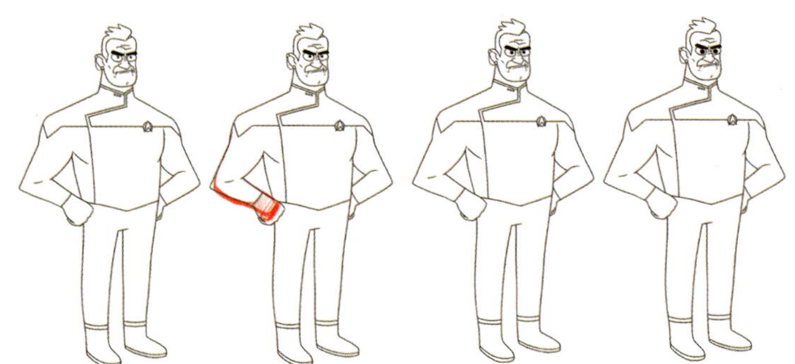

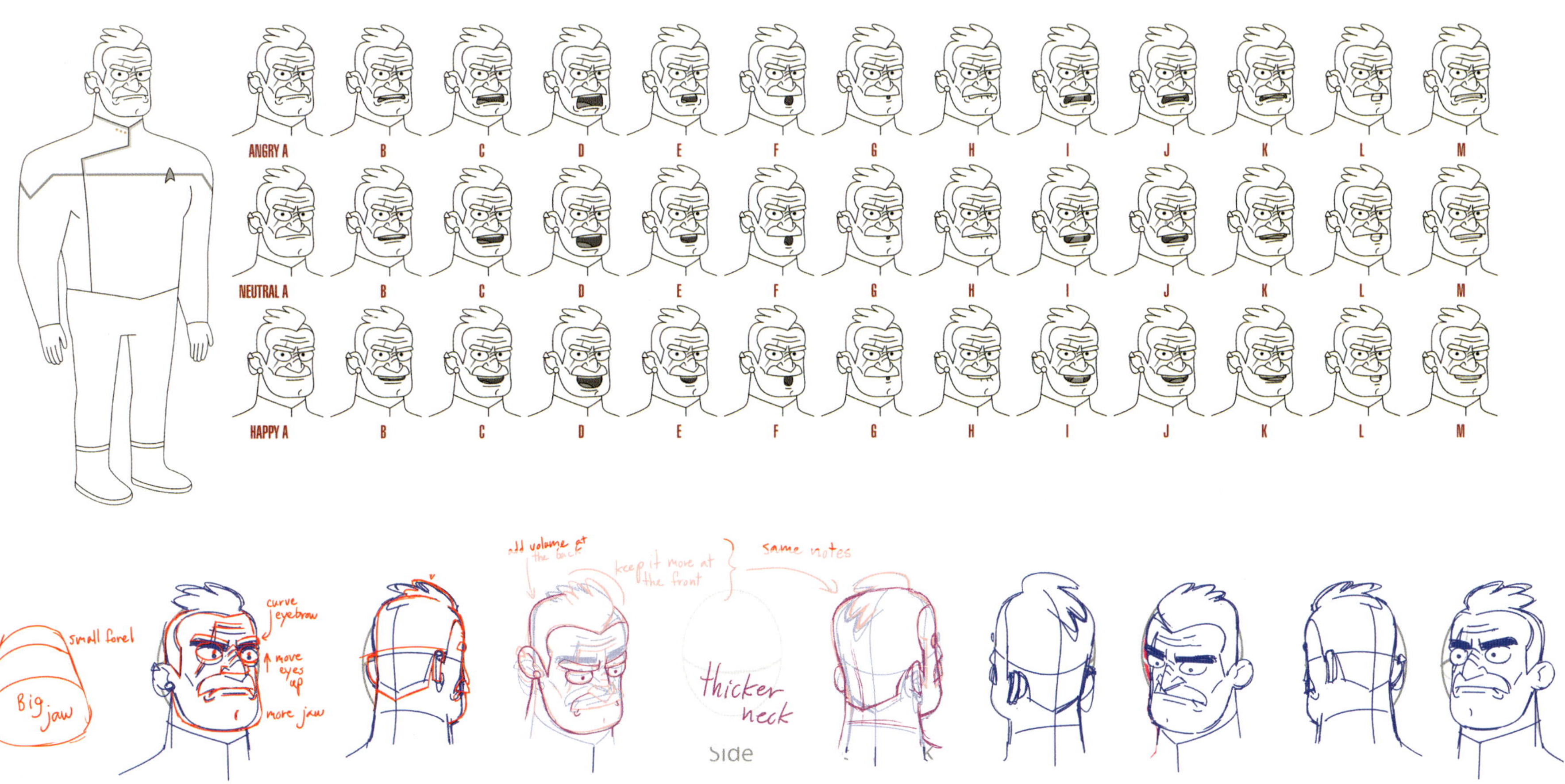
ANGRY A
B
C
D
E
F
G
H
I
J
K
L
M
NEUTRAL A
B
C
D
E
F
G
H
I
J
K
L
M
HAPPY A
B
C
D
E
F
G
H
I
J
K
L
M
small forel
Big jaw
curve eyebrow
move eyes up
more jaw
add volume at the back
keep it more at the front
same notes
thicker neck
Side

LIEUTENANT COMMANDER ANDARITHIO "ANDY" BILLUPS

HYSPERIAN

Billups is our super sweet, bright-eyed, mustachioed chief engineer.

VOICED BY

PAUL SCHEER

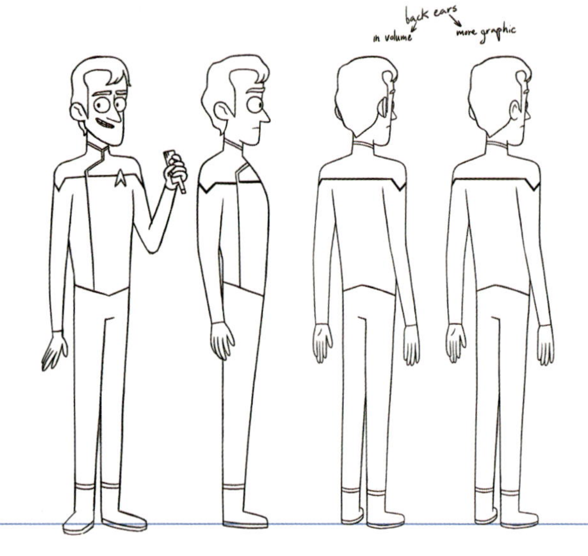

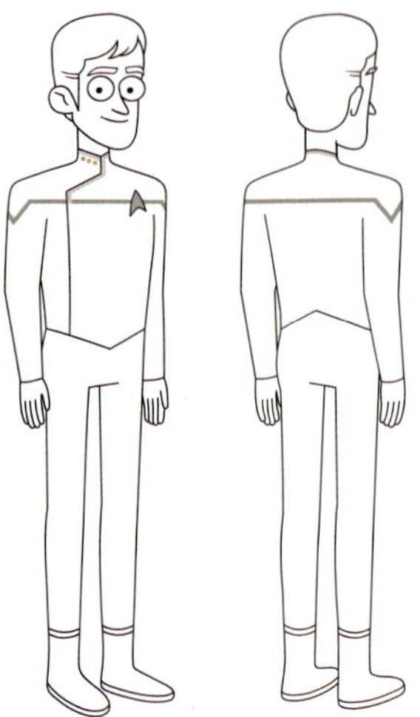

LIEUTENANT JUNIOR GRADE

KAYSHON

TAMARIAN

We wanted Kayshon to look like Captain Dathon from TNG: "Darmok." And all Tamarians carry a dagger, so we needed to make sure Kayshon had his.

VOICED BY

CARL TART

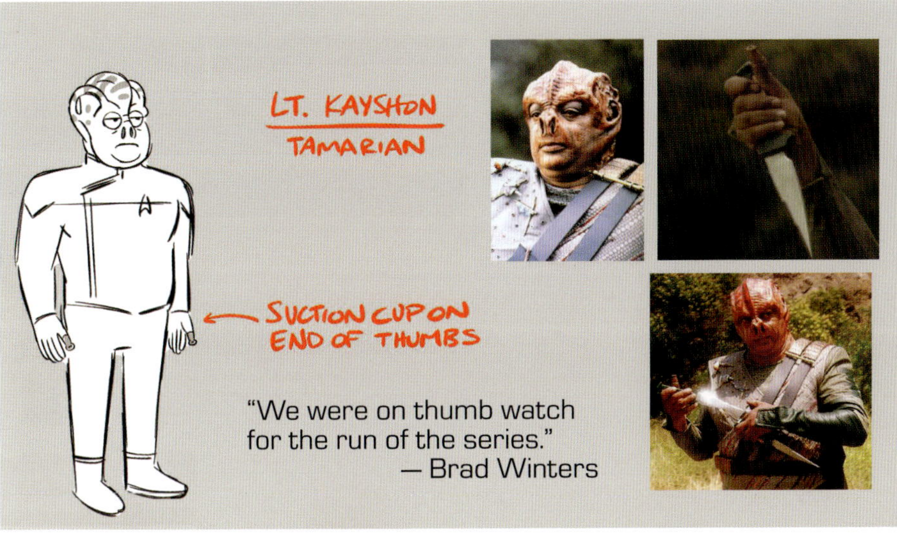

"We were on thumb watch for the run of the series."
— Brad Winters

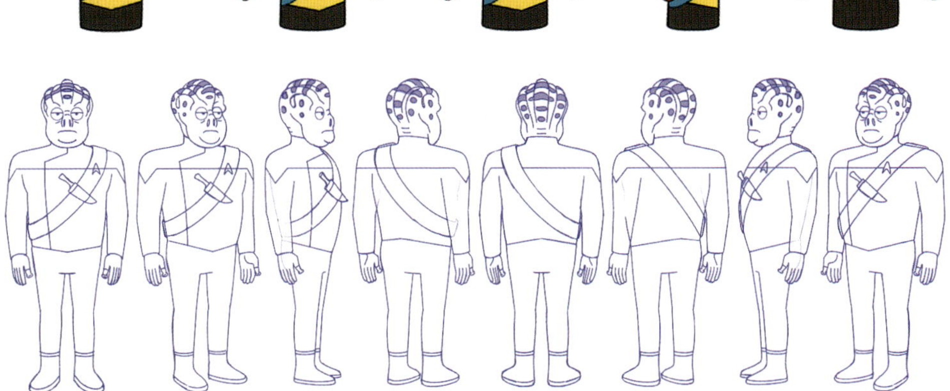

"Kayshon was a pretty easy design to get through because it's like you put these suction cups on the end of the thumbs, and that orange color just sells it. He was great. He was cute."
— Barry J. Kelly

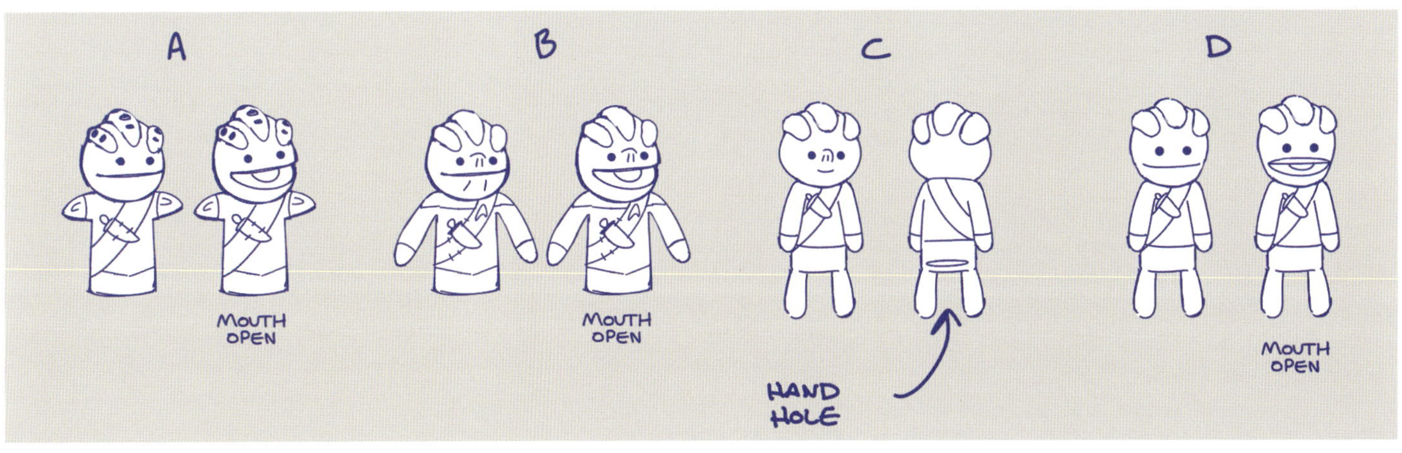

CHAPTER 03

LCARS 40274

02-654598

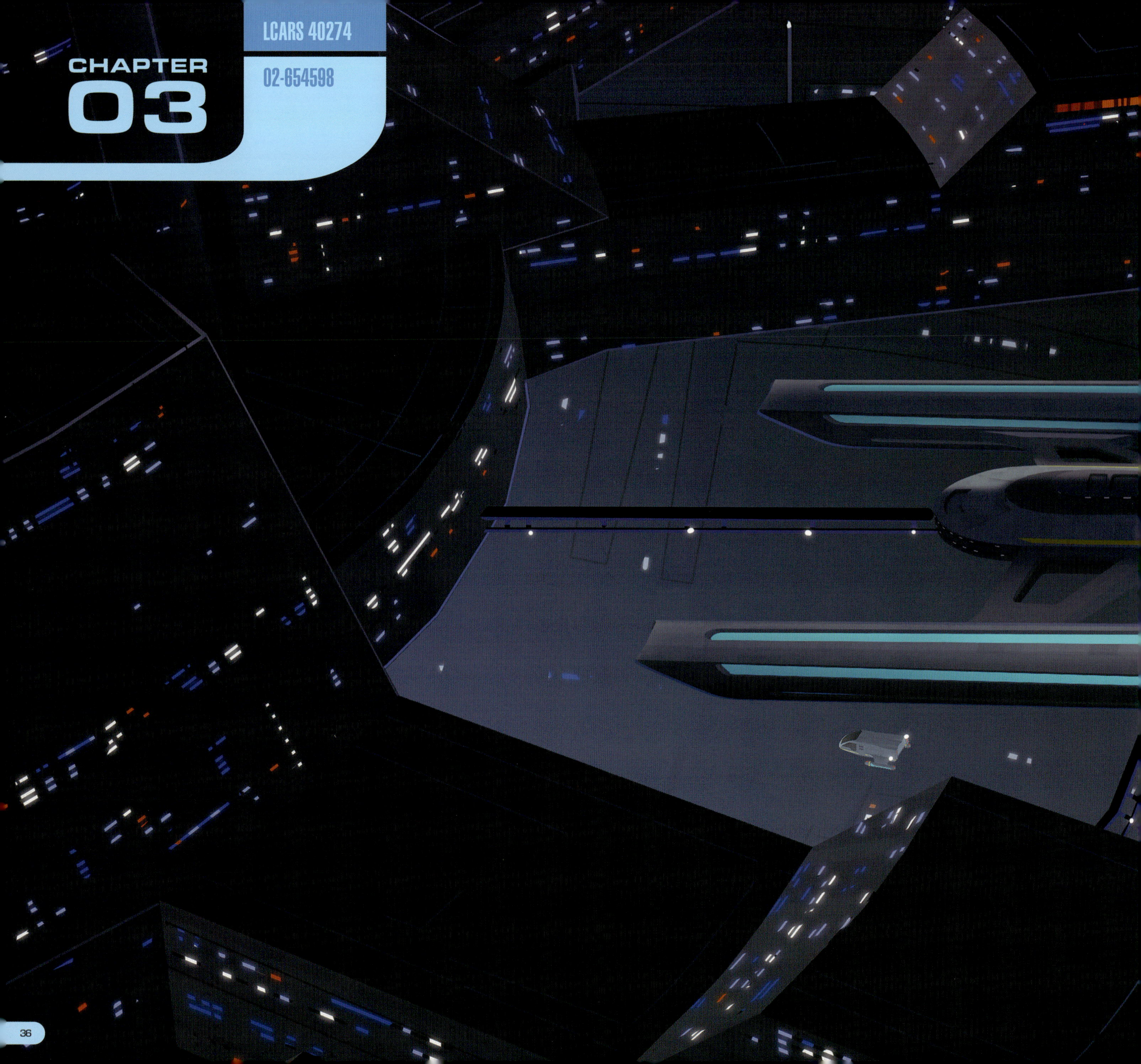

LCARS 40274

02-654598

U.S.S. CERRITOS

CALIFORNIA-CLASS STARSHIP

REGISTRY NUMBER: **NCC-75567**

We initially thought that we had to build a ship based on what already existed, like what a *Galaxy*-class ship would look like now, but then we realized that we could make our own ship.

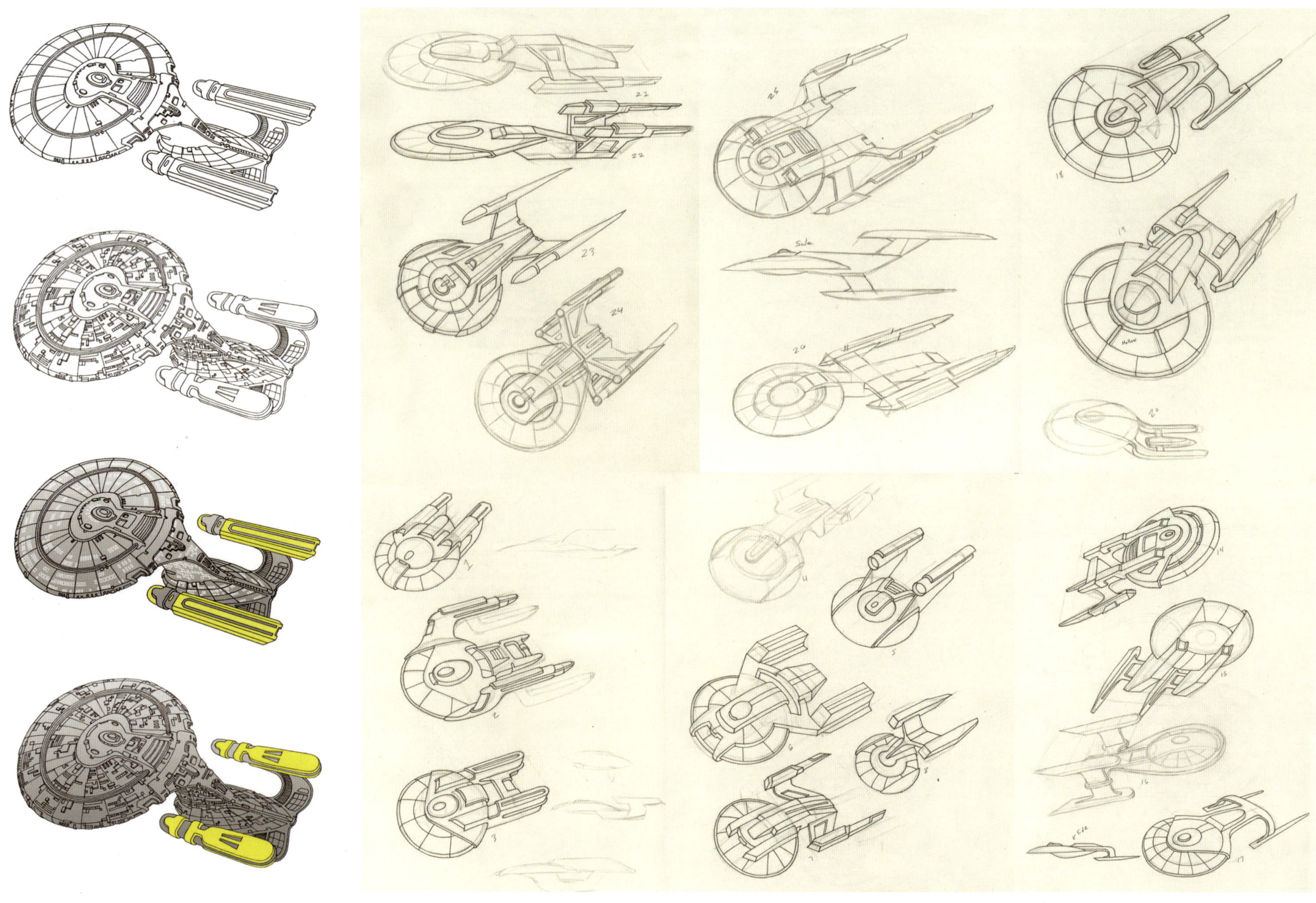

We wanted the silhouette to look like a ship we've never seen before, but still Starfleet. The struts that connect the nacelles to the dish are utilitarian and look like clunky, industrial construction equipment. We made the nacelles look like skates.

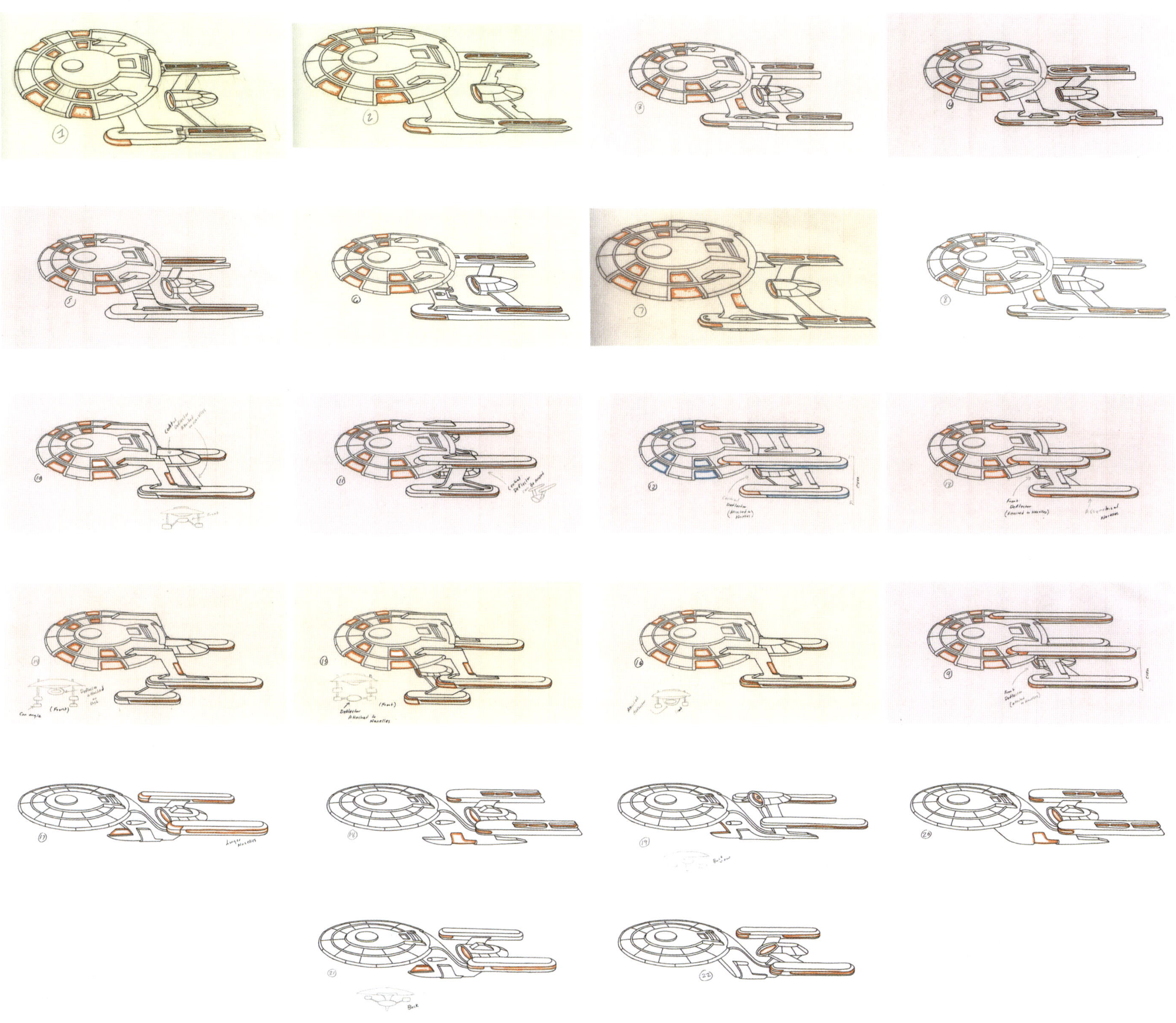

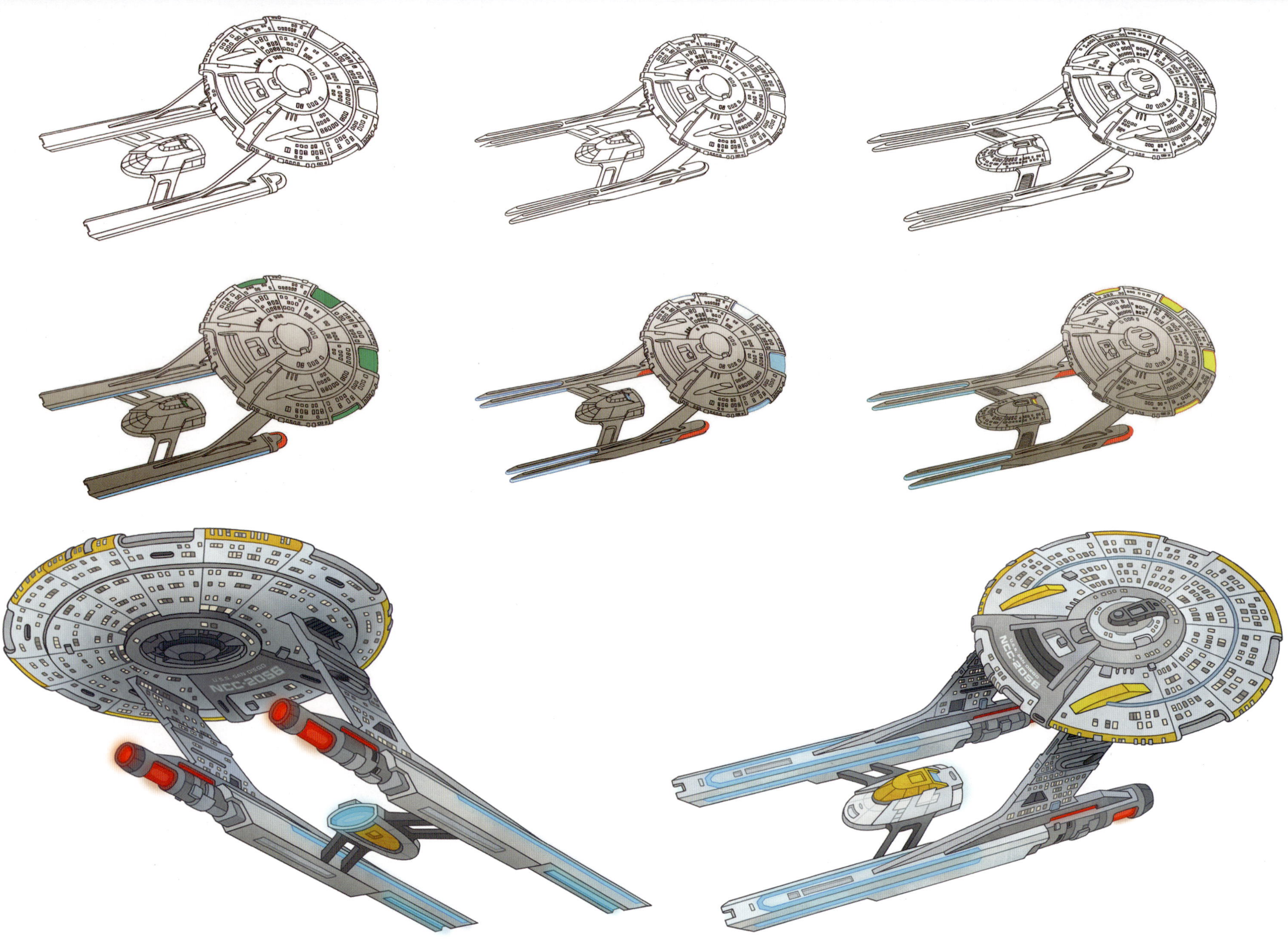

Mike McMahan always wanted colorful paint on the hull. This allowed us to have one ship design that we could differentiate with accent colors and build out a whole *California*-class fleet. We also added the *Cerritos* name on the back to look similar to a tow truck or a lower-back tattoo that we see whenever the ship leaves.

“In season two, we gave the *Cerritos* a bit of a ‘glow-up.’ We were avoiding using too much 3D in season one, but then we found ourselves with a model that didn’t have enough details in close-up shots that we needed. So we took a moment to revise the details and greebles so that we could go in tighter and not be as vague.”

— Barry J. Kelly

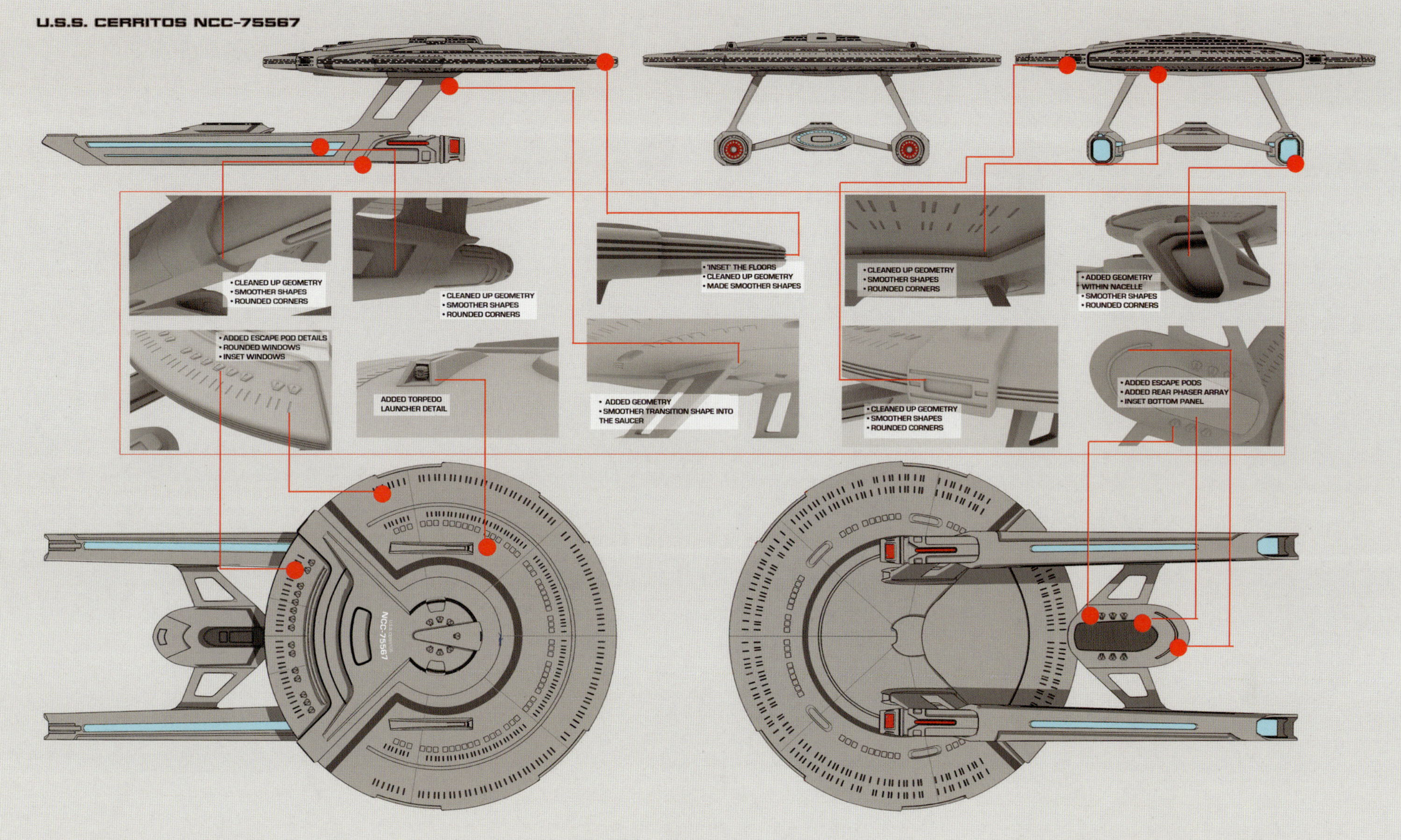

“The geometry was a lot simpler in season one. We did a whole overhaul of the geometry, such as adding details to torpedo launchers on top. We suggested escape pods in season one but defined them in season two.”

— Barry J. Kelly

“In season one, the lights in all of the windows were on the entire time, but the crew needed to sleep. So we updated it to not have all windows on at the same time. We also knew we were getting a captain’s yacht, so we wanted to suggest panels for that.“

— Barry J. Kelly

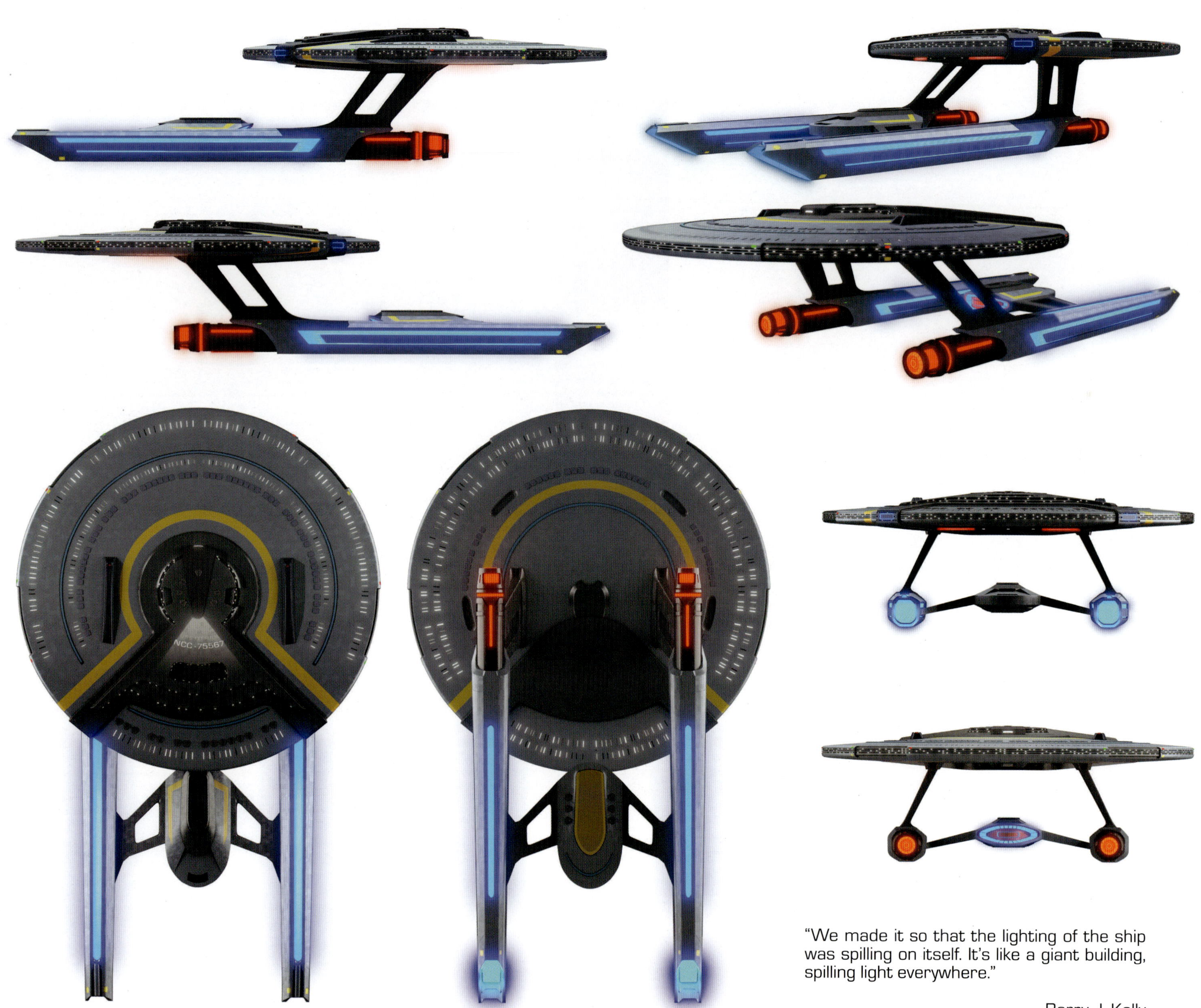

"We made it so that the lighting of the ship was spilling on itself. It's like a giant building, spilling light everywhere."

— Barry J. Kelly

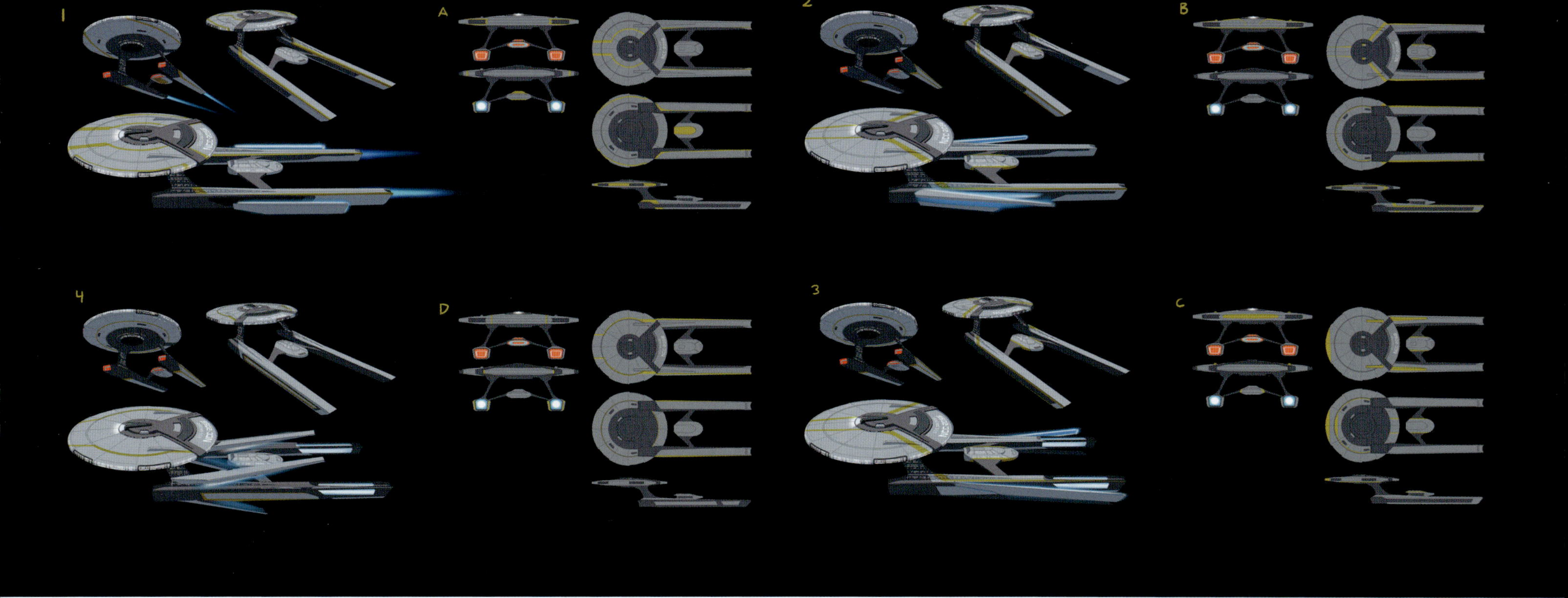

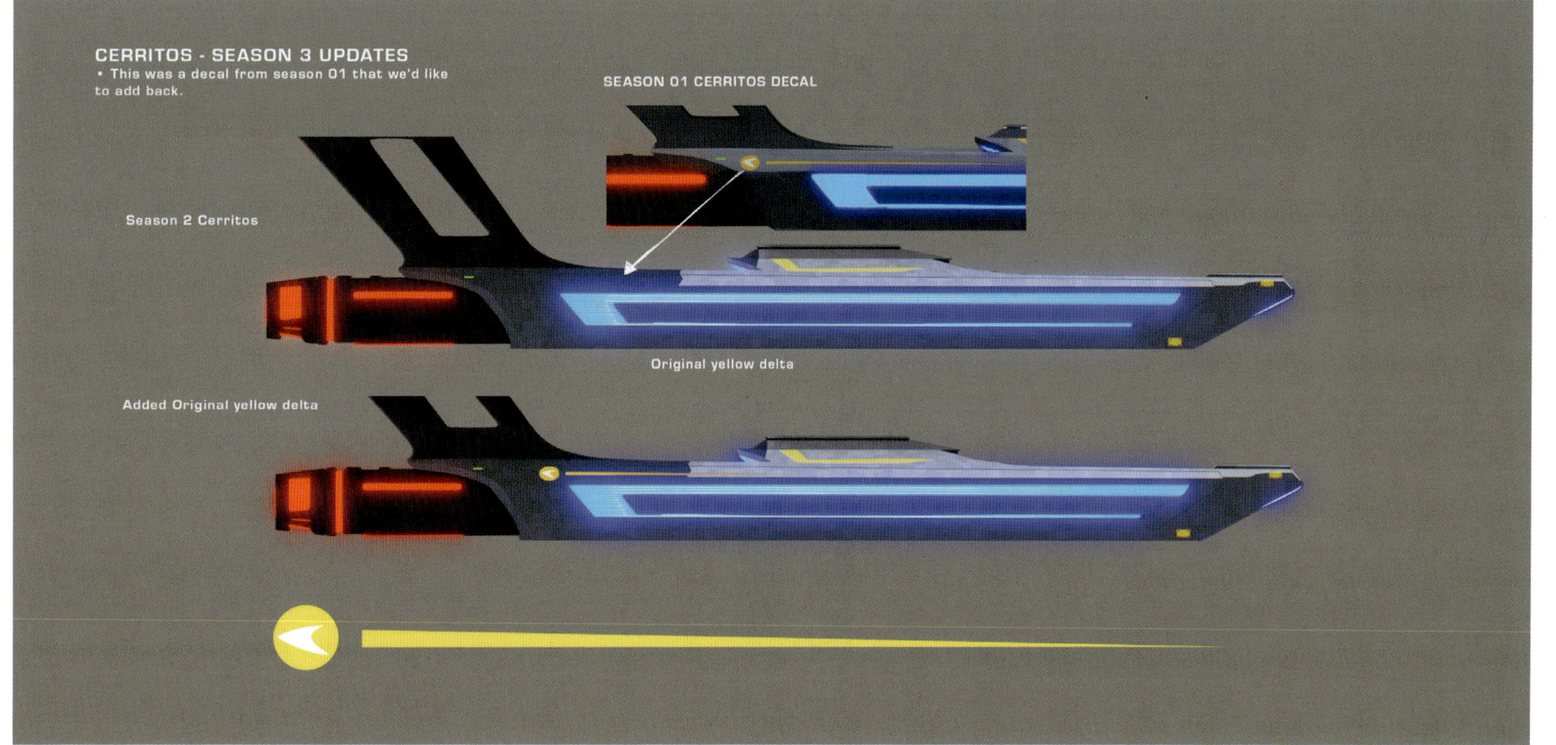

CERRITOS - SEASON 3 UPDATES
• This was a decal from season 01 that we'd like to add back.
SEASON 01 CERRITOS DECAL
Season 2 Cerritos
Original yellow delta
Added Original yellow delta

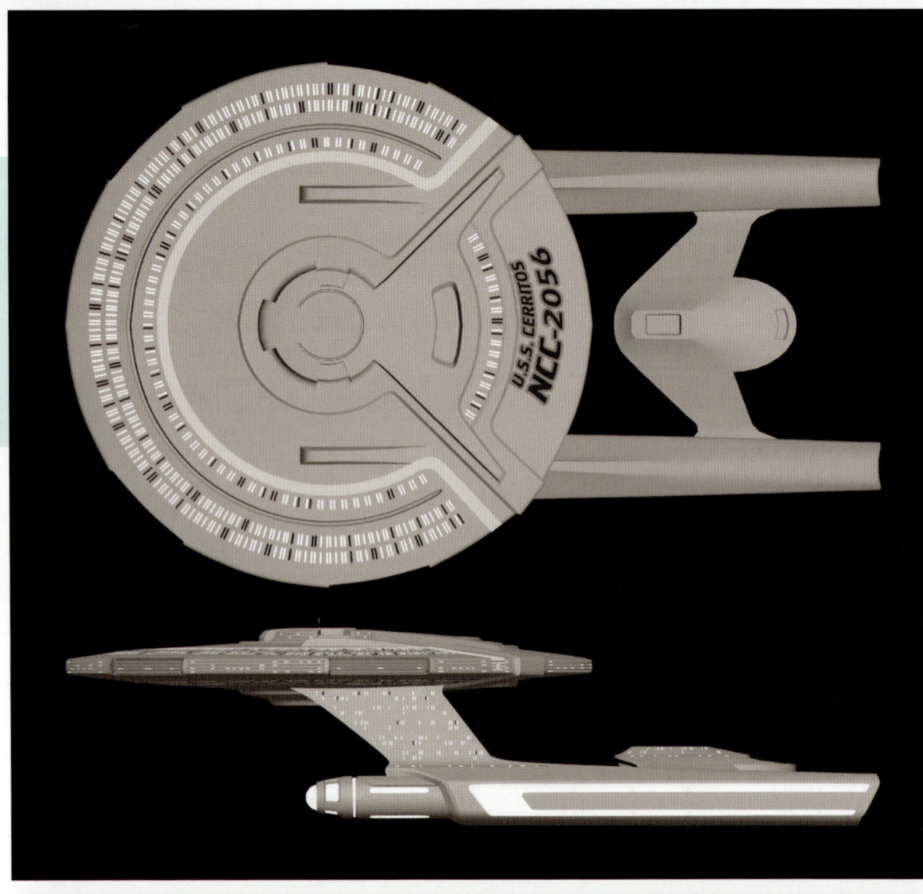
U.S.S. CERRITOS
NCC-2056

NCC-75567
U.S.S. CERRITOS

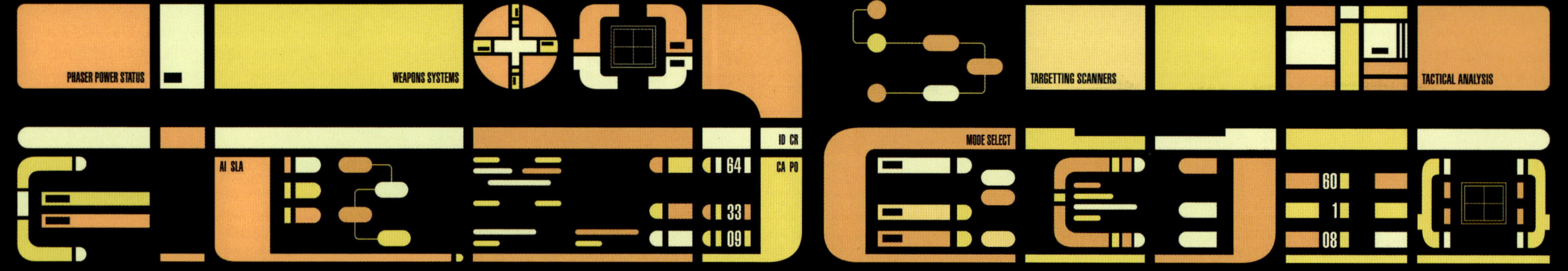
PHASER POWER STATUS
WEAPONS SYSTEMS
TARGETTING SCANNERS
TACTICAL ANALYSIS
ID CR
AI SLA
CA PO
MODE SELECT
64
33
09
60
1
08

ALERT
CONDITION:RED

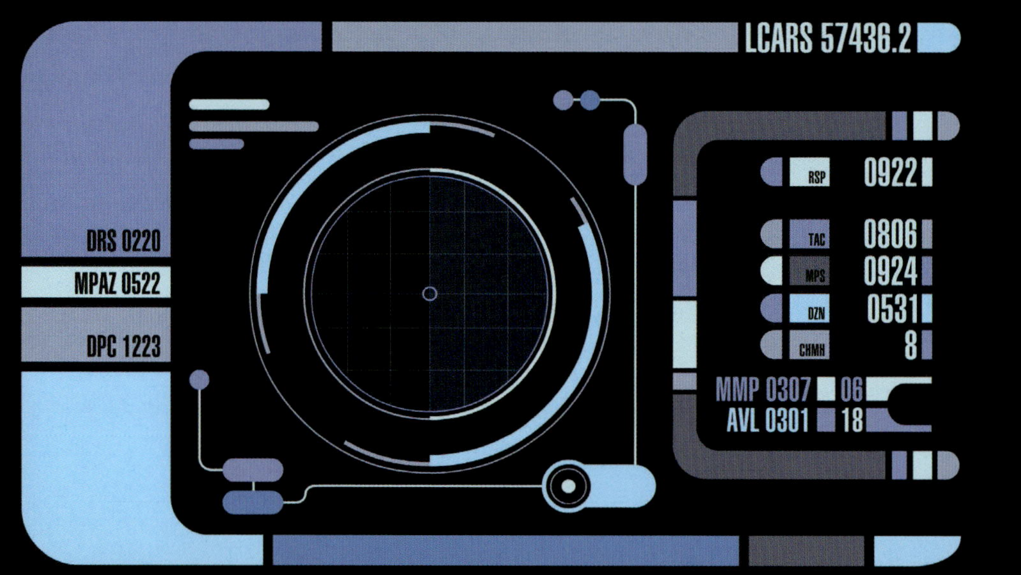
LCARS 57436.2
DRS 0220
MPAZ 0522
DPC 1223
RSP 0922
TAC 0806
MPS 0924
DZN 0531
CHMH 8
MMP 0307 06
AVL 0301 18

The Titmouse designers really took the lead and expanded the look of the LCARS to the lighting and carpet patterns around the ship.

BRIDGE

LCARS 40274

SYS 8554.1
SCIENCE

BRIDGE

LCARS 40274

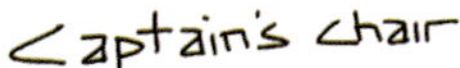

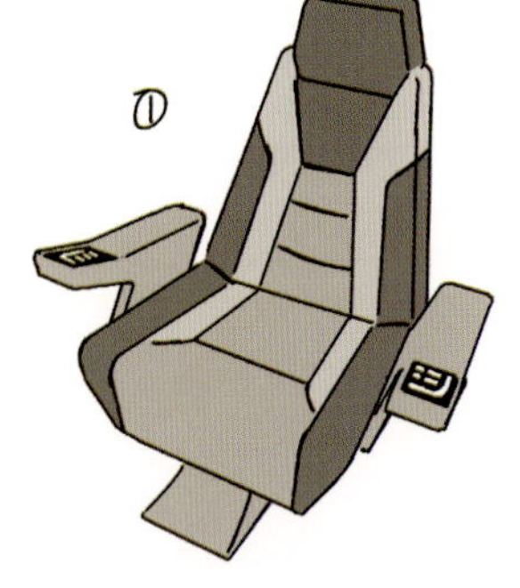

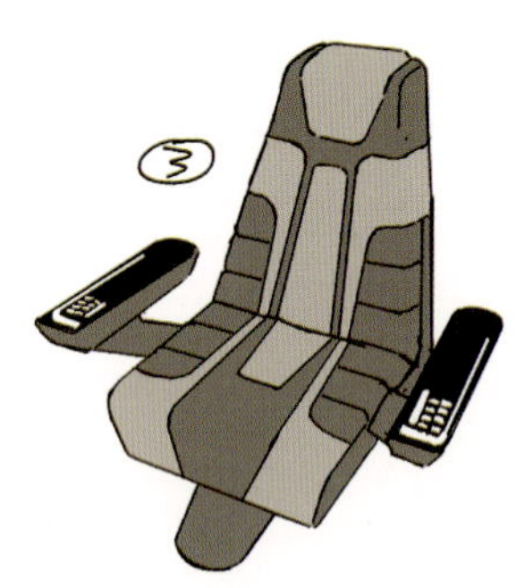

Command chairs

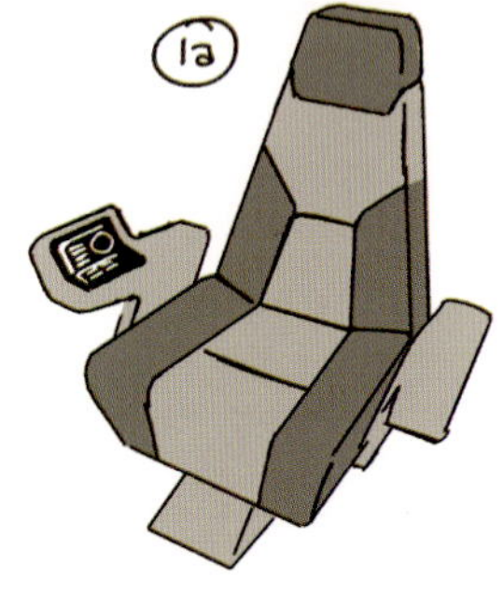

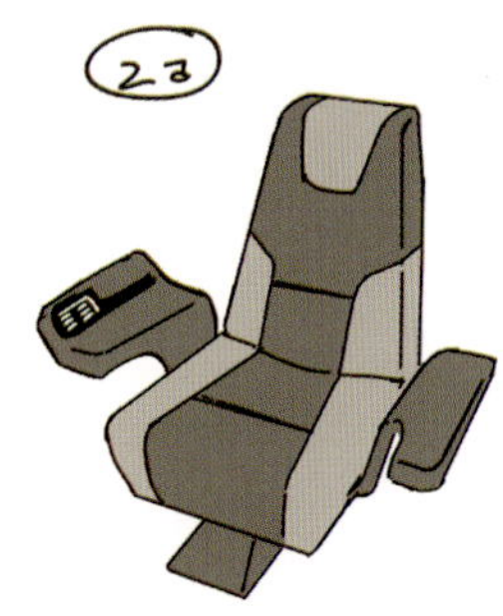

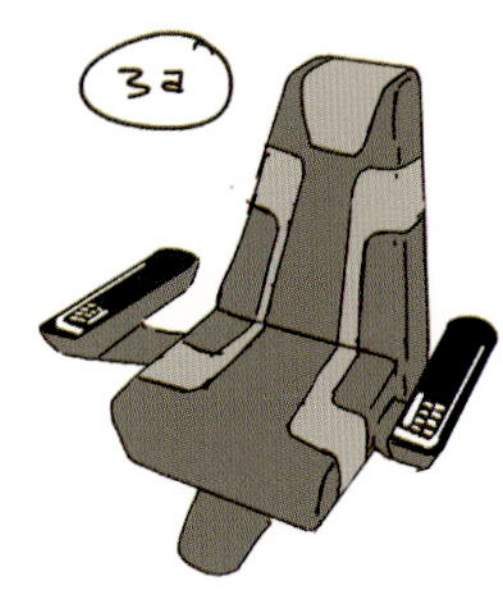

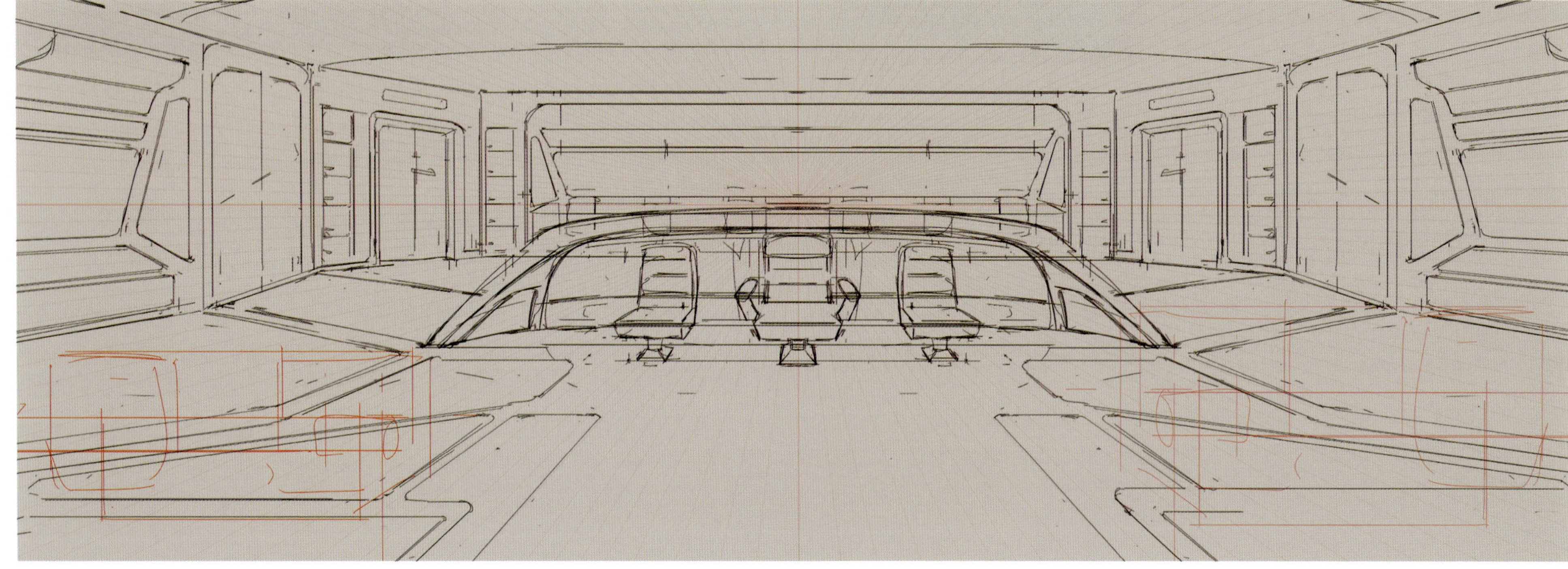

"The bridge is the most important part because we visit it so much, and it needs to look iconic and consistent throughout the show."

— Khang Le

LCARS 40274

CAPTAIN'S READY ROOM

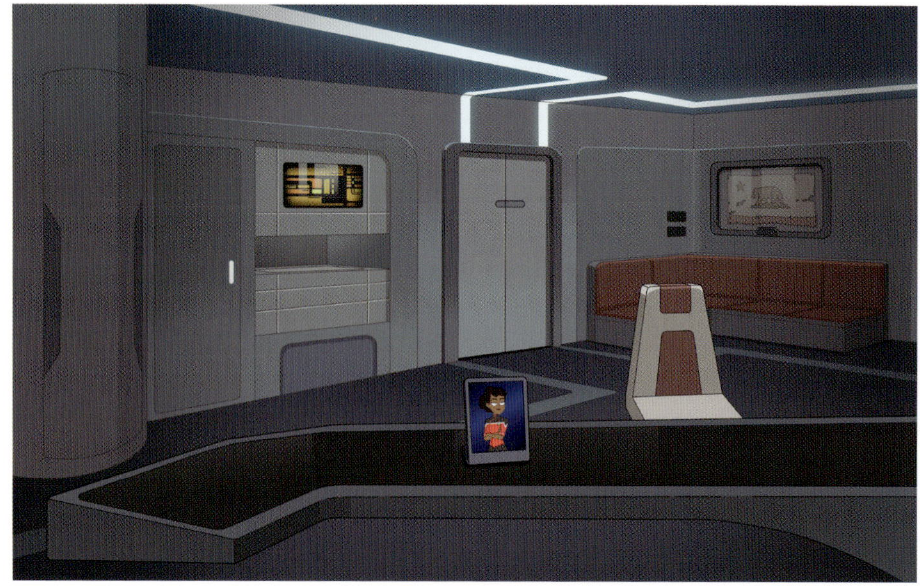

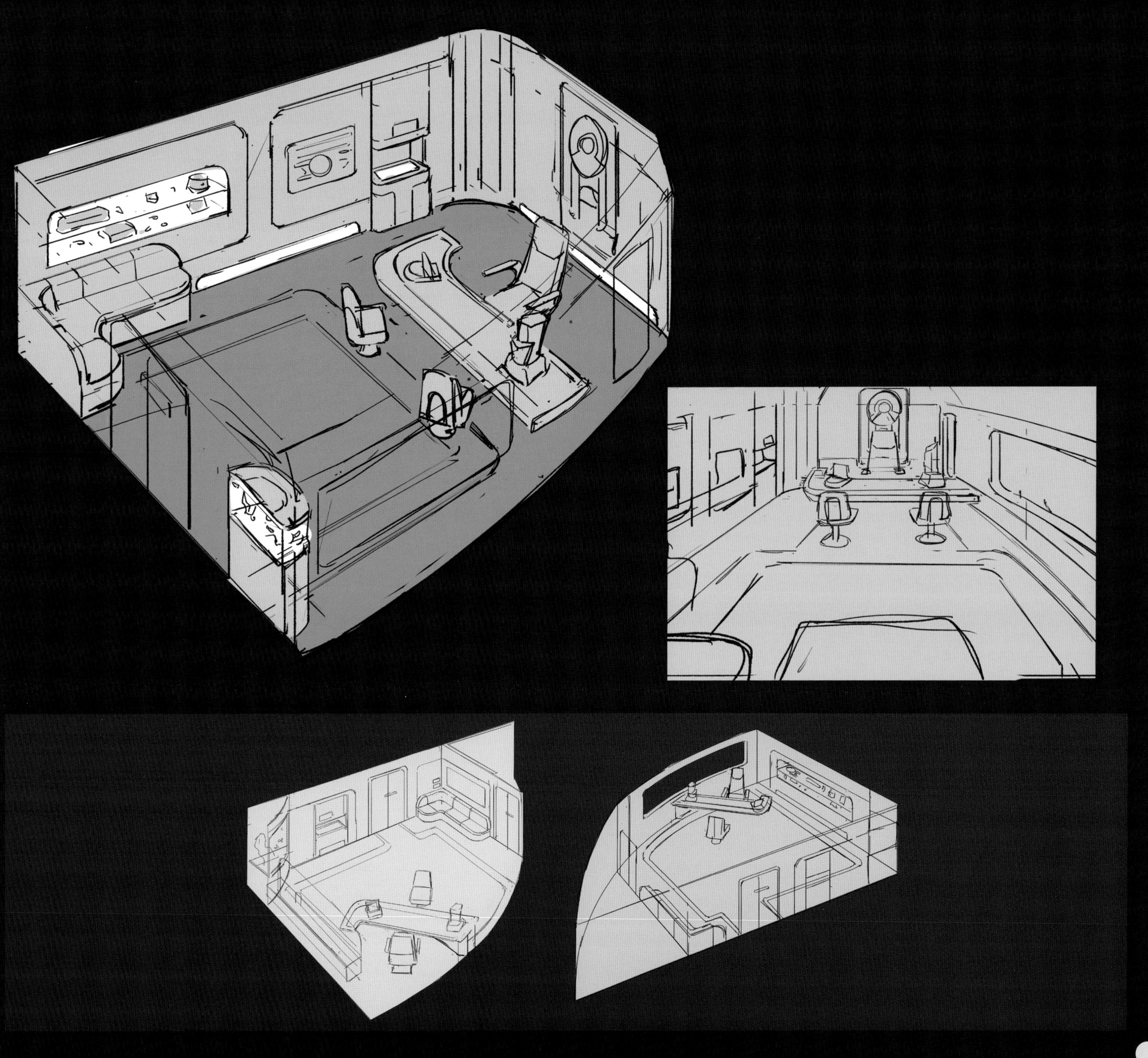

CAPTAIN'S YACHT

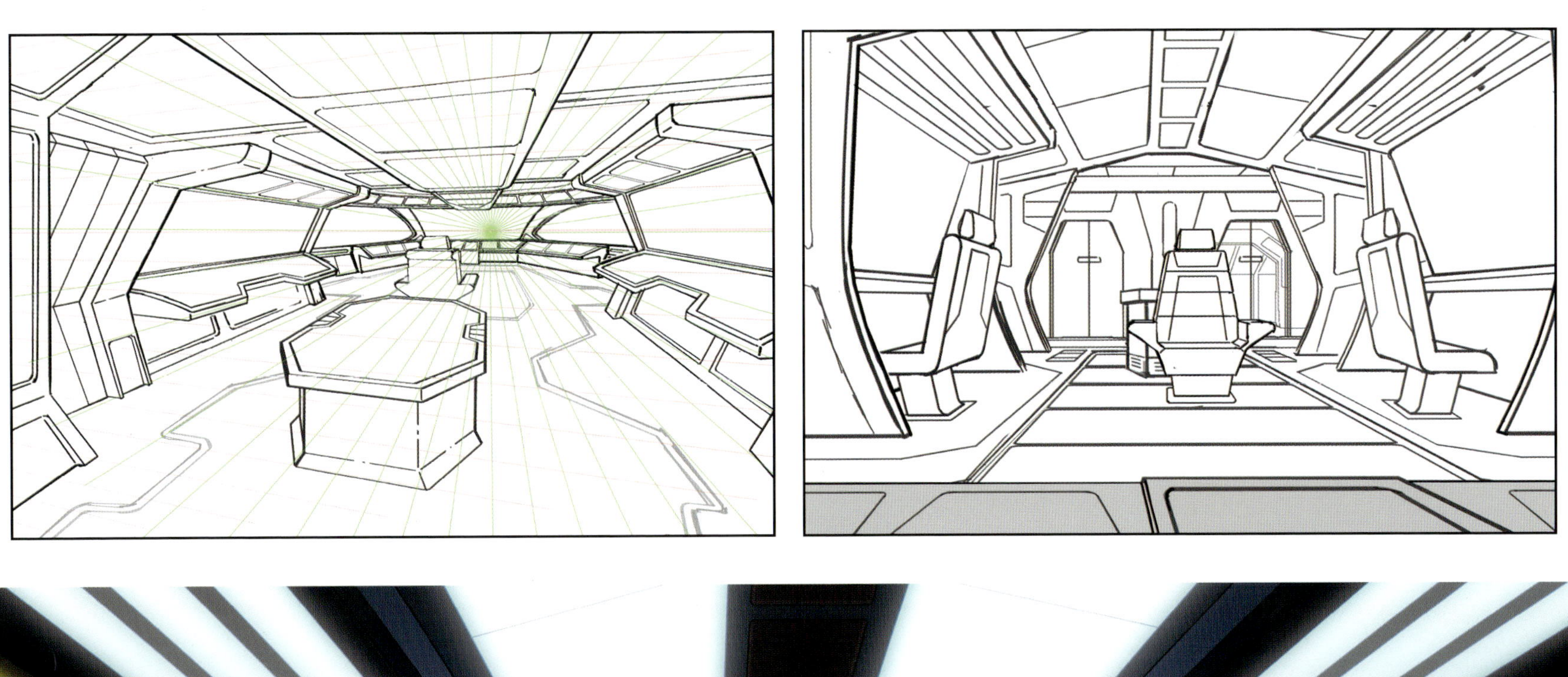

LCARS 40274

BAR

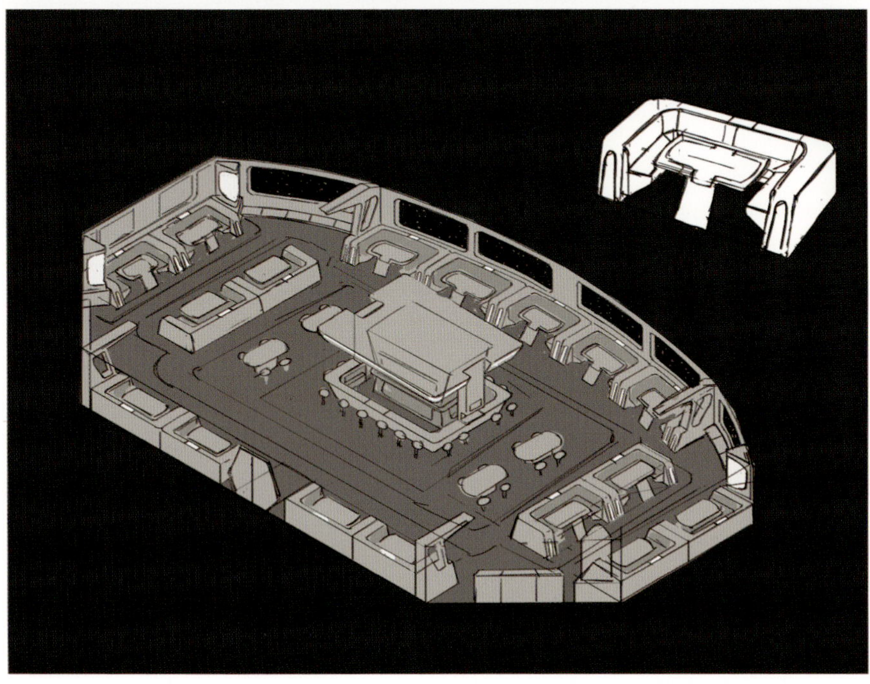

CAFETERIA

WINDOWS/SPACE
DOOR
DOOR
WALL
USS CERRITOS - CAFETERIA
QUADRUPLE REPLICATORS
TABLE & BENCH
(Lower, shorter than the bar area)

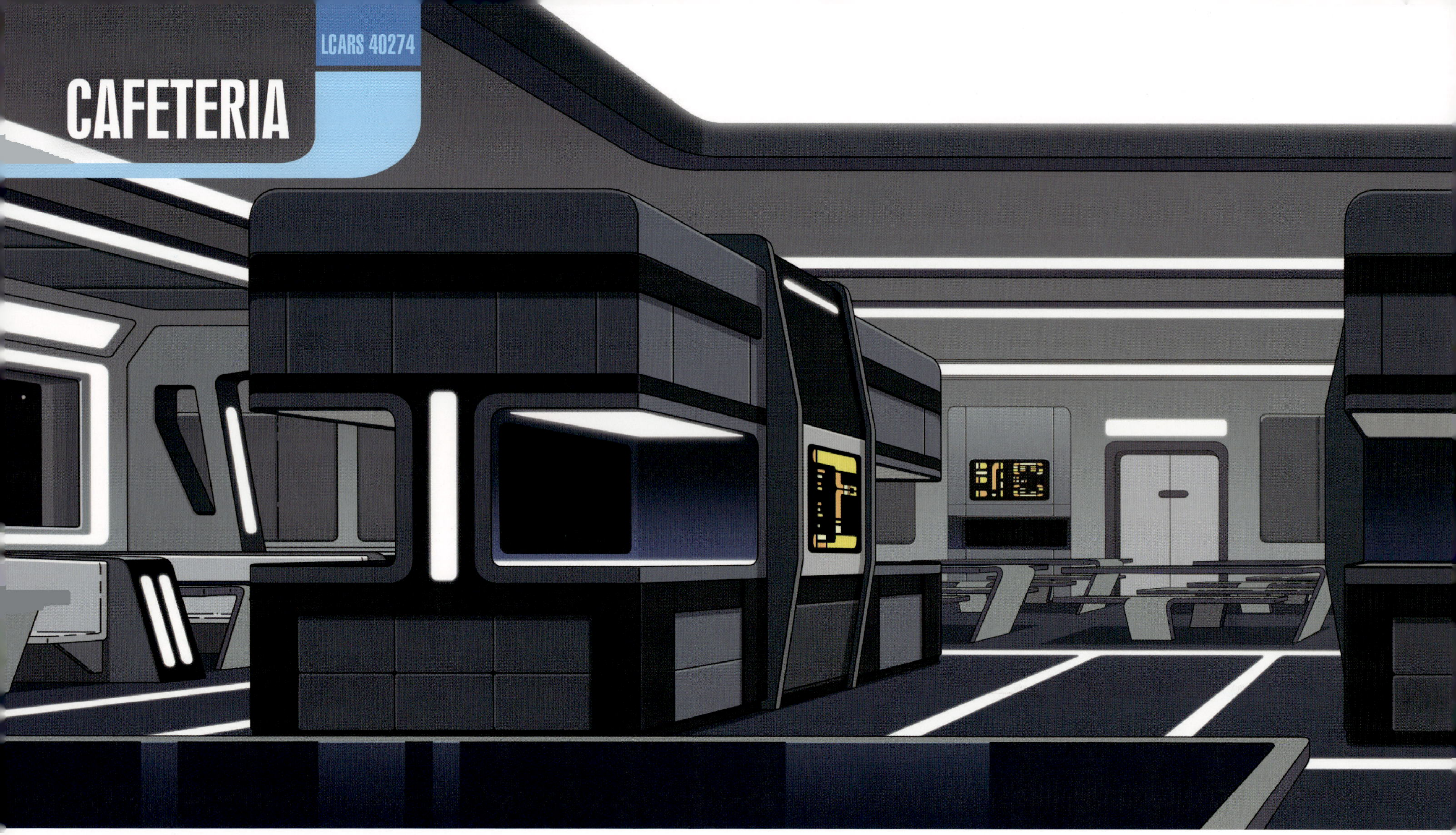

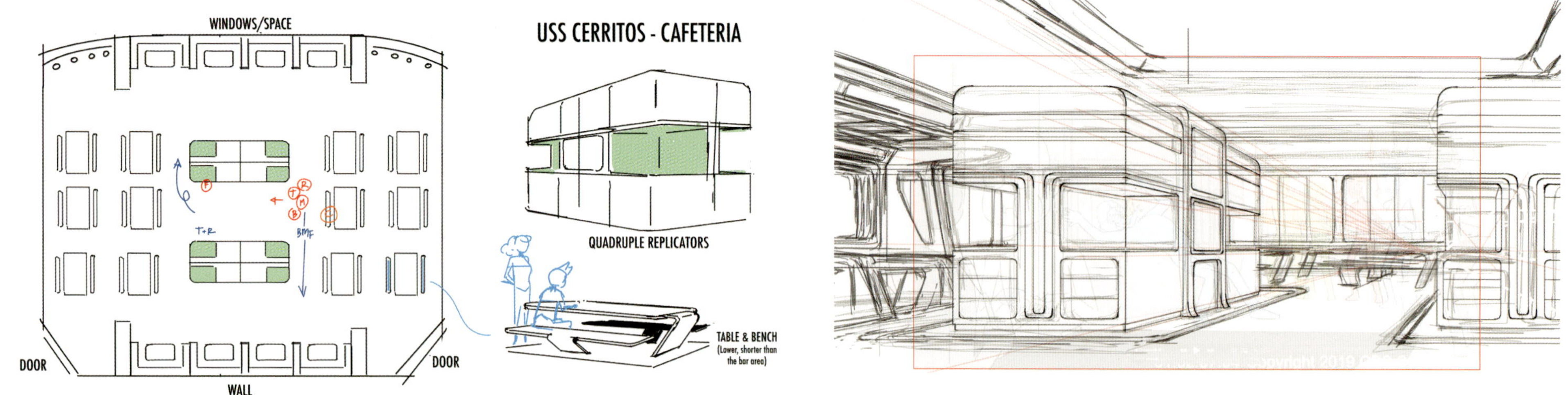

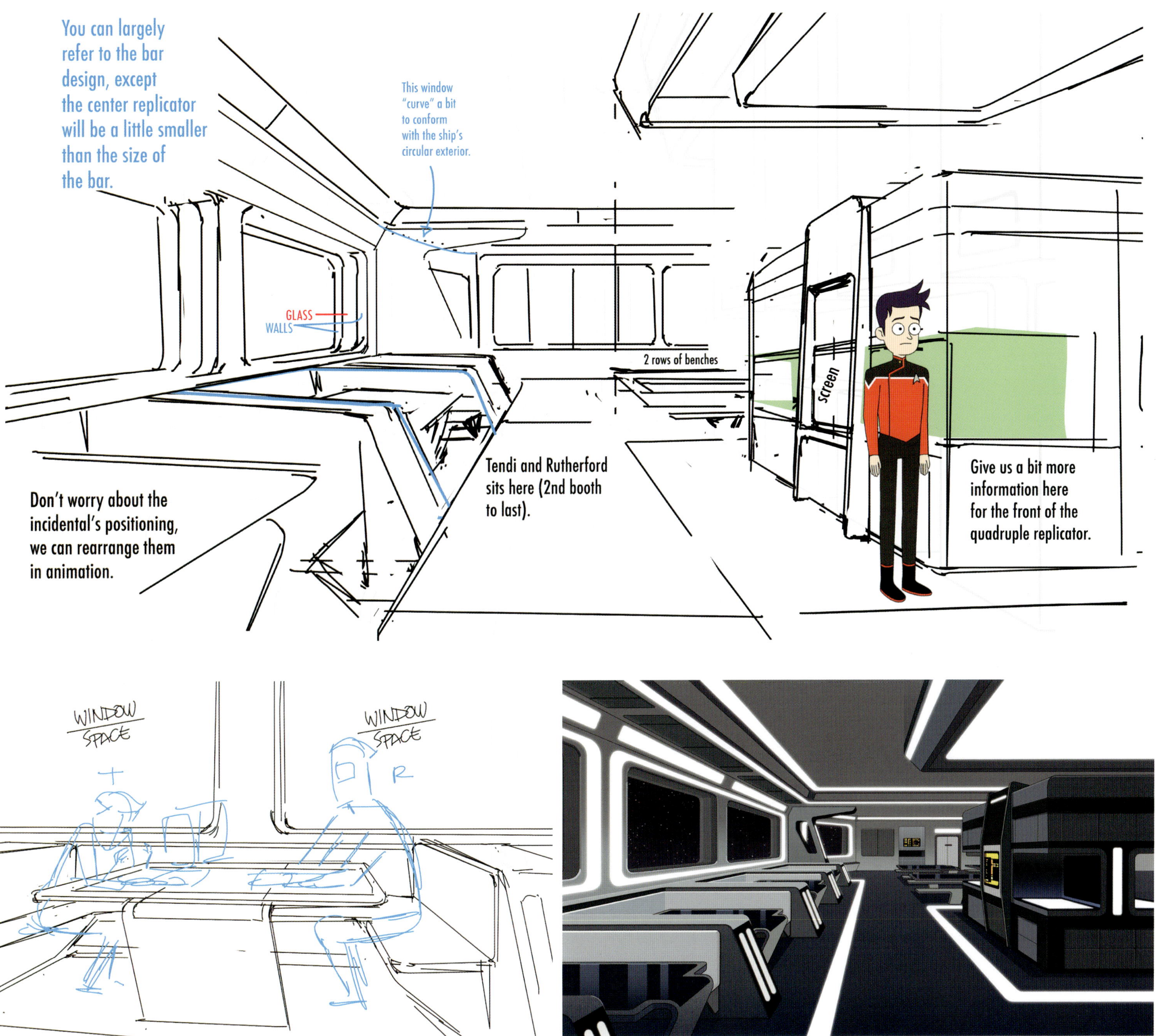
You can largely refer to the bar design, except the center replicator will be a little smaller than the size of the bar.
This window "curve" a bit to conform with the ship's circular exterior.
GLASS
WALLS
2 rows of benches
screen
Tendi and Rutherford sits here (2nd booth to last).
Give us a bit more information here for the front of the quadruple replicator.
Don't worry about the incidental's positioning, we can rearrange them in animation.
WINDOW SPACE
T
WINDOW SPACE
R

LCARS 40274

SHUTTLE BAY

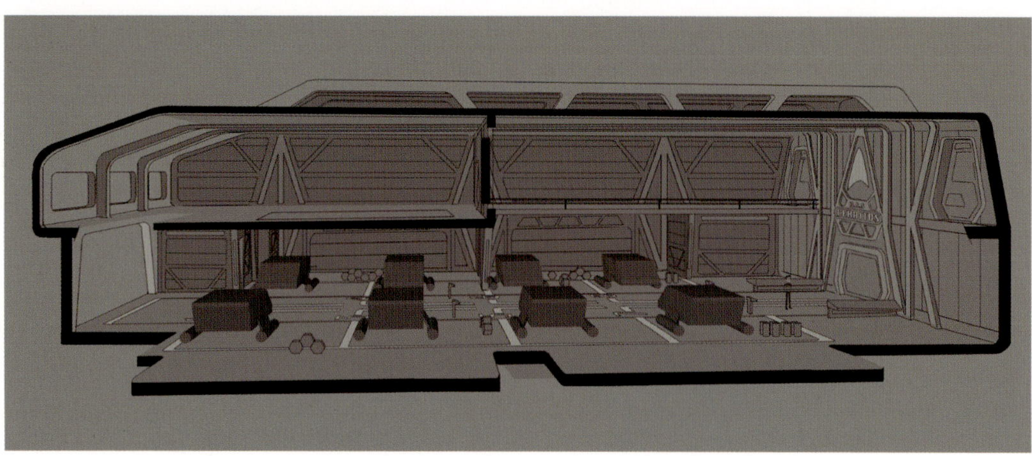

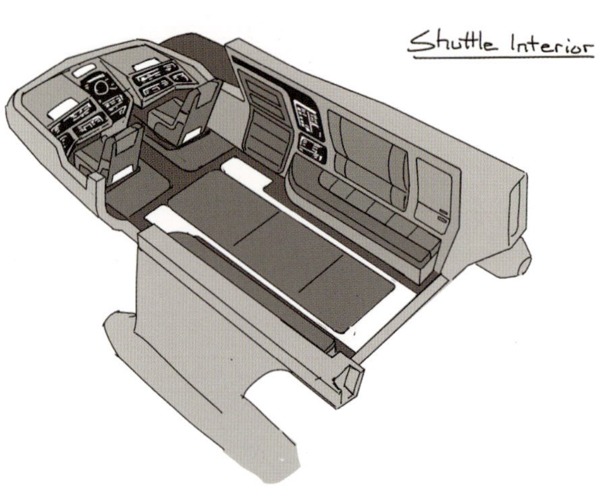

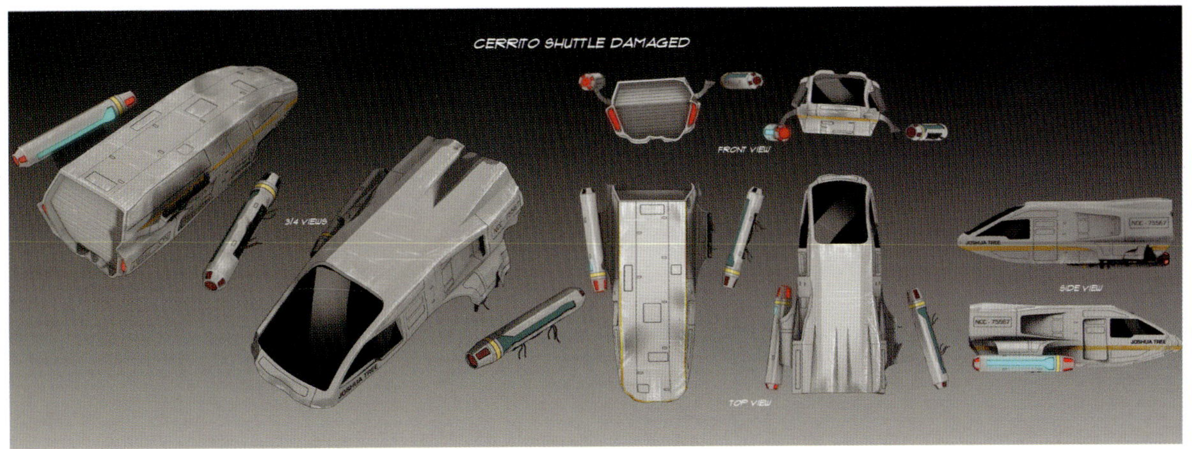
CERRITO SHUTTLE DAMAGED
3/4 VIEWS
FRONT VIEW
TOP VIEW
SIDE VIEW
JOSHUA TREE
NCC-75567

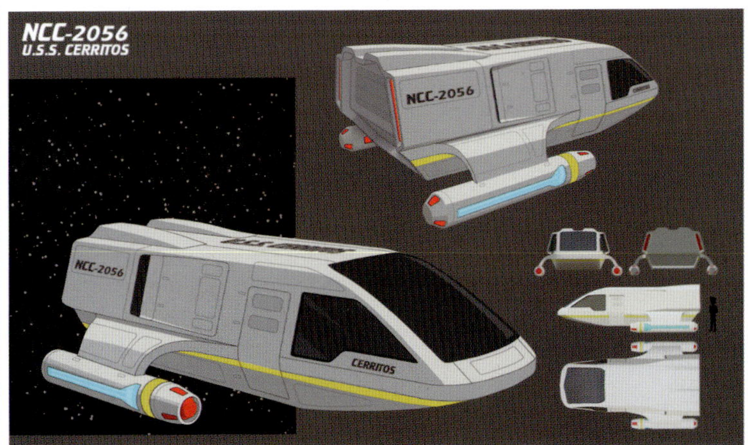
NCC-2056
U.S.S. CERRITOS
NCC-2056
NCC-2056
CERRITOS

TRANSPORTER BAY

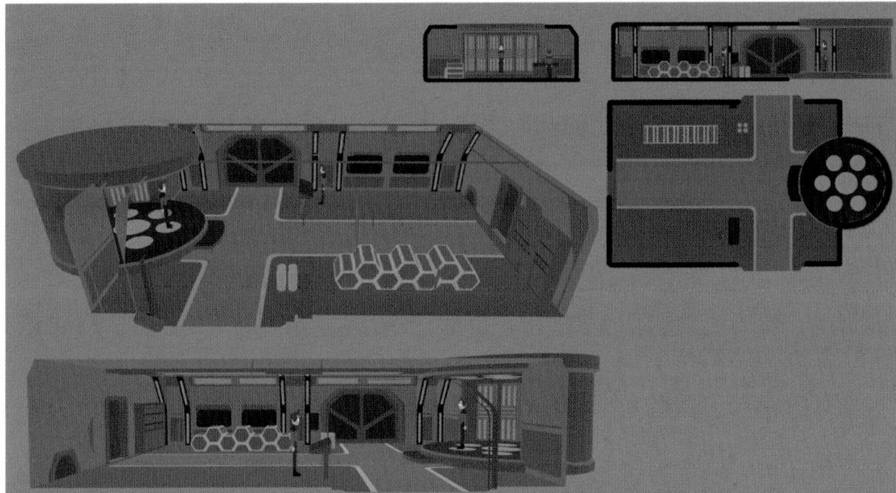

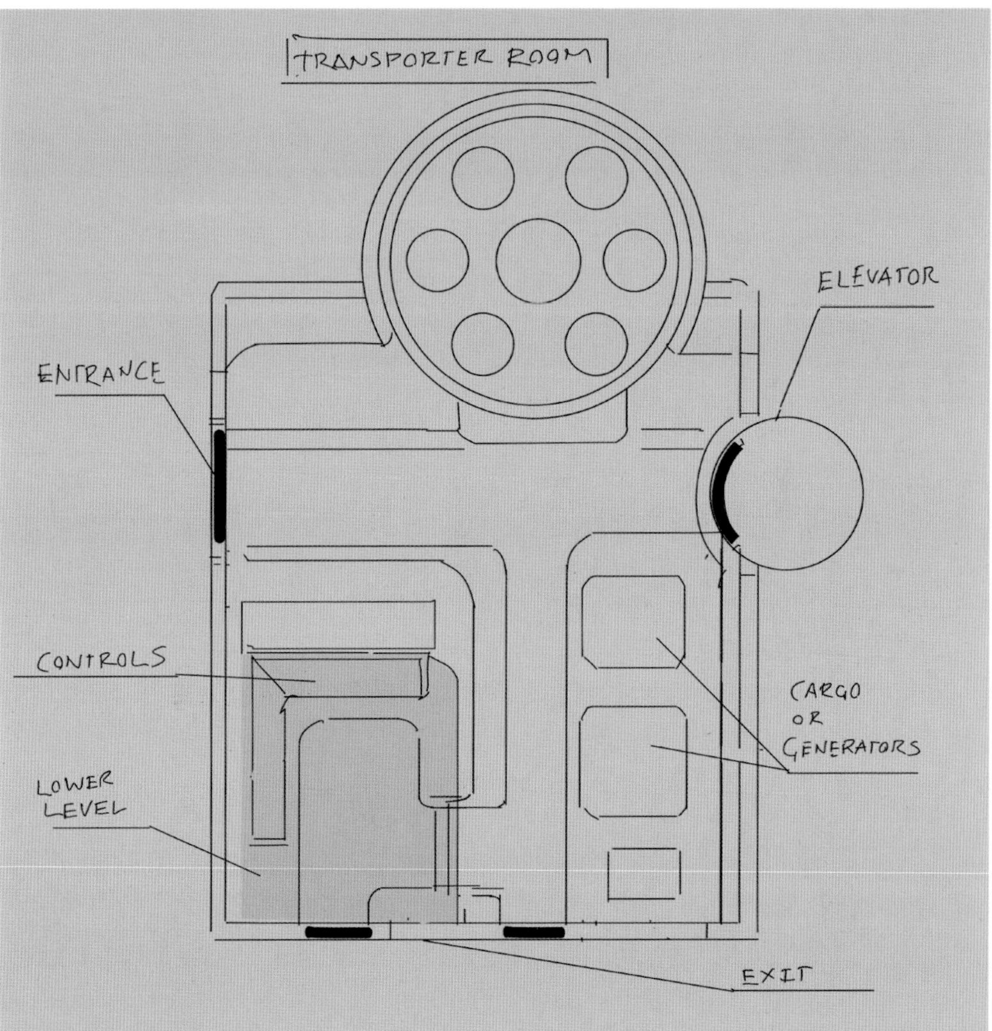
TRANSPORTER ROOM
ELEVATOR
ENTRANCE
CONTROLS
CARGO
OR
GENERATORS
LOWER
LEVEL
EXIT

SICKBAY

LCARS 40274

BRIG

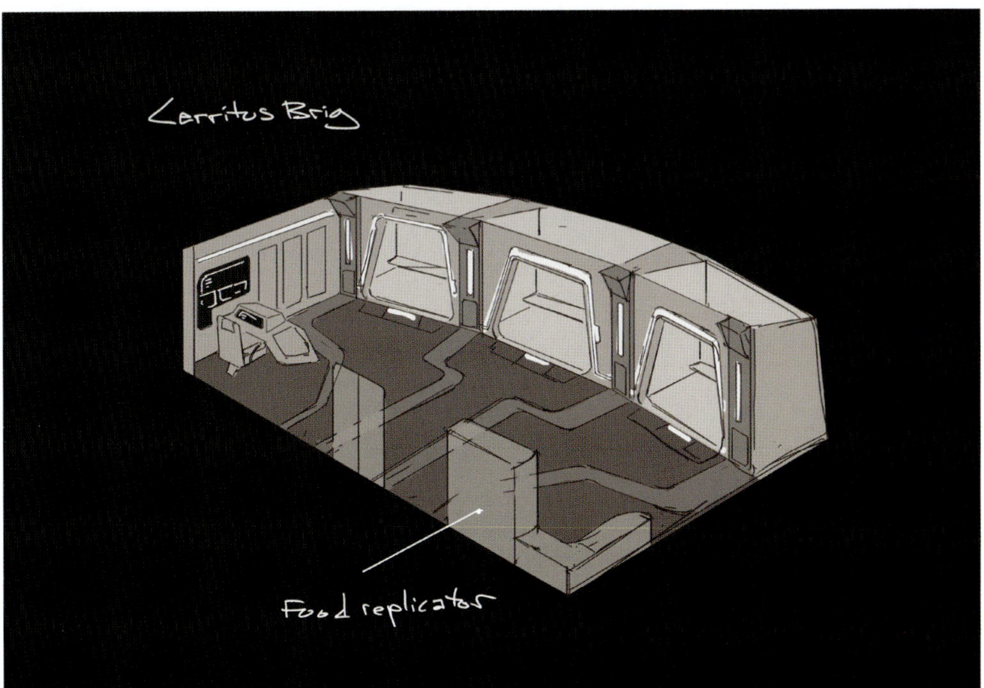

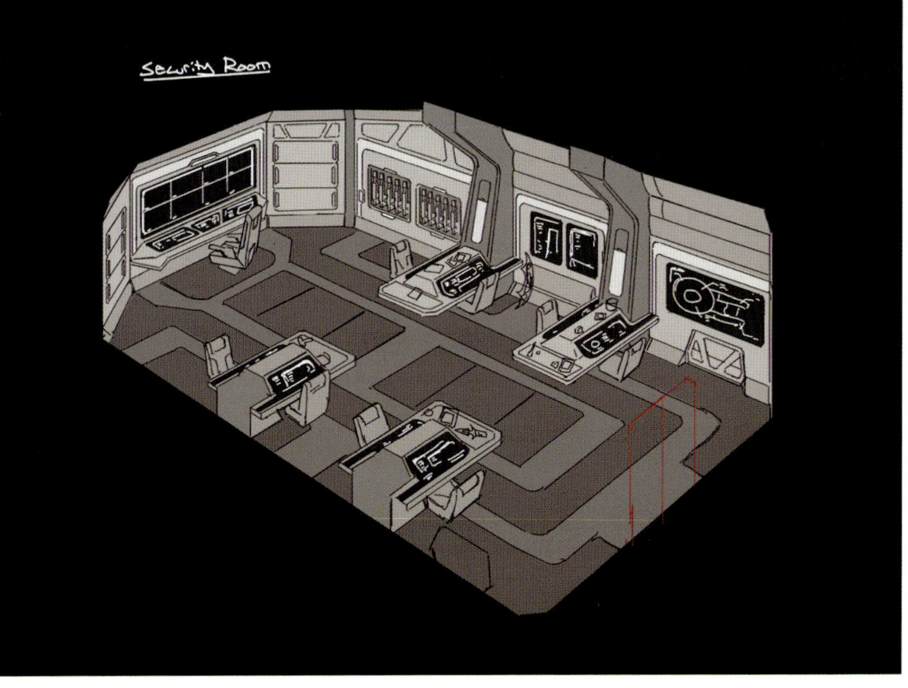

ENGINEERING BAY

LCARS 40274

LCARS 40274

CORRIDORS

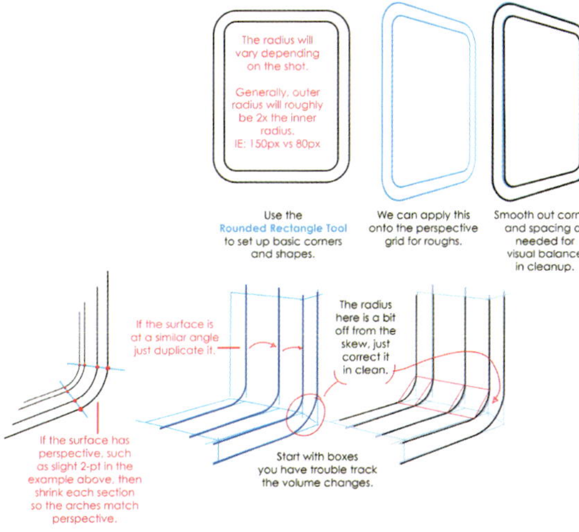

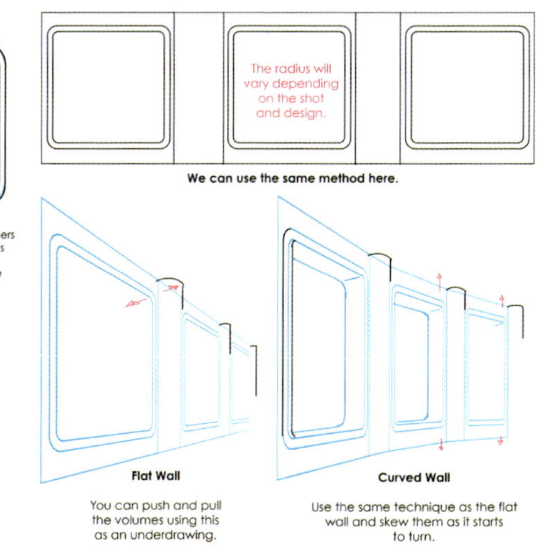

LCARS 40274

CETACEAN OPS

"The whales are also fun. They're always bickering with each other, so we wanted to always put in an element of fun into the room like their toys and a bucket of fish. Pool noodles. But throughout the series it's known for other officers to go into the pool and have fun with the whales. It was important to show that the whales were officers. So we had to equip the room with screens so that they could just do their job. And the pool is filled with screens. It's not just a room with a pool. It has to be functional. It has to be where these whale officers can go in there and do their work."

— Nollan Obena

"Cetacean Ops was always talked about. It was in Michael Okuda's master systems display of the *Cerritos*. He left out room for the Cetacean Ops, and we got to design it for episode 210."

— Nollan Obena

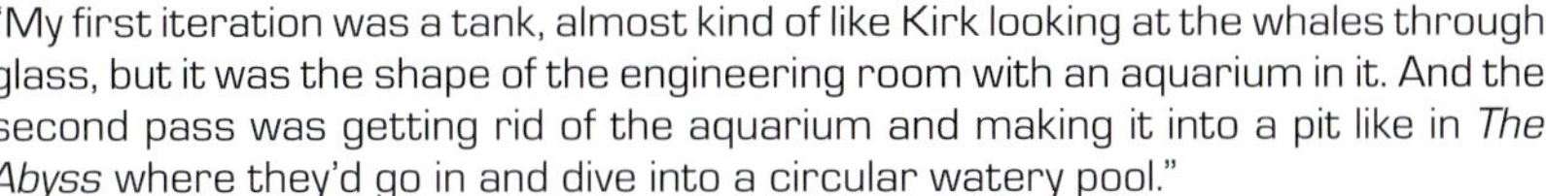

"My first iteration was a tank, almost kind of like Kirk looking at the whales through glass, but it was the shape of the engineering room with an aquarium in it. And the second pass was getting rid of the aquarium and making it into a pit like in *The Abyss* where they'd go in and dive into a circular watery pool."

— Nollan Obena

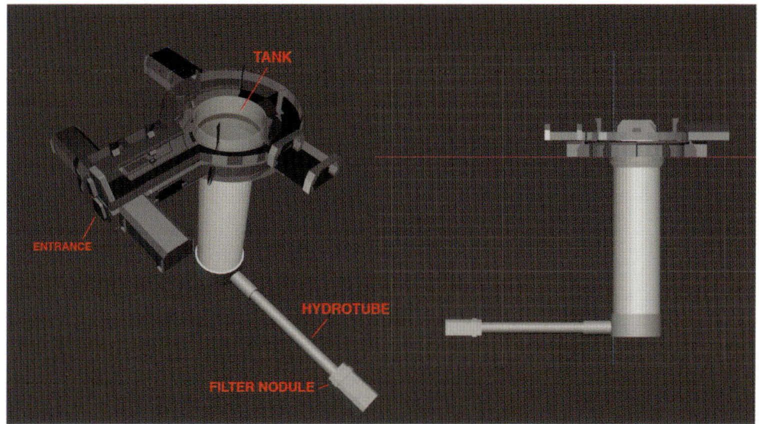

"Boimler had to dive and then go somewhere once he went down ("First First Contact"). So we had to design how deep the pool was in Cetacean Ops and where it leads. We made a diagram to show where the Ops is, the pool, the length of the pool, and going into the vent area."

— Nollan Obena

LCARS 40274

JEFFERIES TUBES

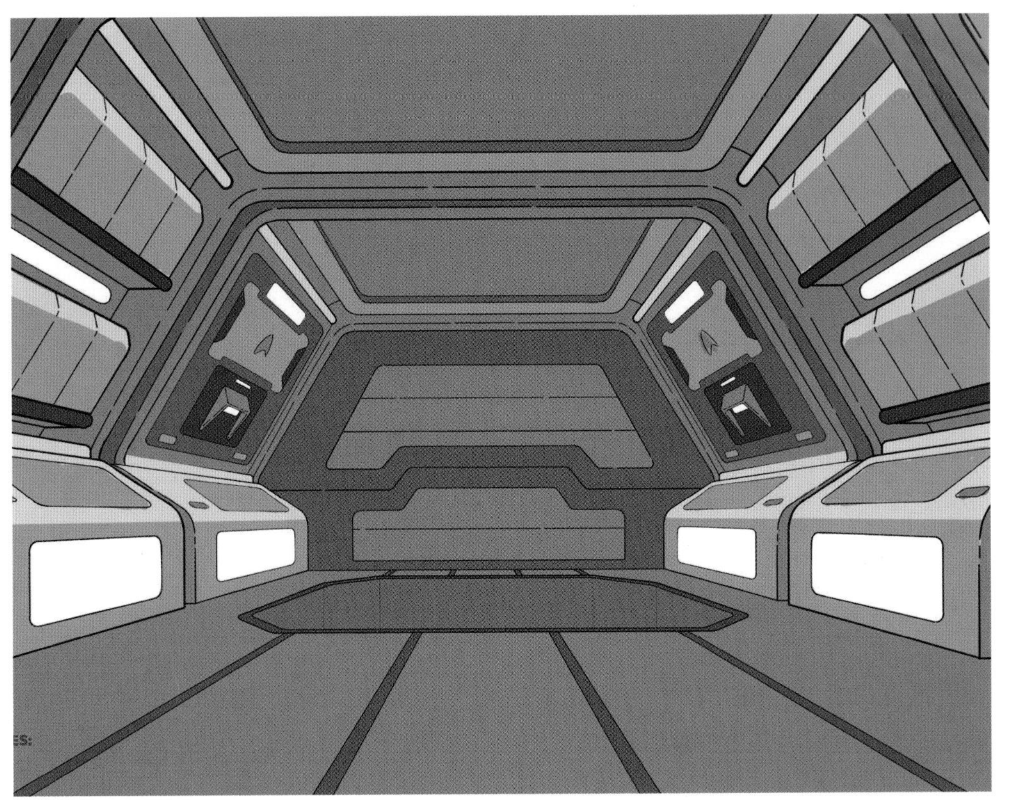

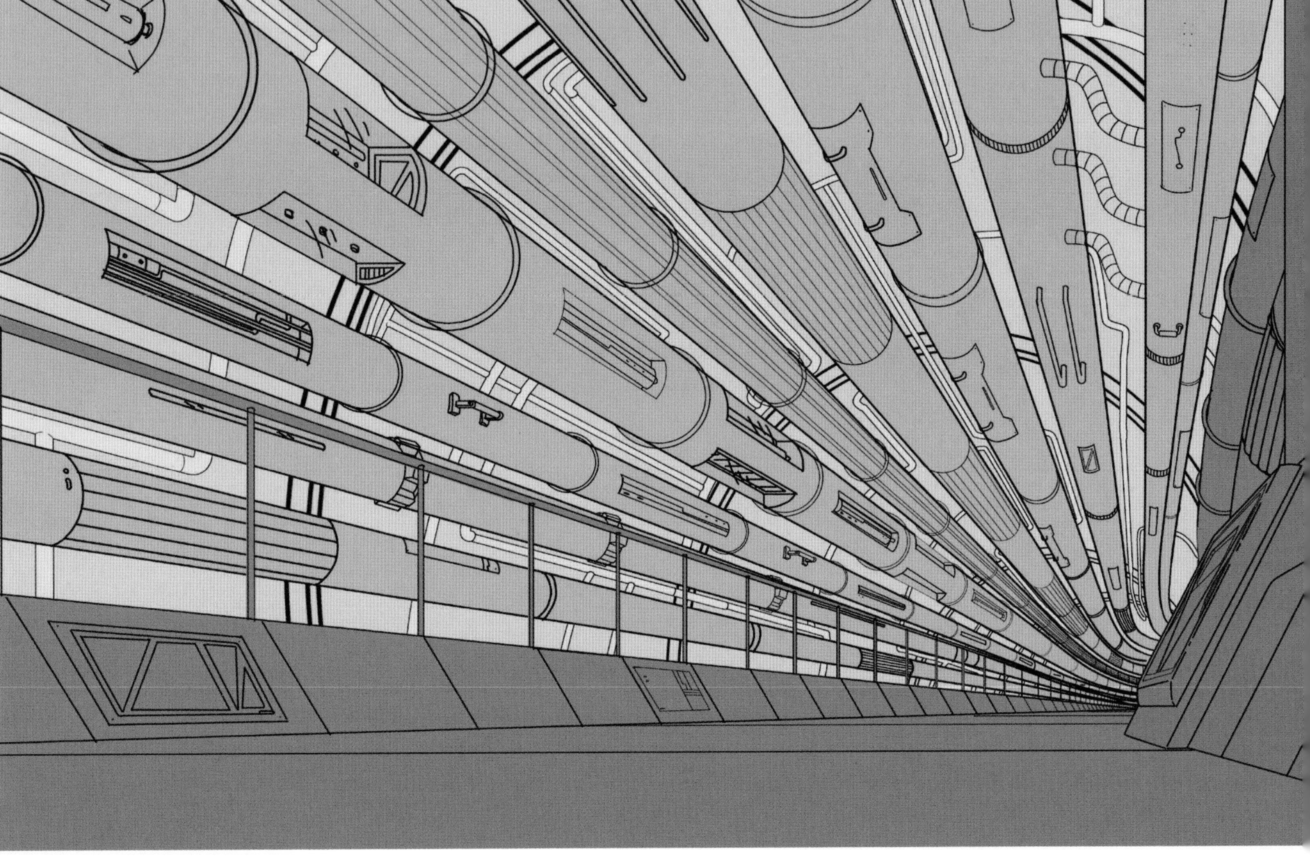

LCARS 40274

BUNKS

"The goal in designing the first image of the show is creating a candid moment. You don't want a complicated scene that will take you too long to design. The style frame could have been simpler, like a close-up of a bunk, but we wanted to show people interacting with their environment."

— Antonio Canobbio

"You live with your teammates on the ship. You come out of the shower and walk down the hall. Where do you store your stuff? I love going to the galley on the plane and seeing where everything is. They have one tiny room to feed about three hundred people, and it all fits somewhere. It's crazy to see the amount of efficiency on the plane. We wanted to see that on the *Cerritos*."

— Antonio Canobbio

"It was mentioned that captains really like talking about themselves, so the monitors above the beds were a funny way of having the captain speak wherever you are. Including in bed."

— Antonio Canobbio

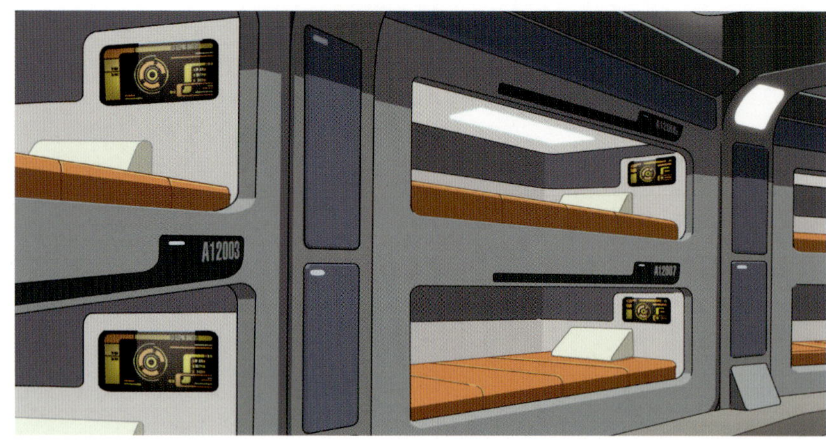

When Tendi looks out the back window in the first episode, it's the opposite of the bridge. We're looking backward and at the nacelles, but it's still very beautiful. Even as a Lower Decker, you get these unique views that you can appreciate that nobody else gets.

"The roof is always at a slant. They are not building the bunks in the best part of the ship. They're on the floors that taper too much. The lower decks. It's still comfortable, but not super-high ceilings. It also gives originality to the design by bringing the exterior shape of the ship into the interior design."

— Antonio Canobbio

U.S.S. CERRITOS

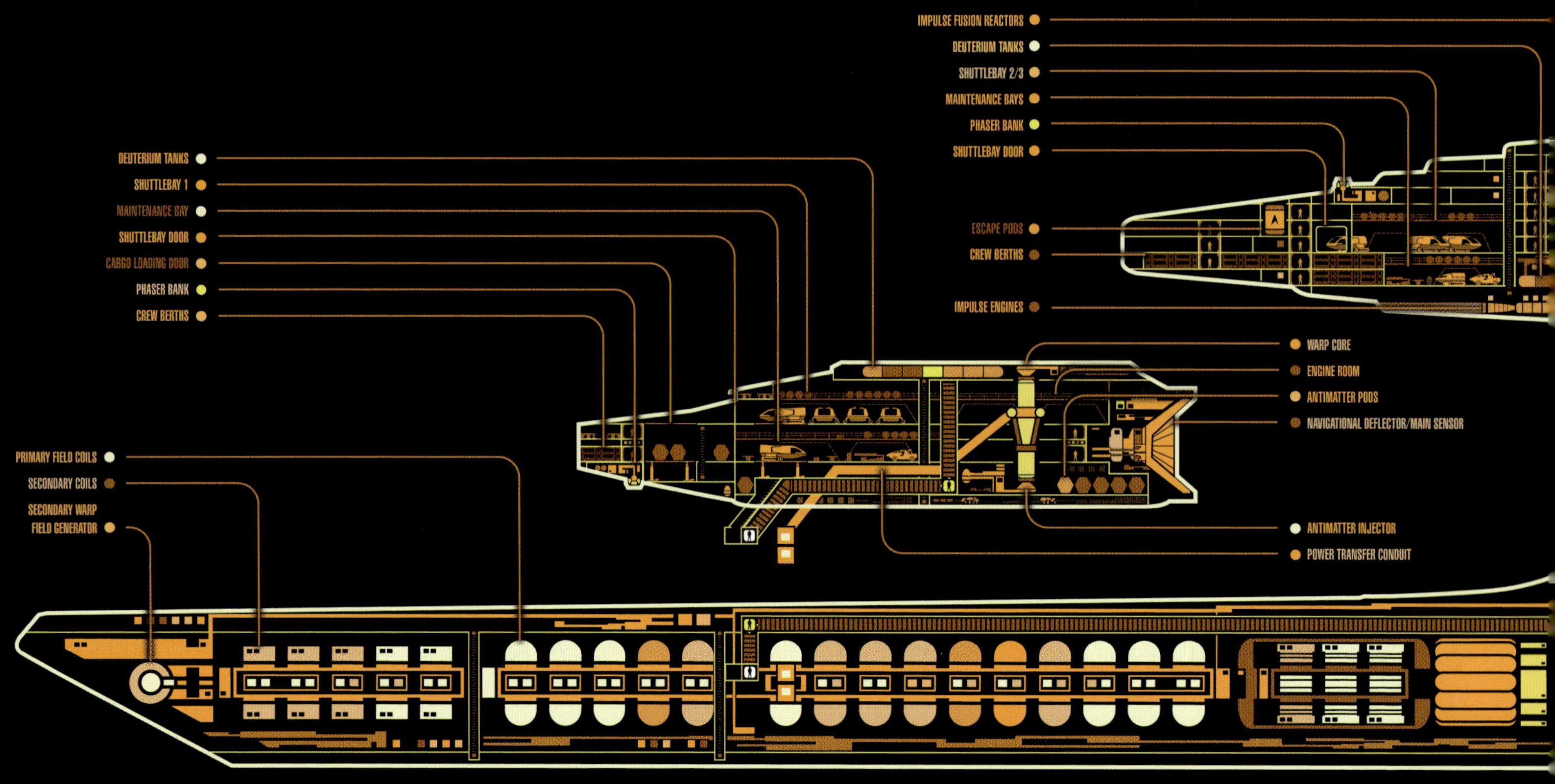

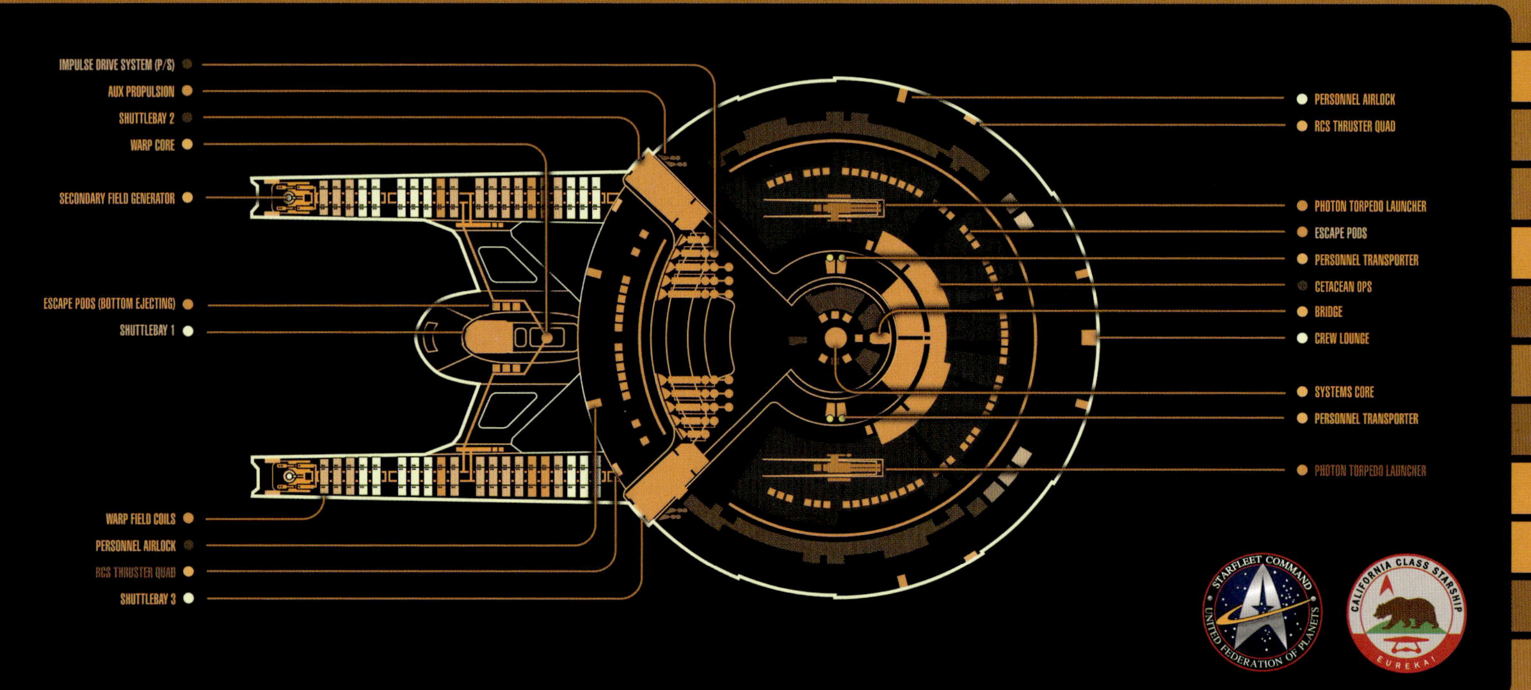

CALIFORNIA-CLASS STARSHIP

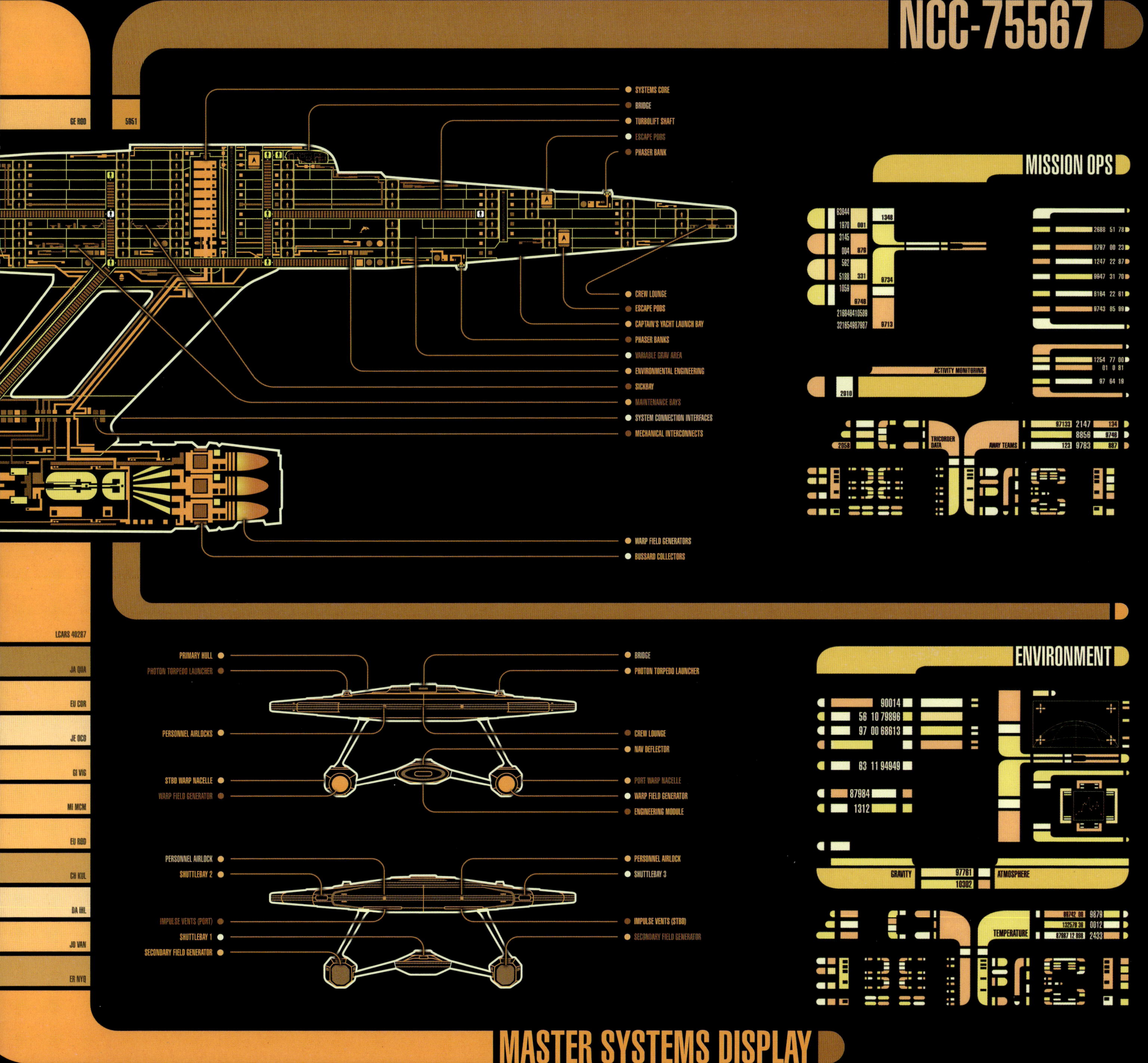

NCC-75567

GE ROD

5951

- SYSTEMS CORE
- BRIDGE
- TURBOLIFT SHAFT
- ESCAPE PODS
- PHASER BANK
- CREW LOUNGE
- ESCAPE PODS
- CAPTAIN'S YACHT LAUNCH BAY
- PHASER BANKS
- VARIABLE GRAV AREA
- ENVIRONMENTAL ENGINEERING
- SICKBAY
- MAINTENANCE BAYS
- SYSTEM CONNECTION INTERFACES
- MECHANICAL INTERCONNECTS
- WARP FIELD GENERATORS
- BUSSARD COLLECTORS

MISSION OPS

63944 1970 001 3145 004 879 562 5188 331 1059 9748 216848410589 321654987987 1348 9734 9713

2688 51 78
8787 00 23
1247 22 87
9947 31 70
8164 22 61
9743 85 99

1254 77 00
01 0 81
97 64 19

ACTIVITY MONITORING

2010

2058

TRICORDER DATA

AWAY TEAMS

97133 2147 134
8858 9748
123 9783 887

LCARS 40287

JA QUA

EU COR

JE OCO

GI VIG

MI MCM

EU ROD

CH KUL

DA IHL

JO VAN

ER NYQ

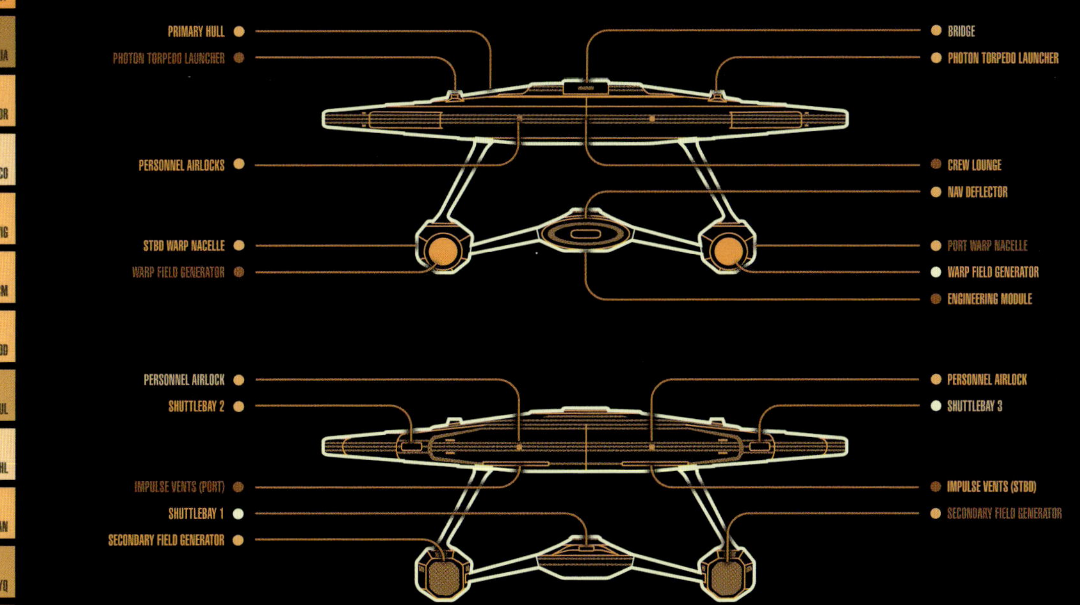

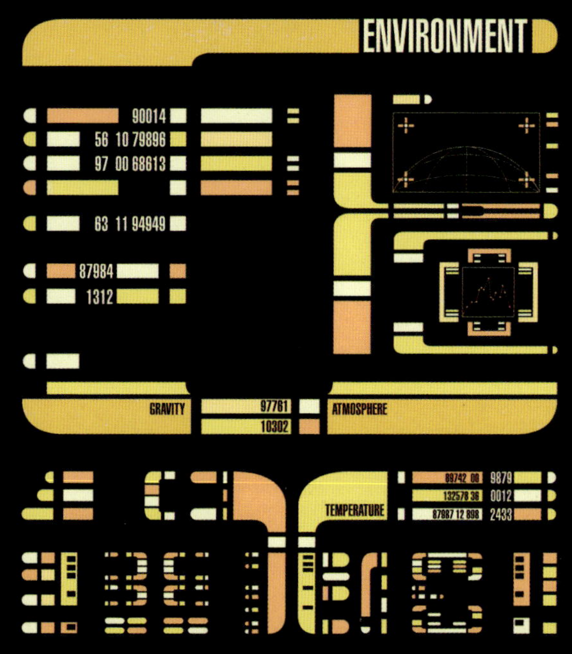

LCARS 40274

02-654598

CHAPTER 04 SEASON ONE

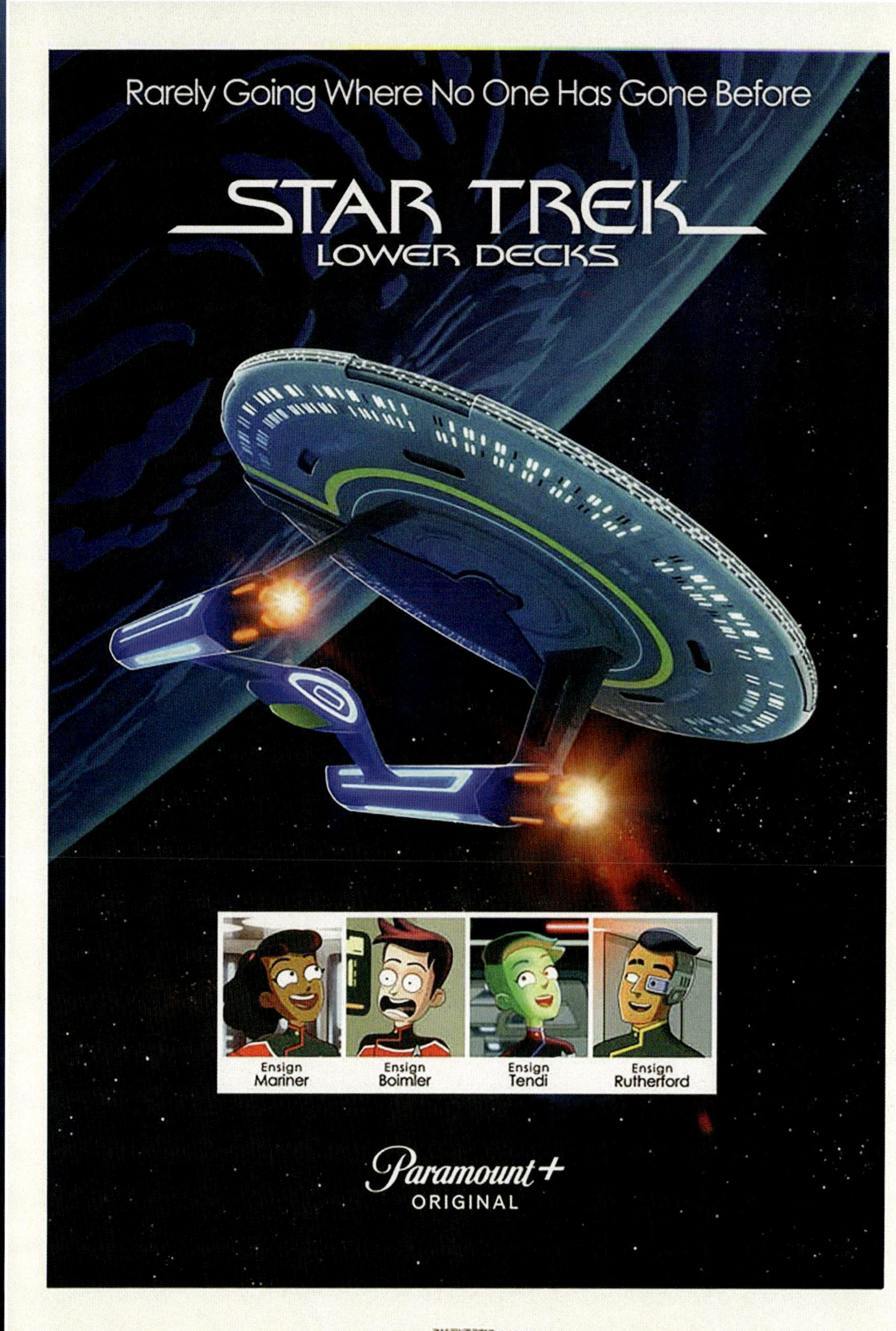
Rarely Going Where No One Has Gone Before
STAR TREK
LOWER DECKS
Ensign
Mariner
Ensign
Boimler
Ensign
Tendi
Ensign
Rutherford
Paramount+
ORIGINAL

LCARS S1E1

AIRDATE: 20200806
STARDATE: 57436.2

"Second Contact"

Series premiere. Ensign Tendi has her first day of work on Starfleet's *U.S.S. Cerritos*, where she meets fellow support crew members Ensigns Mariner, Boimler, and Rutherford. Meanwhile, Boimler is tasked with a secret special assignment and Rutherford attempts to keep his dating life intact while a sci-fi disaster strikes the ship. Meanwhile, an alien bug bite turns into a violent outbreak on the ship.

GALARDONIANS

The first episode welcomes you to the world and the characters. We see a lot of the *Cerritos* and meet all our heroes. If you pay close attention, you see that we're following the rules set up by TNG and other existing *Star Trek* shows. We see Starfleet technology like the little pods they put down to create a larger beaming location.

GALARDON

The Galardonians needed to be rural to align with Mariner's story, but in order for them to join the Federation, they also needed to be warp capable. So we walked a fine line between the two.

U.S.S. CERRITOS WORKSHOP

To build up stakes, we made the zombified crew look gruesome and scary, as well as the spider cow. It needed to look monstrous.

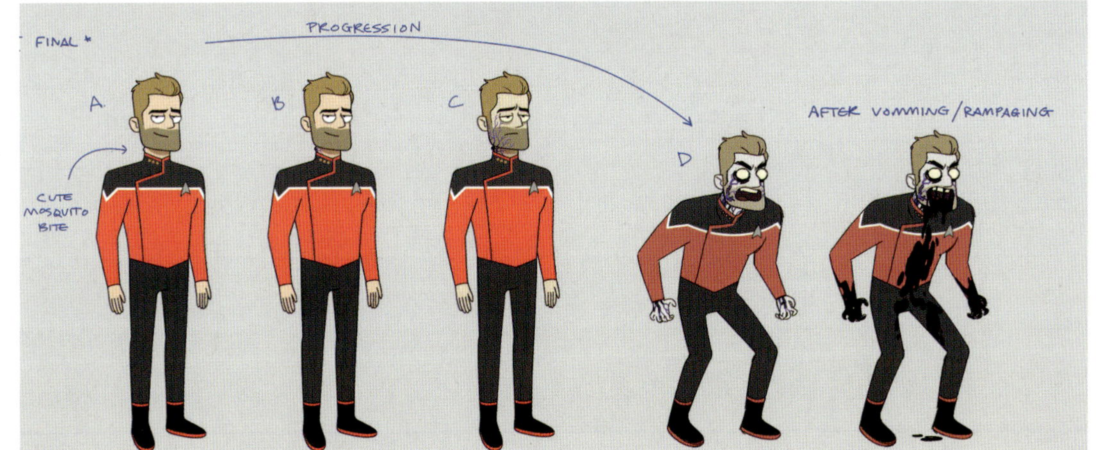

STARFLEET UTV

GALARDON TOWN CENTER

We had a minor setback with the original designs of the Galardonians because Legal was concerned that they looked too similar to other space properties. Legal ended up being a huge ally to the show after this. Although the final Galardonian designs look the most unlike any existing *Star Trek* species, it gave us an opportunity to bend the design rules every once in a while.

GALARDONIAN BUREAUCRATS

GALARDONIAN FARM

GALARDONIAN SPIDER COW

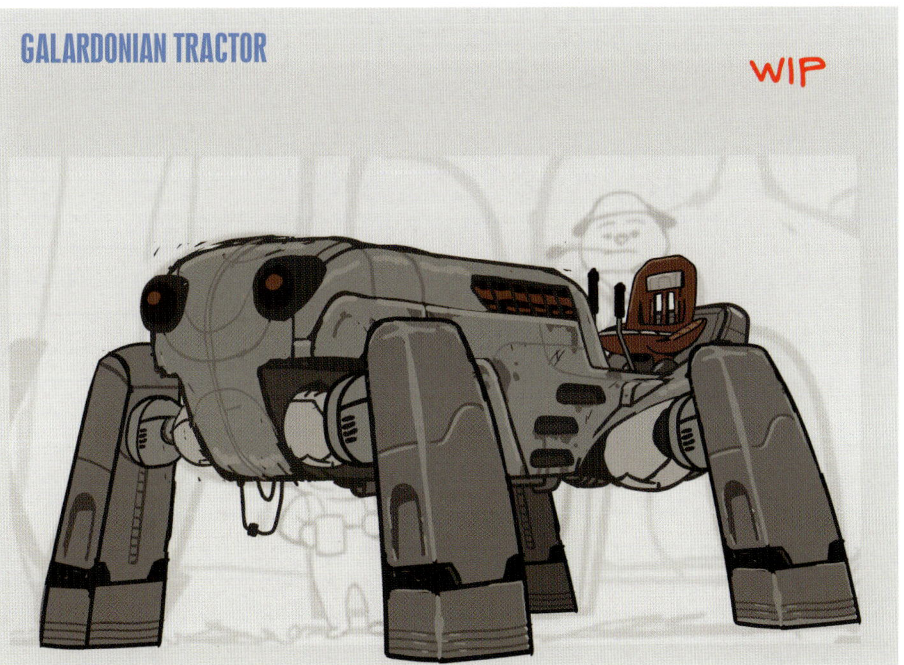

The tractor looks reminiscent of the spider cow, which tells you more about the alien species. The Galardonians base their own designs off existing stuff in their world.

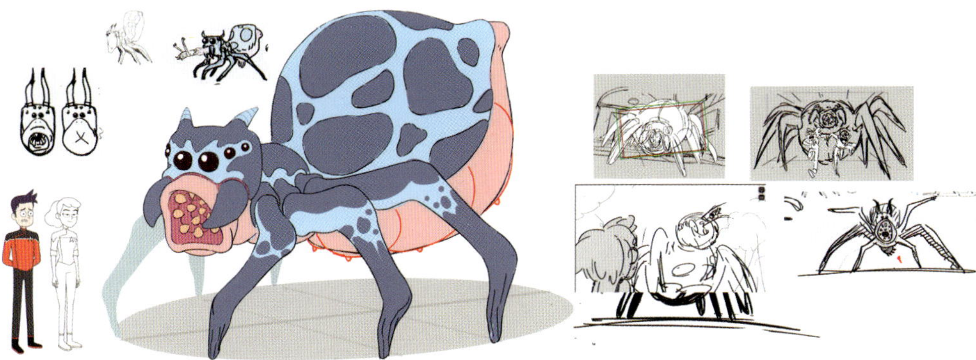

LCARS S1E2

AIRDATE: 20200813
STARDATE: UNKNOWN

"Envoys"

After a high-profile mission goes awry, Boimler is further plagued with self-doubt when Mariner proves herself to be a more naturally talented sci-fi badass than he.

"The layout and central spire were meant to be reminiscent of Farpoint Station from TNG: 'Encounter at Farpoint.'"
— Brad Winters

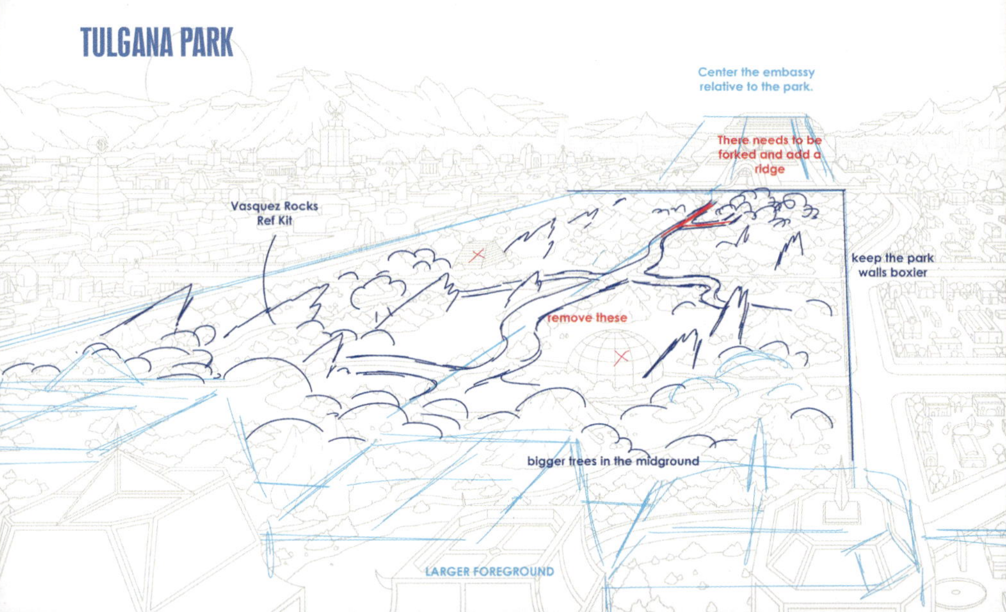

We haven't really seen familiar *Star Trek* species in the show yet. So we send Mariner and Boimler on a mission to an international airport-type planet. A lot of species land here to then go on to other places. We have Little Qo'noS, Little Risa, an Andorian district, and hints of other alien architecture throughout the episode.

LITTLE QO'NOS BAZAAR

We discovered the intricacies of the Klingon language in this episode when we reached out to Marc Okrand to translate some marketplace signage and dialogue.

GENERAL K'ORIN

FERENGI

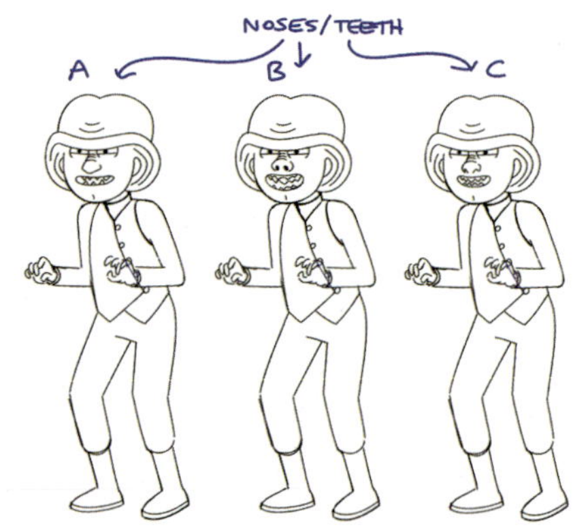

We wanted to show a menacing TNG season one Ferengi, but then reveal at the end of the episode that he's more of a *Deep Space Nine* Ferengi. We wanted to keep the fans on their toes.

BLUE- HORNED ALIEN

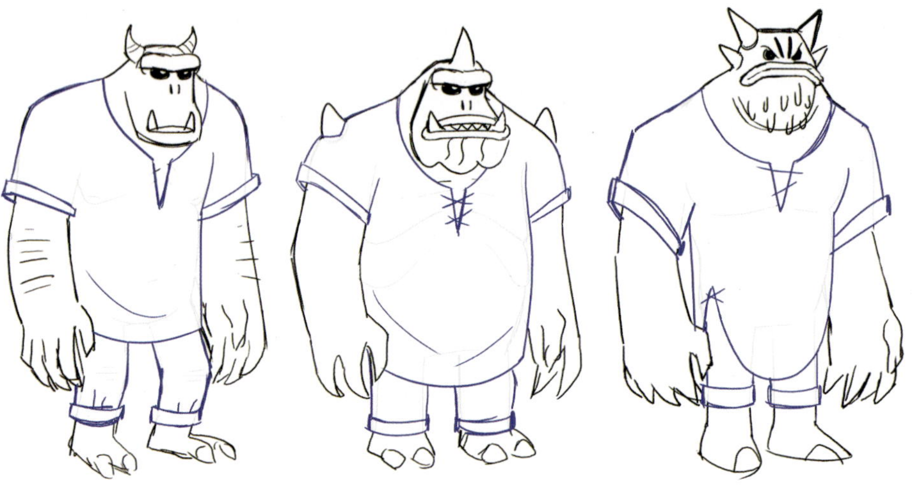

This episode is the first time someone drew Jennifer the Andorian. She's an incidental character laughing at Mariner at the end of the episode. Mike really liked her design, so when Tawny improvised "Move, Jennifer" in episode 105, we used that design and later made her a bigger character.

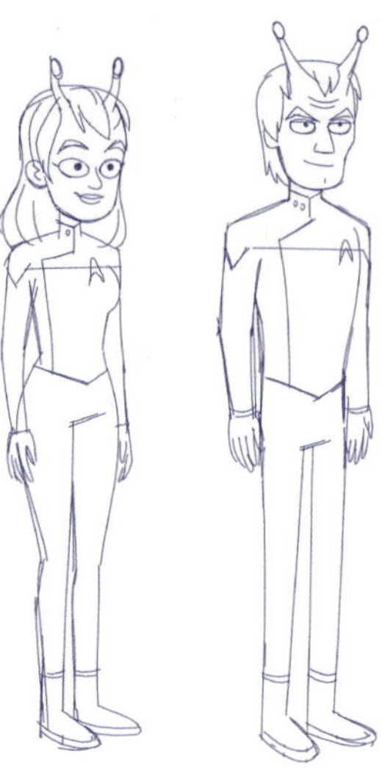

MILNA ALIEN

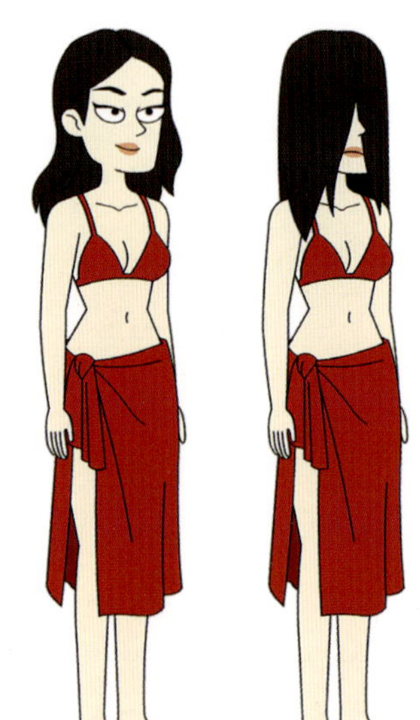

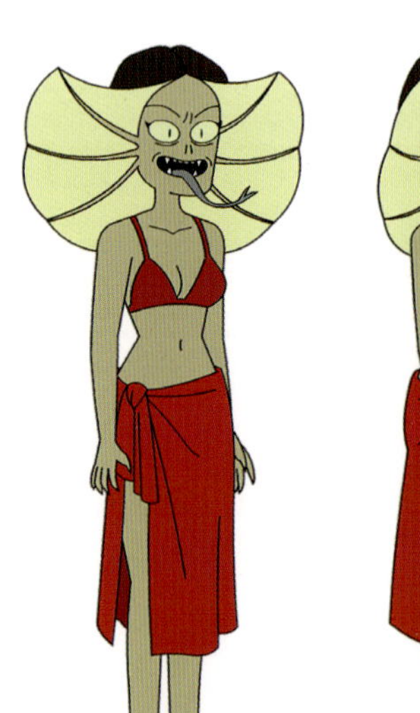

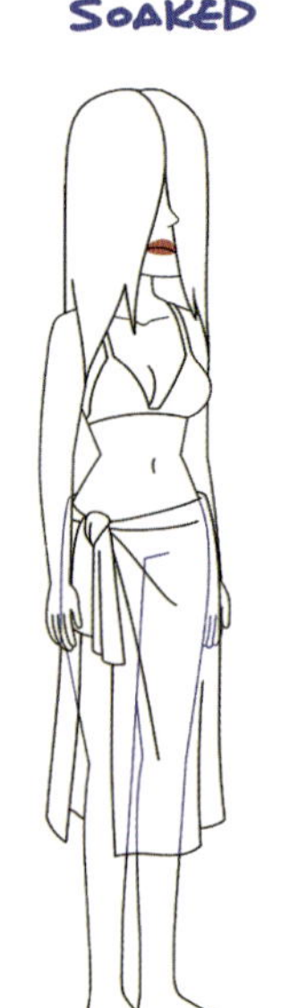

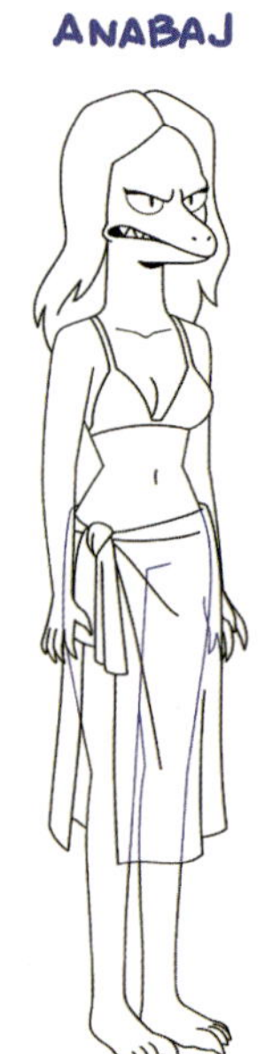

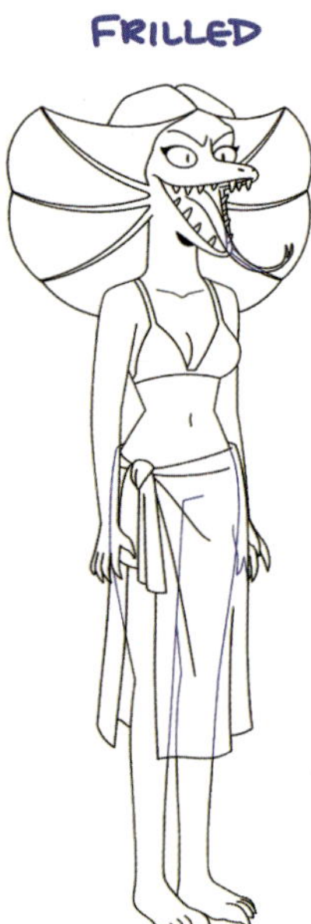

TULGANA BAZAAR ALIENS

We see familiar species like Klingons, Andorians, and Ferengi, but we also came up with a lot of new aliens. We had our cake and ate it, too.

TULGANA BAR ALIENS

LCARS S1E3

AIRDATE: 20200820
STARDATE: 57501.4

"Temporal Edict"

A new work protocol eliminating "buffer time" has the ***Lower Decks*** crew running ragged as they try to keep up with their tightened schedules.

Gelrak V is a planet that feels very classic original series *Star Trek* (TOS).

The inspiration of this episode was that we are in a tough situation on an original series planet where Mariner and Ransom are not seeing eye to eye. The threat on the planet made sense, but we had to figure out the stakes on the ship and how the Gelrakians could take over the *Cerritos*. Because Captain Freeman was trying to control everyone's time, we showed clocks everywhere, making the crew overtly aware and exhausted, which allowed the Gelrakians to infiltrate the ship. We added graffiti throughout the ship and on the hull, which was a great way to show their take-over.

"On this planet we see the structures are very much integrated with the environment, with an exception for a few key locations like the colosseum."

— Khang Le

GELRAK ARENA

GELRAK OBJECTS

"Because it's very rocky and barren, the Gelrakians tend to carve out of these mountains and create structures where they live.

"Most of the inhabitants live inside the mountains, in which they almost become skyscrapers."

— Khang Le

GELRAK ARENA

GELRAKIAN SHIPS

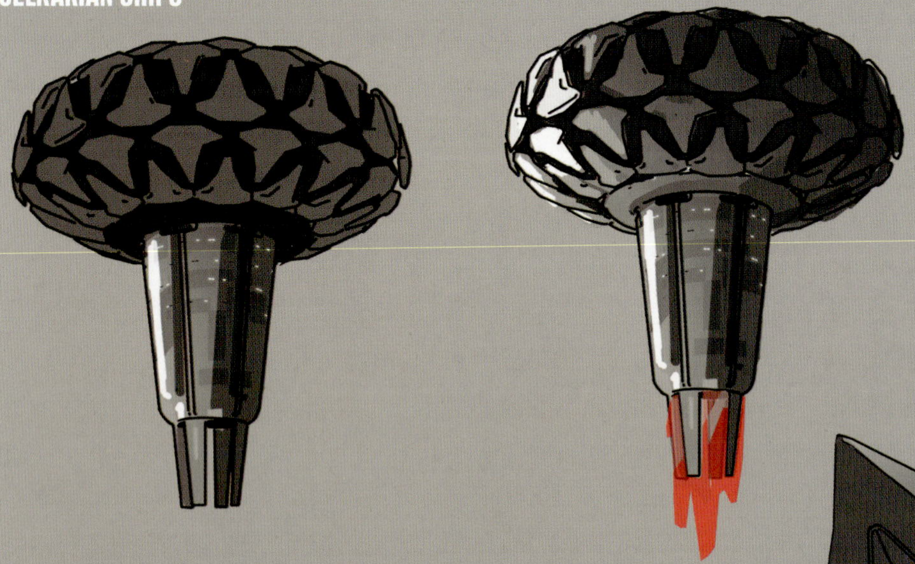

"The crystals are used to power technology for civilization. It looks barren at first, but all the crystals are a very vast source of energy that they can utilize throughout their landscape, including their living utilities and even spaceships."

— Khang Le

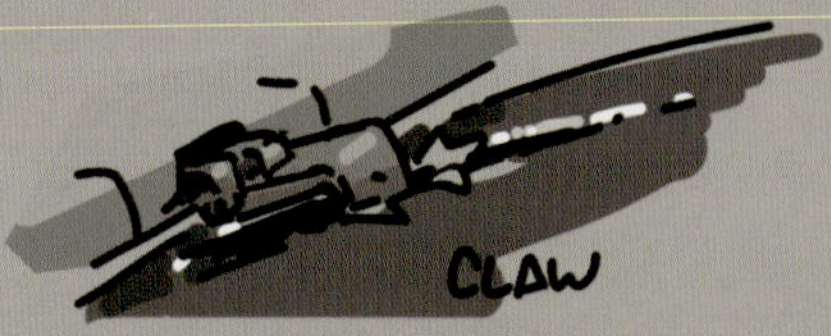

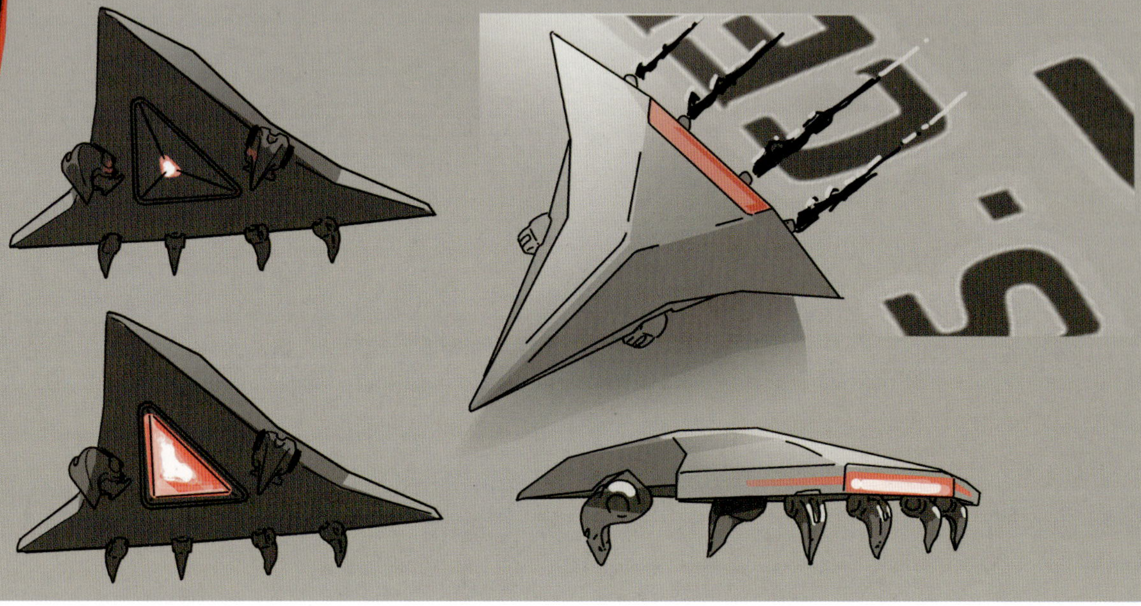

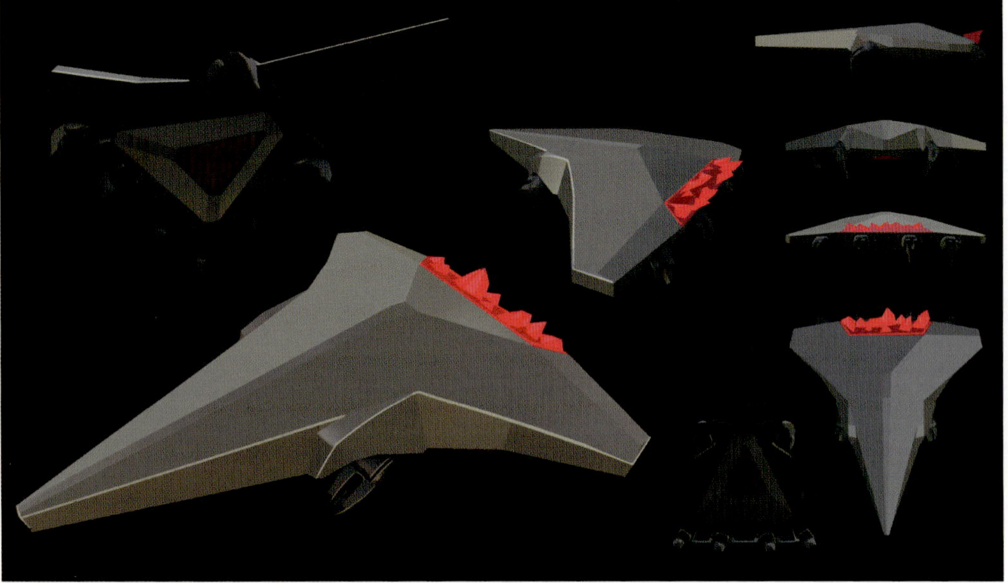

VINDOR

GELRAKIANS

"With the Gelrakians, we explored different animal pupils like goats and frogs."

— Alexandre Pelletier

MILES O'BRIEN

The statue of Miles O'Brien as "the most important person in Starfleet history" at the end of the episode became one of the first art moments in the show when the fans realized that *Lower Decks* was on their side. We were starting to earn our stripes.

LCARS S1E4

AIRDATE: 20200827
STARDATE: 57538.9

"Moist Vessel"

Captain Freeman seeks the ultimate payback after Mariner blatantly disrespects her in front of the crew.

It was really hard to come up with bad jobs for Mariner because the ships are all made to look cool and fun. How could we dramatize something we've never seen before?

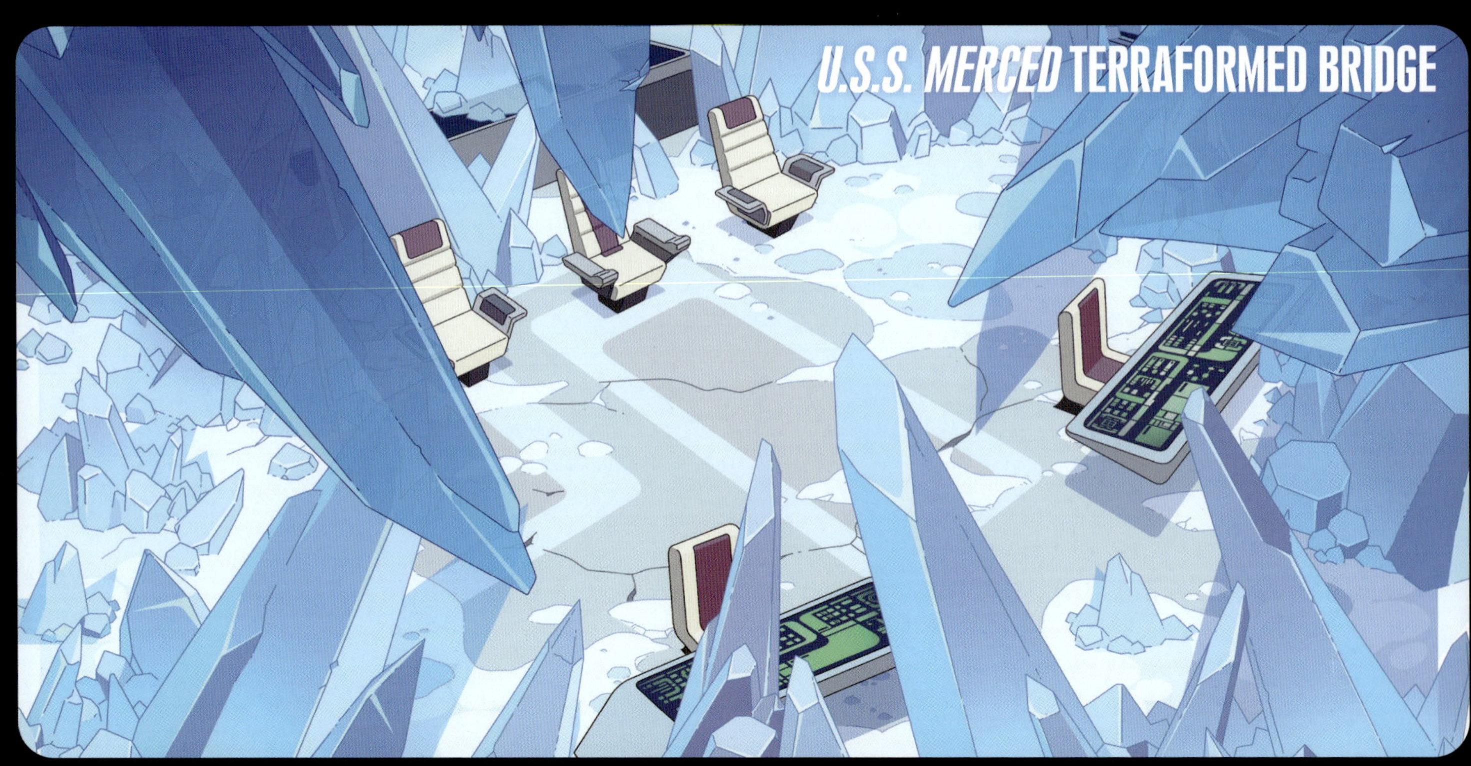

U.S.S. MERCED TERRAFORMED BRIDGE

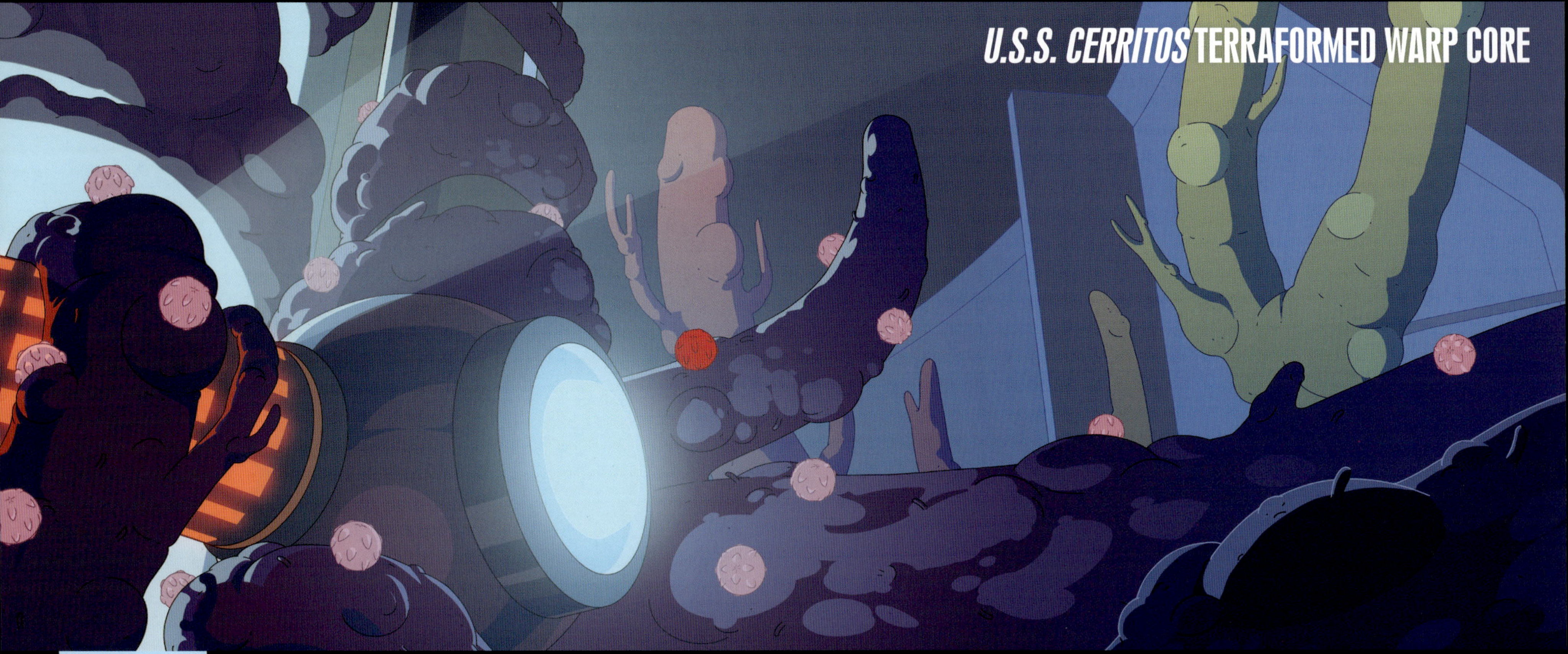

U.S.S. CERRITOS TERRAFORMED WARP CORE

CERRITOS TERRAFORMED INTERIORS

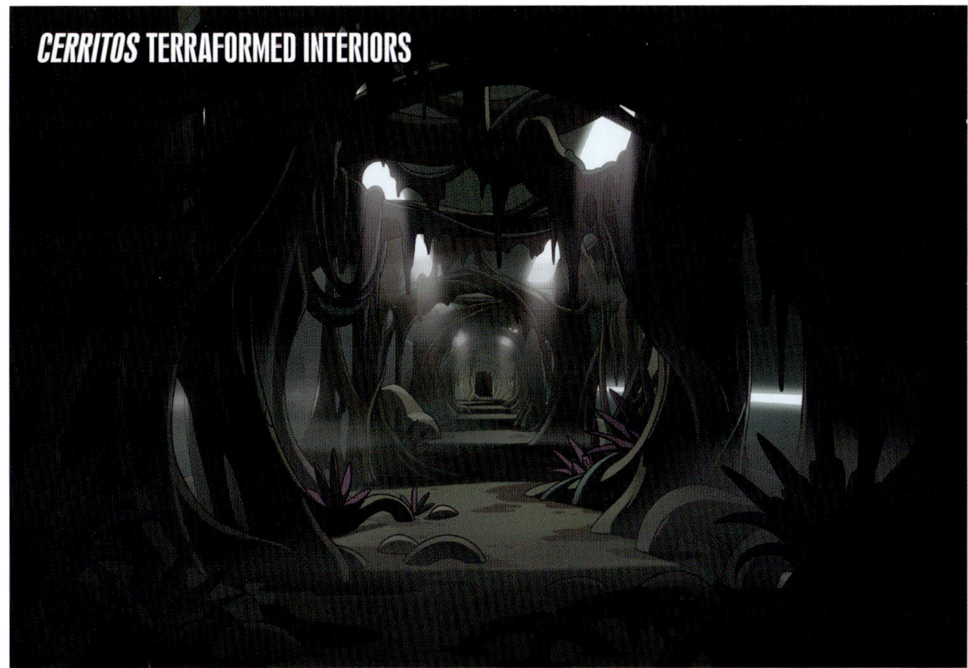

What's more fun than destroying a ship? We wanted to fill the *Cerritos* with water and terraform it with different environments. We wanted a fun ship-in-peril episode with everyone working together amongst the chaos.

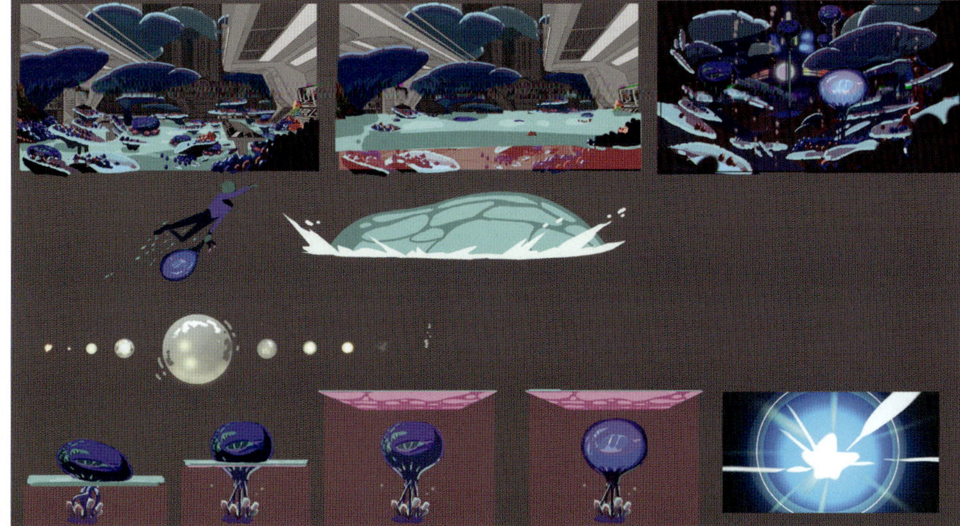

ANCIENT GENERATION SHIP

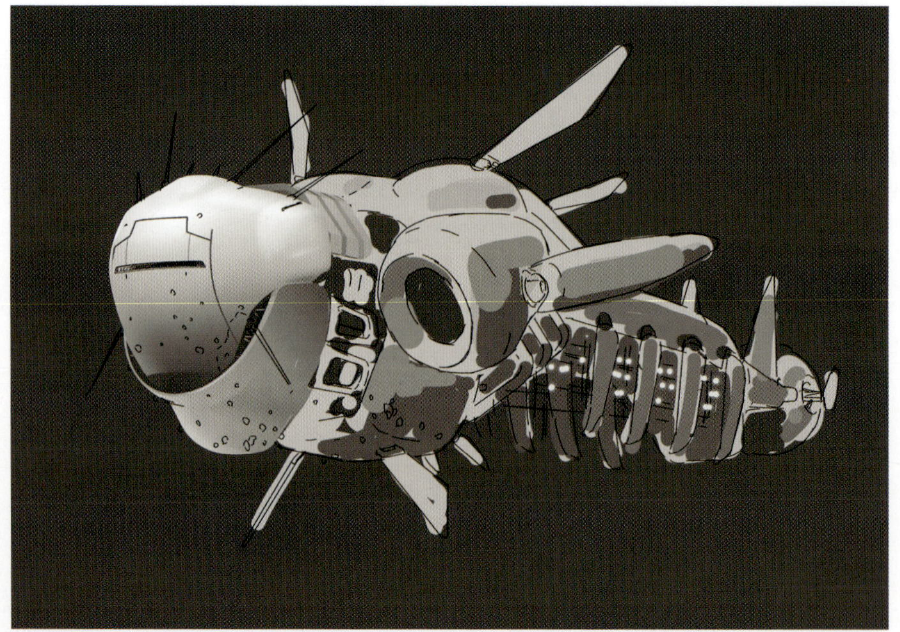

ANCIENT GENERATION SHIP SHUTTLE BAY

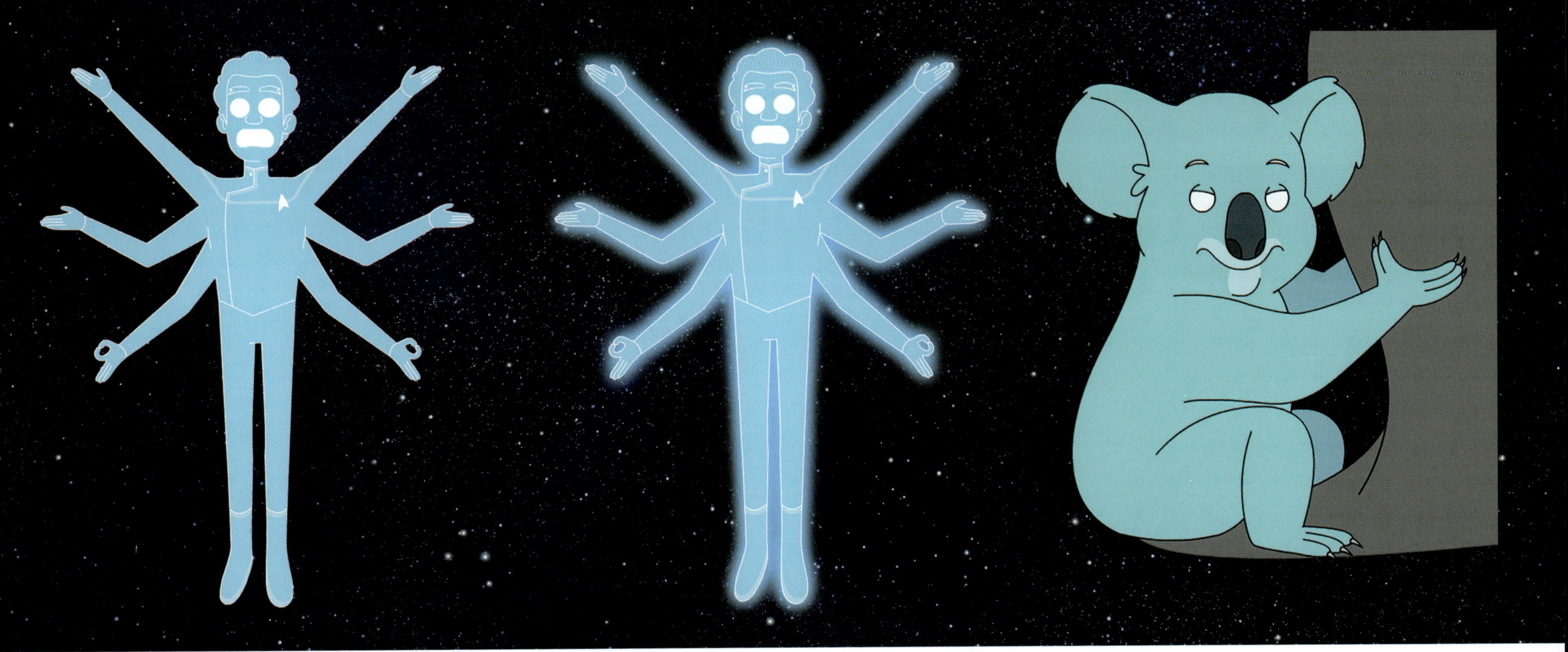

We meet the koala for the first time in this episode, which several crew members later report seeing during near-death experiences. It's also the first time we see another *California* class, the *U.S.S. Merced*, led by Captain Durango.

LTJG. O'CONNOR

CAPTAIN DURANGO

LCARS S1E5

AIRDATE: 20200903
STARDATE: 57601.3

"Cupid's Errant Arrow"

Mariner is suspicious of Boimler's new girlfriend, Lieutenant Barbara Brinson. Tendi and Rutherford grow jealous of a bigger starship's gear on the *U.S.S. Vancouver.*

We needed the *U.S.S. Vancouver* to read as a new ship, but not a capital-class ship. It's essentially the same as the *Cerritos* with different colors, but everyone is impressed.

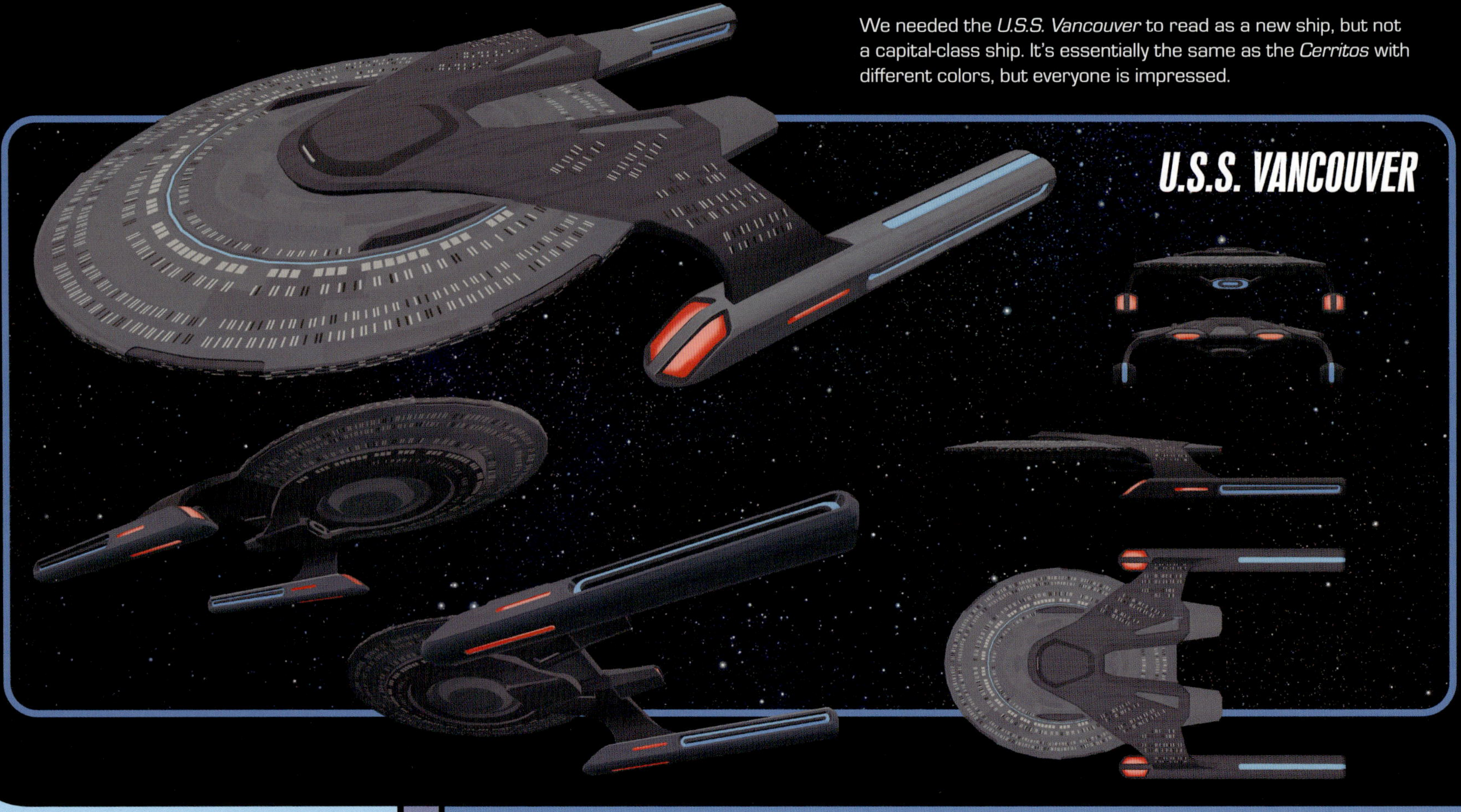

U.S.S. VANCOUVER

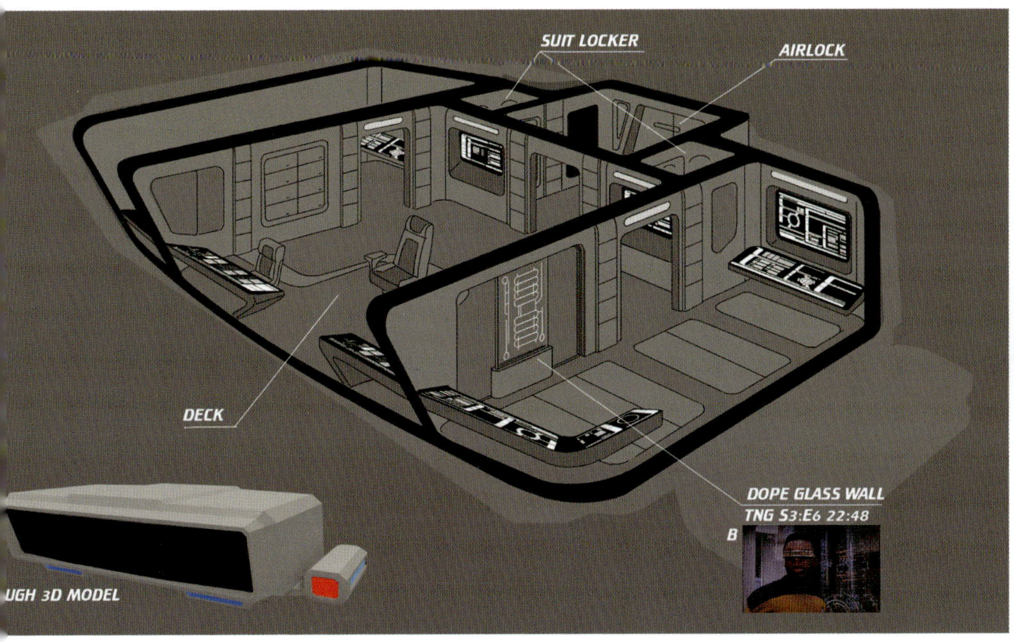

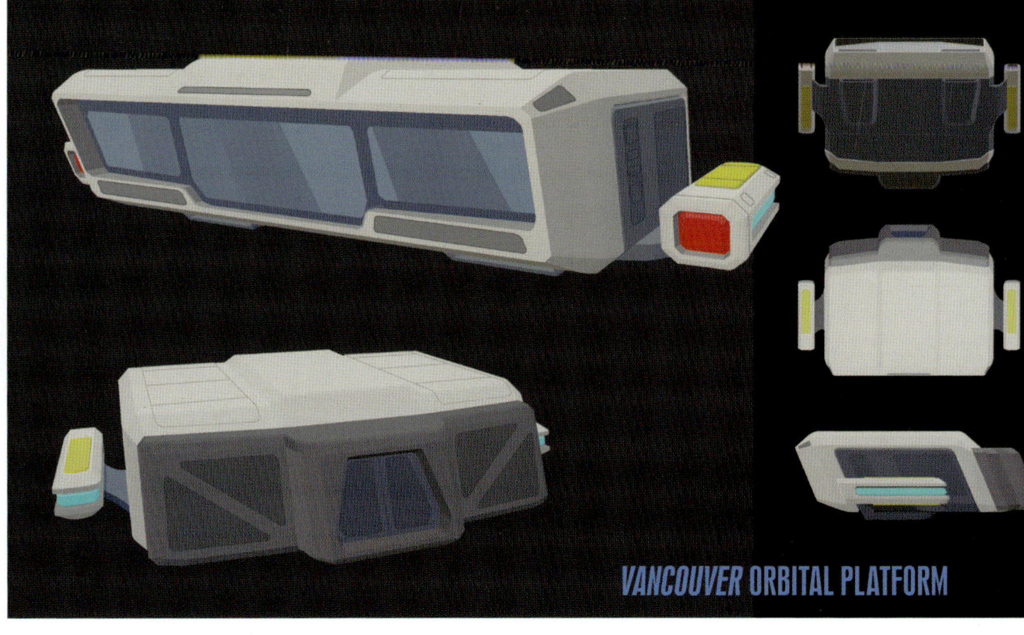

CAPTAIN NGUYEN

LT. BARBARA BRINSON

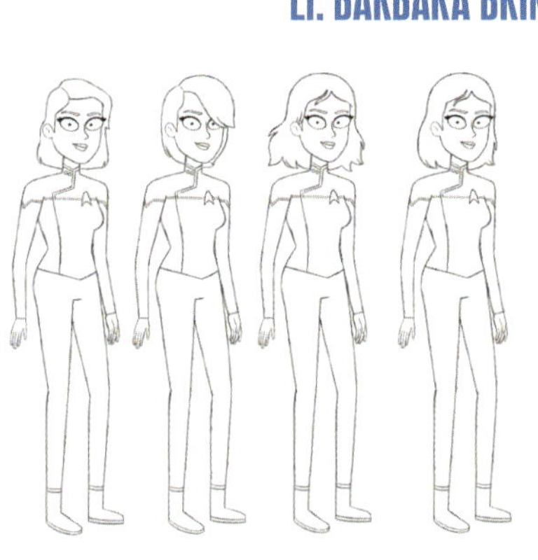

We see the dynamic between Starfleet captains, and how Captain Freeman and her crew are seen as lesser than the *Vancouver*. This episode sets up that the *California* class is seen as lesser than the rest of the ship classes. Part of the DNA of the show is about the *Lower Decks* crew, but now the bridge crew are also lower deckers, and the *Cerritos* is a lower-decker ship compared to other ships in the fleet.

ENS. NIKO
ENS. ANGIE

NIKO · CREATURE
MORPHING?
A.
B.
C.
NIKO'S HUMAN TEETH

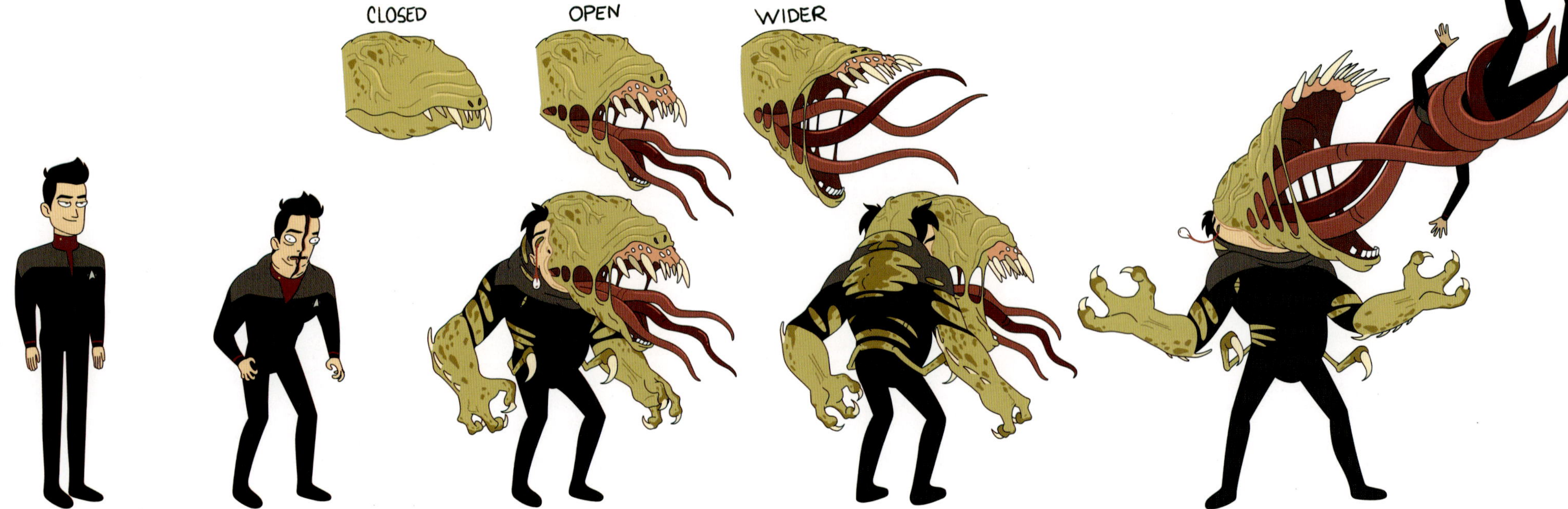
CLOSED
OPEN
WIDER

PURPLE AND RED ALIENS

This episode is a play on classic episodes where some alien thing is happening to someone, but nobody knows about it. However, in this situation, a non-alien thing is happening, but Mariner is hyper focused on it.

PARASITE

A B C

COCOON

Husk

Cocoon

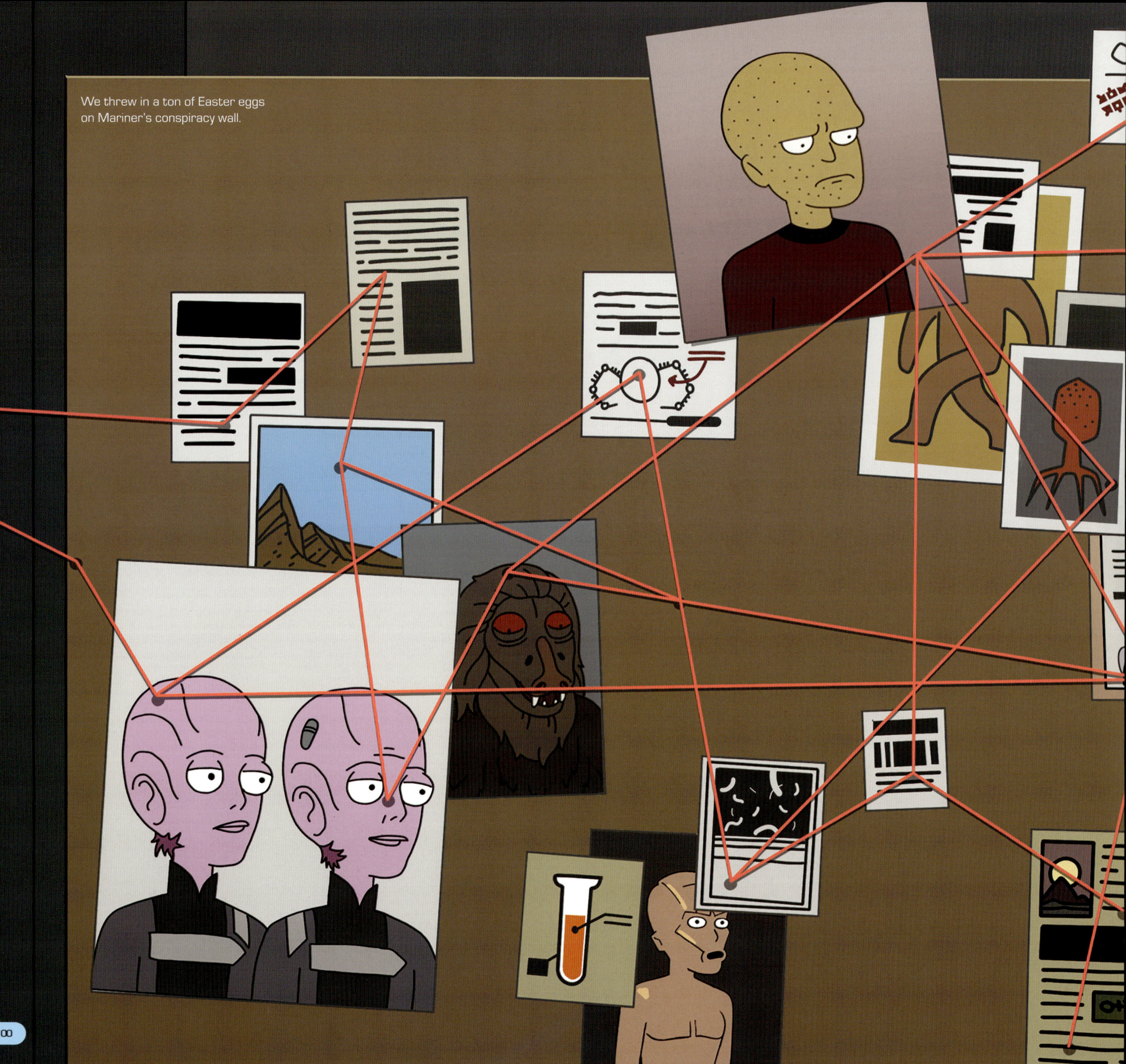

We threw in a ton of Easter eggs on Mariner's conspiracy wall.

LCARS S1E6

AIRDATE: 20200910
STARDATE: 57663.9

"Terminal Provocations"

The lovable, but awkward, Ensign Fletcher makes work difficult for Mariner and Boimler. Rutherford introduces Tendi to a holodeck training program he created.

This episode is the first time we meet the Delta shifters, who are designed like our main cast, but slightly different. They're the ones who work when our guys are sleeping.

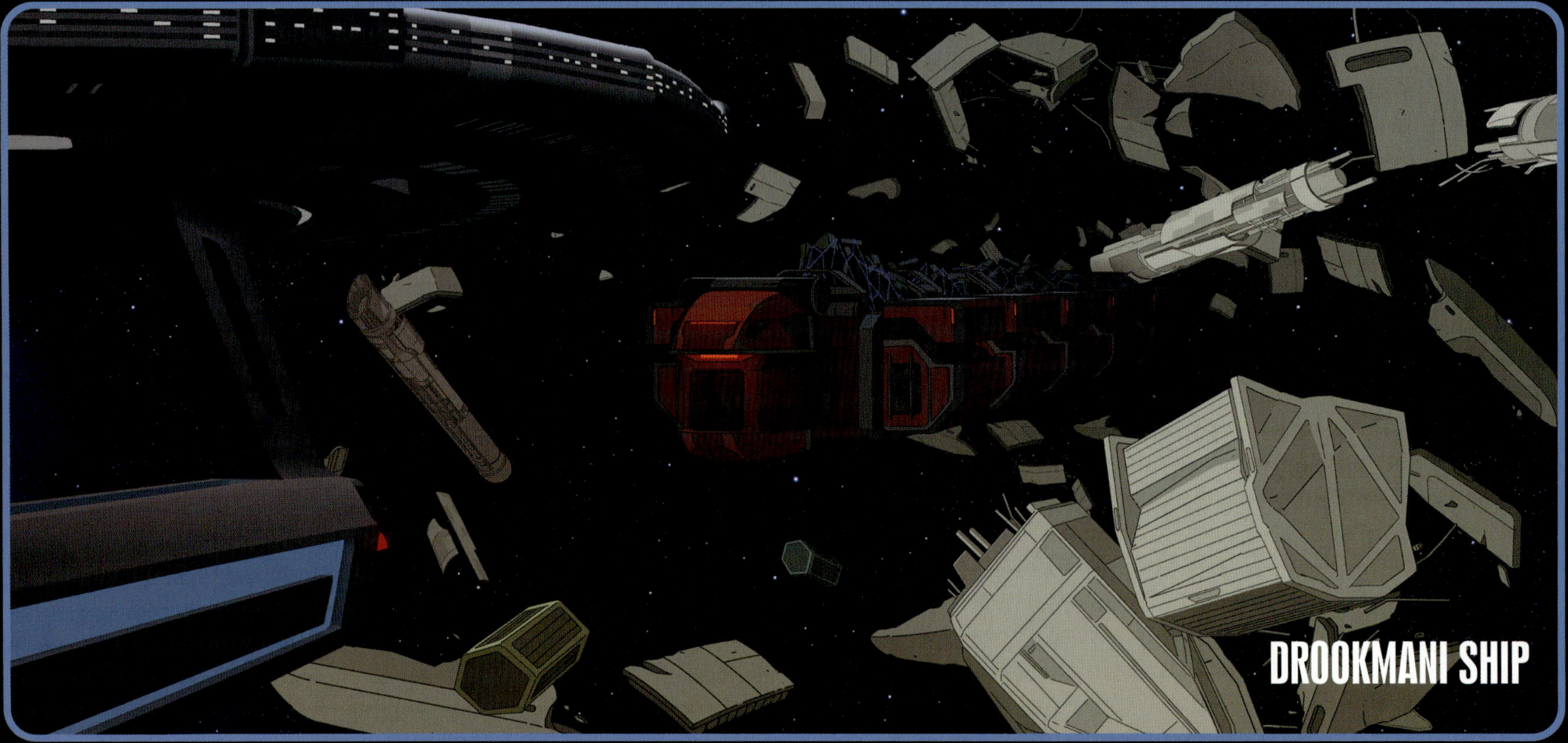

BAJORAN MARKETPLACE

DROOKMANI SHIP

DROOKMANI SHIP CAPTAIN

The logistics of the Drookmani being in a big, clunky scavenger ship and not being equipped with weapons created a challenge in how to make them a threat. We designed their ship so the front command center could detach and maneuver around the cargo in space, then throw it at the *Cerritos*.

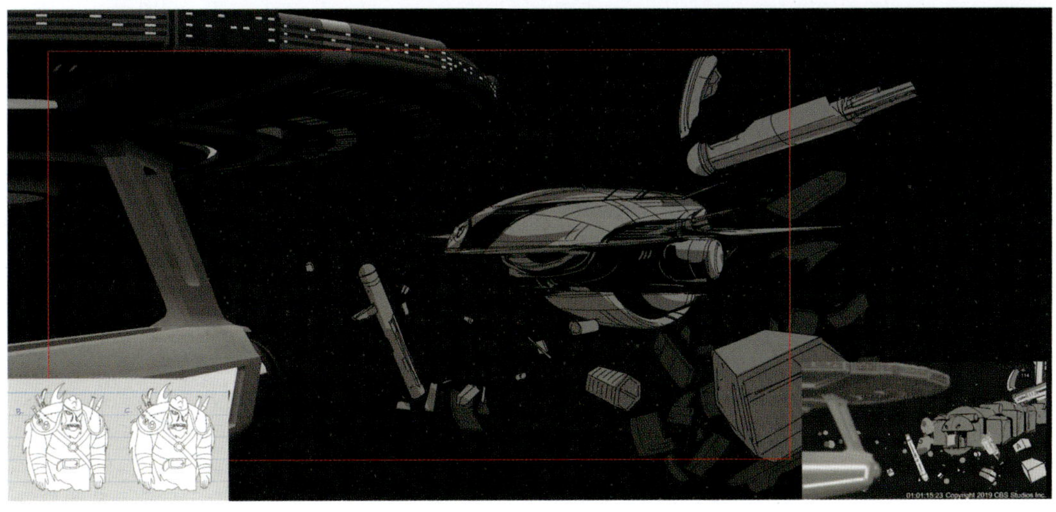

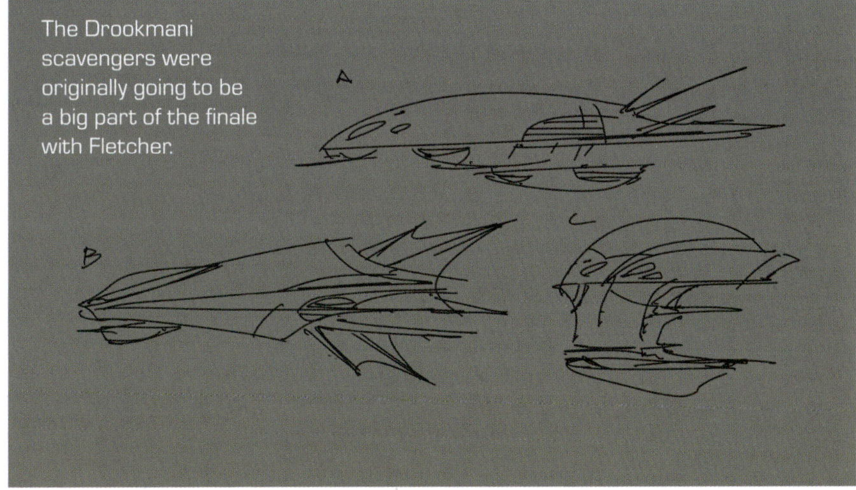

The Drookmani scavengers were originally going to be a big part of the finale with Fletcher.

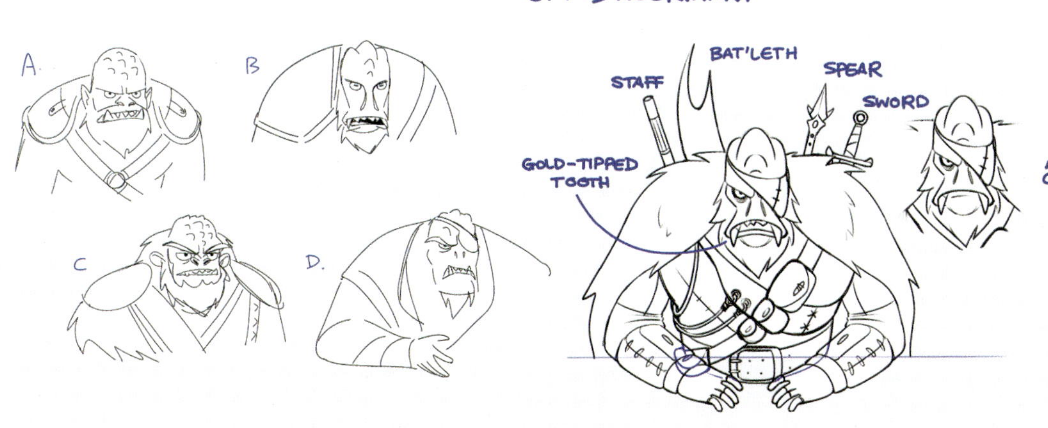

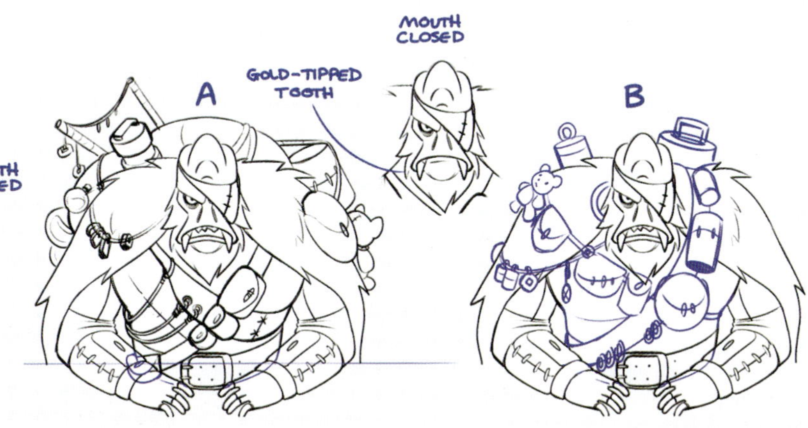

BAJORAN MARKETPLACE

We had to figure out the design language of the Bajoran marketplace.

This episode is a classic trouble-on-the-holodeck, safety-protocols-are-deactivated story.

Mariner and Boimler's friendship starts to crystallize in this episode as they bond over the Chu Chu dance and wear matching T-shirts.

BADGEY

Badgey is our version of Microsoft's Clippy but gone wrong. He's cartoonishly violent, which couldn't happen in another *Star Trek* show. He only belongs in an animated show.

We wanted Rutherford's tinkering with the holodeck training program to be something like what Geordi would do, but he still has much to learn and accidentally developed a catastrophic creation.

ENS. FLETCHER

If our ensigns are imperfect, what does an ensign that should not be in Starfleet look like? Fletcher was a bad ensign that our Lower Deckers assumed had the best intentions. We based some of his actions on Lieutenant Barclay, like plugging himself into a computer. Fletcher was voiced by Tim Robinson. So we matched his character and animation to his performance.

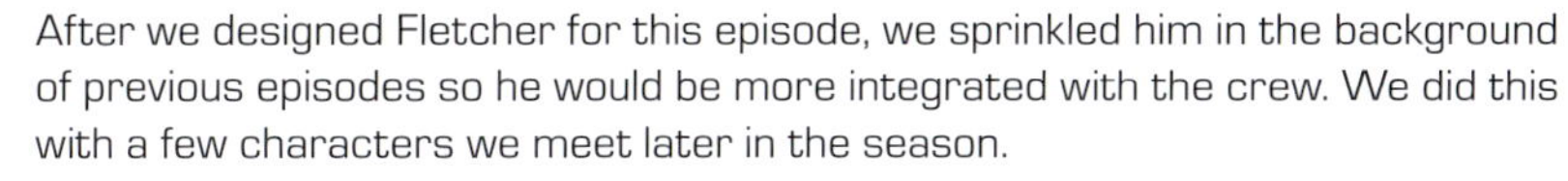

After we designed Fletcher for this episode, we sprinkled him in the background of previous episodes so he would be more integrated with the crew. We did this with a few characters we meet later in the season.

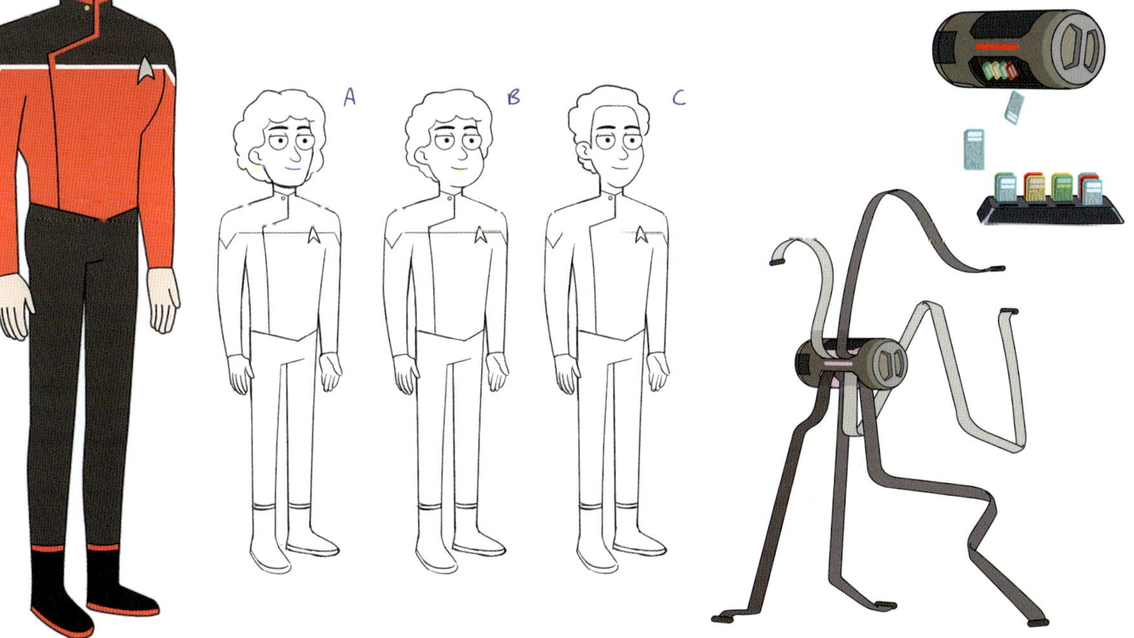

LCARS S1E7

AIRDATE: 2020917
STARDATE: 57752.6

"Much Ado About Boimler"

Mariner tries to impress her best friend from Starfleet Academy, visiting captain Amina Ramsey.

The storyline was in the original pitch—what if someone got stuck in the beaming mode with the loud sparkles and how annoying that would be.

In our balance of comedy and *Star Trek*, comedy bubbled more in this one. What if we put all of the freakish accidents together on a ship with Boimler?

U.S.S. CERRITOS AND U.S.S. RUBIDOUX

KING PHIBEAS

KHWOPIANS

KHWOPIAN WATER FILTRATION SITE

ANTHONY THE SALAMANDER

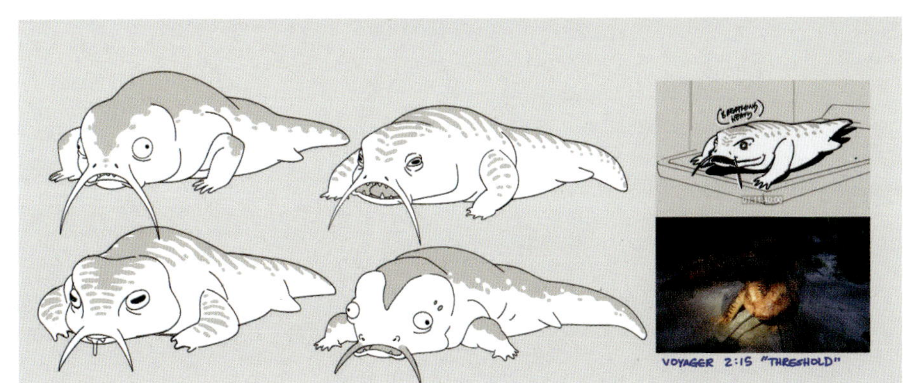

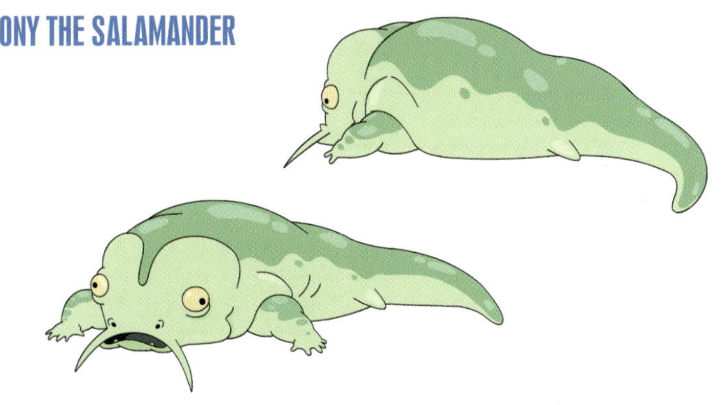

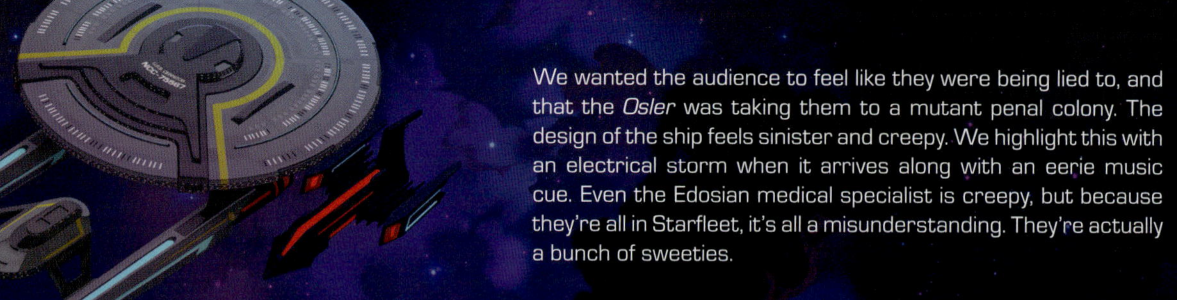

We wanted the audience to feel like they were being lied to, and that the *Osler* was taking them to a mutant penal colony. The design of the ship feels sinister and creepy. We highlight this with an electrical storm when it arrives along with an eerie music cue. Even the Edosian medical specialist is creepy, but because they're all in Starfleet, it's all a misunderstanding. They're actually a bunch of sweeties.

Tendi's dog stuff came from when we were auditioning actors. Mike wrote a monologue of Tendi remaking the DNA of a dog from scratch, but she's never actually seen a dog before. That's how we found Noël Wells, who was precise, but also funny and exuberant. All of that stuff made it into the show.

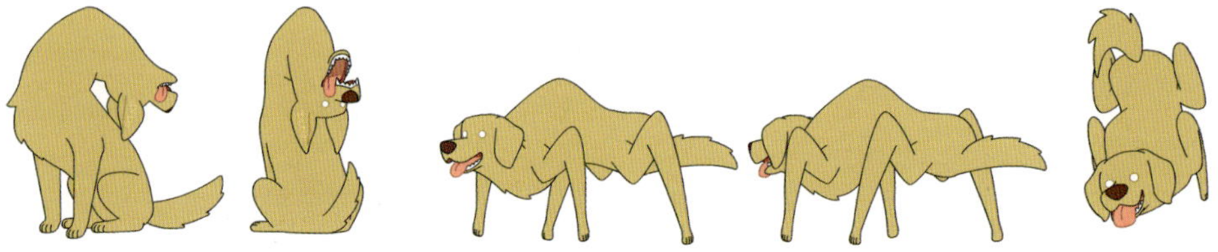

TENDI'S DOG

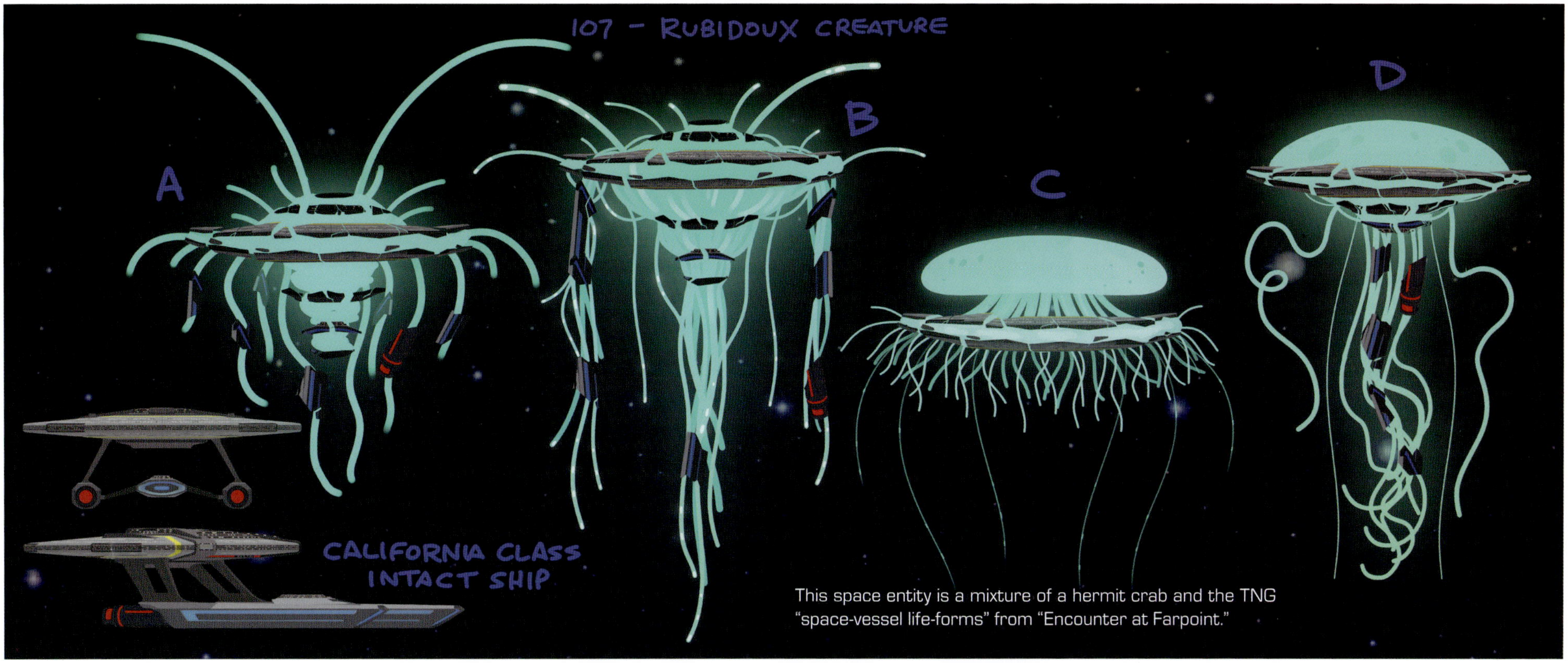

107 - RUBIDOUX CREATURE

A

B

C

D

CALIFORNIA CLASS
INTACT SHIP

This space entity is a mixture of a hermit crab and the TNG "space-vessel life-forms" from "Encounter at Farpoint."

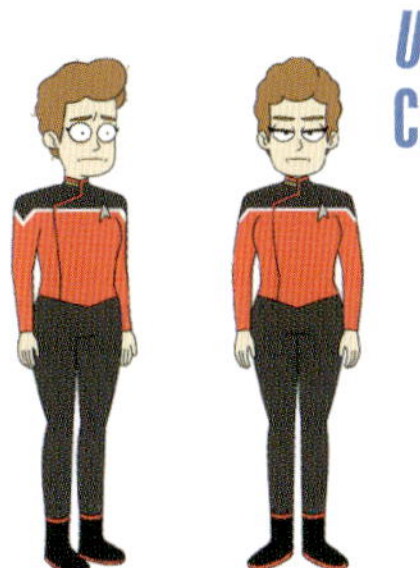

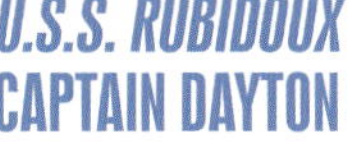

LCDR. DURGA

LT. DREW PRACHETT

LT. OTTESSA WARREN

CAPTAIN AMINA RAMSEY

U.S.S. OAKLAND CREW

With Mariner's story, we see her bristling at being put in a bridge-crew situation when an old friend comes to the *Cerritos*. We see Mariner take a dive on a bog planet with the sweet Khwopians. Then it escalates on the *U.S.S. Rubidoux* when a space entity tears the ship apart and they emergency beam everyone out of there.

RUBIDOUX BRIDGE

LCARS S1E8

AIRDATE: 20200924
STARDATE: UNKNOWN

"Veritas"

Mariner, Boimler, Tendi, and Rutherford are caught off guard when aliens force them to testify about a series of seemingly unrelated events.

"We used elements from TNG warbirds and used the TOS Bird of Prey colors to make a new bridge."
— Brad Winters

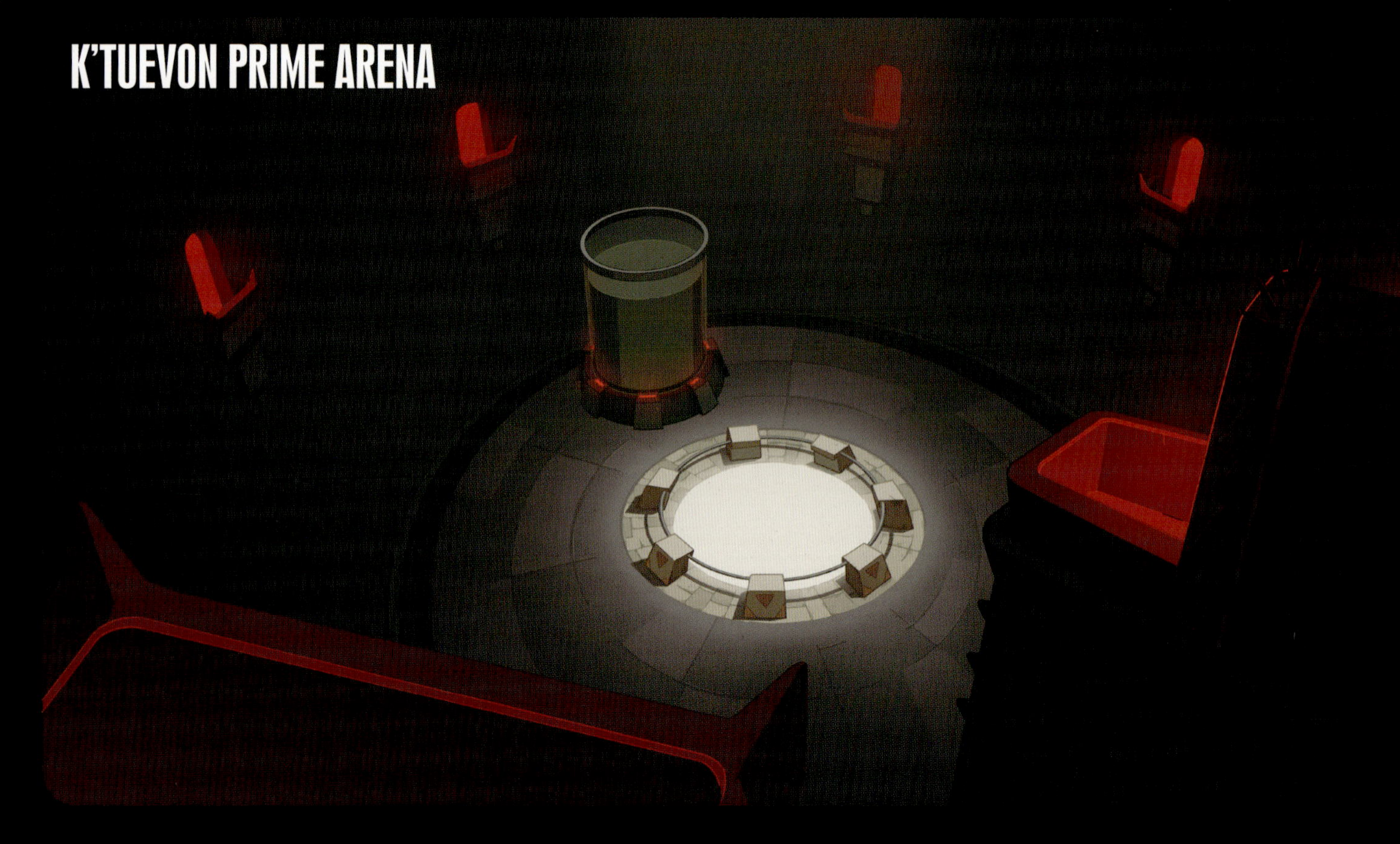

K'TUEVON PRIME ARENA

CESTUS III GORN WEDDING

K'TOEVON PRIME COUNCIL CHAMBER

"If you look closely, you see a balloon. Basically, we're telling you it's a party from the first shot."
— Brad Winters

All of season one of *Lower Decks* was inspired by playing all the big hits. What do you need in a *Star Trek* show? You need a trial episode. We wanted an episode that was inspired by when you were a kid, and you turned on the TV to an episode of *Star Trek*, but you missed the first five to seven minutes. For the rest of the episode, you're trying to piece it together and figure out the story. It's a trial clip show, but the audience and the Lower Deckers don't have any of the context for what is going on.

It's a sketch-comedy episode with different set pieces like the cleaning crew, the Clickets, the *D'deridex* class, and the Gorn wedding. All the art in the episode needs to support these.

U.S.S. ALHAMBRA CREW

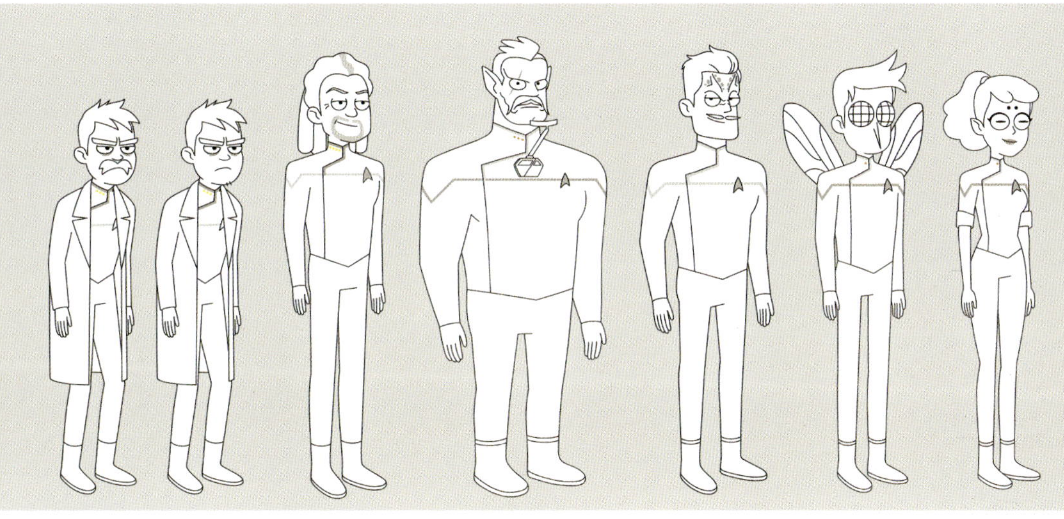

TACTICAL STEALTH TEAM

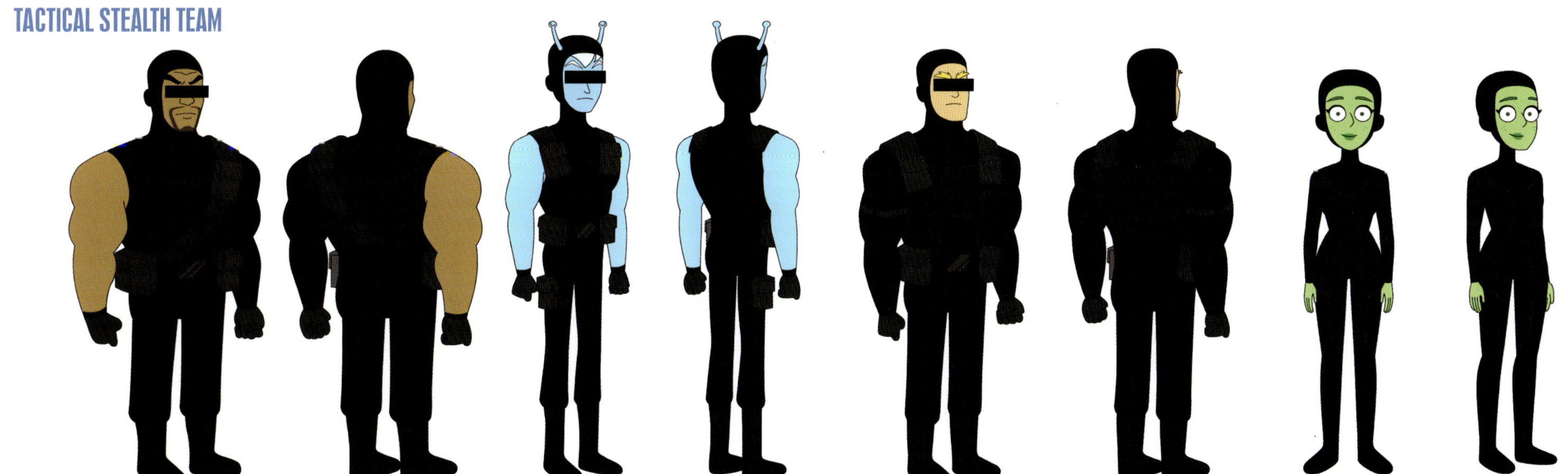

LCARS S1E9

AIRDATE: 20201001
STARDATE: UNKNOWN

"Crisis Point"

Mariner repurposes Boimler's holodeck program to cast herself as the villain in a *Lower Decks*-style movie.

We wanted a movie adaptation of a show we were making that is a loving parody of the *Star Trek* movies.

CERRITOS BAR

This was a big Mariner episode. We had three Mariners: Vindicta, real Mariner, and holodeck Mariner, all played by Tawny.

VINDICTA'S SHIP

VINDICTA'S SHIP DESIGNS

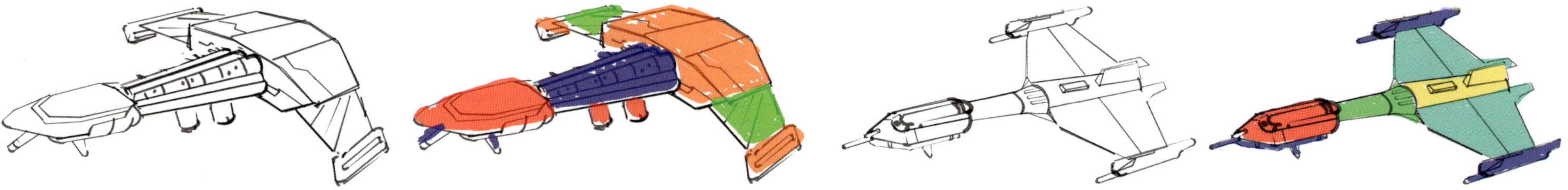

SHAXS' PHASER BAZOOKA

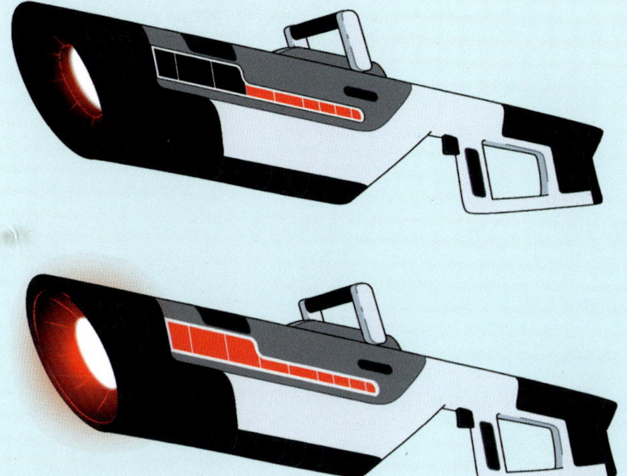

To separate this episode from the rest of the season, we updated our familiar locations on the *Cerritos* with a more dramatic color palette, changed the aspect ratio of the framing, and even added film grain and cigarette burns in post.

VINDICTA'S PHASER

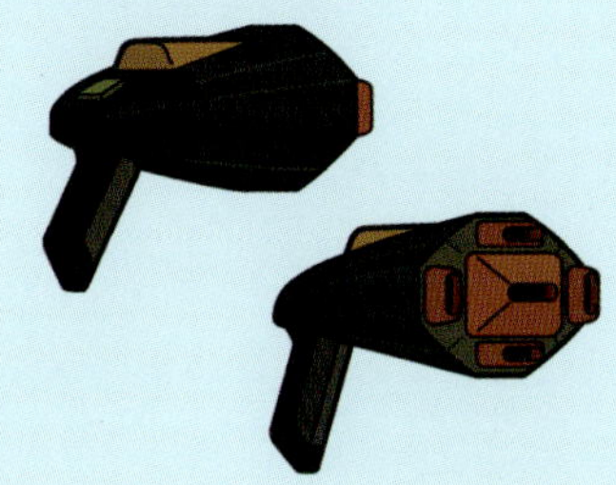

VINDICTA

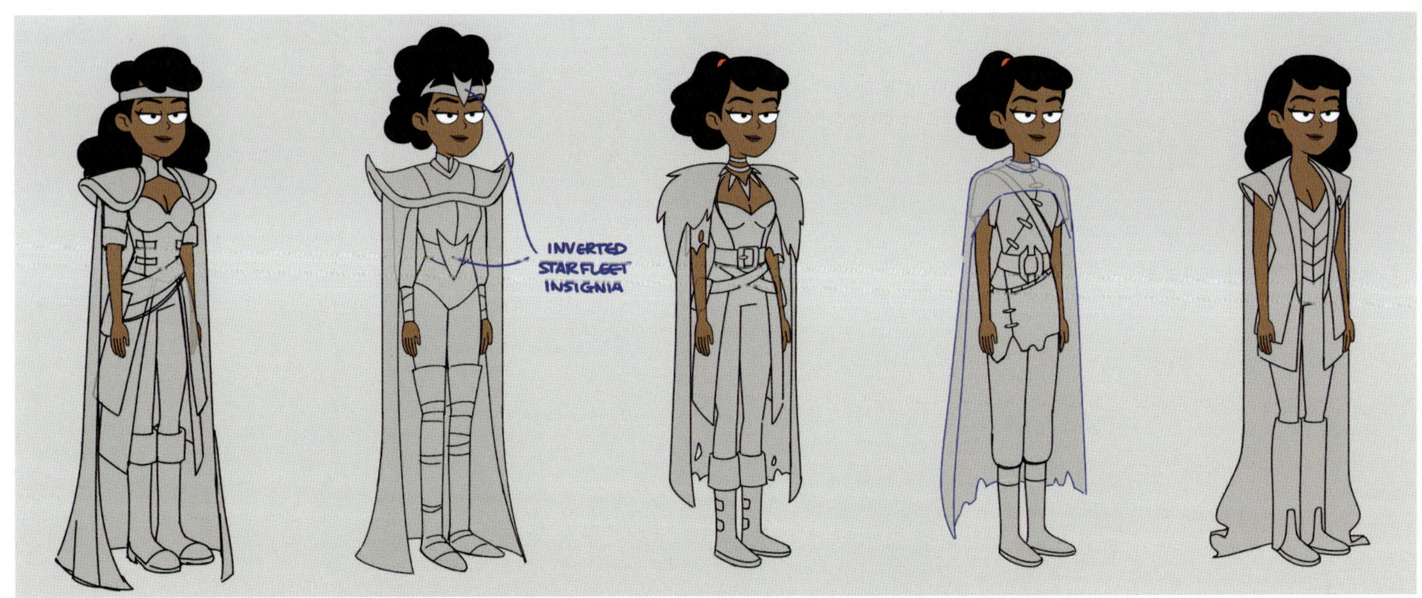

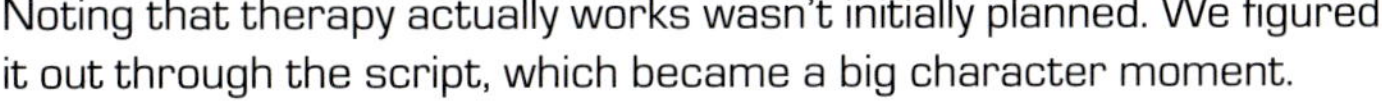

Noting that therapy actually works wasn't initially planned. We figured it out through the script, which became a big character moment.

This is the first time we meet Dr. Migleemo, who is an annoying, incapable, but lovable academic whose methods don't work for Mariner.

We also hint at Tendi's complicated Orion background of pirating, and the *Cerritos* crew learns of Mariner's relationship with the captain.

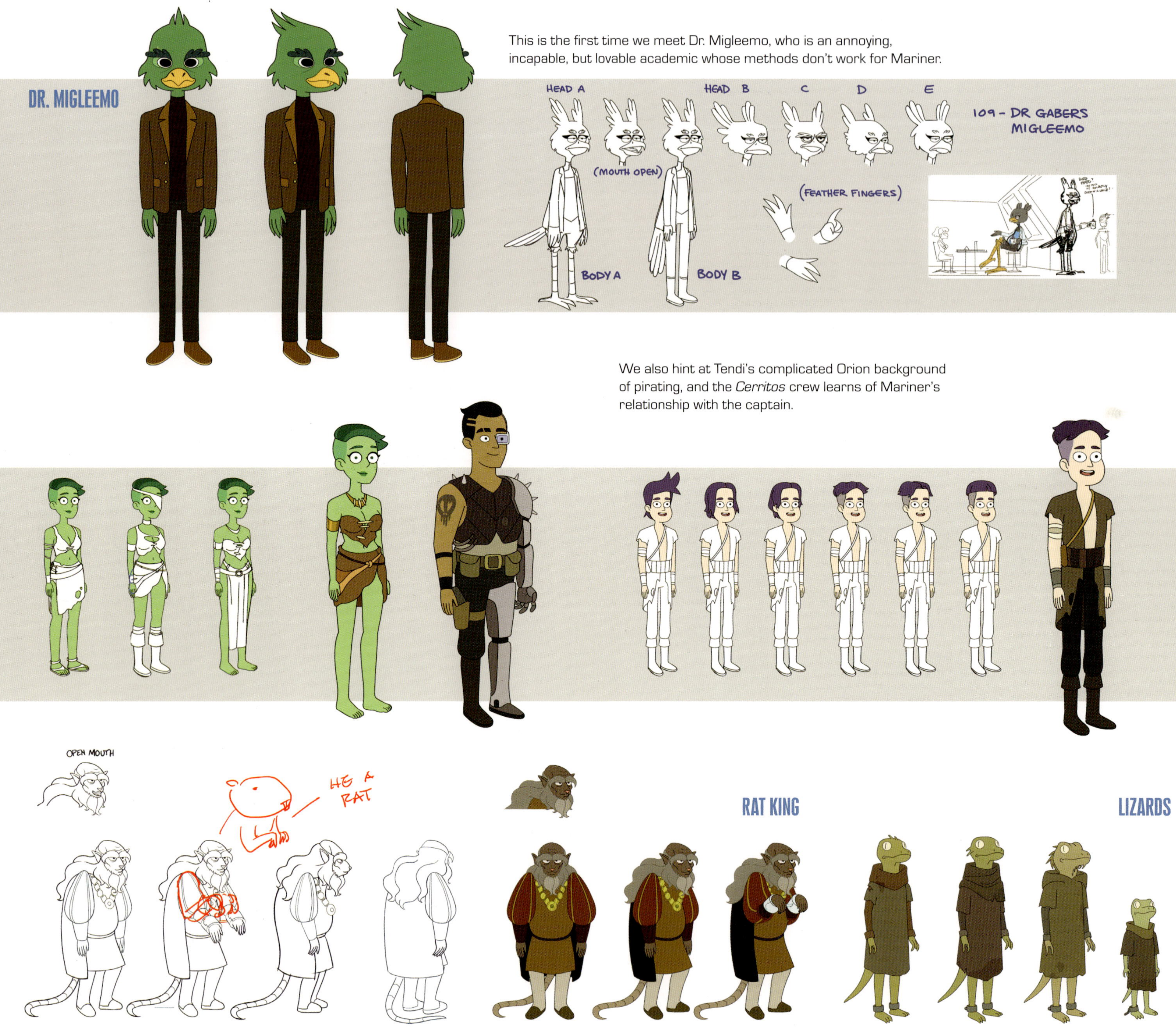

Inspired by comic books when X character kills the universe. We wanted this to feel like it's a huge battle, but it's all on the holodeck, so nobody gets hurt.

LCARS S1E10

AIRDATE: 20201008
STARDATE: UNKNOWN

"No Small Parts"

The *U.S.S. Cerritos* encounters a familiar enemy. Tendi helps a struggling recruit find her footing.

This episode had to feel like a *Star Trek* finale: big and unresolved.

There's a poignant moment in the beginning when we see the *U.S.S. Solvang* destroyed. This sets up the stakes for the episode.

PAKLED SHIP

We called back to alien villains that were underestimated, which were the Pakleds. These villains are so stupid, but they are great for the rise of fascism. Their lack of intelligence was misinterpreted as weak, but they've been gaining power and acquiring technology that could pull you apart.

We put Riker on the *U.S.S. Titan*, a ship that had not yet been seen on screen. So we used the contest-winning book-cover design by Sean P. Tourangeau, and made the ship canon.

U.S.S. TITAN

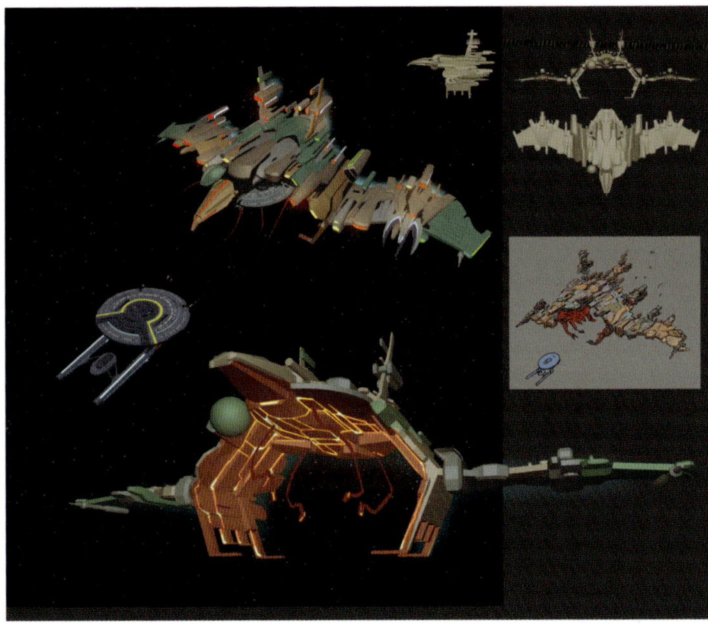

PAKLED SHIP

"The Pakled ship was crazy in concept and in building it. There were a lot of moving parts and functionality. The Pakleds are known for acquiring technology from various sources, so their ships are kitbashed." — Khang Le

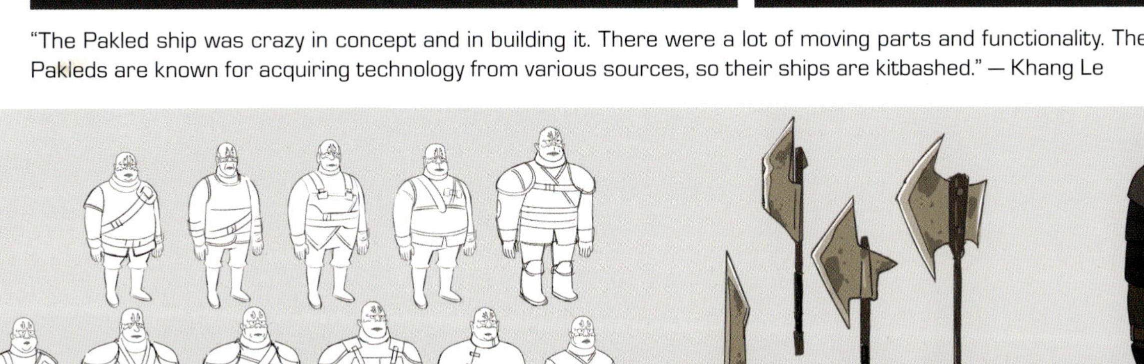

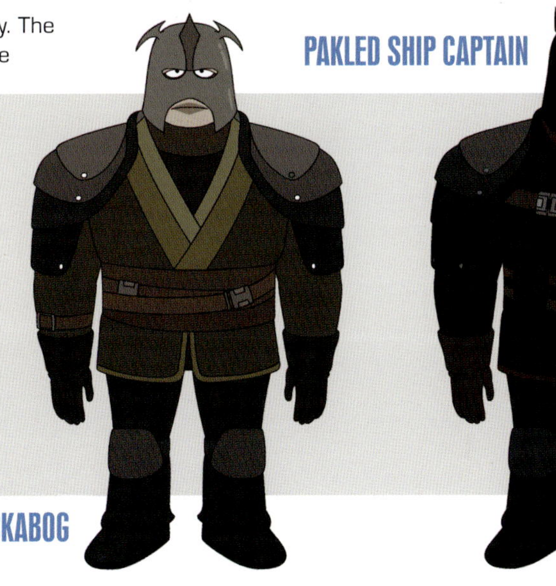

PAKLED SHIP CAPTAIN

PAKLED SHIP CREW

PAKLED WEAPONS

JACKABOG

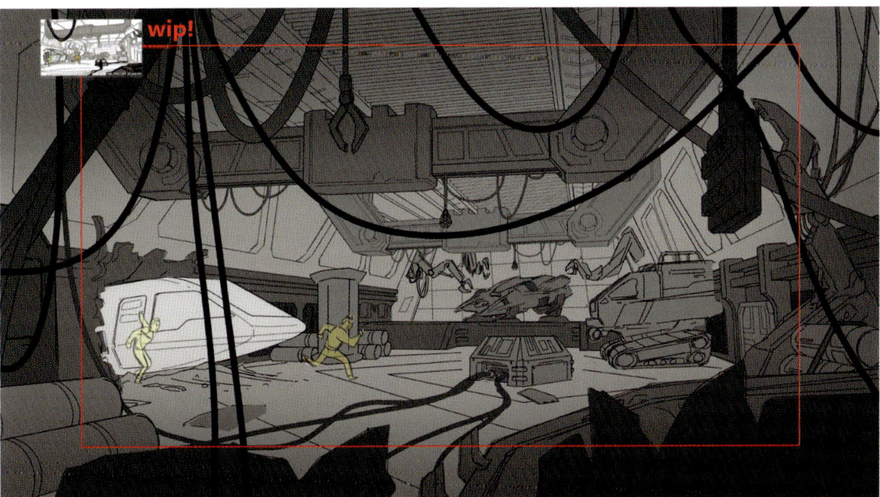

PAKLED SHIP INTERIOR

CAPTAIN RIKER AND CMDR. DEANNA TROI

Mike met Jonathan Frakes when their paths crossed and pitched *Lower Decks* to him with the intent to have him as a guest on the show. Frakes loved that idea. But we were now at the end of the season and hadn't figured out how to make that work.

If we were getting Riker, we of course wanted Marina Sirtis to play Deanna Troi. We gave her character design bigger pupils to match her black contact lenses on TNG. And we designed Riker based on how he would look in this era.

TITAN BRIDGE

At the end of the episode, we see Boimler in his new uniform. Throughout the season, Mariner and Boimler have become close friends, but then he messes it up, betrays her, and undoes it all by leaving her behind.

TITAN SKETCHES

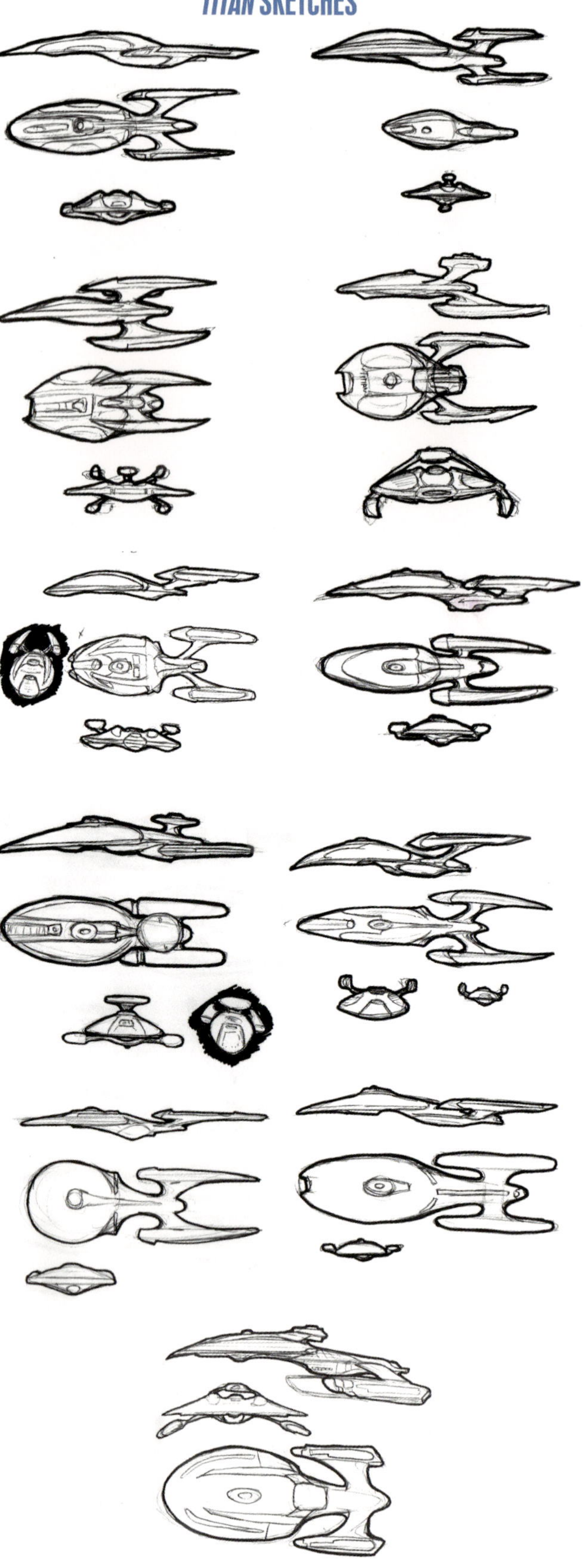

A big *Star Trek* theme we've left out until here was that the show had to be saying something. At the time we were making this, fascism was rising in Europe again, and it was being mirrored in American politics, so we wanted to do a villain that matched that.

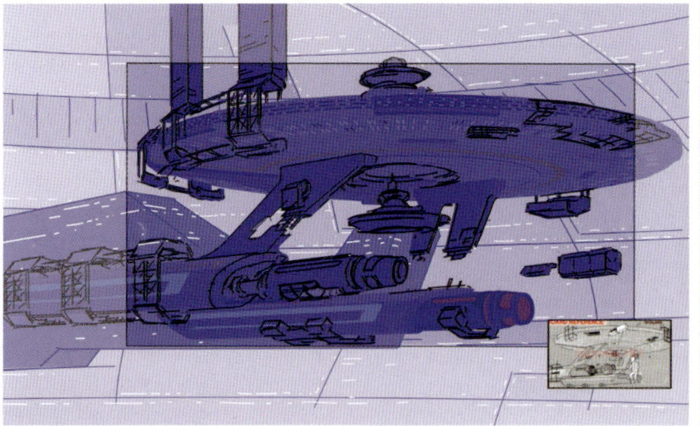

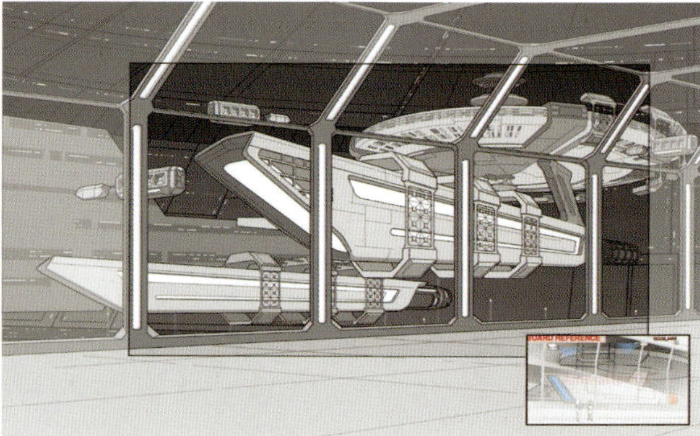

ENSIGN PEANUT HAMPER

Tendi got through the whole season starting out brand-new on the *Cerritos*. With Peanut Hamper joining the crew for the first time, this was Tendi's chance to help with her new-gained knowledge, only to be comically betrayed.

We copied the exocomp design from TNG and matched its movement. We made it a cute hovering robot with a sweet voice by Kether Donohue, but who was ultimately manipulative and a terrible ensign that shouldn't be in Starfleet.

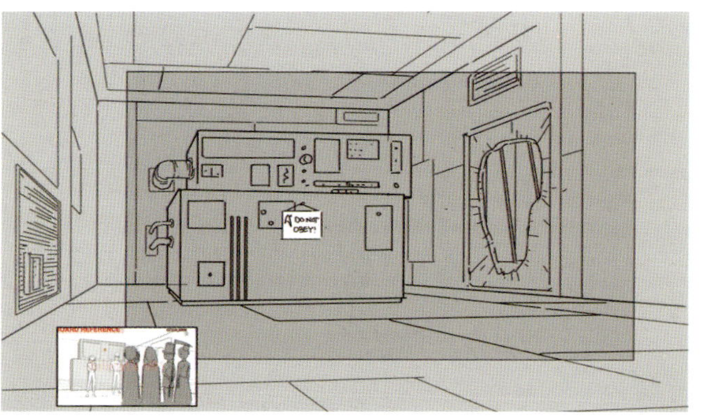

CHAPTER 05

LCARS 40274

02-654598

SEASON TWO

Paramount+
ORIGINAL
STAR TREK
LOWER
DECKS
II

LCARS S2E1

AIRDATE: 20210812
STARDATE: 57995.8

"Strange Energies"

Season premiere. Approximately three months after the events of the season one finale, the *U.S.S. Cerritos* is dispatched on a mission where it ends up in a sci-fi event resulting in "strange energy," which Commander Ransom inadvertently absorbs.

Apergos had to feel like an advanced planet that got really dirty.

APERGOSIAN CITY

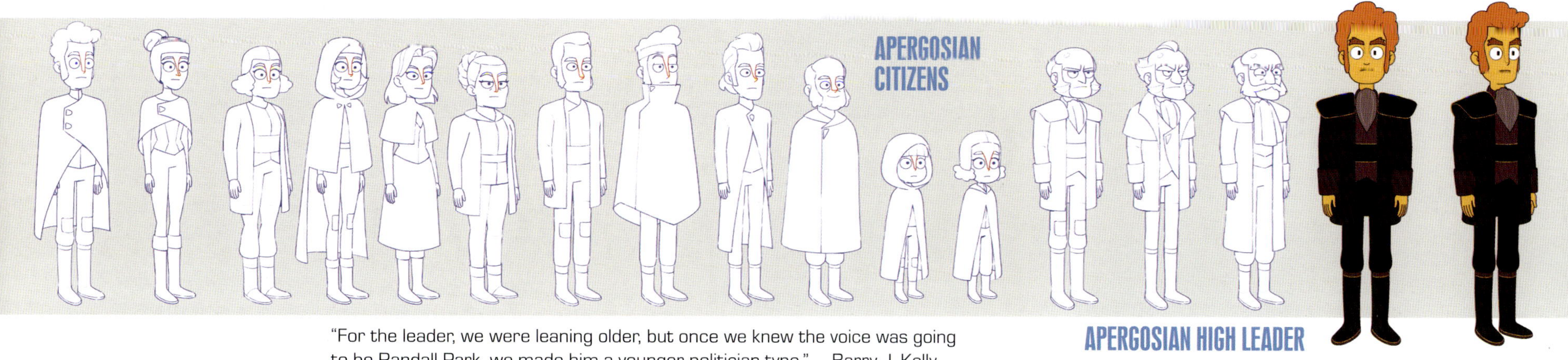

"For the leader, we were leaning older, but once we knew the voice was going to be Randall Park, we made him a younger politician type." — Barry J. Kelly

"In the beginning, we tried out a lot of stuff. Maybe the species evolved from apes, lizards, or rats?" — Barry J. Kelly

"The clock tower and archway were anchors to know where we were in any shot."
— Barry J. Kelly

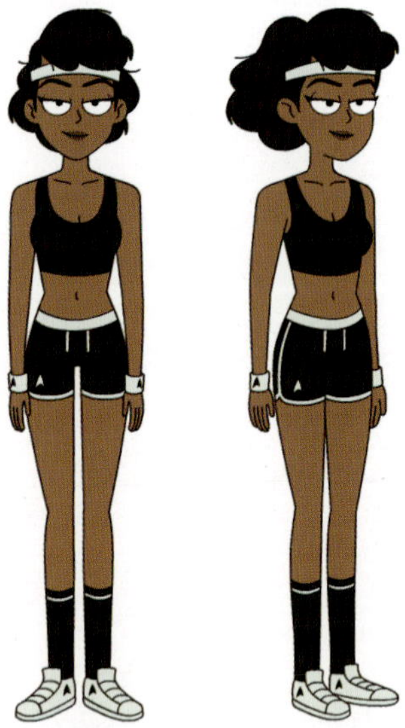

This is where we get Mariner's workout outfit.

CARDASSIANS

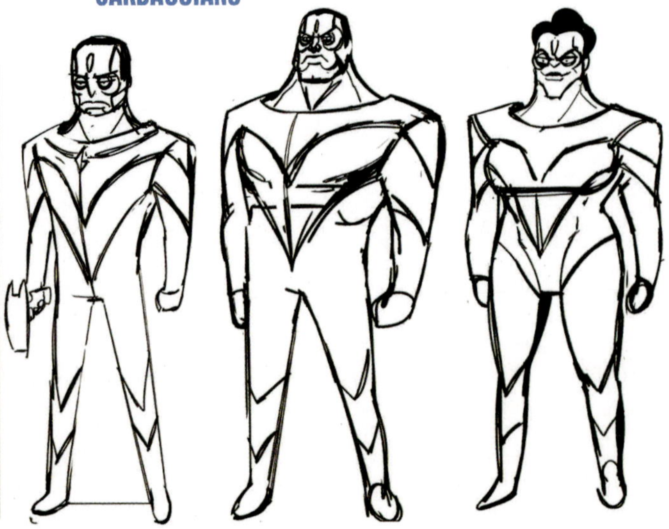

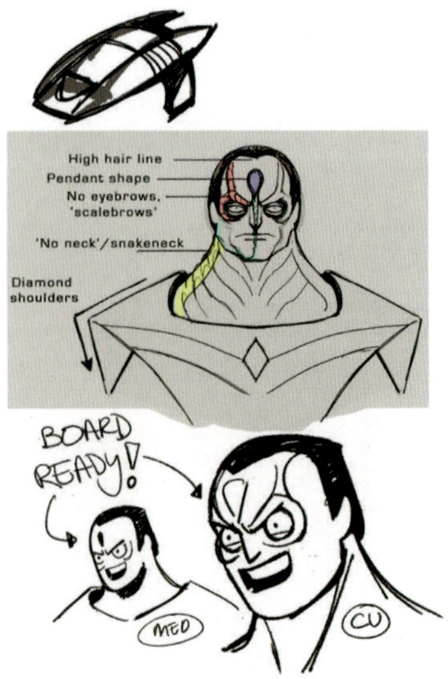

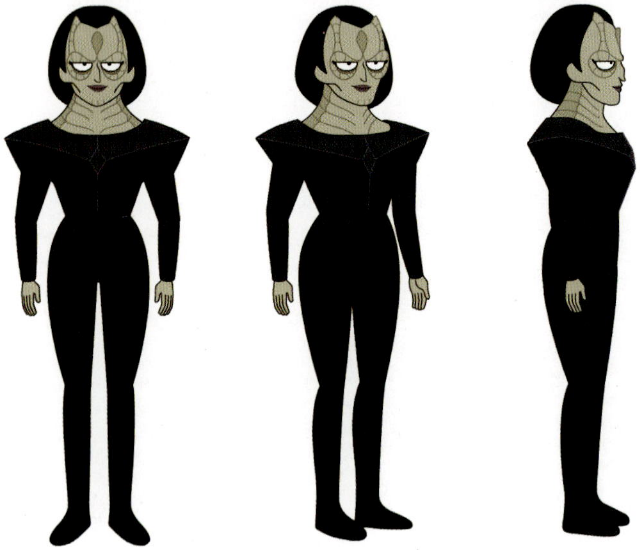

High hair line
Pendant shape
No eyebrows, 'scalebrows'
'No neck'/snakeneck
Diamond shoulders

BOARD READY!

INTERROGATION TOOLS

CARDASSIAN INTERROGATOR

"Our character designers did special poses to make sure we had the correct angles to make the interrogator look more intimidating. A lot of these poses were done because we weren't sure how the armor would work. So we had to test it out to give the animators reference."

— Barry J. Kelly

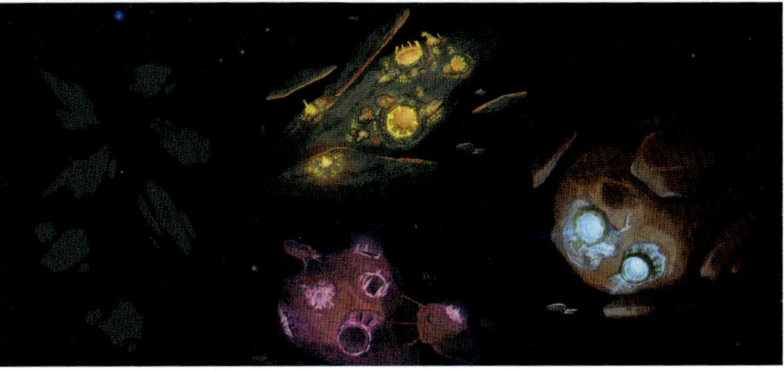

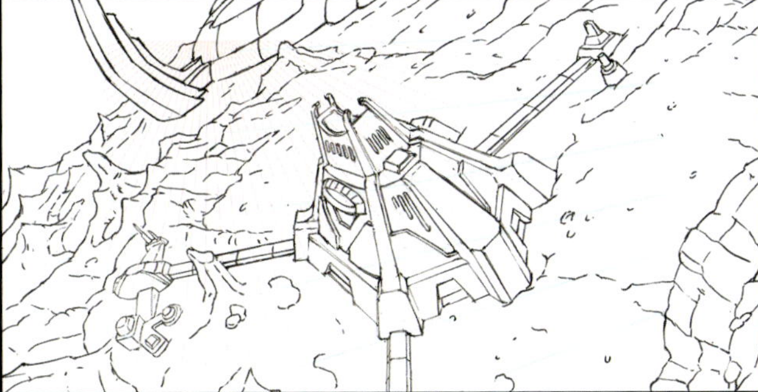

"We took a cue from Ralph McQuarrie's painting of a starbase inside an asteroid for *Star Trek: The Motion Picture*, and that was like one of the coolest paintings ever. So we were trying to channel that kind of energy."

— Barry J. Kelly

"We wanted to make a perfect holodeck room from TNG's 'Chain of Command' episode so the fans knew exactly what scene we were referencing."

— Barry J. Kelly

"For the Cardassian fighters, we wanted to make a stingray-style ship with sea-urchin shapes. I wanted little darts flying around the *MacDuff*."

— Barry J. Kelly

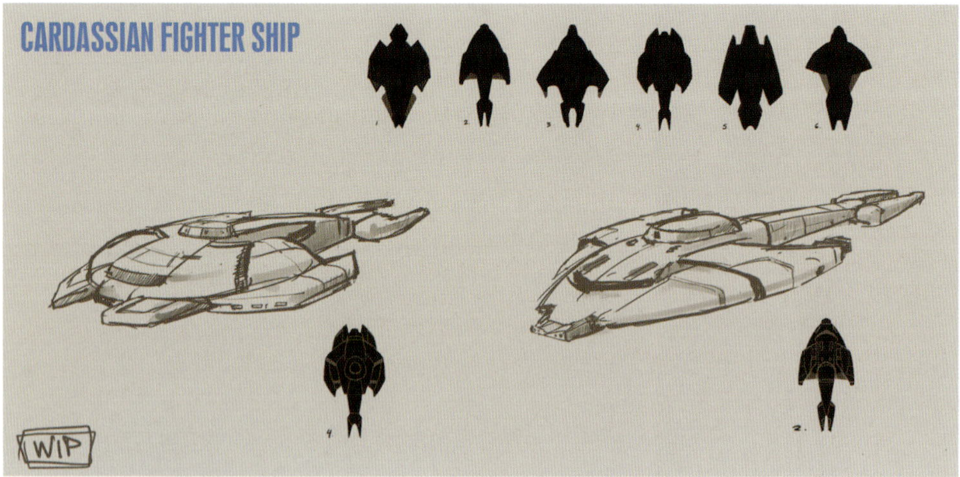

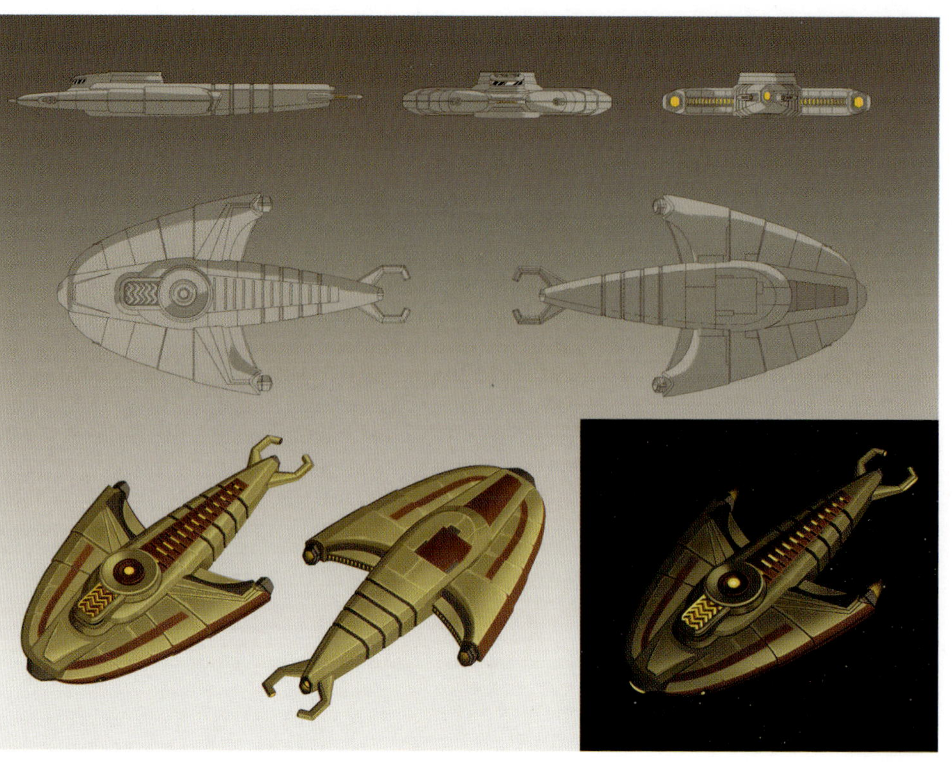

APERGOSIAN SHUTTLE

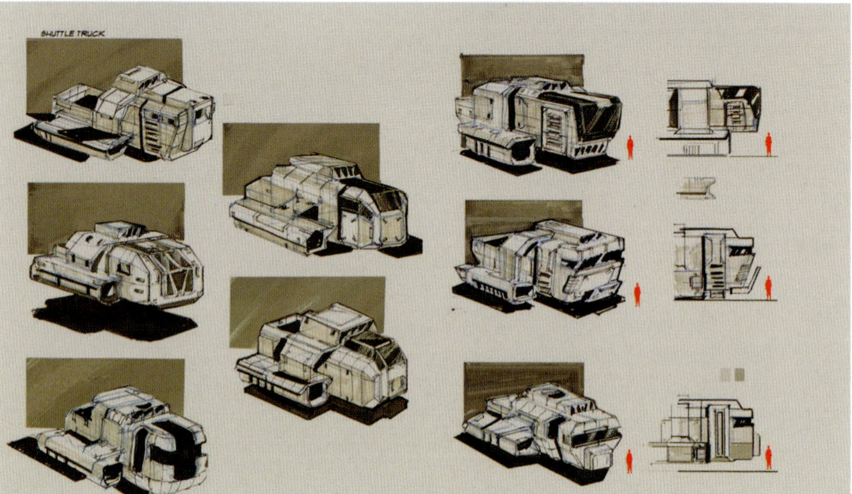

We didn't always have the opening sequence, but the network wanted to start the show with a big, exciting moment. So we made a hodgepodge of a prison escape, *Wrath of Khan*, and "four lights." The interruption of Jennifer and resetting Mariner is a classic holodeck pause. Not only was the network right, but we did this way better. If you like *Star Trek*, there's no way you wouldn't like this.

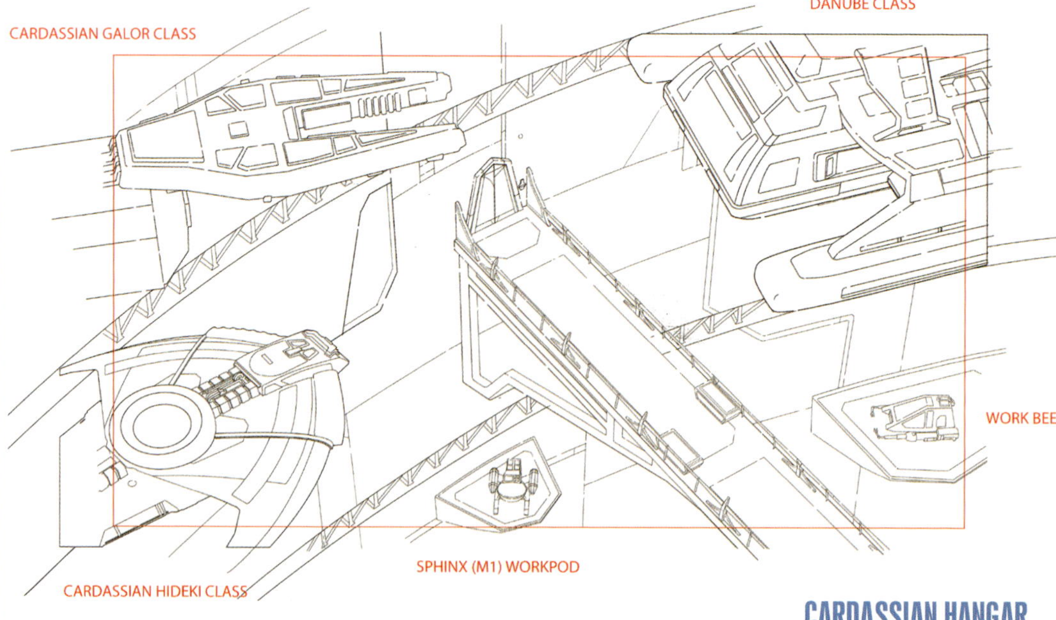

CARDASSIAN HANGAR

"For the *MacDuff*, we used old-school screens and LEDs. We made it feel old, scuffed up, and dirty."
— Barry J. Kelly

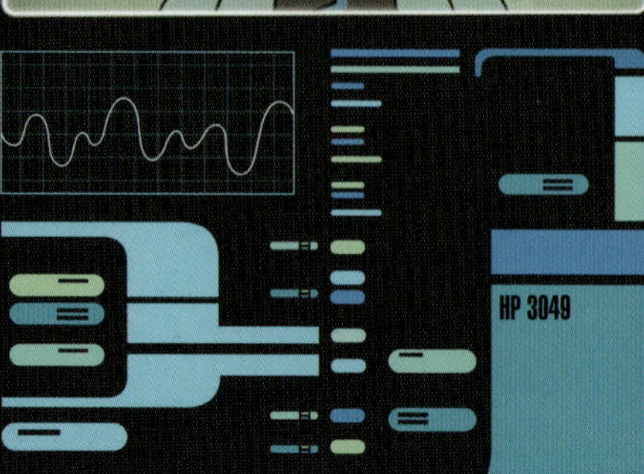

"It was awesome to get to draw Gary Mitchell in our style."

— Barry J. Kelly

"Strange energies were more geometric and less erratic and natural like lightning."

— Barry J. Kelly

"Ransom's robes are inspired by Sybok from *Star Trek V*."

— Barry J. Kelly

"We wanted to flash between skull and flesh head so he didn't feel like a flat cartoon."

— Barry J. Kelly

"When Ransom is so big, we needed to make him feel more like a background instead of a flat cartoon, especially when in shots with the 3D *Cerritos*. So we added more details to him and even painted parts of him."

— Barry J. Kelly

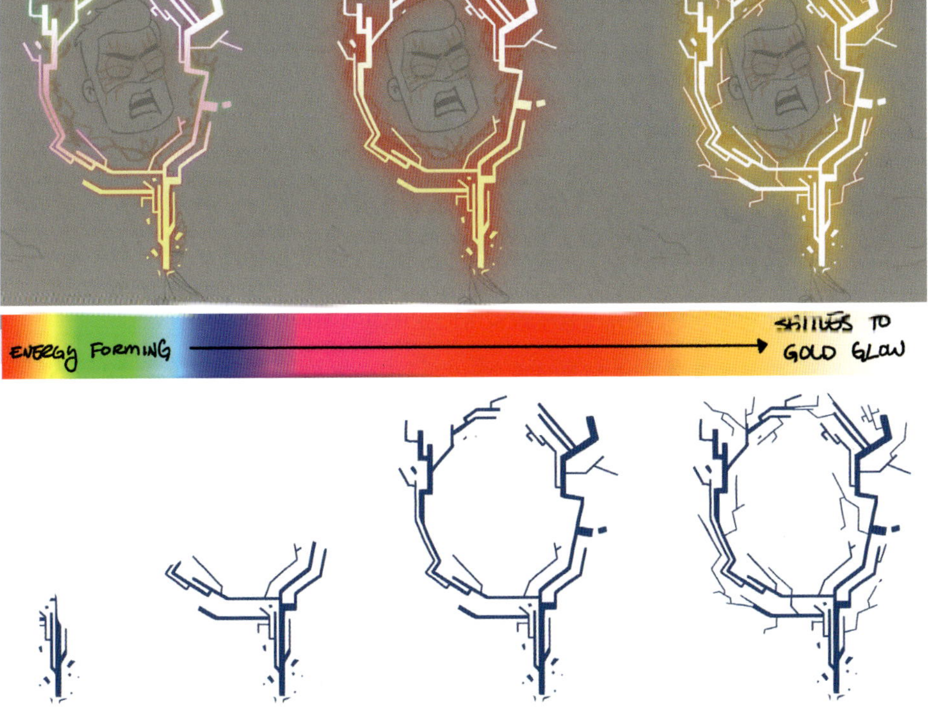

"I always like doing rainbow effects or going through the RGB spectrum for effects. It feels more like the cameras are reacting to the light. It's not really the energy color. The camera can't handle what's happening, and it's like breaking the camera using 'illegal colors.'"

— Barry J. Kelly

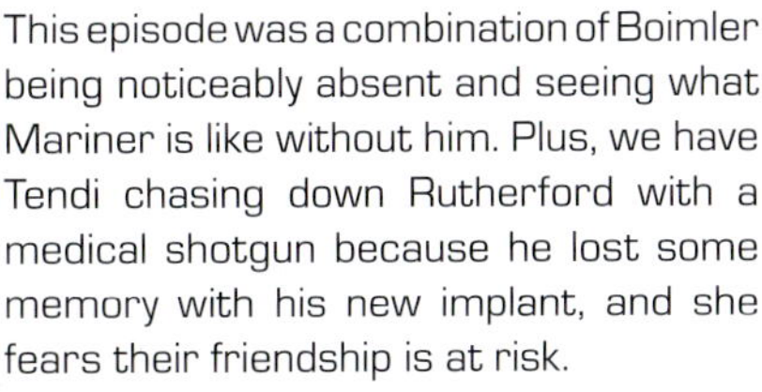

This episode was a combination of Boimler being noticeably absent and seeing what Mariner is like without him. Plus, we have Tendi chasing down Rutherford with a medical shotgun because he lost some memory with his new implant, and she fears their friendship is at risk.

LCARS S2E2

AIRDATE: 20210819
STARDATE: 58001.2

"Kayshon, His Eyes Open"

Our Lower Deckers have trouble bonding with Ensign Jet Manhaver, who has been assigned Boimler's bunk and shift duties. Meanwhile, we get a glimpse of Boimler's life on the *U.S.S. Titan,* which is more intense than he thought it would be.

"This was my second episode as a background designer, and I think I was able to show my range here. There is a skeleton based on a mugato and one based on a Gorn and the giant Spock skeleton was a reference to 'The Infinite Vulcan,' a TAS episode from the 1970s."

— Denny Fincke

COLLECTOR SHIP SKELETON GALLERY

COLLECTOR SHIP

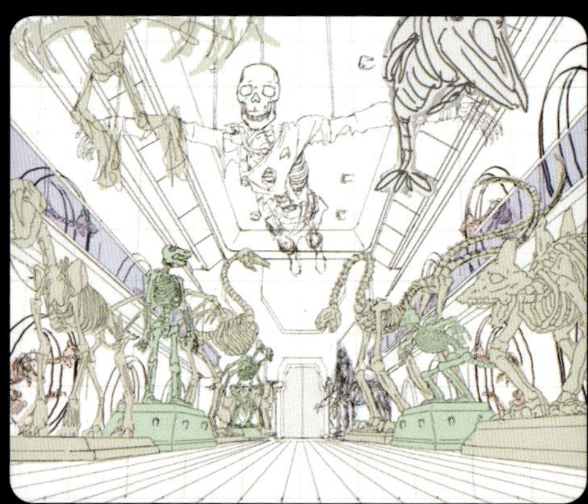

"This was super fun. A lot of these are made-up creatures. We needed to make sure Spock's skeleton was the thing that read the most clear."

— Barry J. Kelly

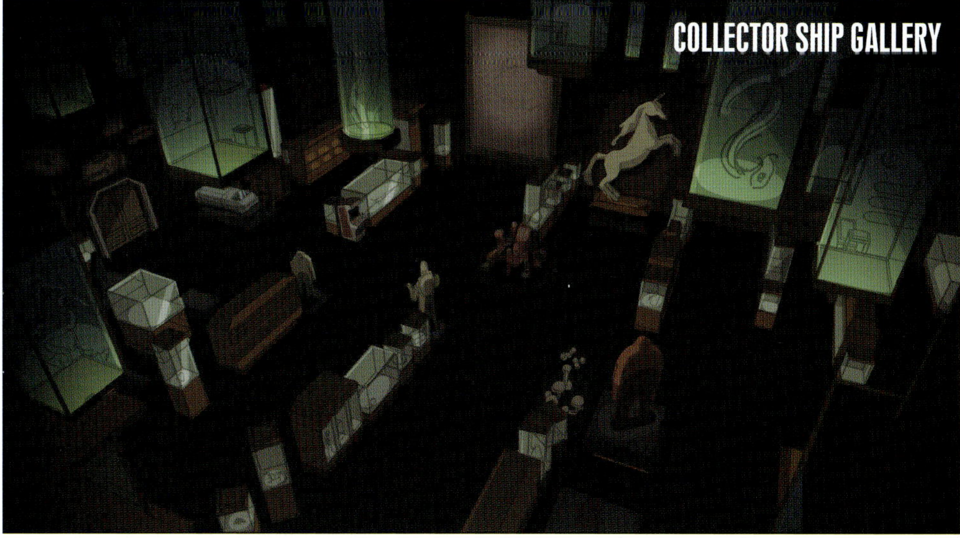

"*Picard* season one just came out, so we added the Château Picard crates. Nollan and I tried to add this in every episode we could."
— Barry J. Kelly

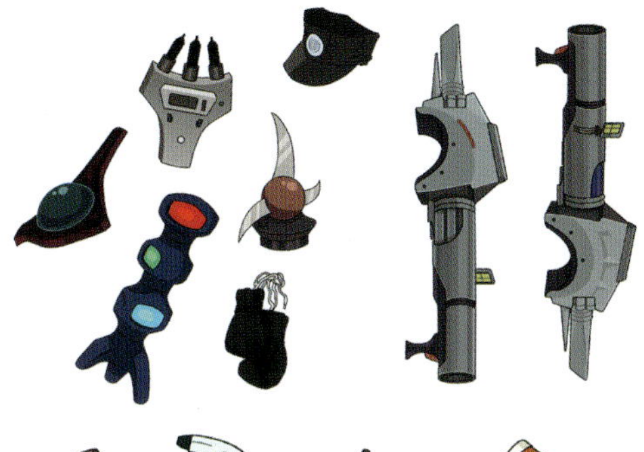

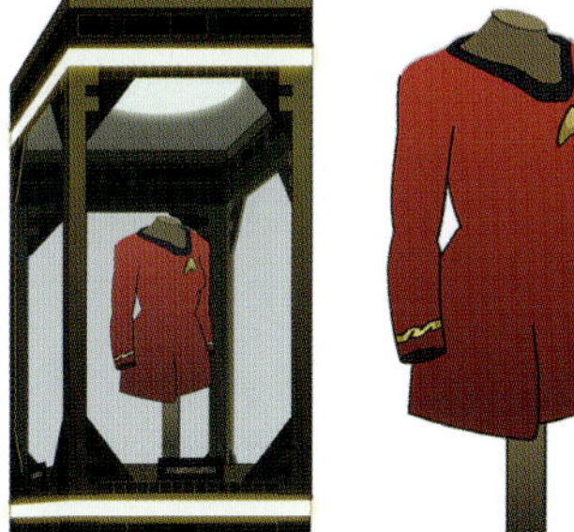

"This is Paul Menegay's contest-winning sculpture for Captain Picard Day (TNG: 'The Pegasus') featuring a Ktarian game headset (TNG: 'The Game')."
— Brad Winters

"This was our first painted portrait. We wanted it to feel almost like it's painted on canvas. So we rendered out the characters a bit more normal." — Barry J. Kelly

CHAIRMAN SIGGI

"Siggi's ship is a fun little truck. He looks like a guy that is always towing stuff."
— Barry J. Kelly

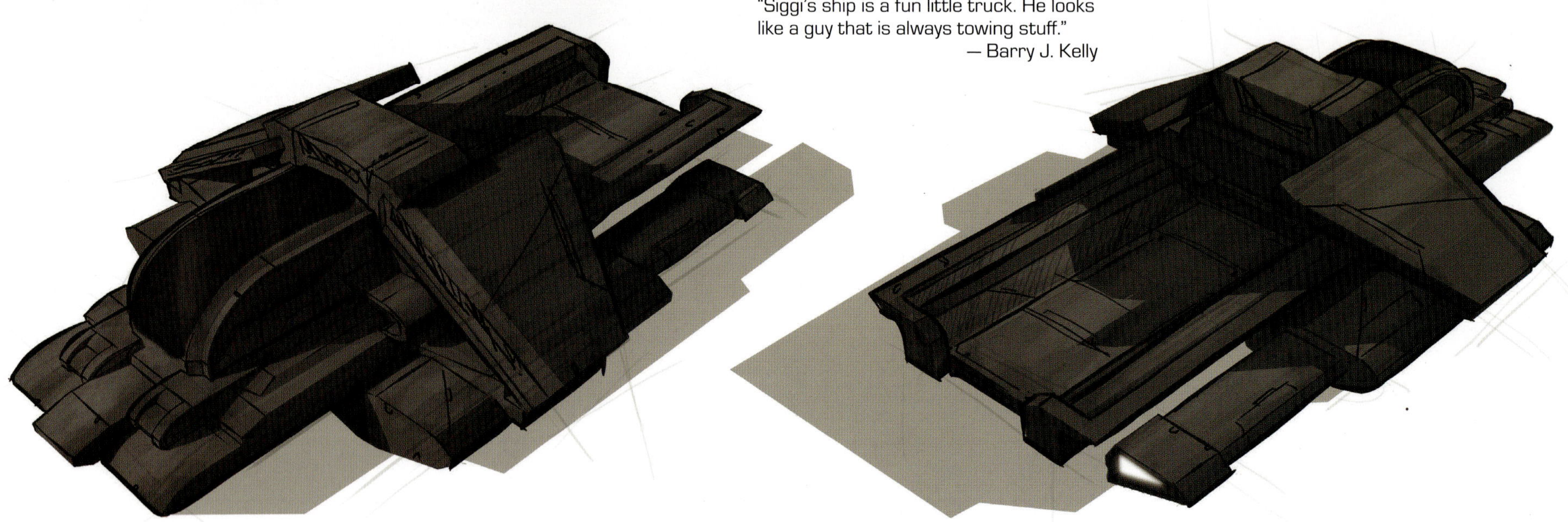

KERNER HAUZE

"Kerner Hauze: We wanted this portrait to feel like the guy from TNG: 'The Most Toys,' but NOT be the same character."
— Barry J. Kelly

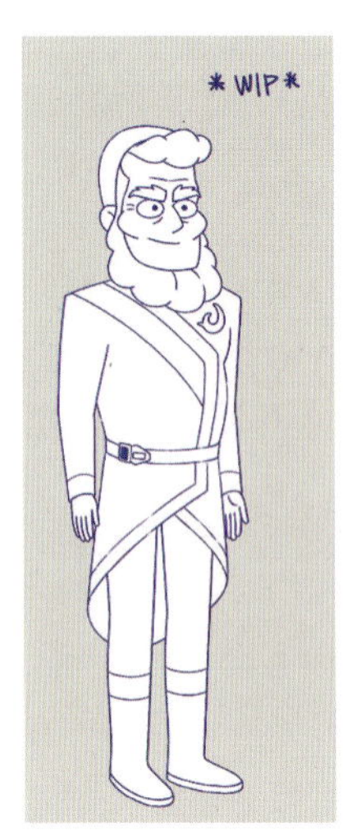

"The control room was a giant laser drilling down. Anything that looked mechanical in the visual development ended up being lasers." — Barry J. Kelly

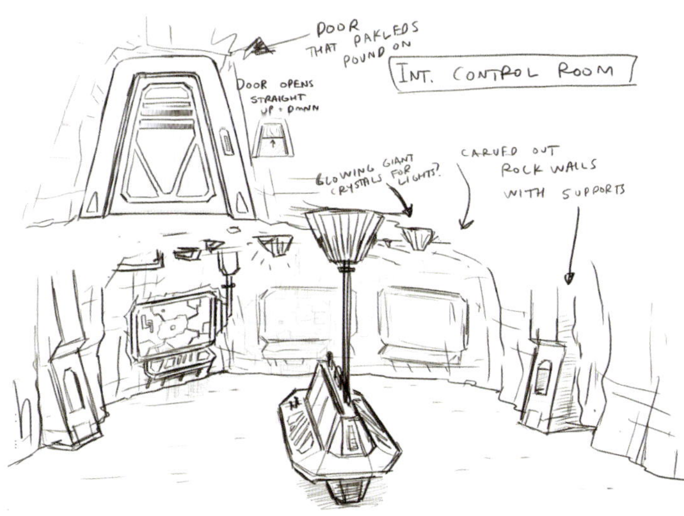

We wanted to show that Boimler made a mistake leaving the *Cerritos*. He thought that he wanted an action-packed life, so we jam-packed this episode with action and Easter eggs, and got a glimpse into his reality.

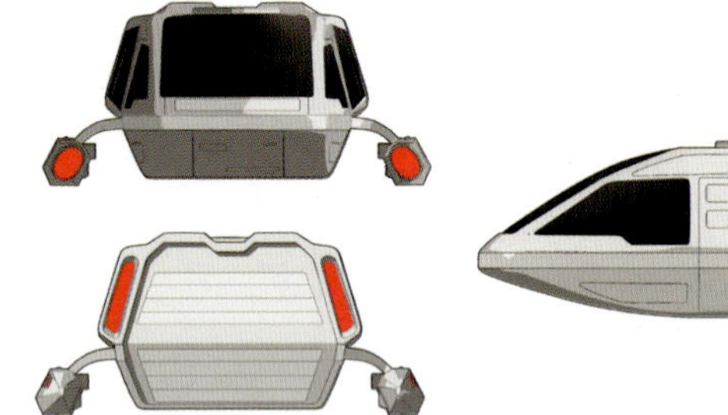

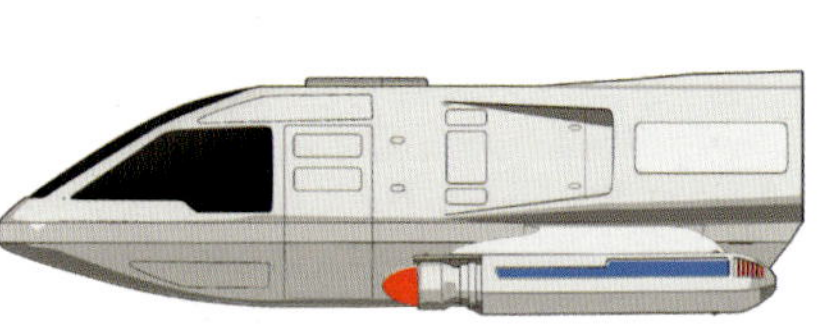

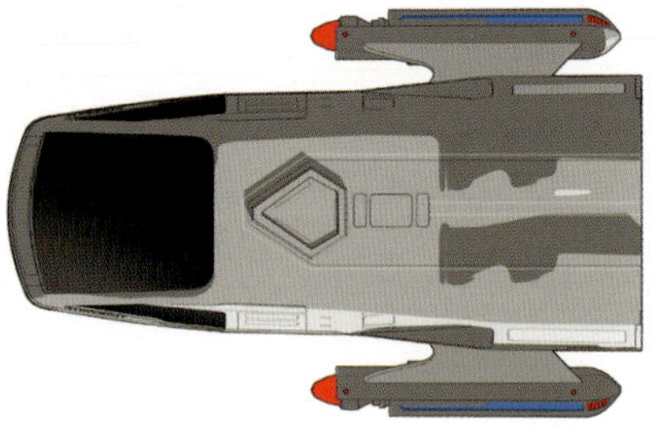

"HELMSWORTH" TACTICAL — "ELBA" ENGINEER — FIRST OFFICER

The crew of the *Titan* are supposed to be inspirational Starfleet officers.

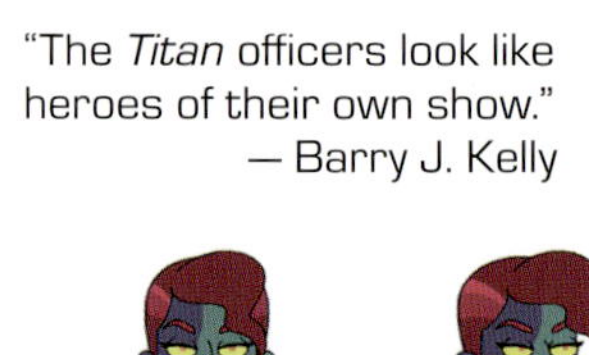

"The *Titan* officers look like heroes of their own show."
— Barry J. Kelly

TITAN TACTICAL OFFICER — *TITAN* CHIEF ENGINEER — *TITAN* FIRST OFFICER

"Riker's office was modeled a little after Picard's."
— Barry J. Kelly

LCARS S2E3

AIRDATE: 20210826
STARDATE: 58018.7

"We'll Always Have Tom Paris"

Assigned a special task by Dr. T'Ana, Tendi enlists Mariner for help. On the *U.S.S. Cerritos*, Rutherford is consumed by a bridge-crew mystery.

"We wanted this to feel like your classic sci-fi bustling city. Like almost an overload of sci-fi stuff."

— Barry J. Kelly

QUALOR II

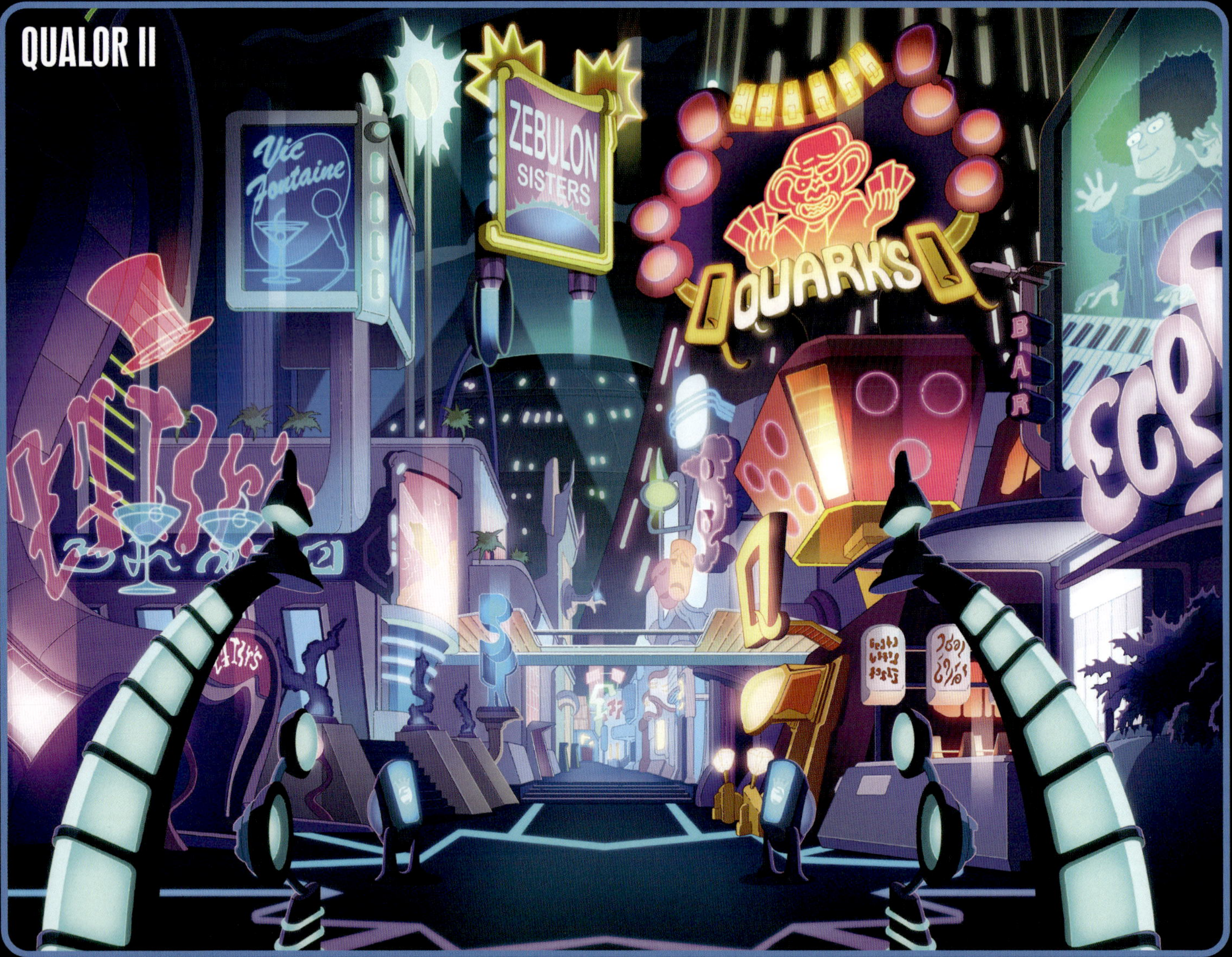

QUALOR II

QUALOR II CAITIAN

When Shaxs comes back from the dead, Rutherford is hyperfocused on how. This gave us a fun scene with a variety of Shaxses in his imagination.

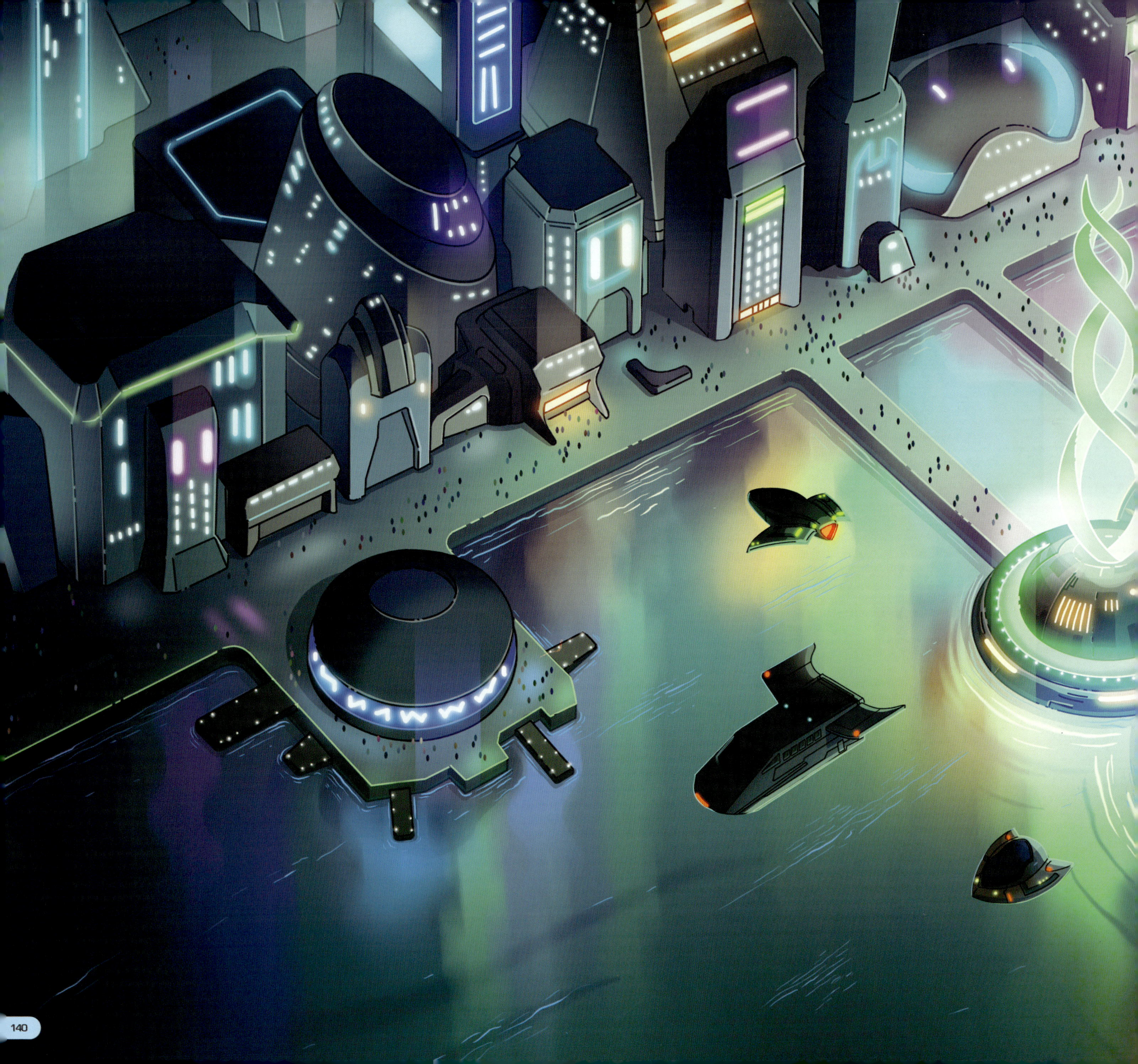

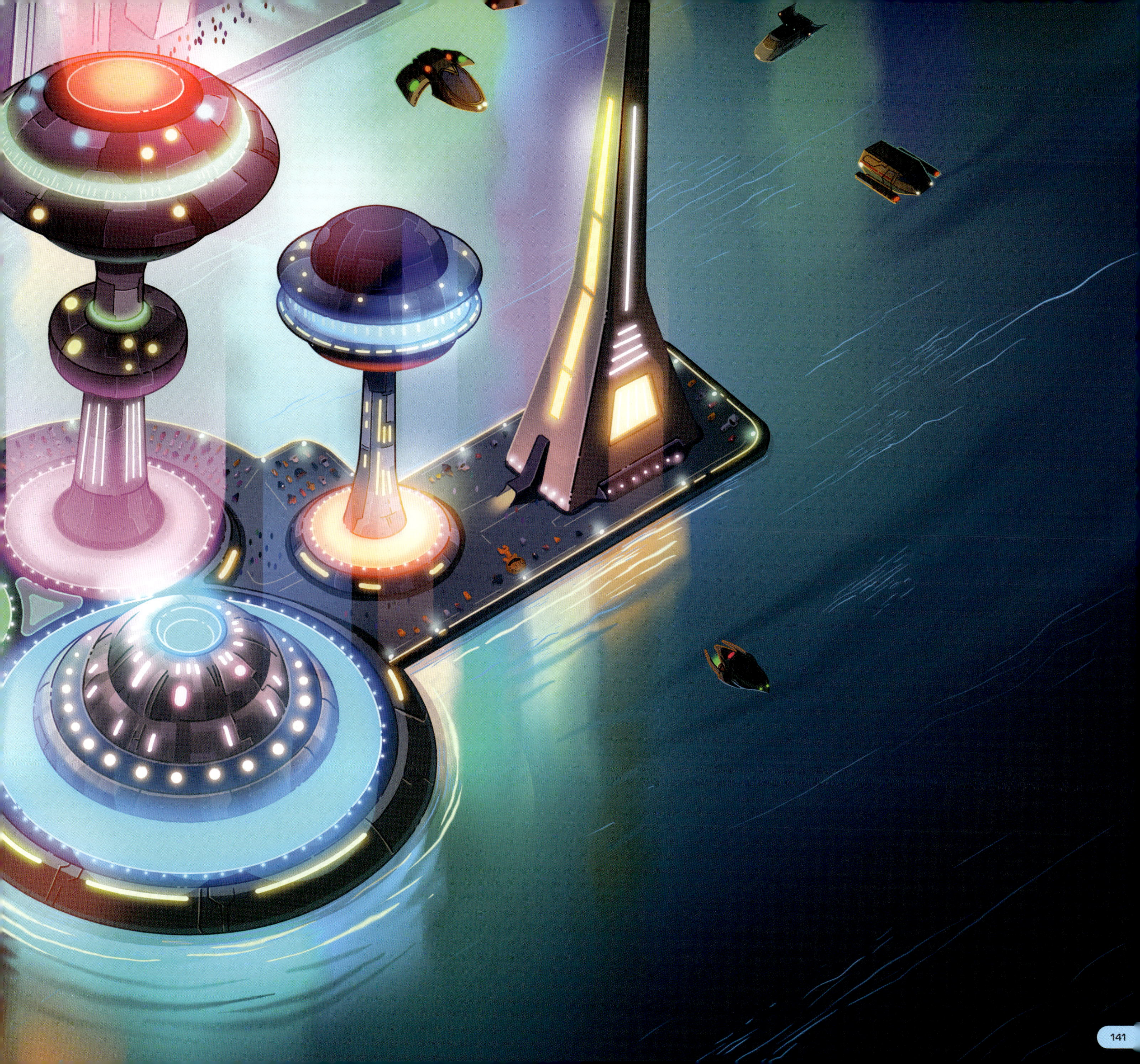

ORION STATION

"We wanted the Orion station to feel as if it was an outpost. Maybe if it's in a hazardous environment, and there are big walls protecting it. The main thing that sticks out is the shuttlebay, so we know easily where the shuttle goes, and the elevator, which we knew could be used as a great set piece later for when they're getting chased. It anchored us so we always knew where we were."

— Barry J. Kelly

"We briefly thought the Orion station was a starbase."

— Barry J. Kelly

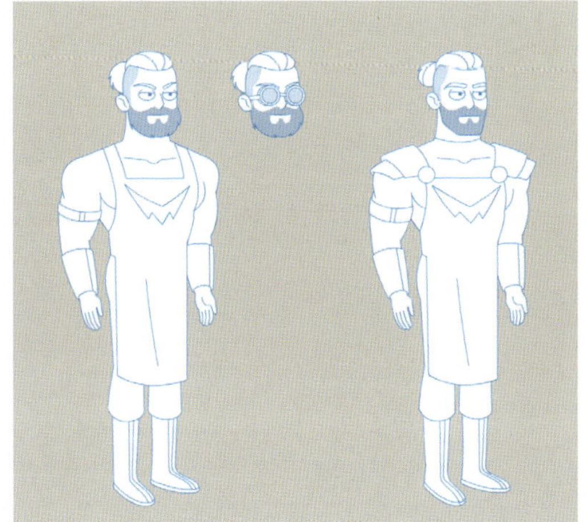

ORION RAT

D'ONNI TENDI

"The symbol on this apron is a nod to the Orion pirate uniforms seen in TAS: 'The Pirates of Orion.'"

— Brad Winters

This is our first girls' trip episode where we paired up Tendi and Mariner and learned more about the two. We often take something that is one-dimensional, like Orions being pirates, and build it out to learn more about Orion. In the end, we see Mariner and Tendi becoming closer friends.

D'ONNI TENDI STALL

BONESTELL RECREATION FACILITY

BONESTELL BAR INTERIOR

"The exteriors of Starbase Earhart weren't really seen in the TNG 'Tapestry' episode, so we used the exteriors of the Starfleet Operational Support Services facility on Relva VII (TNG: 'Coming of Age') as a reference."

— Brad Winters

BARTENDER

NAUSICANS

ADDIX

"Addix was from a new species that we created for the series that would go on to be called 'those tall silver guys.'"

— Brad Winters

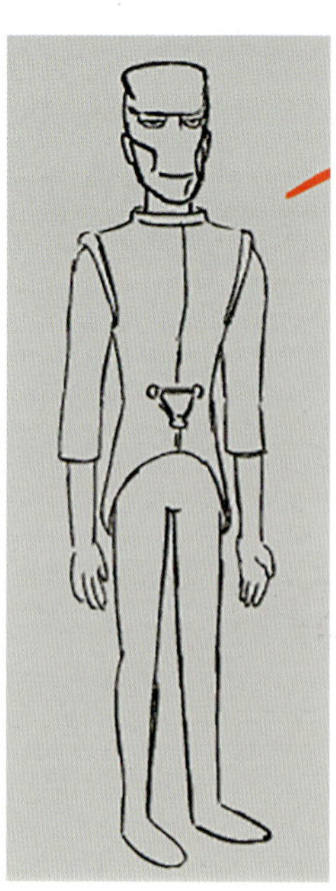

INCIDENTAL BONESTELL ALIENS

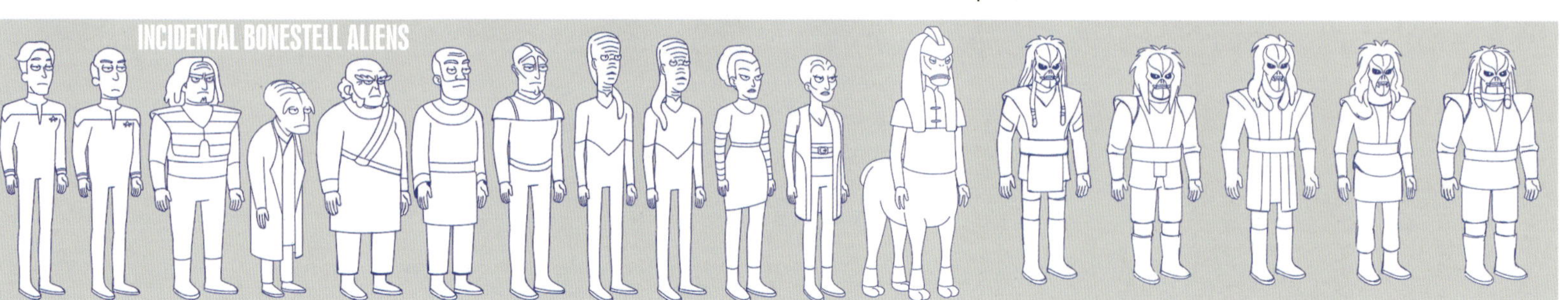

"The plate talking to Boimler was so good. We had original ideas like maybe it's the group on the commemorative plate, and Tom Paris is the only one that talks to him."
— Barry J. Kelly

LT. TOM PARIS

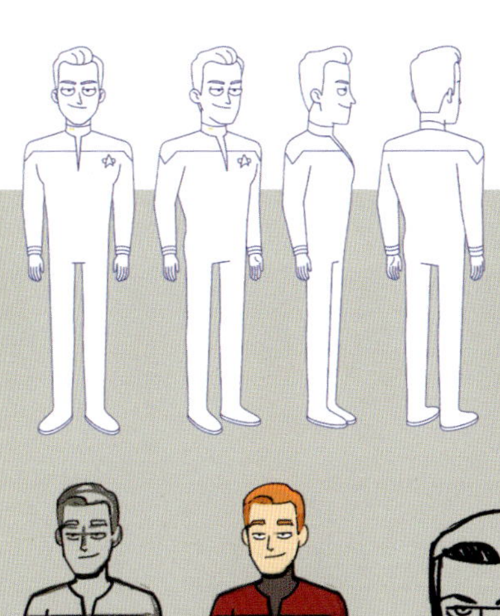

We brought Robert Duncan McNeill back as Tom Paris. Not only does he get to play the man, he gets to play the man on a plate.

In this episode, Boimler is back on the *Cerritos*, but the ship's systems are not responding to him

We wanted Boimler to carry a fragile thing throughout the ship while the ship is out to get him like a haunted house.

CAITIAN LIBIDO POST

LCARS S2E4

AIRDATE: 20210902
STARDATE: 58036.4

"Mugato, Gumato"

The *U.S.S. Cerritos* is dispatched to a planet to investigate an unexplained sighting of a dangerous mugato.

MUGATOS

We really wanted to bring mugatos back.

FERENGI BASE

KYNK

KYNK SIDEKICK

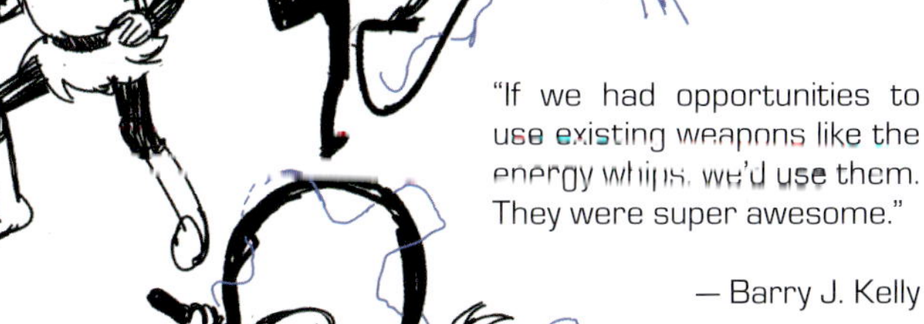

"If we had opportunities to use existing weapons like the energy whips, we'd use them. They were super awesome."

— Barry J. Kelly

"We have to figure out with design all the action that needs to happen in the episode. If a character needs to escape, he can't run a mile to get to where he needs to be. The ship needs to be nearby for clarity."

— Barry J. Kelly

FRYLON IV

"One of our background designers, Kip Noschese, loves designing organic landscapes, so this was his jam. We wanted to make it feel like a monster island where the vegetation could kill you like the creatures."

— Barry J. Kelly

"The painters add the lightning into the backgrounds, and then the compositors flash them on and off."

— Barry J. Kelly

"Patingi is a Tellarite. He needed short shorts like 'the Crocodile Hunter.' Very practical."

— Barry J. Kelly

MUGATOS

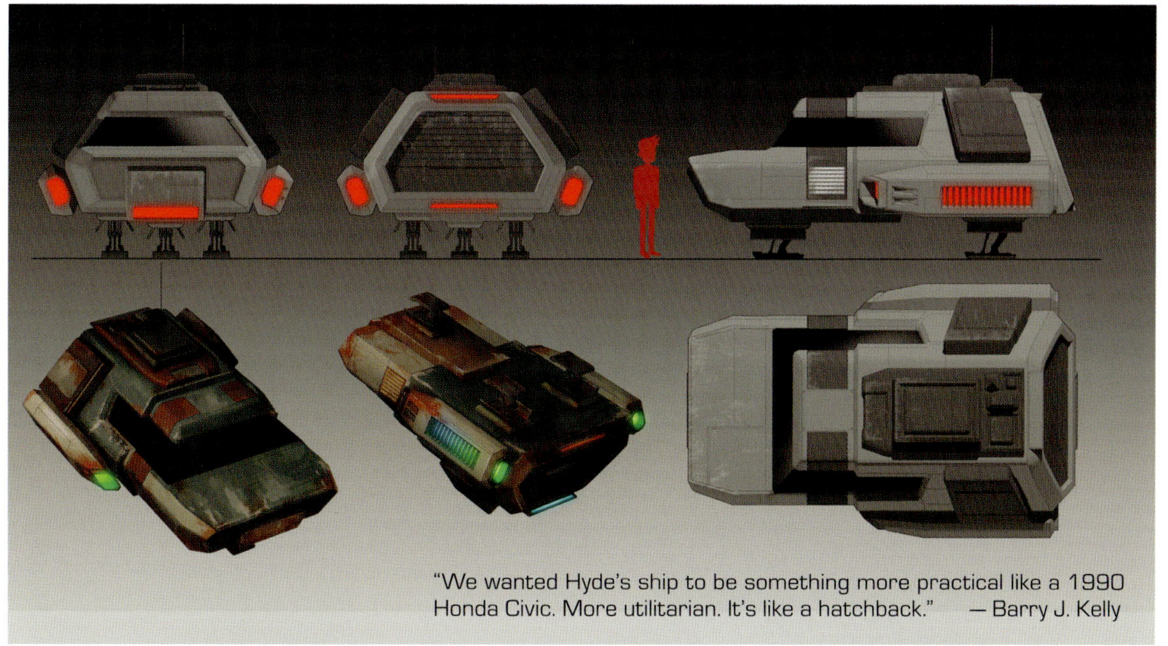

"We wanted Hyde's ship to be something more practical like a 1990 Honda Civic. More utilitarian. It's like a hatchback." — Barry J. Kelly

HYDE

ANBO JYUTSU GEAR

"I love the chance of bringing back weird obscure TNG references, especially the 'ultimate evolution of martial arts.'"
— Barry J. Kelly

DENOBULANS

"Denobulans are perfect for animation. I love their reactions when they're scared."
— Barry J. Kelly

LCARS S2E5

AIRDATE: 20210909
STARDATE: 58053.9

"An Embarrassment of Dooplers"

Mariner and Boimler try to track down the location of a legendary Starfleet party while the bridge crew deal with an insecure alien diplomat.

This episode was our version of a classic tribbles episode, along with an older starbase, a *Blues Brothers* car chase, and a lot of fun cameos, including the crew that makes *Lower Decks*.

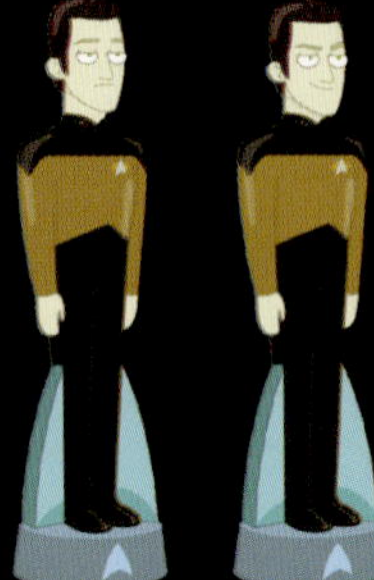

This was our first Data likeness with one Lore who is smiling.

STARBASE 25 MALL

"We wanted a *Blues Brothers*-level chaotic car chase, so we built a mall in 3D."
— Barry J. Kelly

STATION ENTRANCE

AVIARY

DIVE BAR

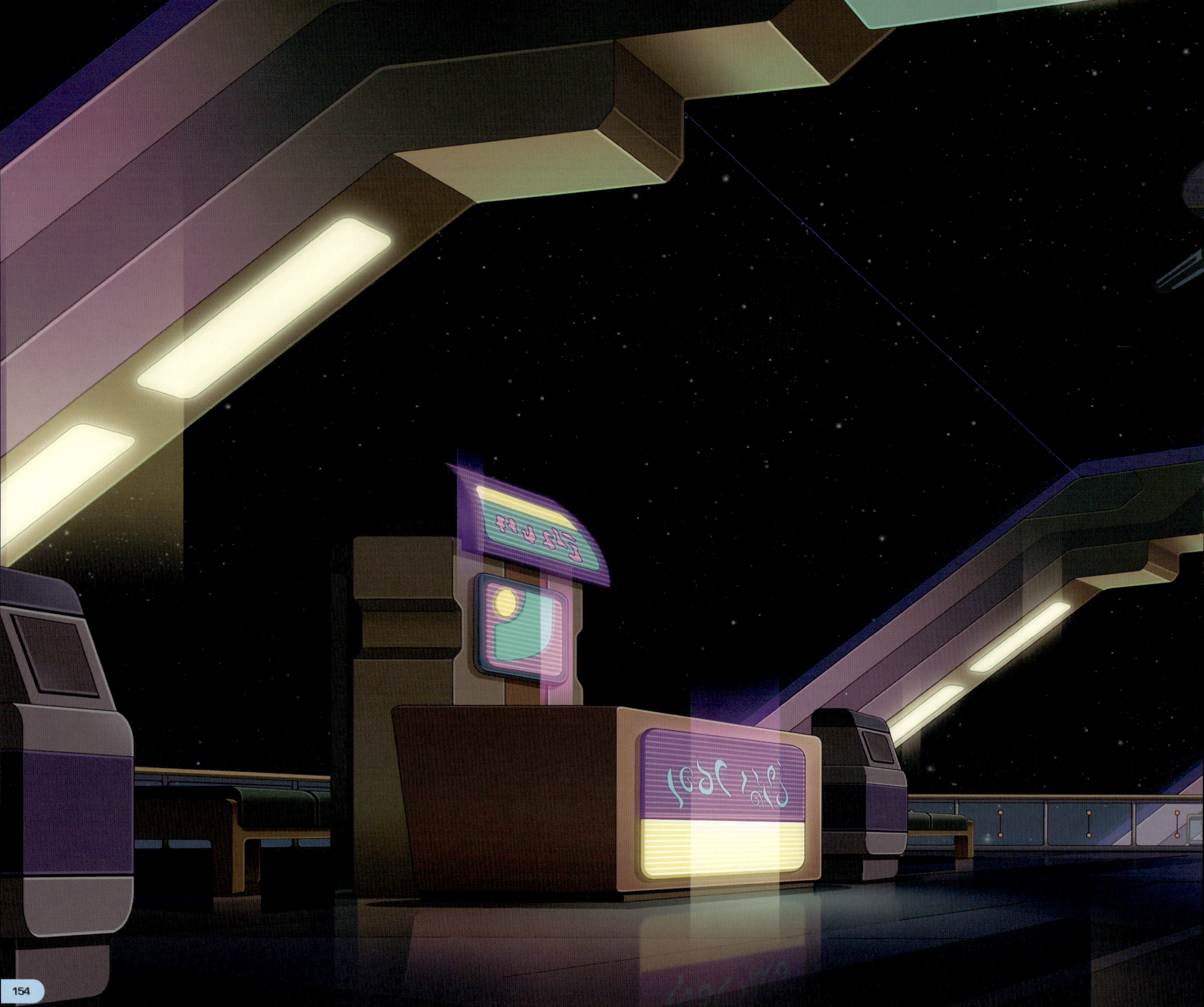

QUARK'S

STARFLEET FORMAL UNIFORMS

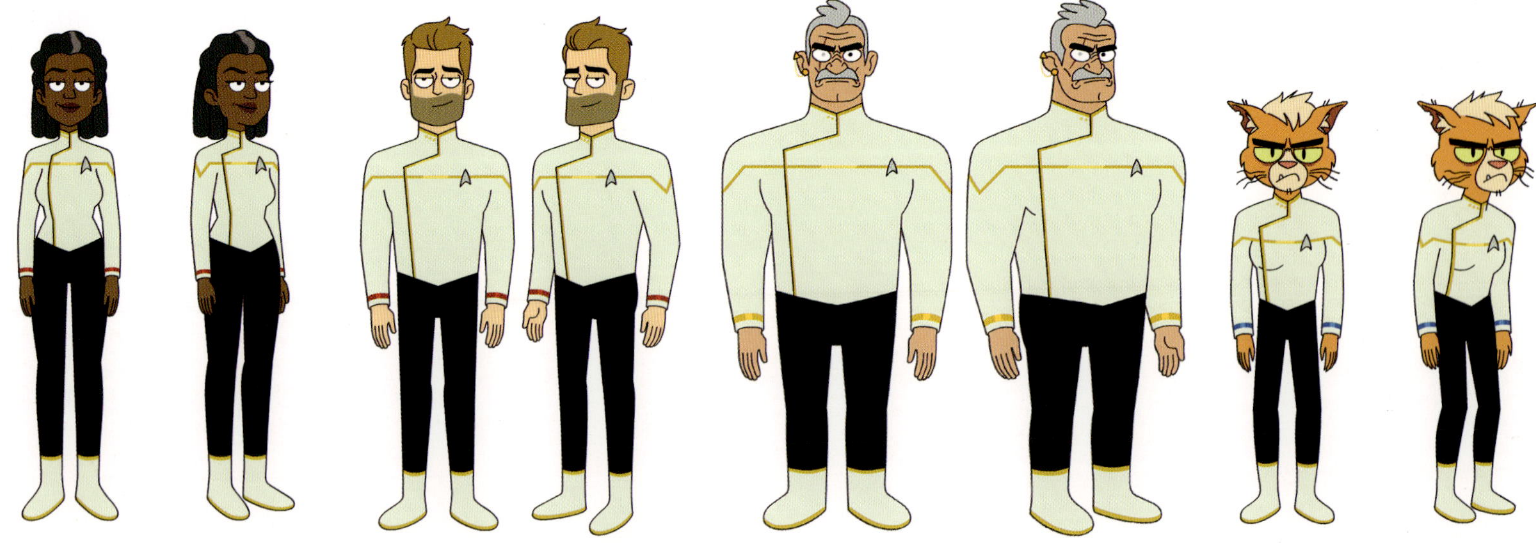

CAPTAIN SHELBY

We designed some really cool formal uniforms for the party.

"Captain Shelby's Number One is inspired by an unused design from *Discovery* for Saru. It's an early Saru look."

— Barry J. Kelly

BOUNCER

"Bouncer is Em/3/Green's species, from TAS: 'The Jihad.'"

— Barry J. Kelly

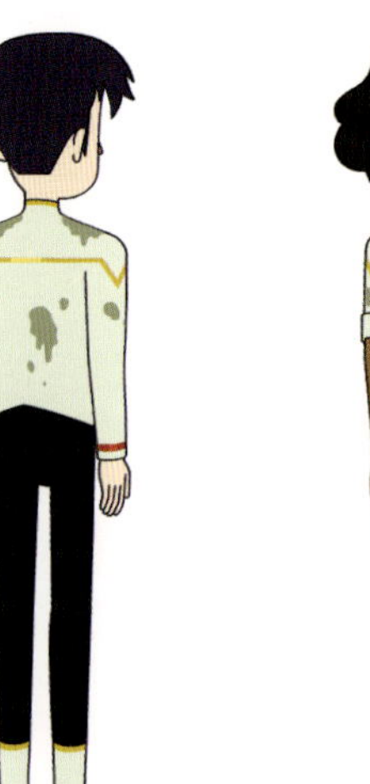

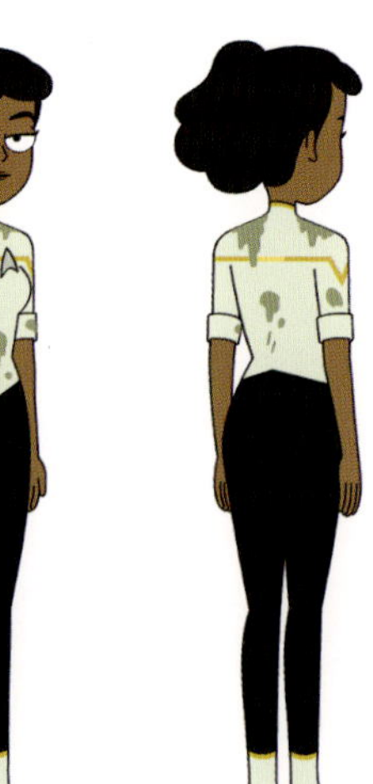

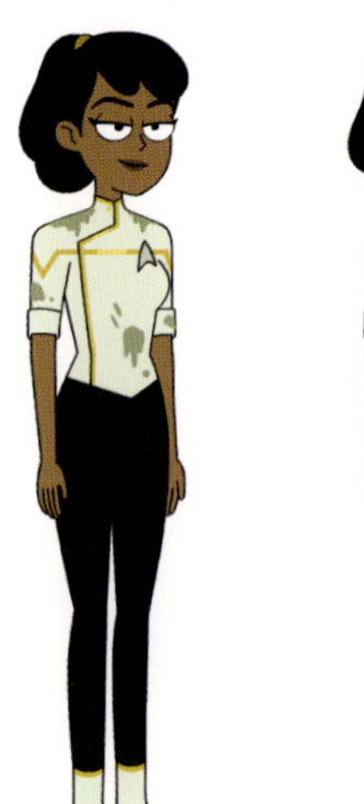

DOOPLER EMMISARY

"We wanted a guy who looked nervous and squeamish just by people looking at him."

— Barry J. Kelly

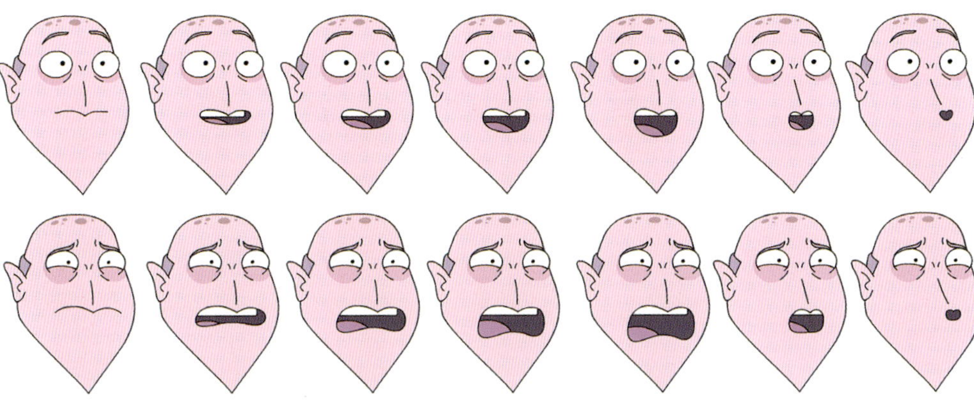

STARBASE 25 DIVE BAR

The bar at the end of the episode is based on an old-time ale house that Mike would go to when he worked at the Second City.

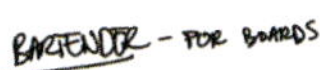

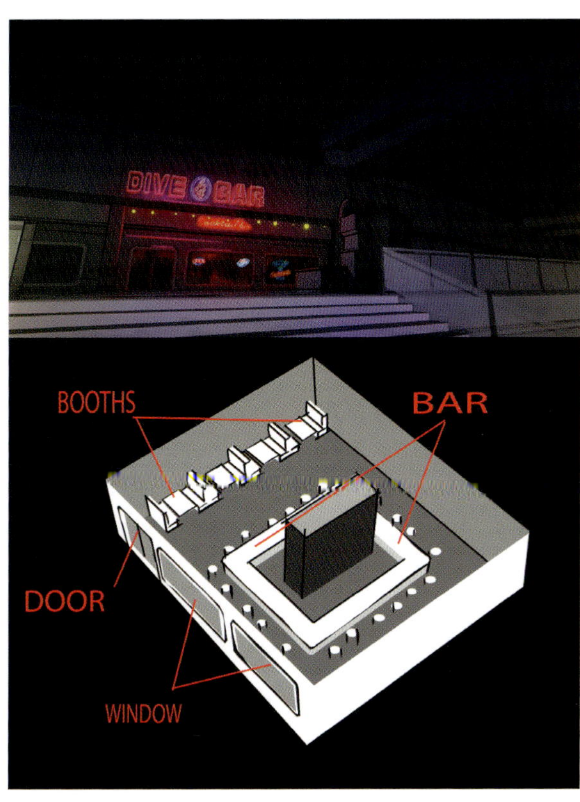

MALVUS

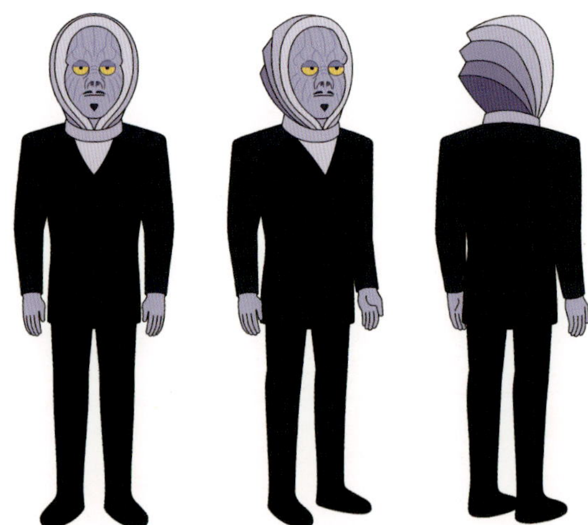

"Malvus was a direct reference to the Mizarians in the TNG 'Allegiance' episode."

— Barry J. Kelly

DRUNK LURIAN

"We referenced Morn from DS9, who frequented Quark's Bar."

— Barry J. Kelly

CAPTAIN THADIUN OKONA

"When *Star Trek: Prodigy* shared the design they'd be using for Okona, we grayed his hair and added the eye patch to line him up with his future *Prodigy* appearance."

— Brad Winters

CAPT. EXLEY
(AND FIRST OFFICER)

AURELIANS

Incidental Aurelian Hunk is referencing Barry J. Kelly and his pet bird, Jack.

ANTEDIANS

"Antedians are a reference from the TNG 'Manhunt' episode."

— Barry J. Kelly

MODEL KITS

The Quark *Cerritos* model ship shows that even in Tendi and Rutherford's downtime they're still working on the ship. Their friendship is really coming through.

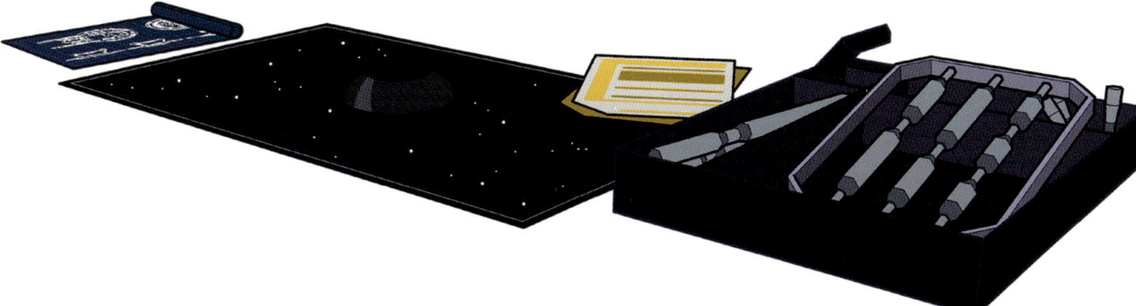

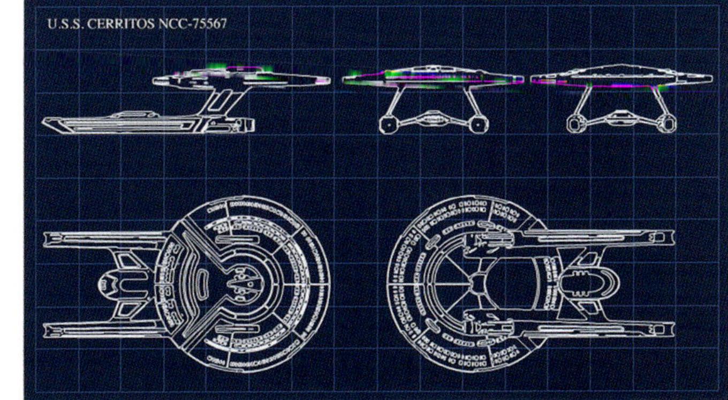

LCARS S2E6

AIRDATE: 20210916
STARDATE: 58105.1

"The Spy Humongous"

Anomaly consolidation day on the *U.S.S. Cerritos* leaves the Lower Deckers with mixed emotions. Captain Freeman attempts to negotiate peace on the Pakled homeworld.

This episode was supposed to be a bottle episode, which is when we stay on the ship to alleviate the need for the design team to create new locations and species. It's a time for the teams to catch up or get ahead onto bigger, design-heavy episodes. However, we ended up designing a bunch of new stuff for this episode.

PAKLED CITY SQUARE

"*Enterprise-D* was a dream background for us to bring into *Lower Decks*. It was a huge benchmark."
— Barry J. Kelly

U.S.S. *ENTERPRISE*-D BRIDGE

THREE PIGS ANOMALY

RUMDAR

It was a lot of fun having Rumdar going around the *Cerritos* and seeing Kayshon and Ransom's friendship as they track him down.

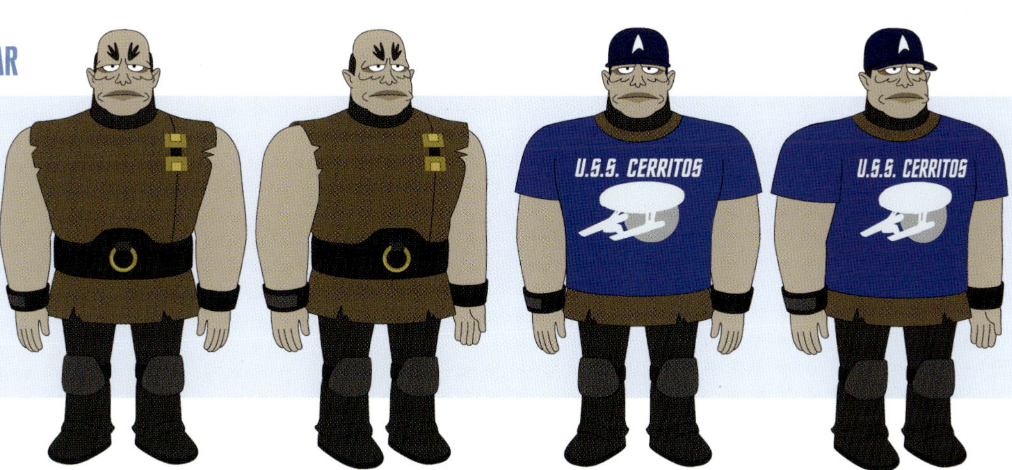

"Rumdar is fun. We don't normally keep the characters' arms down, but we did for Rumdar because it helped him look more dopey."

— Barry J. Kelly

We wanted to start setting up a recurring Pakled threat while making fun of fascists.

AMBASSADOR GRUBDIN | PAKLED REBEL LEADER | PAKLED QUEEN | PAKLED KING | PAKLED EMPEROR

PAKLED DIPLOMATIC ASSEMBLY HALL

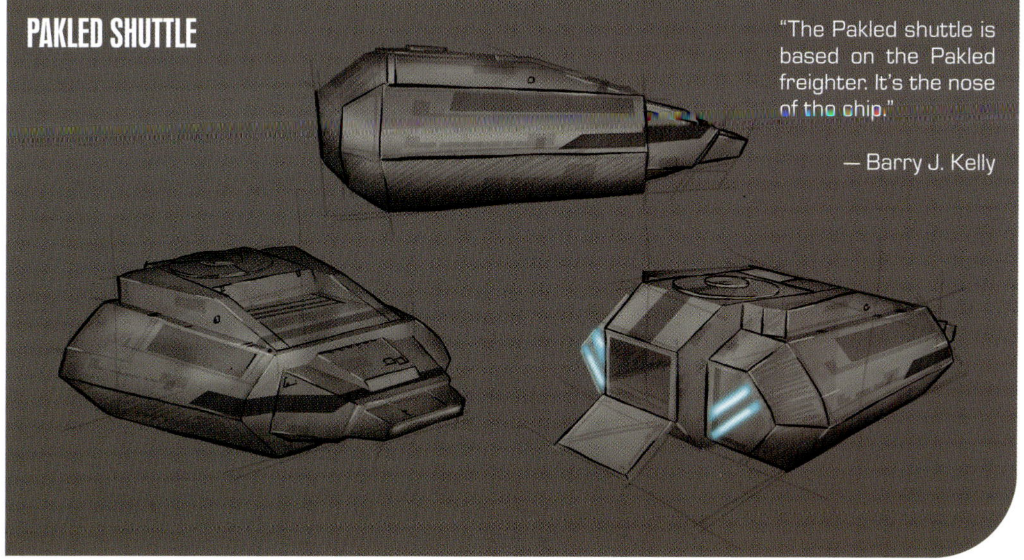

PAKLED SHUTTLE

"The Pakled shuttle is based on the Pakled freighter. It's the nose of the chip."

— Barry J. Kelly

U.S.S. *CERRITOS* CREW ANOMALIES

GIANT FURRY SLUG

We had to come up with a dirty, unappealing job for the three Lower Deckers while Boimler went off and did Redshirt stuff, so we made the anomaly collections.

TENDI TRANSFORMATION

We transformed Tendi to have a visual representation of her getting upset.

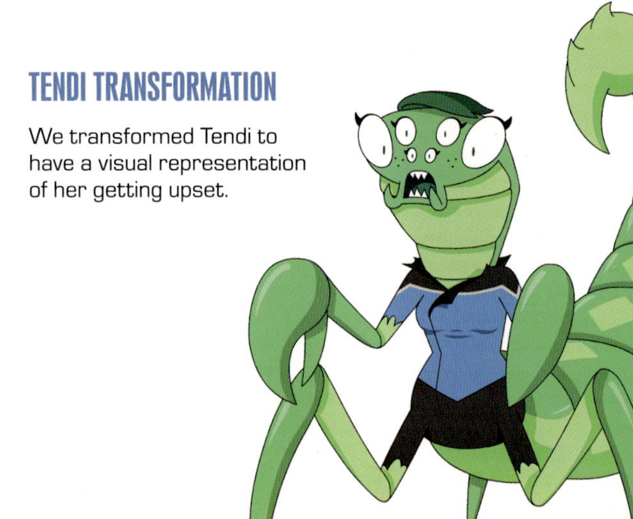

"The tricky part with Tendi as an alien insectoid was that she needed to laugh, and how can we make that clear?"

— Barry J. Kelly

We brought back the *Star Trek* "redshirts," but with a twist. The *Cerritos* "Redshirts" is a club of ensigns that help each other rank up to be captain.

We gave Boimler a muscle suit and a new hair style. He left the *Titan*, where he didn't fit in with the action-packed life, but even on the *Cerritos*, he finds people that he doesn't quite fit into either.

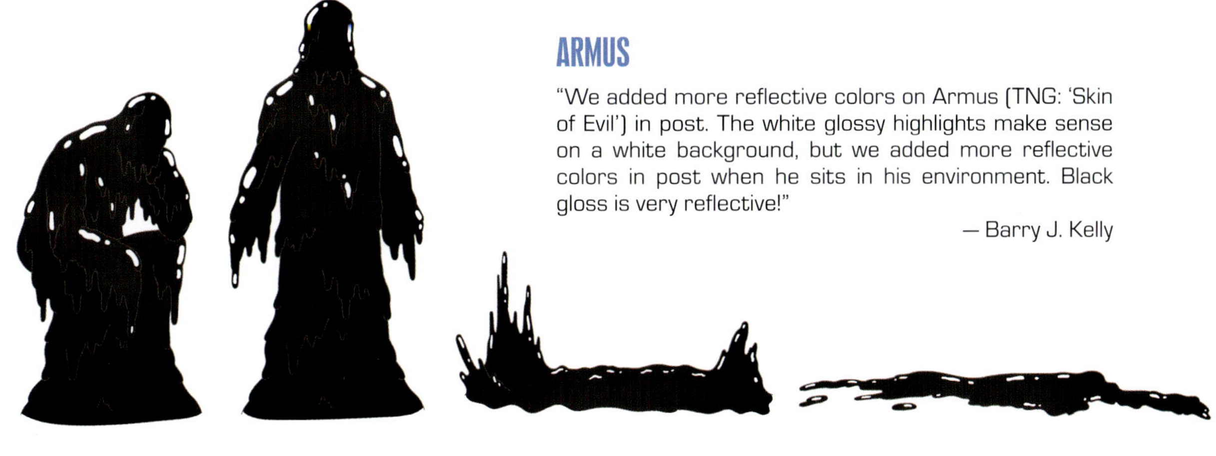

ARMUS

"We added more reflective colors on Armus (TNG: 'Skin of Evil') in post. The white glossy highlights make sense on a white background, but we added more reflective colors in post when he sits in his environment. Black gloss is very reflective!"

— Barry J. Kelly

LCARS S2E7

AIRDATE: 20210923
STARDATE: 58109.3

"Where Pleasant Fountains Lie"

Mariner and Boimler are stranded on an uninhabited planet with a sentient computer. On the *Cerritos*, Lieutenant Commander Billups must prove his engineering abilities to an old adversary.

This episode is partially based on when Lwaxana Troi shows up in TNG and creates trouble.

AGIMUS VISION

"The drones were designed to be reminiscent of the Minosian Echo Papa 607 drones from TNG: 'The Arsenal of Freedom.'"

— Brad Winters

HYSPERIAN CRUISER *MONAVEEN*

"We were making everyone attractive because we wanted to add more of a 'Why would you ever leave this place?' It makes going to Starfleet even more meaningful. Like everyone's hot and there's dragon stuff. Didn't know you had it so good."

— Barry J. Kelly

QUEEN PAOLANA BILLUPS

HYSPERIAN ROYAL GUARDS

"Billups' mourning sash is actually green in the show. We changed it last minute so it wouldn't look too similar to Kayshon's sash."

— Barry J. Kelly

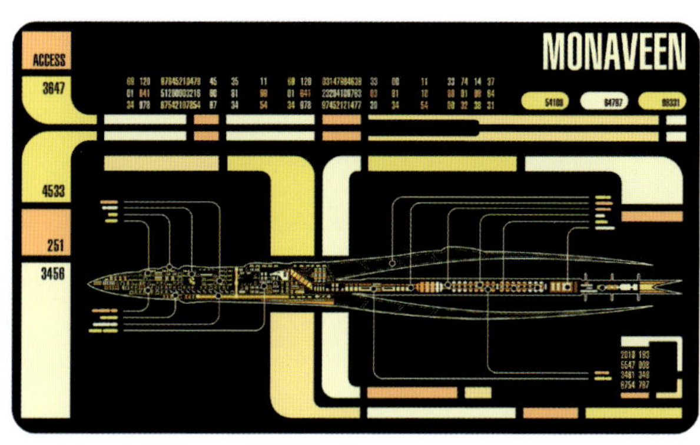

MONAVEEN ENGINE ROOM

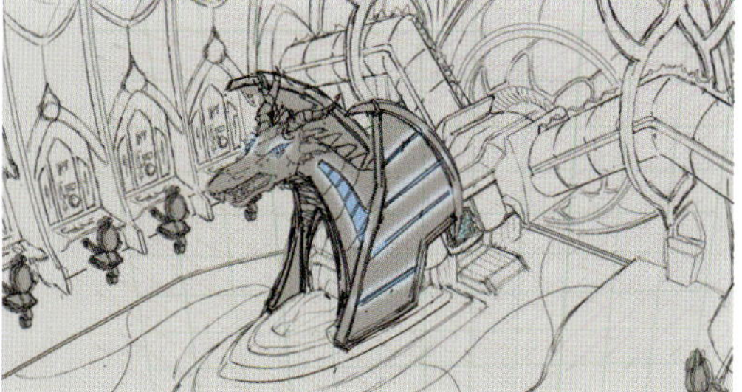

"Even though it looks like a fantasy room with a dragon engine, it still needed a base with a connection to nacelles."

— Barry J. Kelly

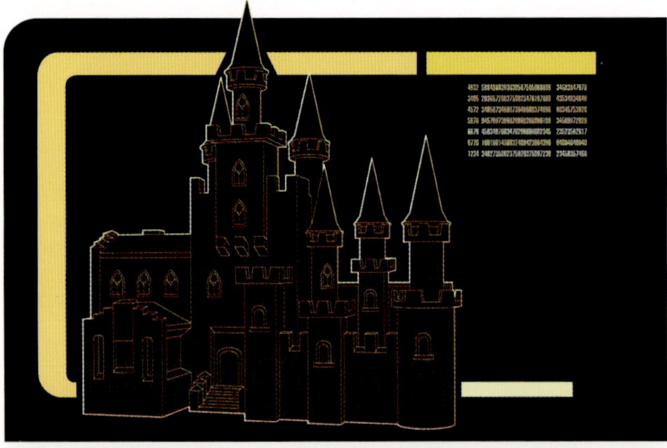

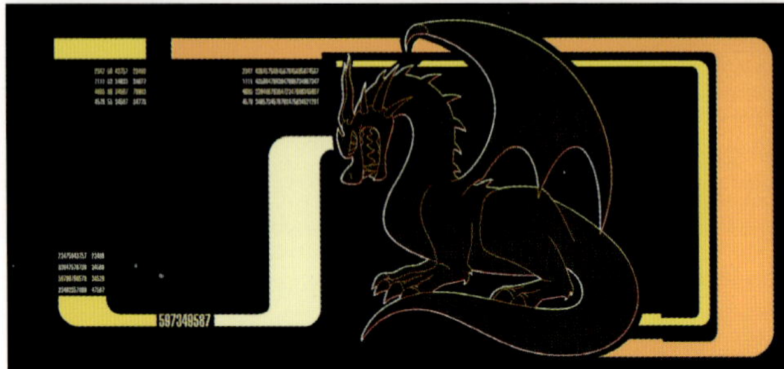

MONAVEEN CORRIDOR PORTAITS

"The painted portraits—we needed to make sure they looked like our style but also emulated brush strokes."

— Claire Lenth

MONAVEEN BRIDGE

DAYSTROM INSTITUTE EVIL COMPUTER WALL

Mariner and Boimler go on their first mission as pals with AGIMUS.

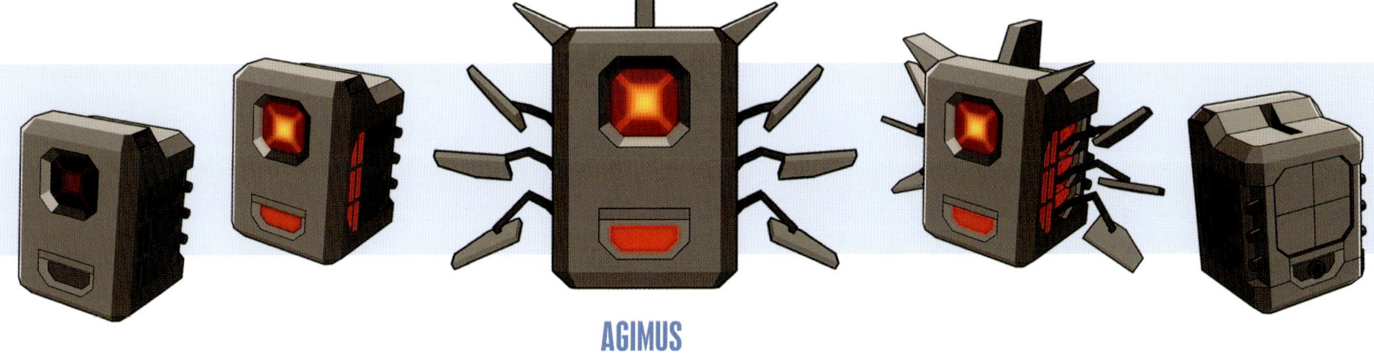

AGIMUS

"We wanted to give AGIMUS a Hannibal Lecter muzzle. We also wanted him to be a PC computer but needed him to be small enough for a Boimler baby carrier."

— Barry J. Kelly

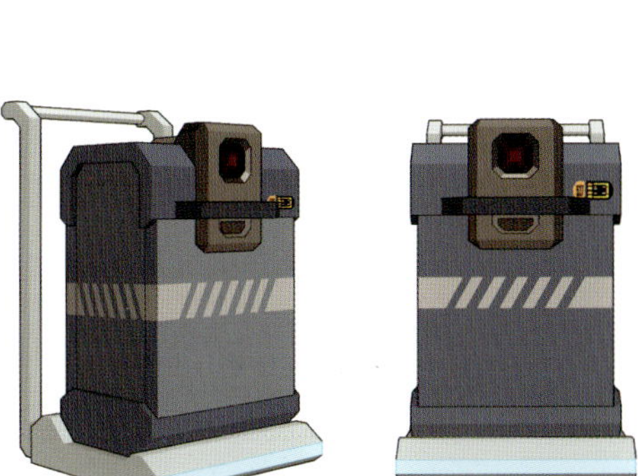

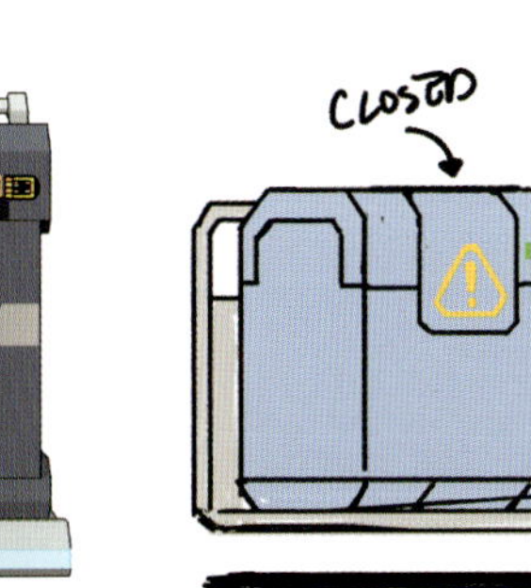

DAYSTROM INSTITUTE SCIENTIST

"The Daystrom scientist's outfit is referencing the TNG 'Home Soil' episode. We wanted a 'go-to' scientist for incidental scientists."

— Barry J. Kelly

DELTORE V

"We needed to make sure this felt like a battle had just happened, and there was propaganda. It's almost like hints of how much of a leader AGIMUS was."

— Barry J. Kelly

"We made this alien wasteland that is pretty at night."
— Barry J. Kelly

"Mike gave us a note at the animatic stage: 'Do not ever cut this crab.'"
— Barry J. Kelly

"Nollan wanted to always have this with an obscured view so that sand was always in the air, and you don't have a clear horizon. It makes it disorienting. It gives you that feeling that you're never clean."
— Claire Lenth

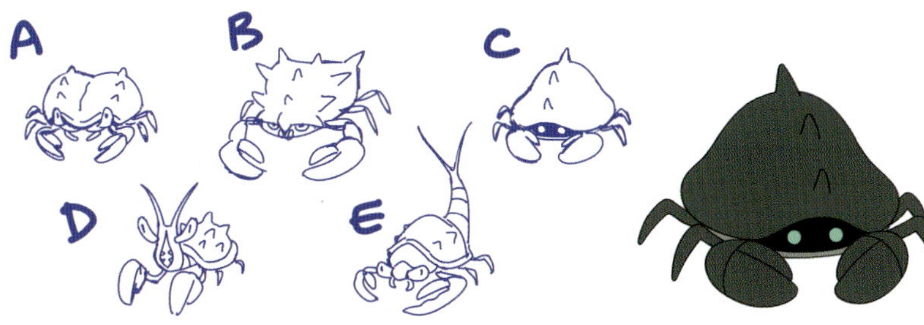

"The little crabs are so f***ing cute."
— Mike McMahan

LCARS S2E8

AIRDATE: 20210930
STARDATE: 58114.8

"I, Excretus"

A Pandronian consultant arrives on the *U.S.S. Cerritos* to run drills that require the Lower Decker and bridge crew to swap duties.

This is our second version of a sketch comedy episode, but with callbacks to famous existing problems from other *Star Trek* shows like Borg babies and the Western planet.

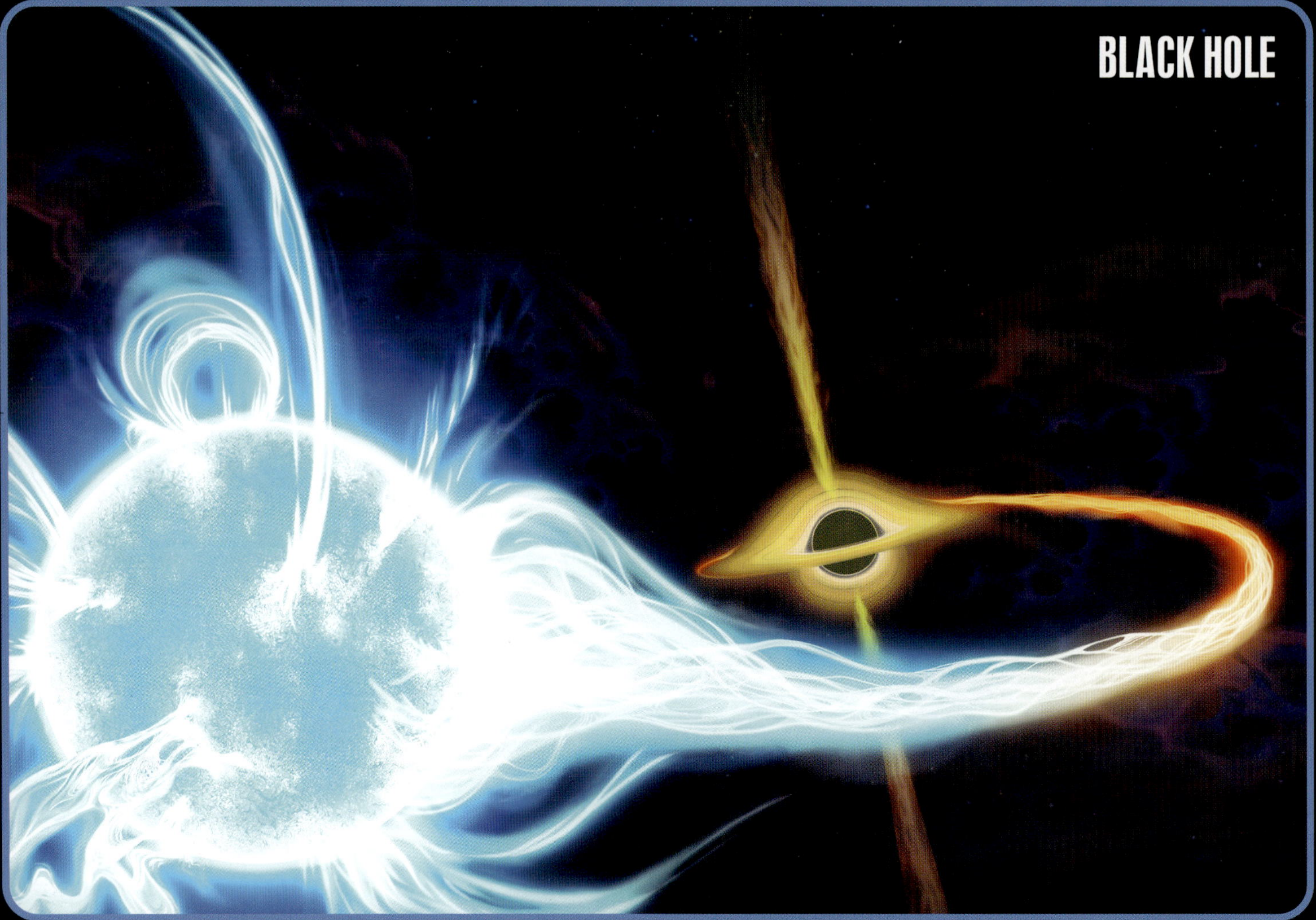

BLACK HOLE

SHARI YN YEM

"The design team extrapolated what a female Pandronian would look like based on the Ari bn Bem design from TAS: 'Bem.'"

— Brad Winters

HOLOPOD-GENERATED MIRROR UNIVERSE CREW

HOLOPOD: OLD WEST

"The Western is based off a classic TOS episode, 'Spectre of the Gun.'"

— Barry J. Kelly

HOLOPOD: CHIEF ENGINEER

"Rutherford's *Star Trek II: The Wrath of Khan* feature-film engineering suits. A Scotty classic."

— Barry J. Kelly

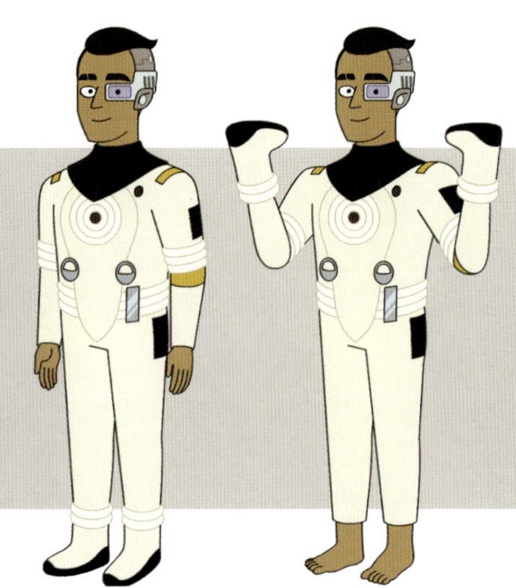

PHASE 1 PHASE 2 PHASE 3

"The Borg babies are a favorite. This was a delight. The animators really plushed them up and made them so cute, especially when the babies are squishing Boimler's little face."

— Marisa Livingston

"It made the most sense to design them directly strapped onto Boimler, which made them extra fun, too. They were endearing right from the get-go. They were never a model sheet baby. They were little things that Boimler was always carrying."

— Marisa Livingston

HOLOPOD: BORG

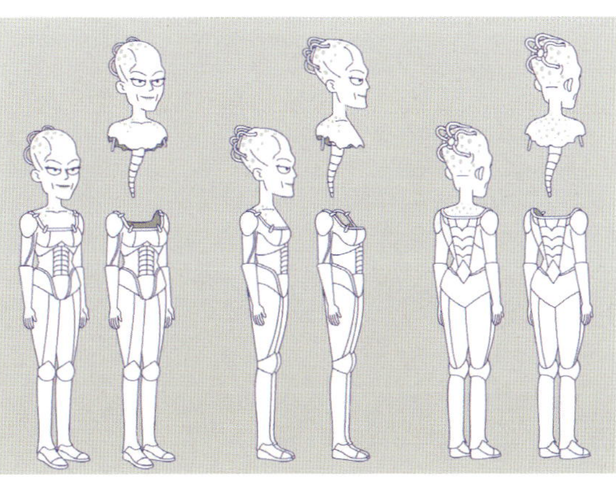

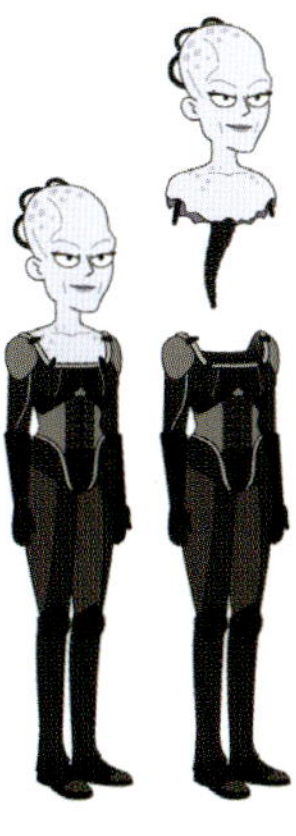

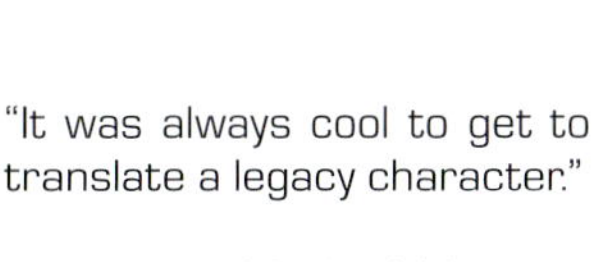

"It was always cool to get to translate a legacy character."

— Marisa Livingston

LCARS S2E9

AIRDATE: 20211007
STARDATE: 58125.3

"wej Duj"

Boimler tries to find a bridge buddy while the *U.S.S. Cerritos* crew has downtime during a long warp trip.

This episode is hitting so above what we were doing in season one, and it was written and produced at the height of Covid.

Wow, we're only nineteen episodes into a series, and we're already doing an all-timer awesome episode.

VULCAN CRUISER VCF *SH'VHAL*

"This was the first time that really struck me while making the show that this would have been a good episode in any *Star Trek*. It's an all-timer in any series. It's still an awesome episode, and it's funny."

— Mike McMahan

KLINGON BIRD OF PREY *CHE'TA'*

SH'VHAL RESEARCH LAB

CREW RECREATION DAY

"We received a note from one of our animators to make our knots accurate."
— Barry J. Kelly

"Nothing was a bigger legal hurdle in all of *Lower Decks* than getting this shirt approved."
— Brad Winters

"We matched Yosemite in the holodeck to *Star Trek V: The Final Frontier*."
— Barry J. Kelly

This is the first time we see the RITOS T-shirt, which you can purchase now.

STARSHIP *CLUE*

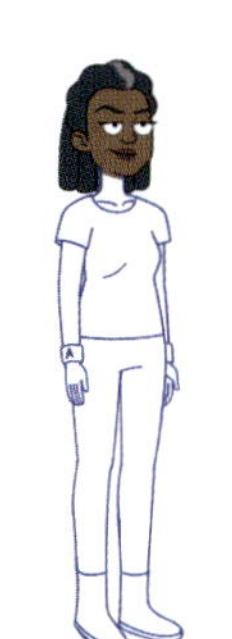

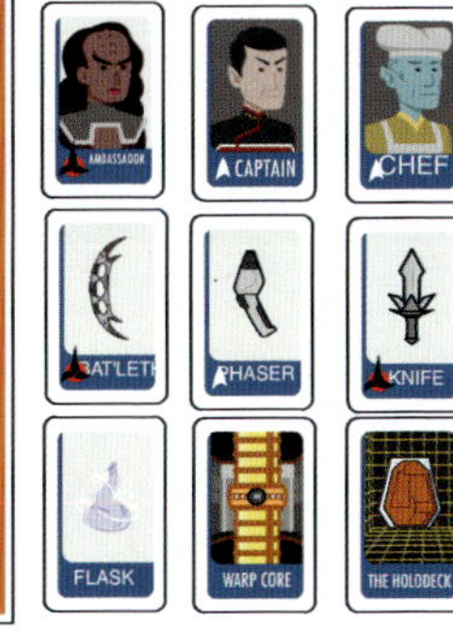

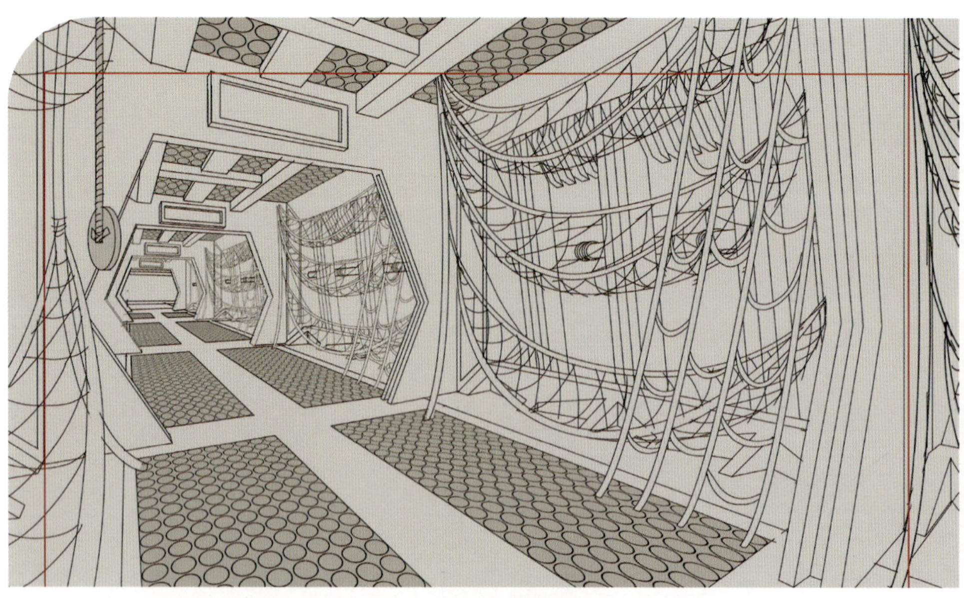

"Klingon lower decks. We needed the equivalence of our Lower Decker bunks."

— Barry J. Kelly

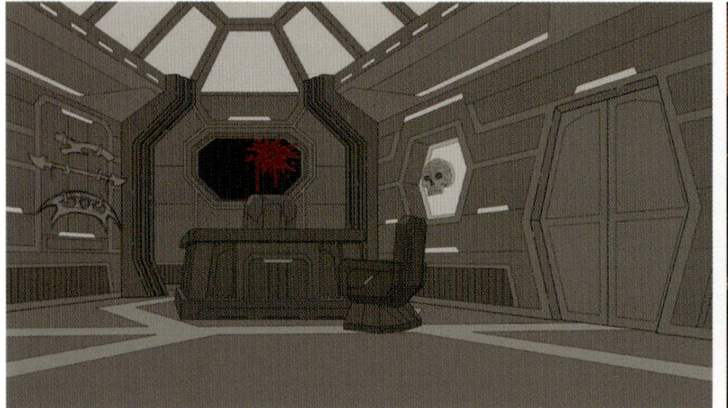

"In the Klingon ships, the colors make it look humid with some heavy mouth breathers and smells."

— Claire Lenth

"I had a lot of fun with Dorg and Ma'ah. They had a cool conflict at the end of the episode where they battled to the death, and we spelled out a lot of it with special poses for animation."

— Marisa Livingston

CAPTAIN DORG

MA'AH

"Ma'ah was supposed to be a Klingon Boimler. We initially designed him to be skinny and dorky, like a huge Klingon dweeb, which is why he had the little almost mustache that he can't really grow. He's trying to imitate the captain but was really unintimidating even amongst his fellow lower deckers. But as we kept building versions of him, it made more sense for him to be a stronger, sturdier-built Klingon dude. He needed to be able to fight Dorg, who was a huge guy, and claim ownership of the ship."

— Marisa Livingston

PAKLED LOWER DECKERS

It was our chance to see the lower decks of other alien ships and tie it all into our overall storyline with the Klingons doing weapon deals with the Pakleds.

TARG

"We wanted it to be scary and frightening. It was the captain's dog. At first, we tried to make it look kind of grotesque or weird or like lovably ugly, but it was better to lean more cute-ugly."

— Marisa Livingston

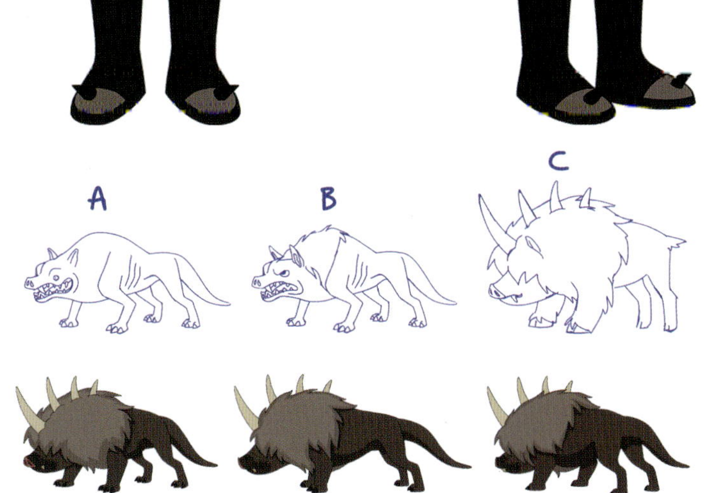

SH'VHAL CAPTAIN'S READY ROOM

BRIDGE

A
B

MEDITATION ROOM

SH'VHAL CREW DESIGNS

T'GAI

T'LYN MESSY HAIR?

"We had a messier version of T'Lyn that was more similar to Mariner, but even a Vulcan Mariner would still be a Vulcan to us."

— Barry J. Kelly

ENS. T'LYN

We meet T'Lyn and Ma'ah for the first time in this episode. Ma'ah is trying hard to do things by the book but can't grow because of it. T'Lyn is an outcast that the others in her crew don't take seriously. We wanted T'Lyn to seem like the Mariner of the Vulcan ship. She's more freewheeling. We loosely tied her and Mariner together with the use of hair accessories. T'Lyn has a headband, and Mariner has a hair tie. "She has lost all control."

CAPTAIN SOKEL

SYVEK

T'GAI

SHARA

SH'VHAL BRIDGE CREW

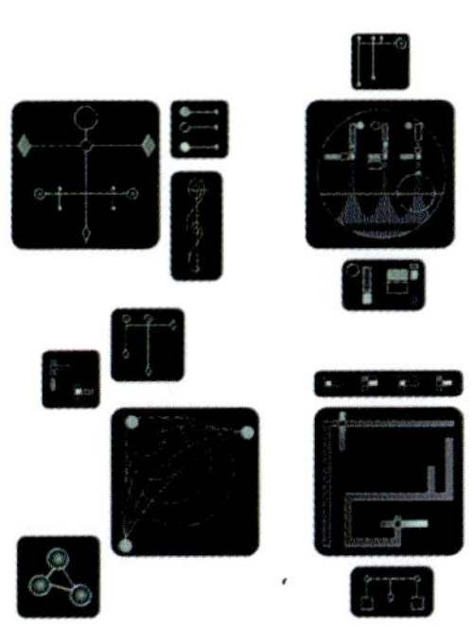

LCARS S2E10

AIRDATE: 20211014
STARDATE: 58130.6

"First First Contact"

In the season two finale, the *U.S.S. Cerritos* is tasked to aid another starship on a first contact mission.

We really wanted to do a ship-based finale, and we wanted the *Cerritos* to be really messed up again. However, this time the *Cerritos* would be doing the rescuing instead of the other way around.

U.S.S. ARCHIMEDES

With the *Archimedes*, we created a whole new class of Federation starships, the *Obena* class, which is named after our art director, Nollan Obena.

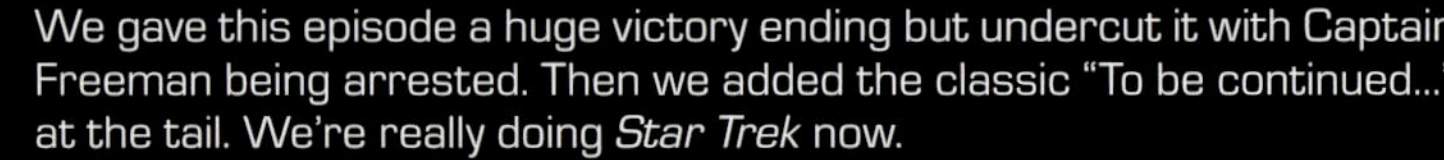

We gave this episode a huge victory ending but undercut it with Captain Freeman being arrested. Then we added the classic "To be continued..." at the tail. We're really doing *Star Trek* now.

ARCHIMEDES BRIDGE

U.S.S. ARCHIMEDES

We brought back an original Lower Decker, Sonya Gomez, the ensign that spilled hot chocolate on Captain Picard in TNG: 'Q Who.' We wanted to show that despite her rocky start, she ended up as a captain of her own ship, the *U.S.S. Archimedes*.

ARCHIMEDES BRIDGE CREW

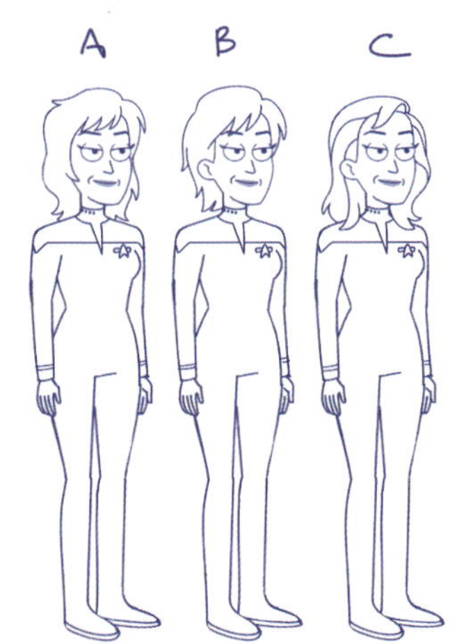

CAPTAIN GOMEZ

CMDR. MANDEL

STARFLEET COMMAND OFFICERS

DAMAGED *U.S.S. CERRITOS*

"We did a lot of research on what it would look like. We looked through those *Star Trek* cutaway books to get an idea of what the nacelles looked like on the inside. Mike wanted a pop of color when they took off the hull, so we made it bronze underneath, which stood out when all the panels were gone."

— Nollan Obena

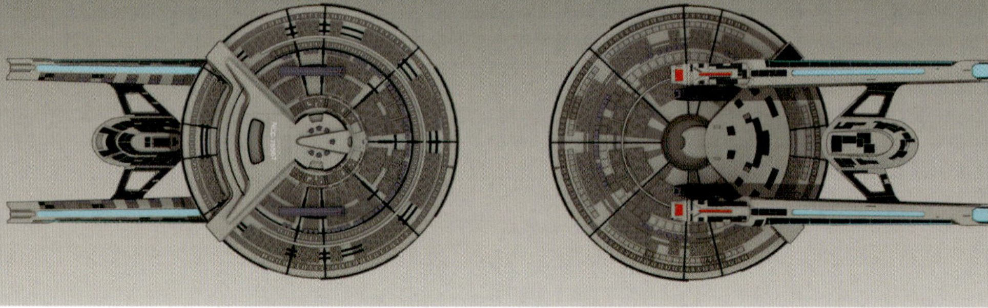

LT. MATT AND LT. KIMOLU

This is the first time we see Cetacean Ops. It's been a mysterious place that we've always wanted to see since the blueprints from the 1980s.

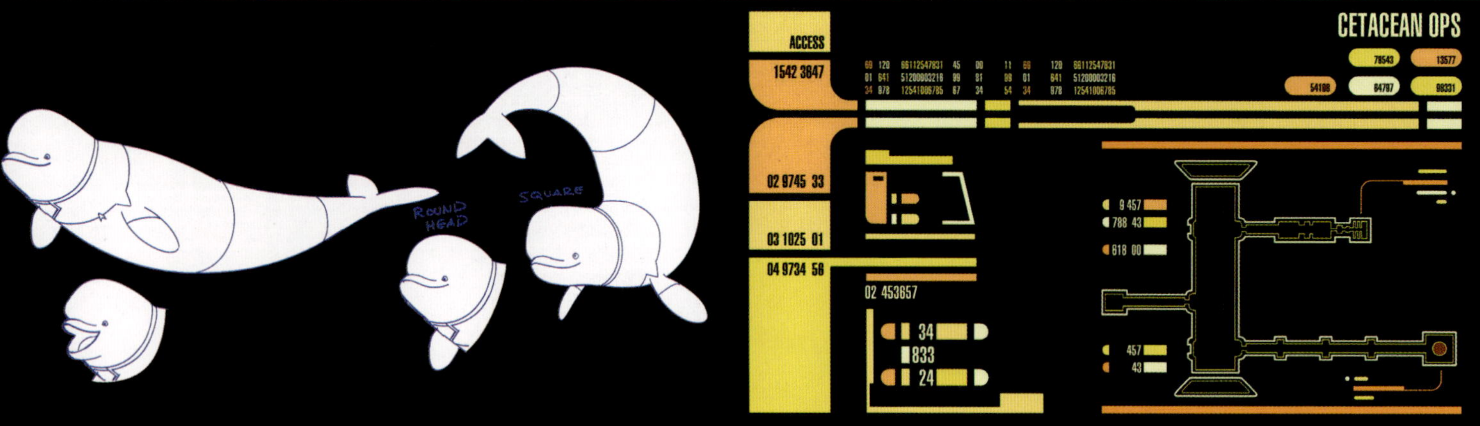

"Connecting the bridge to the exterior once that screen was taken out was a challenge. We had to figure out the scale. How big was the bridge in the upper saucer dome?"

— Nollan Obena

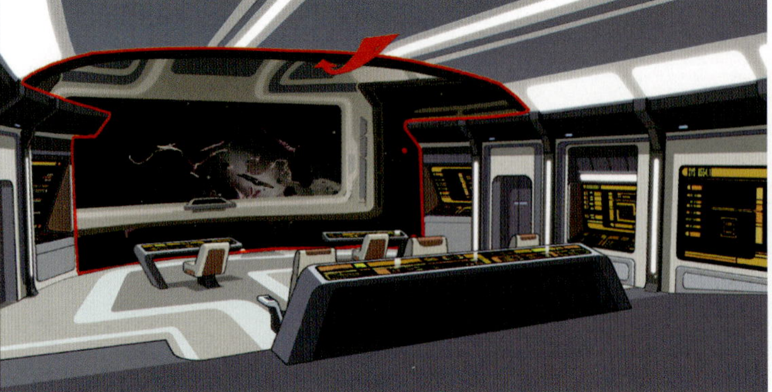

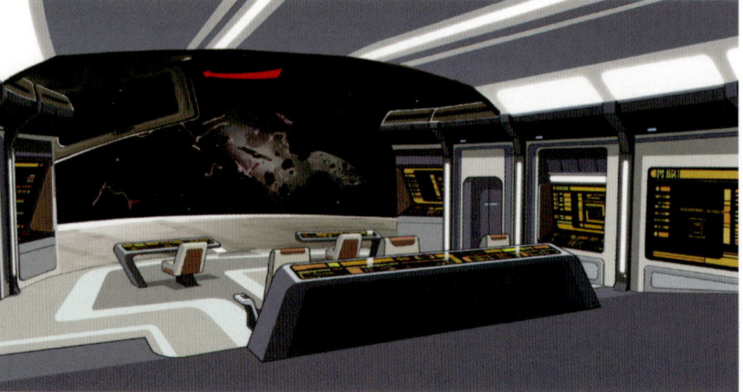

"When we designed the whales, we didn't realize they would be returning. We looked for ways to differentiate the characters when they're a singular species. So we gave one a square head and one a round head."

— Marisa Livingston

LAAPERIAN CITY

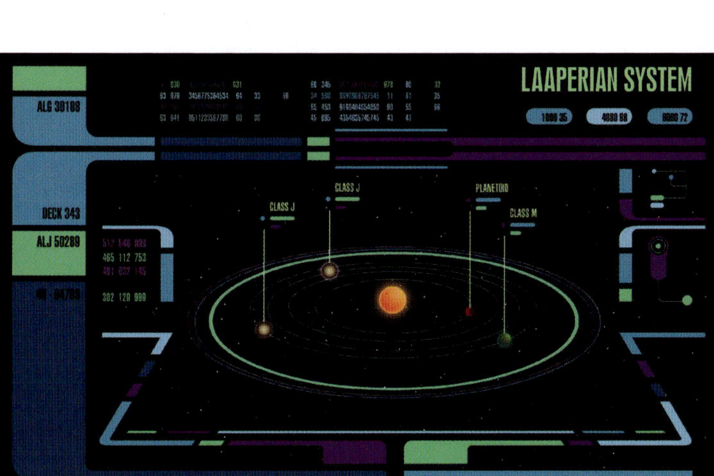

LAAPERIAN LEADERS

LAAPERIAN CITIZENS

CHAPTER 06

LCARS 40274

02-654598

SEASON THREE

STAR TREK
LOWER DECKS
III
SEASON 3

LCARS S3E1

AIRDATE: 20220825
STARDATE: UNKNOWN

"Grounded"

Mariner enlists her friends on a rogue mission to exonerate her mother, as Captain Freeman faces a military tribunal for the destruction of Pakled Planet.

This was our homage to *Star Trek: First Contact* and rescuing someone in prison. It had to feel like Earth. Seeing Sisko's restaurant, Boimler's vineyards, and being in San Francisco, seeing Mariner's dad's place. This is a "we're on EARTH episode," doing fun Earth stuff.

BOZEMAN PARK

"When making the 'ride' version of the Phoenix, first we make the movie-accurate pass and then we add some extra LEDs and more contrast to the paintjob to make it feel more like a cleaner, newer version of the legendary ship. This is the initial design; as we approach the modeling, the animation, and final composite, we tend to make tweaks and adjustments at each stage to make sure it flies effectively across the screen.

"What's easy to forget is that we have to make different 'states' of props or backgrounds for when things break. A normal state and a 'broken' state."

— Barry J. Kelly

PHOENIX ROCKET REPLICA

"James Cromwell himself returned to voice Zefram Cochrane. Legendary! We needed that classic hat and gave it to Ruthie and Tendi to wear as merch!"

— Barry J. Kelly

ZEFRAM COCHRANE

GAVIN

"We had a lot of fun going through TNG and picking out the wildest outfits. Rutherford's sweater is based on Jake Sisko's outfits."

— Nollan Obena

"With the exception of the extra seats, we matched every detail we could to the cockpit set in *First Contact*."

— Barry J. Kelly

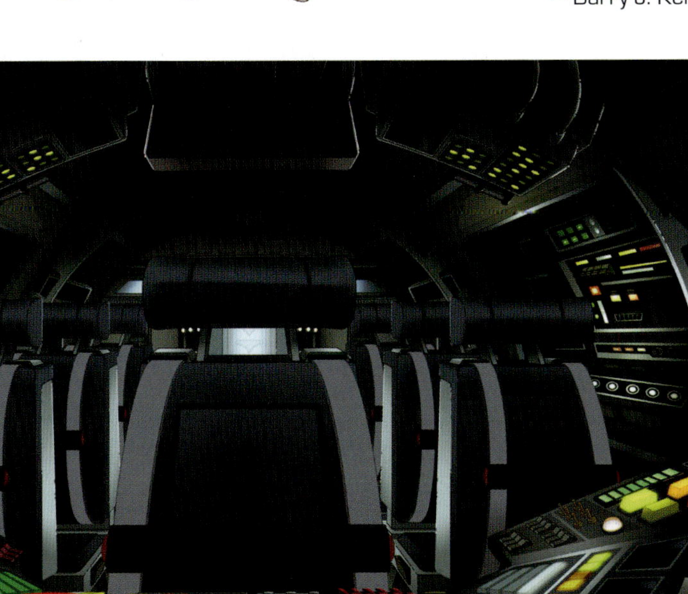

"The statue of Cochrane was based on Archer's statue of him in *Star Trek: Enterprise*, which was designed by Doug Drexler."

— Barry J. Kelly

THIRST
CONTACT
B B

"The reason Modesto is so hilly in the 2380s is because of all the carnage from World War III. That's how I made these backgrounds make sense."

— Brad Winters

"I believe we had a Boimler Vineyard water tower here at one point, but we removed the layer to not give it away too soon."

— Barry J. Kelly

RAISIN FARM

"The Boimler farm was fun. It's all raisins. It's an homage to Picard, but it's raisins."

— Nollan Obena

LIANNE

GENEVIEVE

MANDOLINA

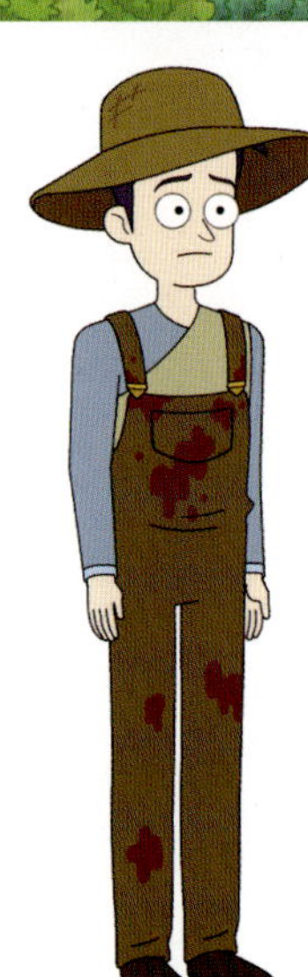

"We wanted a classic sun maid to hit the nose on the head with our pack of hot raisin maids for Boimler to 'not' be into."

— Barry J. Kelly

SISKO'S

"Sisko's! Classic, iconic location from DS9! We love getting to paint these backgrounds. We even get to expand the shot as the originals were shot in standard definition, and we are in a high-definition world today."

— Barry J. Kelly

"We had to come up with corners in this restaurant that haven't been seen before, meanwhile making sure we had the right props like the TV monitor needed for this episode. This back area of the restaurant felt more like a café, and a TV wouldn't feel out of place."

— Barry J. Kelly

"The San Franscisco skyline outside of Admiral Freeman's office window is very reminiscent of admirals' offices from DS9."

— Barry J. Kelly

VERUGAMENTS

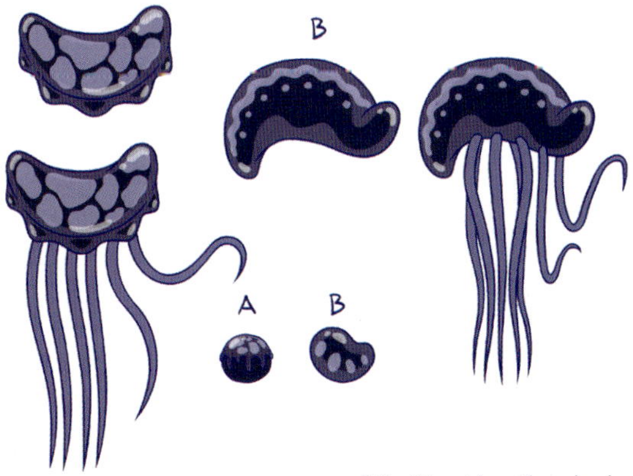

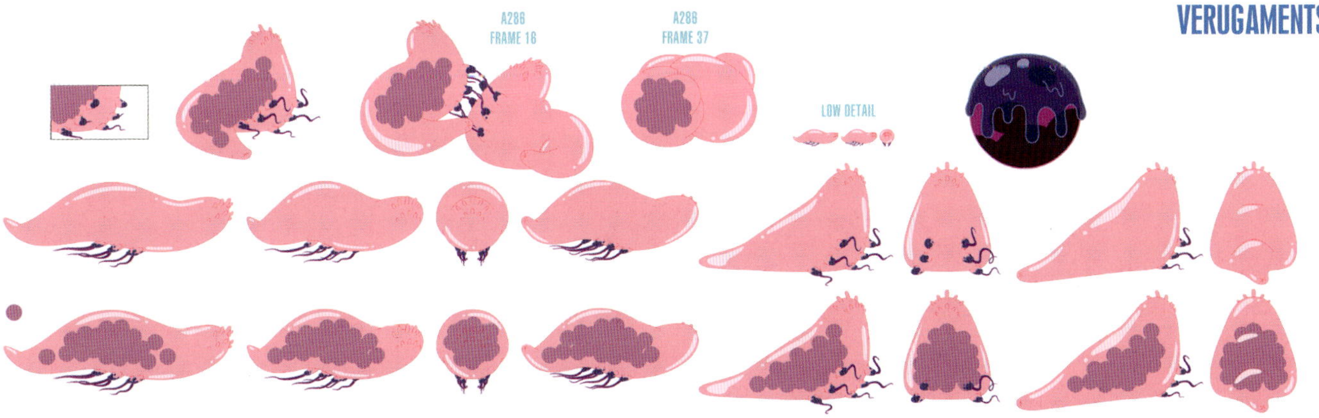

"You'll notice the design is fairly graphic compared to the final look in the show; that is because we add translucency and noise to the animation in composite. The creatures are constructed in layers so that in composite we can make the eggs feel like they are inside the body, with layers of noise to make it feel like jelly, then add a glow to the highlights so they have a 'wet' surface."

— Barry J. Kelly

"This version is what we would feel is too 'stagey.' It has the information we need for the scene, but—when presented with the question 'Why is this room set up this way? Who would be using it?'—you realize it needs to feel more natural and practical."

— Barry J. Kelly

TRANSPORTER FACILITY HANGAR

DENNY

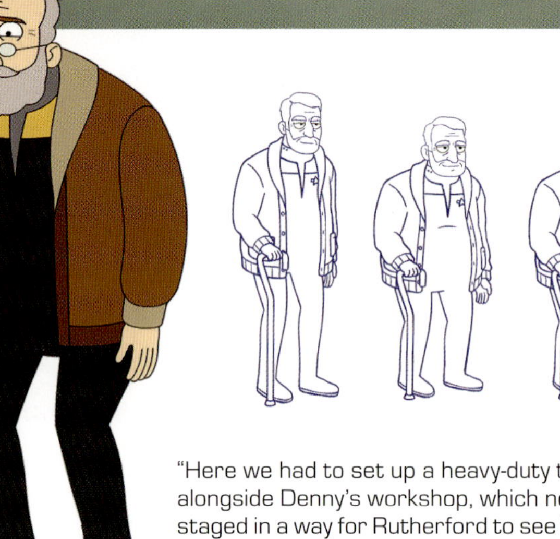

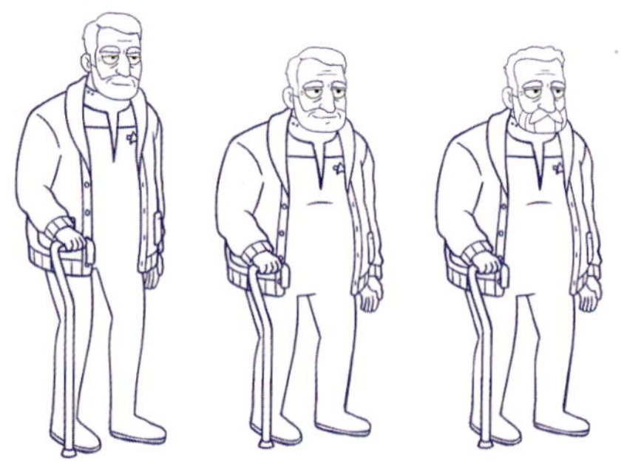

"Here we had to set up a heavy-duty transporter alongside Denny's workshop, which needed to be staged in a way for Rutherford to see it almost as a museum of transporters."

— Barry J. Kelly

DENNY'S QUARTERS

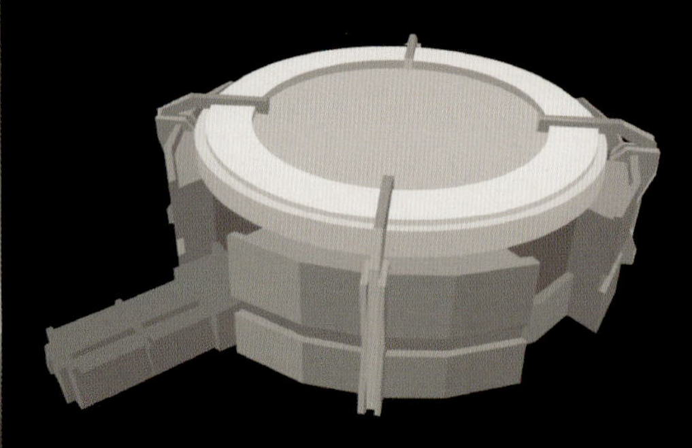

"Great still painting by Amanda Turnage here. We don't always get to do painted still frames, but we try to capture all the excitement of an animated scene."

— Barry J. Kelly

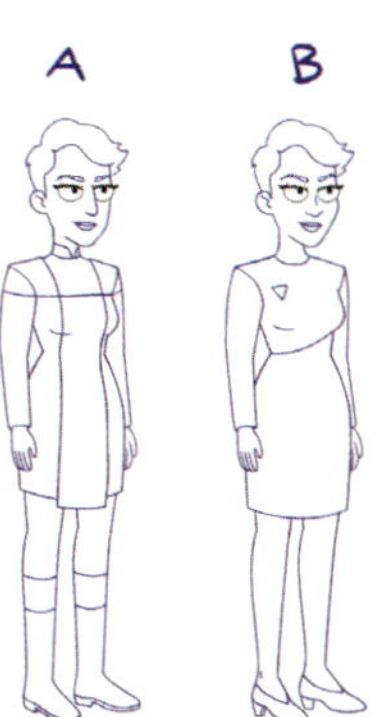

SYLVIA RONT

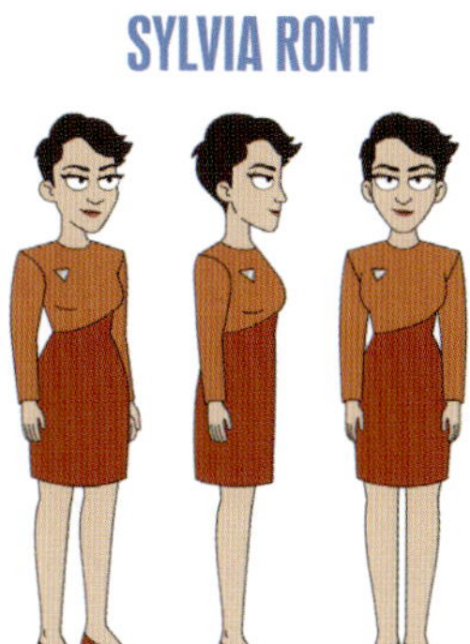

"When we needed 'courtroom attire' for the bridge crew, that San Francisco sun definitely motivated some cool outfits. Everyone needs sunglasses."

— Barry J. Kelly

"We only see Pakled Planet at night once in this flashback, but it was fun to make."

— Barry J. Kelly

PAKLED PLANET

LCARS S3E2

AIRDATE: 20220901
STARDATE: UNKNOWN

"The Least Dangerous Game"

On a tropical paradise planet, Mariner questions Commander Ransom on how he structures his away team. Boimler makes a bold career decision.

Dulaine has the best system of checks and balances with a telekinetic baby, a beeping evil computer, and a talking sentient volcano.

DULAINE SPACE STATION

The orbital lifts were first described to us as "space elevators" that looked like pylons coming out of a tropical beachy planet that stretched into orbit.

DULAINE VOLCANO

DULAINE ISLAND

ORBITAL LIFT

DULAINIAN CITIZENS

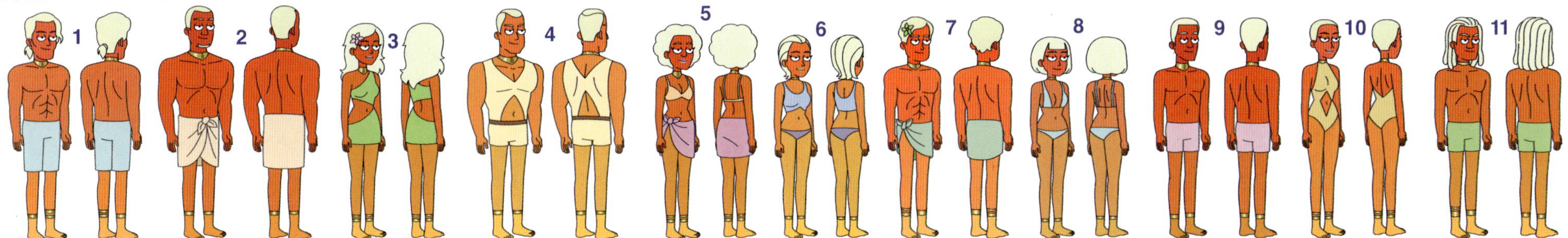

Mike wanted the Dulainians to look like tropical cocktails, like mai tais, with a gradient of skin tone from head to toe. This was a hard task for animation, because in our software, patterns and gradients can make the characters look flat, like a sticker stuck on the screen, when their arms and legs move. The joints like shoulders, knees, and wrists of the characters break the pattern. We wanted them to look good without jeopardizing their volume. So we created a cheat by breaking up the gradient with clothing and jewelry.

MENDRICK

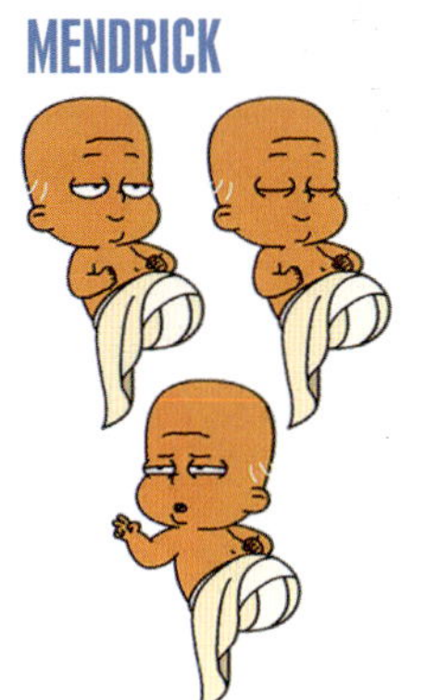

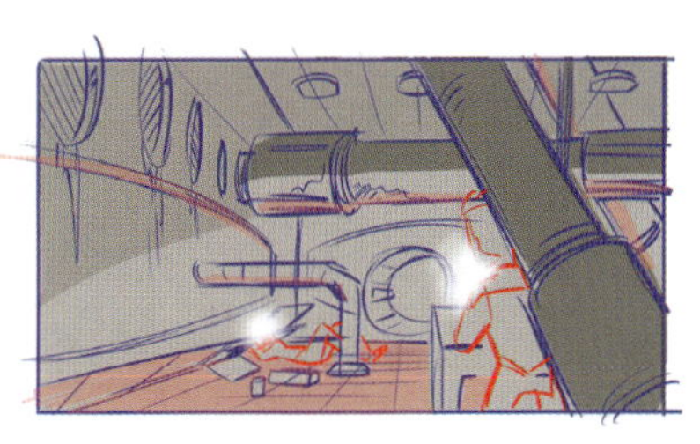

Big pistons and cables crowd the room
Working space is tight and uncomfortable
Signs of wear on all surfaces, dripping oil
Underlit by red emergency light?
Officers carry flashlights

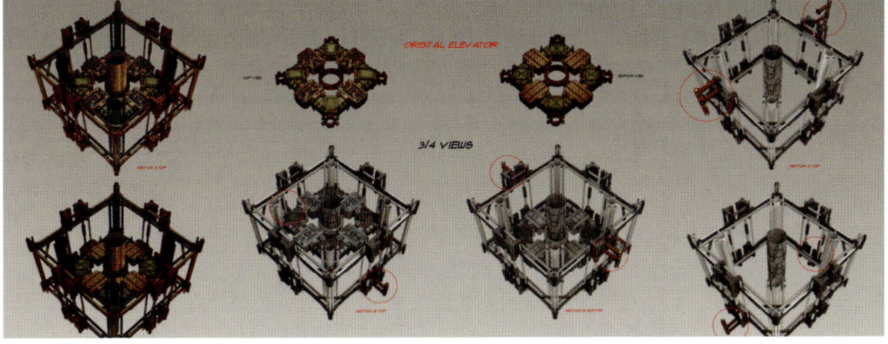

ORBITAL LIFT

"We make one section of the elevator shaft in 3D that is repeated vertically to create the structure."

— Barry J. Kelly

"K'Ranch was so much fun because in *Star Trek,* a lot of the time, the aliens are humans with simple facial prosthetics. Big eyebrows, nose ridges, spots, which we carried over to animation. But it was cool to have characters like K'Ranch where it was a complete alien. A human could not fit into his suit. He's bloodlusty. He's shivering for the hunt. He's uncomfortable. He has to hunt someone aboard the *Cerritos.* So it was fun to make him as scary of an alien as we wanted but also have room for him to be quite the charmer. He has mimosas with the captain."

— Marisa Livingston

"There is clearly a famous alien predator that was the inspiration for K'Ranch, but we always need to make our own *Lower Decks* signature creature. What helps make scary alien monsters is adding revealing details in every scene to create surprises. In the movie *Alien*, the alien is almost a different form in every scene. First an egg, then a facehugger, then small biped, and finally a huger biped. With K'Ranch, first he's intimidating in a helmet, then revealing the face, then he's naked with tattoos, and then he's friendly?"

— Barry J. Kelly

K'RANCH

This is the start of bold Boimler's arc, which he doubles down on at the end of the episode instead of learning a lesson.

This episode was partially inspired by the free-spirited Edo in TNG's "Justice" and by Tosk and the Hunters in DS9's "Captive Pursuit."

We brought back J. G. Hertzler to play Martok in the tabletop game we see the Lower Deckers playing in this episode.

BAT'LETHS & BIHNUCHS

"Super fun logo for *Bat'leths & BiHnuchs* from our painter, Anthony Benedetto, who also happens to be a graphic designer."

— Barry J. Kelly

"When it comes to making games or toy props in the show, we always want the designers to make what they would want or what would be fun to see fans wear in these costumes."

— Barry J. Kelly

B&B GAME PIECES

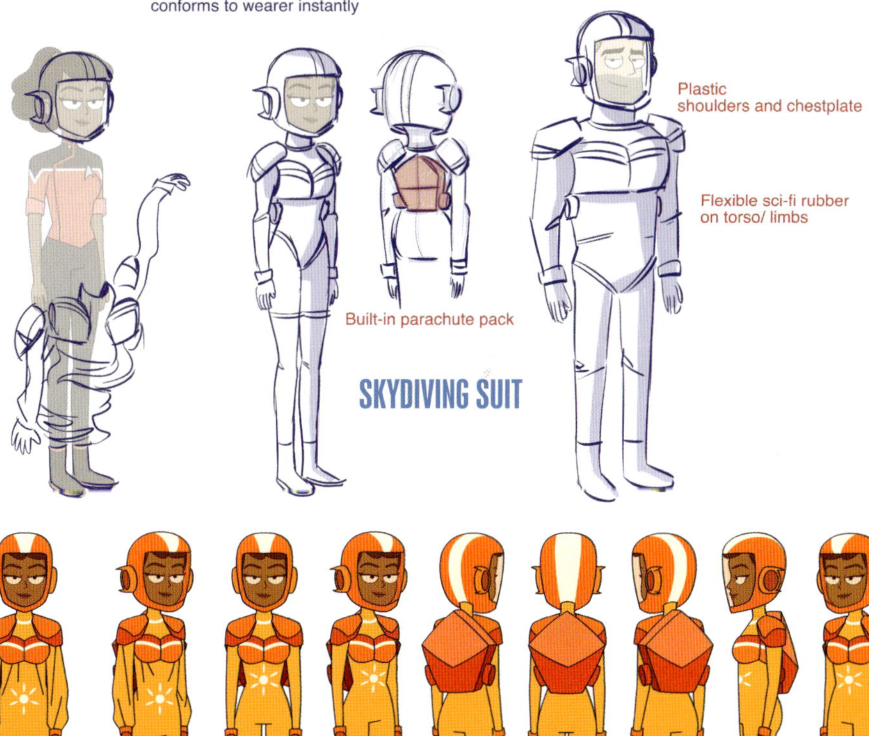

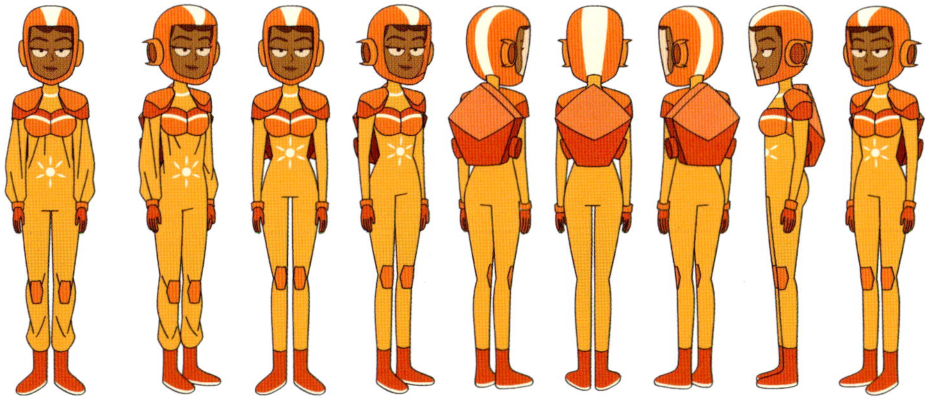

LCARS S3E3

AIRDATE: 20220908
STARDATE: 58256.2

"Mining the Mind's Mines"

On a remote science outpost, stone orbs are bringing fantasies to life. Tendi starts her first day as a senior science officer trainee.

In this episode, it's supposed to feel like a mystery on a planet where our Lower Deckers are coming in to clean up after an episode we didn't see.

U.S.S. Hood and Jengus IV

Jengus IV Crystal Cavern Room

JENGUS IV

"We get dorky where we can. This is a super fun retro hover bike. Check out those NCC-1701 nacelles and deflector dish!"

— Barry J. Kelly

Through Mariner's fantasies of Jennifer, we learn that they don't have the best relationship.

CERRITOS CREW ILLUSIONS

We brought back Susan Gibney to play Rutherford's fantasy Leah Brahms.

DR. HOLDEN

OUTPOST SCIENTIST

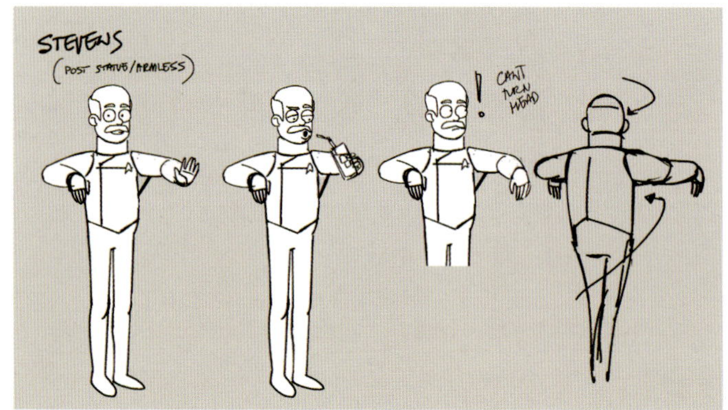

LTJG. STEVENS

SCRUBBLE EMISSARY

U.S.S. CARLSBAD

NCC-73110

U.S.S. *CARLSBAD* CREW

We designed the *Carlsbad* crew to look slightly cooler and more slick than our heroes as a misdirect because we learn that the *Cerritos* is considered the coolest of the *California*-class fleet.

"Cor'Dee is a Zaldan, and their species' bluntness helps the misdirection: him being competitive with the Lower Deckers when he's actually fond of them. The only giveaway is the webbed fingers!"

— Barry J. Kelly

LCARS S3E4

AIRDATE: 20220915
STARDATE: UNKNOWN

"Room for Growth"

Mariner, Boimler, and Tendi clash with their archrivals: Delta Shift. The *Cerritos* engineers go on mandatory relaxation leave.

The cold open of this episode is referencing "Masks" from TNG, which interrupts the Lower Deckers' personal space through their bunks.

This is another false bottle episode—we don't visit another planet, but the ship has so much more to explore.

U.S.S. CERRITOS ANTI-GRAVITY ROOM

The Lower Deckers go on an adventure in the bowels of the *Cerritos* to alter their chances for better quarters. We wanted it to feel similar to a *Stand by Me* coming-of-age journey, with a group of friends building stories to tell years from now. Meanwhile, the engineers, including Rutherford, go on a mandatory spa day with Captain Freeman.

LOWER DECKS BUNKS MINOOKI TRANSFORMATION

CERRITOS BOTANICAL GARDEN

MINOOKI STONE IDOL AND MASK

GOOPY

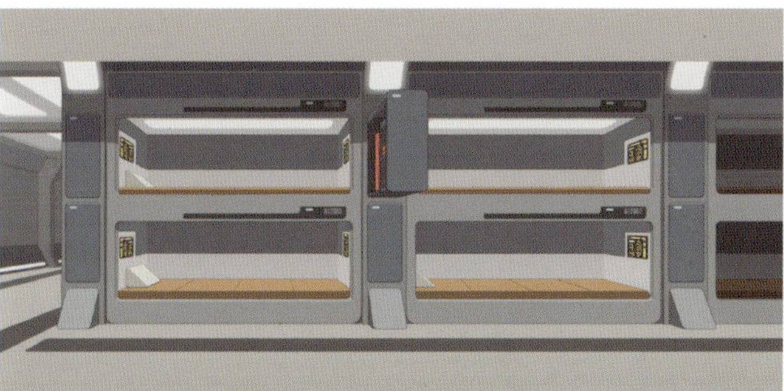

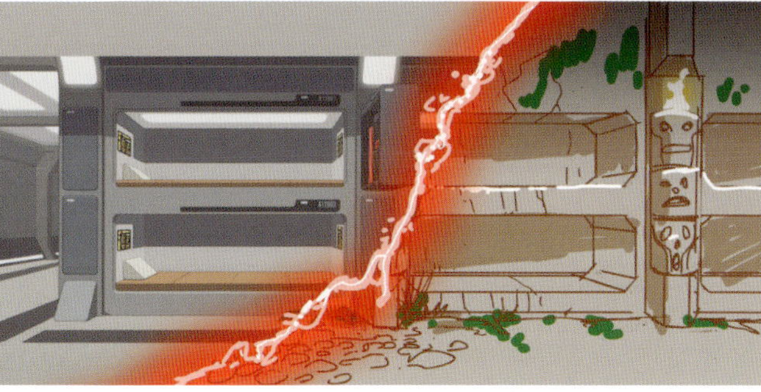

"This temple version of the bunks is drawn right on top of our key bunk background so we can wipe to reveal the temple over the bunks in composite."

— Barry J. Kelly

ENGINEERING MINOOKI TRANSFORMATION

If you look closely in the swamp scene under the hydroponics bay, you'll see a Doopler must have gotten lost and never made it out.

CERRITOS HOLODECK

We painted the holodeck backgrounds, props, and characters in color, then converted them into black and white.

"These are early keyframes I drew to get the vibe for the board artist. It's usually the shot we need the most, then we build the scene around it."

— Barry J. Kelly

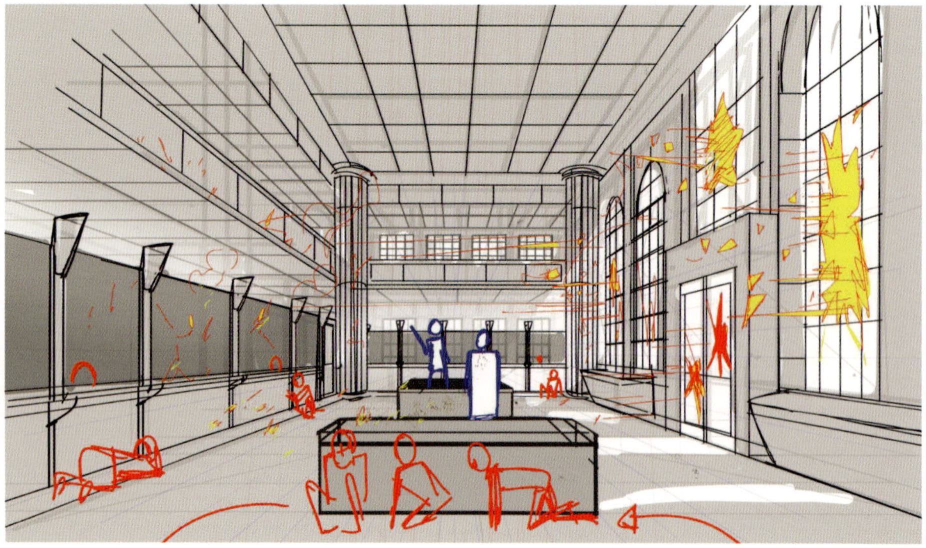

This is the first time we meet Ensign Meredith, played by Charlotte Nicdao, who brought so much charm to the character, we wanted to see more of her in the future.

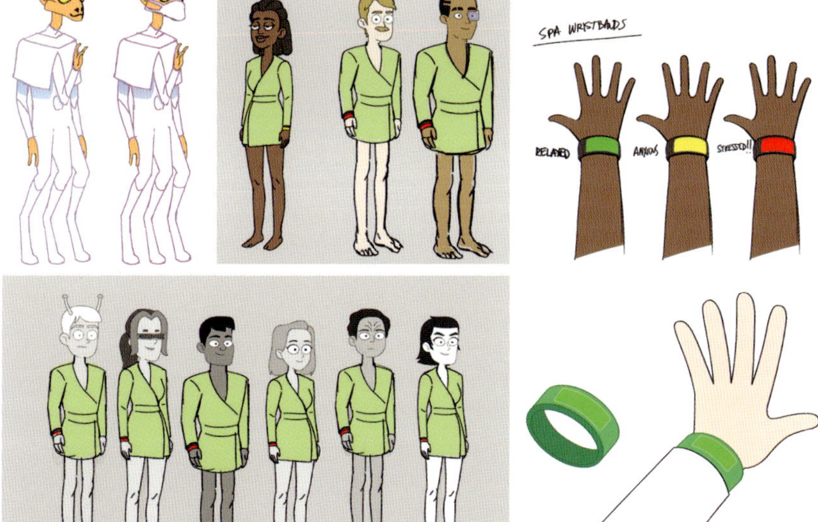

LCARS S3E5

AIRDATE: 20220922
STARDATE: 58354.2

"Reflections"

Mariner and Boimler work the Starfleet recruitment booth at an alien job fair. Rutherford challenges himself.

In this episode, we dig into some of Rutherford's past, with Eugene Cordero playing two different versions of the same character that race against each other.

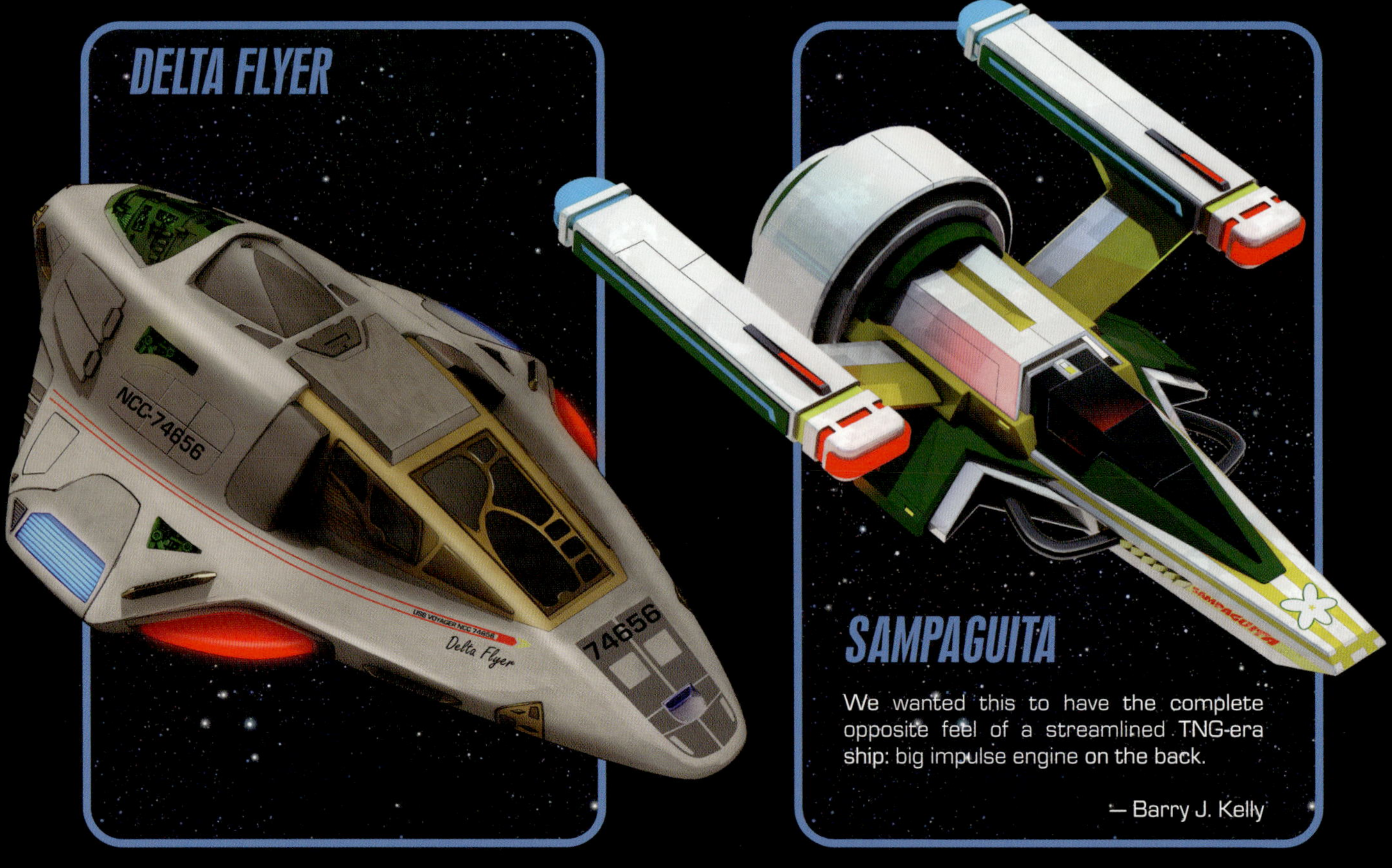

DELTA FLYER

SAMPAGUITA

We wanted this to have the complete opposite feel of a streamlined TNG-era ship: big impulse engine on the back.

— Barry J. Kelly

DELTA FLYER WORKSHOP

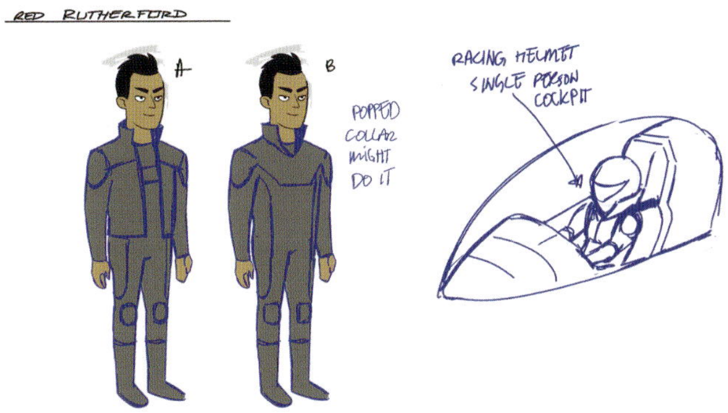

RED RUTHERFORD

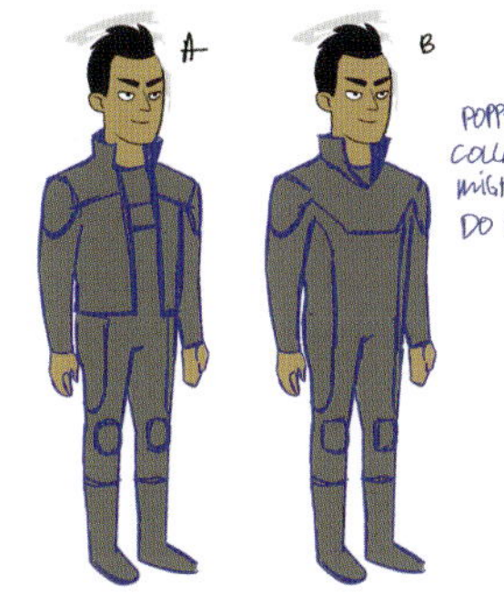

RACING HELMET SINGLE PERSON COCKPIT

DELTA FLYER LOWER DECKERS

NO PIPS!

Barry J. Kelly mocked up the mirror treatment so we could see our usual Rutherford through reflecting surfaces.

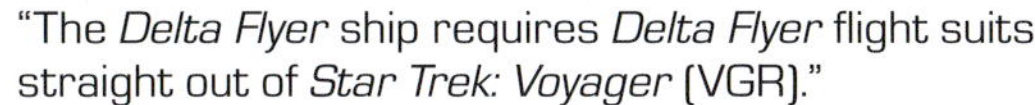

"The *Delta Flyer* ship requires *Delta Flyer* flight suits straight out of *Star Trek: Voyager* (VGR)."

— Barry J. Kelly

We brought the *Delta Flyer* and its costumes into the *Lower Decks* style.

RUTHERFORD IN SICKBAY

SAMPAGUITA DESIGNS

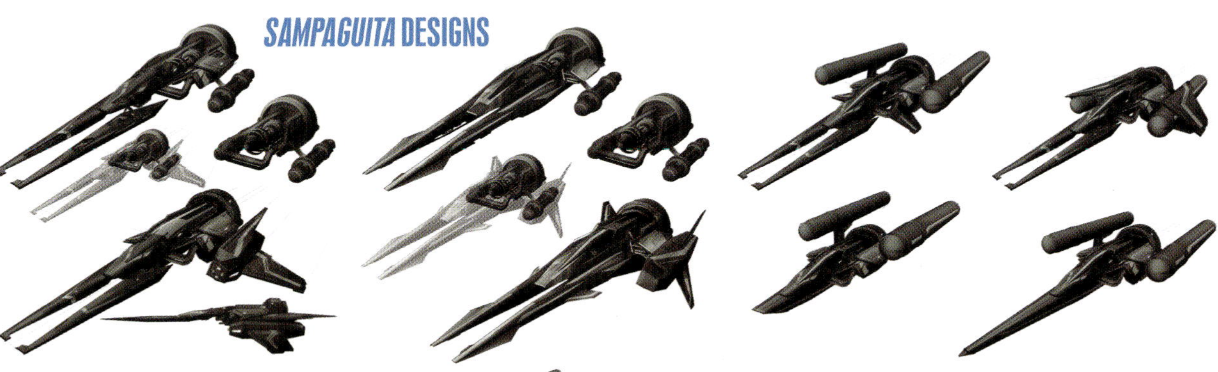

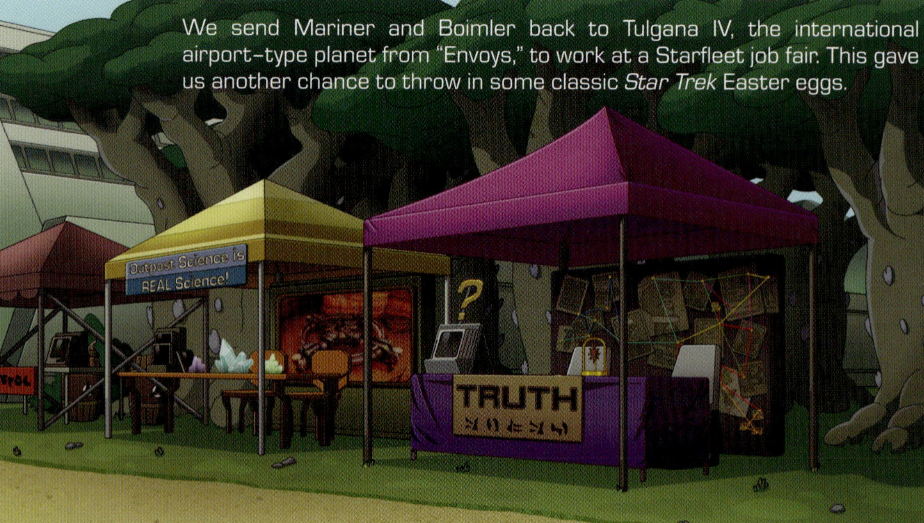

We send Mariner and Boimler back to Tulgana IV, the international airport-type planet from "Envoys," to work at a Starfleet job fair. This gave us another chance to throw in some classic *Star Trek* Easter eggs.

TULGANA IV

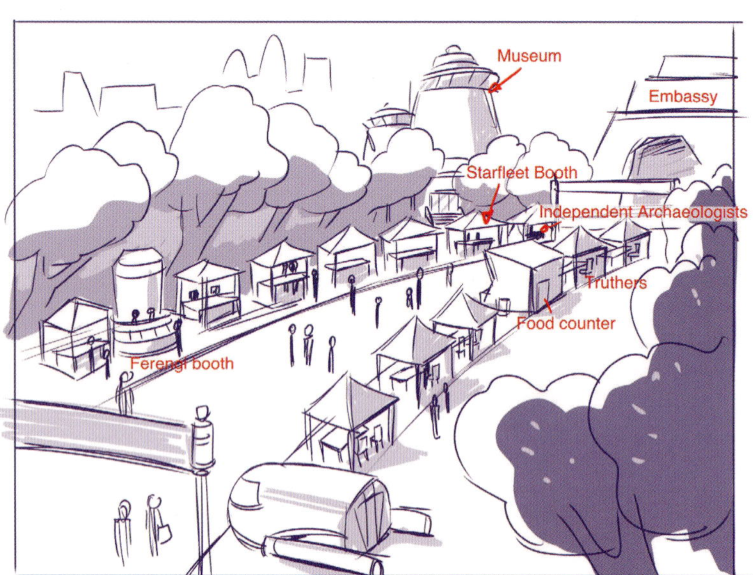

"These were sketches by the director, Mike Mullen, for the board artists to start with. We needed that classic job-fair setup so you could quickly read what the scene was."

— Barry J. Kelly

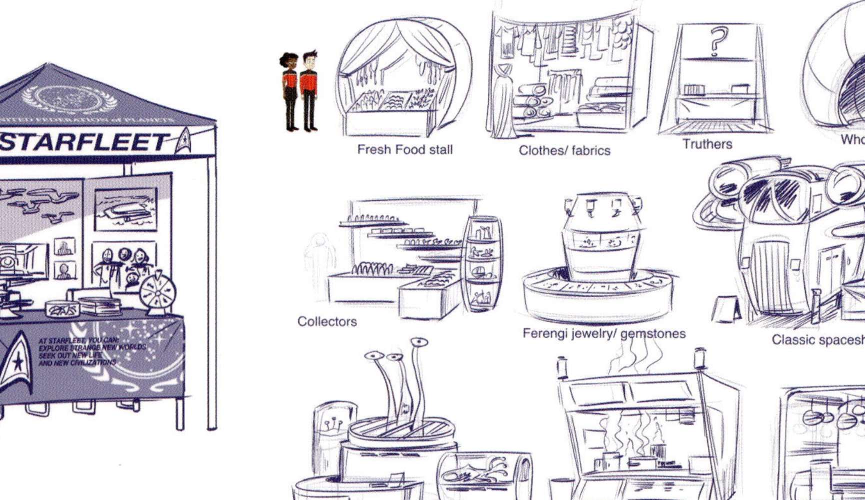

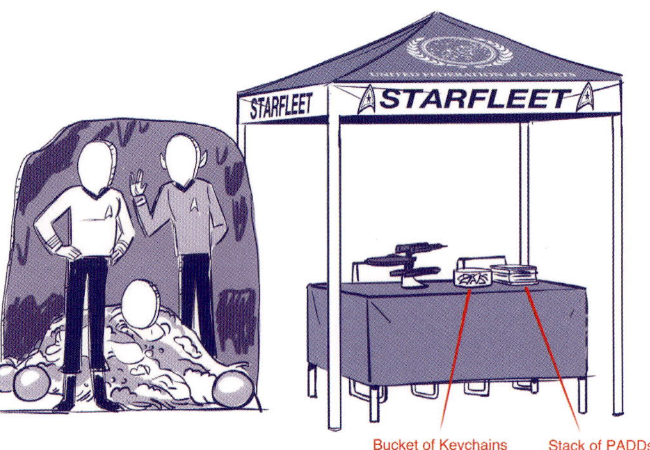

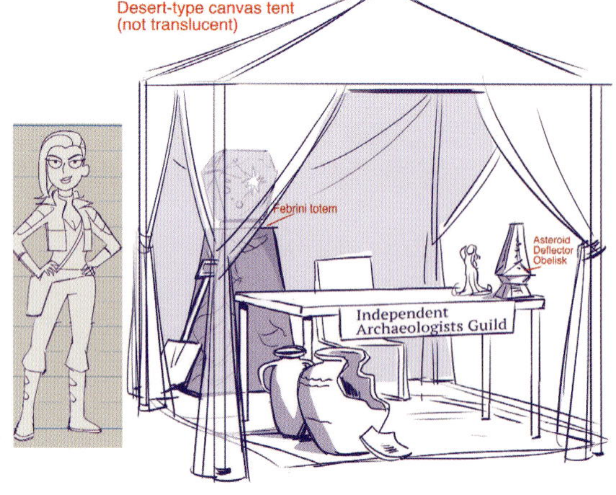

PETRA

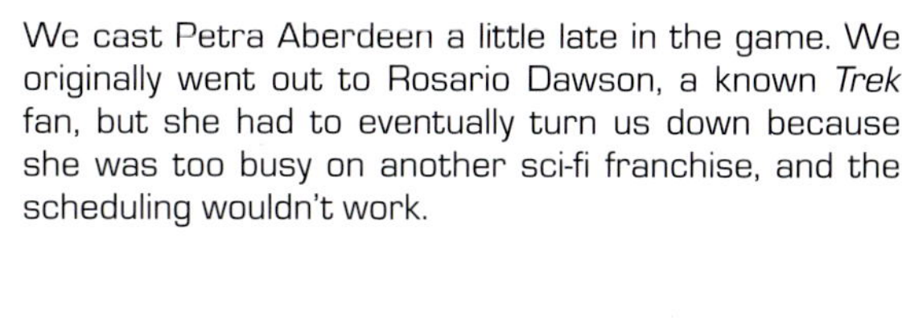

We cast Petra Aberdeen a little late in the game. We originally went out to Rosario Dawson, a known *Trek* fan, but she had to eventually turn us down because she was too busy on another sci-fi franchise, and the scheduling wouldn't work.

We luckily were able to get Georgia King to play our free-spirited archaeologist shortly before we shipped the episode to get animated.

"TNG-era uniforms are always a pleasure when we get to do them. Somehow in design his shirt waist got extra high on his chest. This was corrected in retakes in the final animation so more red area covers the chest."

— Barry J. Kelly

LCARS S3E6

AIRDATE: 20220929
STARDATE: 58456.2

"Hear All, Trust Nothing"

The *Cerritos* crew unexpectedly spends a day on Deep Space 9.

"We worked really hard to get the details as accurate as possible for DS9. It is a privilege to be able to put this baby on screen. We tried to cover the discrepancies across the TV show, the guide books, and model kits to encompass them all."

— Barry J. Kelly

QUARK'S BAR

This was a cast and crew favorite episode. We wanted to treat DS9 and other *Star Trek* series like a national park. Enjoy it, but don't leave our trash behind and completely change it. That success is debatable.

DEEP SPACE 9 OPERATIONS ROOM

We expanded on what we heard in the documentary *What We Left Behind: Looking Back at Star Trek: Deep Space Nine* with Quark and Kiera on the station.

It was already established that Mariner had been on DS9 before. This in turn made it difficult for her to turn down Jennifer's invite to get to know her friends better at Castro's party in her quarters.

"The tiny Alamo is meant to be an Easter egg on a rewatch hinting at the *Texas* class."
— Brad Winters

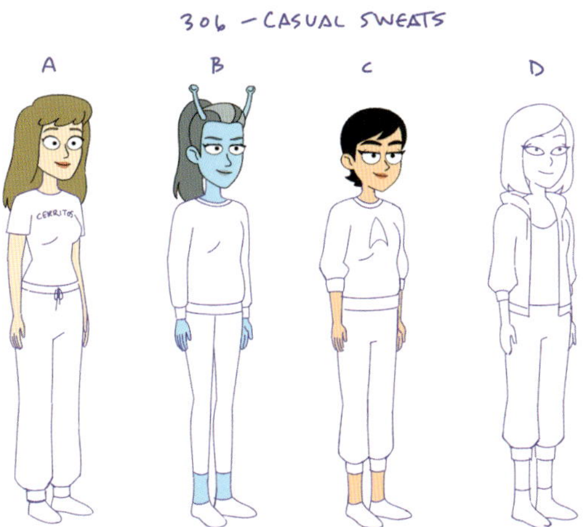

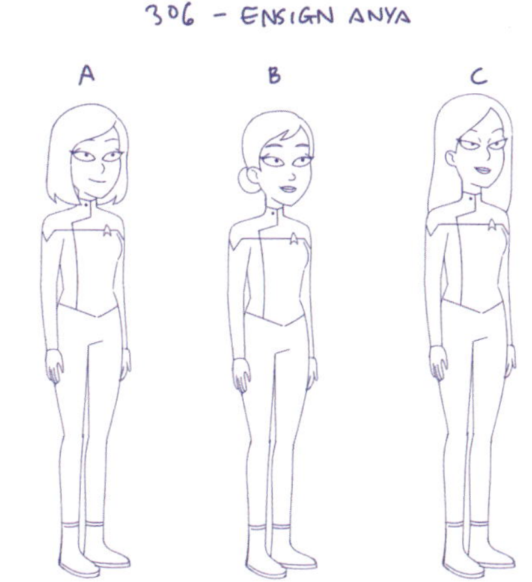

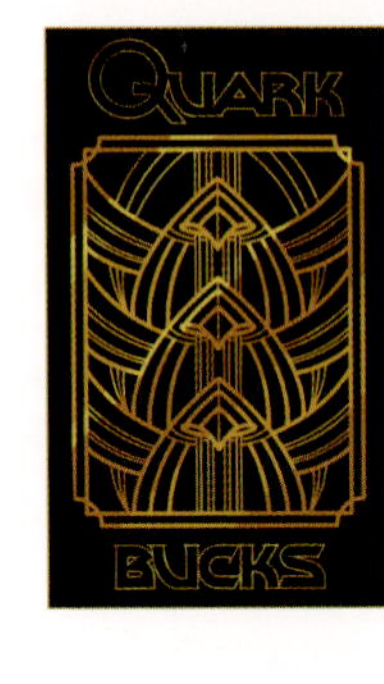

We brought back Nana Visitor and Armin Shimerman, who brought his costume teeth to record the voice of Quark!

"Profile views are always tricky. If you compare Quark's profile heads to the final animated shots, we definitely add more dome to that head."

— Barry J. Kelly

QUARK'S
QUARK'S BAR
QUARK'S BAR

"Kira! My DS9 crush! To do Nana Visitor justice, we went with an iconic Kira look here, crimson body suit with the pixie cut. Once we got into animation, we realized we scaled her head too big on her body in design. We had to do a whole retake pass across the episode to resize her head to make better proportions."

— Barry J. Kelly

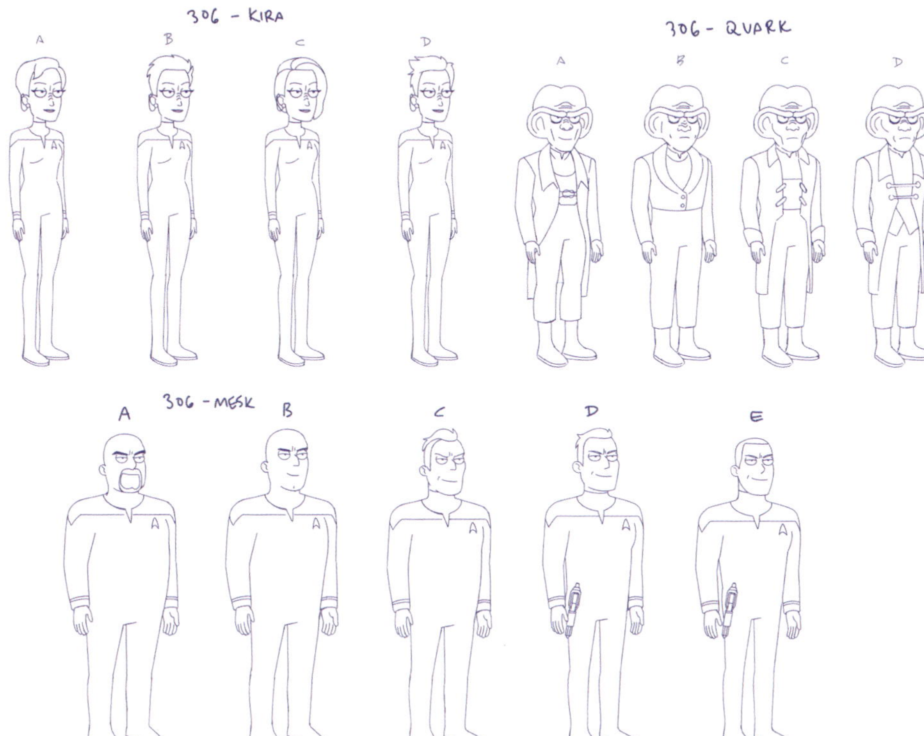

"Morn! He was actually one of our early test designs in season one, and now we got to design THE Morn! This guy is having an adventure off-screen, we're just always too late to catch him in action."

— Barry J. Kelly

QUARK'S BAR

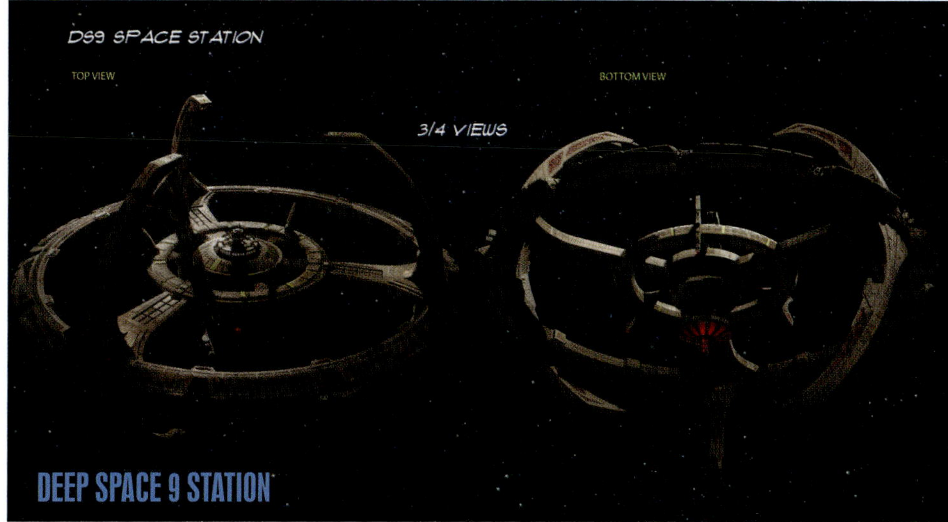

DEEP SPACE 9 STATION

DEEP SPACE 9 CONFERENCE ROOM

KAREMMA SHIP

TOP

BOTTON

SIDE

FRONT

BACK

"The Karemma ships seen in DS9 had some inconsistencies. The *Lower Decks* version includes elements from all the versions seen in DS9."

— Brad Winters

STORAGE ROOM

ENGINE ROOM

KAREMMA DELEGATION

A

B

DELEGATES

REGULARS

GUARDS

306 TOMINKI

306 KORZAK

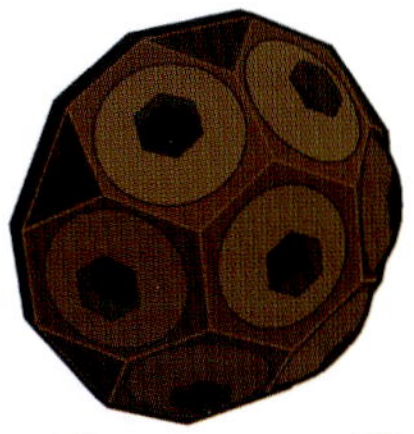

KAREMMA GRENADE

TOMINKI

KORZAK

LCARS S3E7

AIRDATE: 20221006
STARDATE: UNKNOWN

"A Mathematically Perfect Redemption"

A wayward Starfleet ensign struggles to find a path to redemption.

This episode has proven to be either the most hated or favorite among the crew and fans.

"This episode was probably the most VisDev (Visual Development) I've ever done for an episode. This episode was a tall order, a completely new location with new bird people where we don't see our cast until the third act."

— Barry J. Kelly

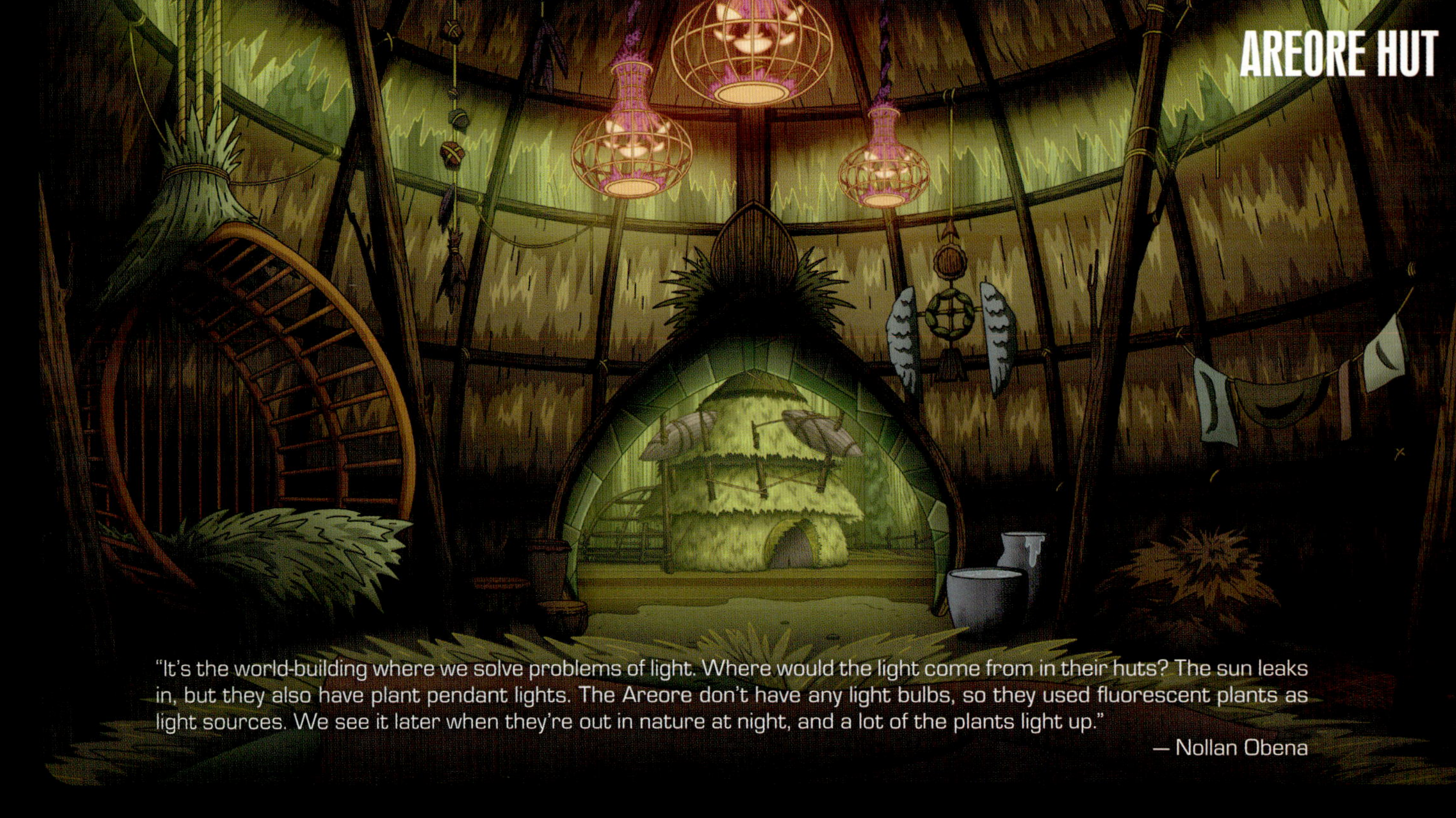

AREORE HUT

"It's the world-building where we solve problems of light. Where would the light come from in their huts? The sun leaks in, but they also have plant pendant lights. The Areore don't have any light bulbs, so they used fluorescent plants as light sources. We see it later when they're out in nature at night, and a lot of the plants light up."

— Nollan Obena

AREORE FOLIAGE

"Due to how many new locations and story beats there were to get across in the episode, I tried to get as many connective story beats roughed out as possible. How the waterfall leads to the cave, then how the cave leads to the buried ships, etc."

— Barry J. Kelly

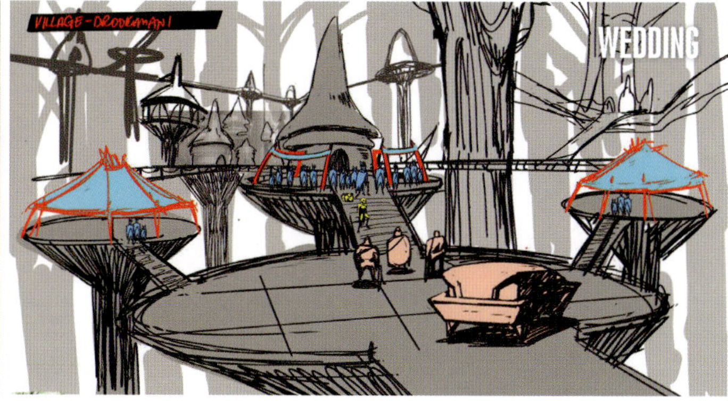

We wanted a departure episode but thematically still tied to *Trek*.

It would have been near impossible to make this in live action.

"We were trying to figure out what a bird race would look like and how they would live. They'd still live in homes but look like nests. They don't have technology, so they use a lot of wood, hay, leaves, etc."

— Nollan Obena

It feels like a classic *Star Trek* episode and somehow a ridiculous divergence from a *Star Trek* episode.

"Their domesticated animals can't be in a normal pen because they would all fly out. So we make it a circular cage like from *Planet of the Apes*."

— Nollan Obena

We put wings on all the species of this planet.

"I designed Rawda's birdlike Areore ship going one direction, but I guess it looks better going the opposite way, because that's how they animated it."

— Marcelo Bonifacio

"Our name for this was 'Wicked Warbird.' Since it's not a normal warbird, we took influence from the Valdore type from *Star Trek: Nemesis* and added a shark fin and a slick paintjob by our painter, Ryan Magno."

— Barry J. Kelly

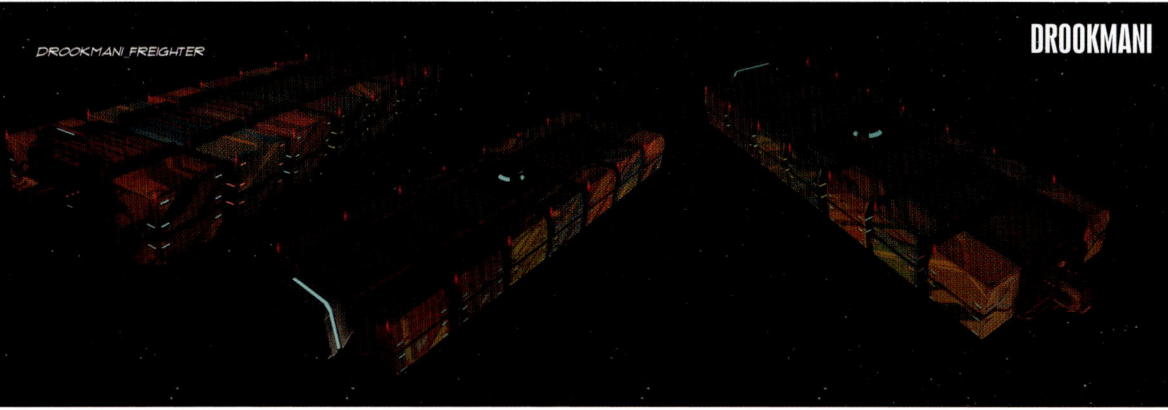

The last time we saw Peanut Hamper, she was floating in space, so we wanted to see what she had been up to since then. What would happen if we put a morally repugnant character with a well-respected leader? She doesn't learn her lesson. Also, showing a lead character as a robot without any facial features, thus no expressions, is funny.

"There were a few other iterations of this Peanut Hamper nacelle. I'm not sure if it was in the outline that a basket was tethered to a nacelle like a chariot, but then Mike was like, no just do this, and he drew this."

— Nollan Obena

SOPHIA

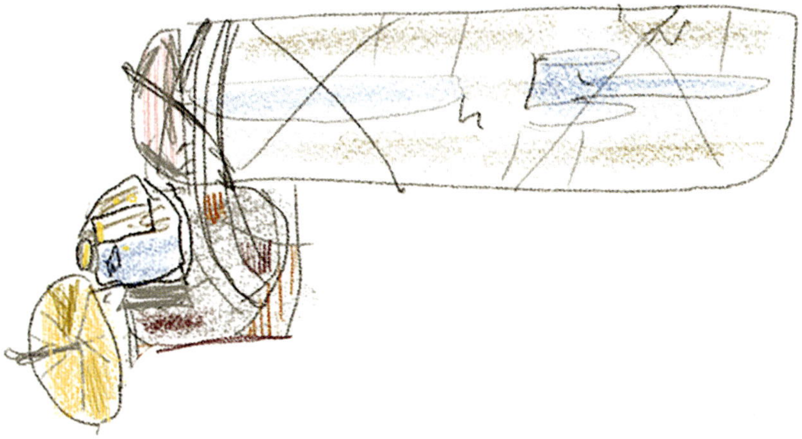

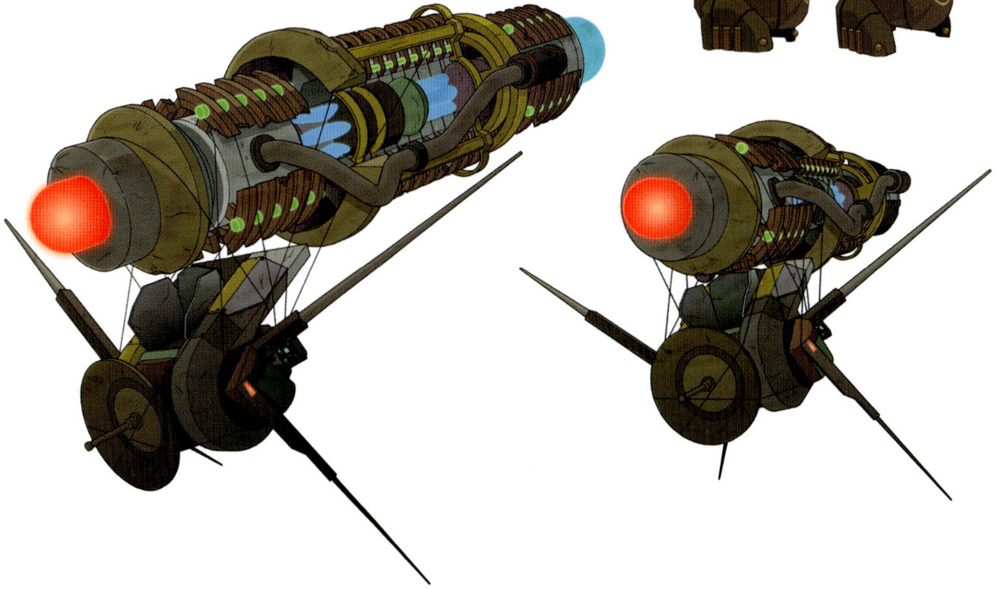

"This was Nollan's first pass based on Mike's design. Mike normally doesn't do this for us, but when he does, we love it. It's a fun drawing, and it especially helps if he already had something in his head."

— Barry J. Kelly

LCARS S3E8

AIRDATE: 20221013
STARDATE: UNKNOWN

"Crisis Point II: Paradoxus"

Boimler's holodeck movie sequel tries to live up to the original.

This was our sequel movie episode, which was based on Shatner's contractual parity with Nimoy, who started to direct *Star Trek* movies. Because Mariner got to make her movie, *Crisis Point*, in season one, Boimler got to make his movie in season three.

TATASCIORE IX

TATASCIORE IX

"We've got Boimler dealing with death but at the same time there's an adventure story going on. We took a lot of the cues from the planet in *Star Trek V: The Final Frontier* with the wasteland stuff. There's a lot of old designs that didn't quite make it into the previous episode that made it into this one."

— Nollan Obena

HOVER CYCLES

KnickKnac

Illustor

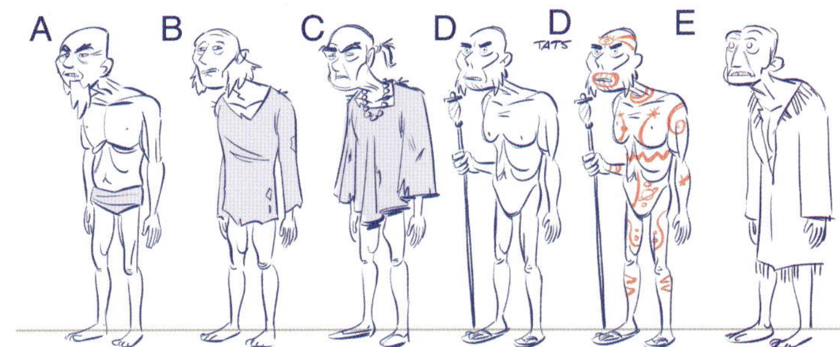

"This is one of the few times we employed animation cheats. It's like we wanted it to be plausible that this huge, buff Knicknac could fit under this little robe, but we did a little bit of an animated fake-out so that his reveal could be more fun and hilarious. The first thing he does is profess his love for Boimler. He's in love with him. We wanted him to be hunky once he was revealed. He's a strong, capable alien that would treat anyone right."

— Marisa Livingston

"Illustor is just so gross and weird. We wanted him to look deranged. A complete lunatic look because he's hiding a dark secret, which is that he has weird, gross tattoos."

— Marisa Livingston

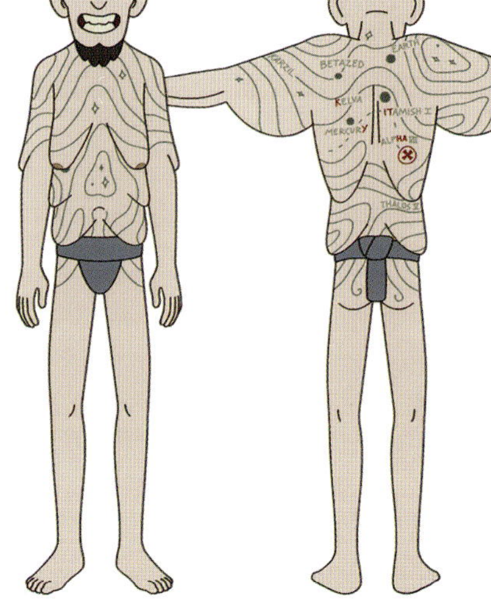

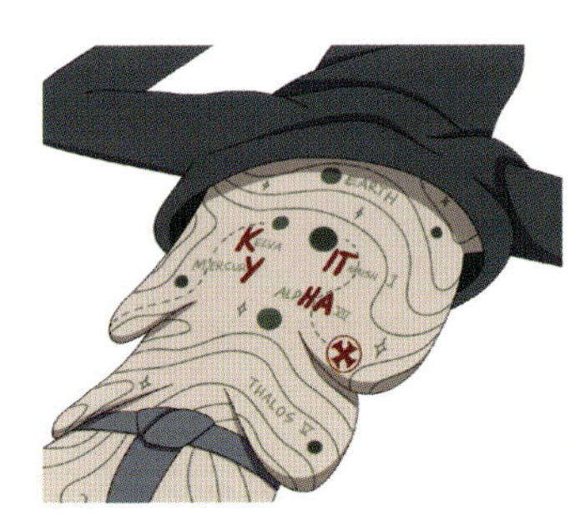

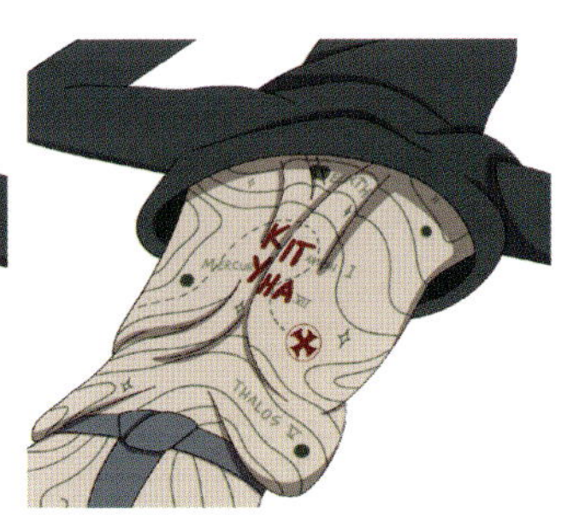

"We based the design on a consistently reused model originally from TNG." — Brad Winters

FREIGHTER

FREIGHTER BRIDGE

EUROPA SPACE STATION

CHRONOGAMI WRIST WATCH

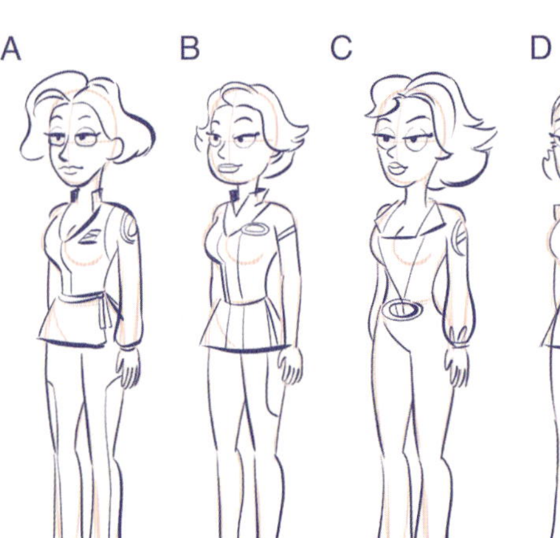

HELENA GIBSON

"I love the retro tech here that was inspired by the Genesis lab in *Wrath of Khan*. We even licensed the computer-graphics overlay, which was a last-minute addition that was totally worth it."

— Barry J. Kelly

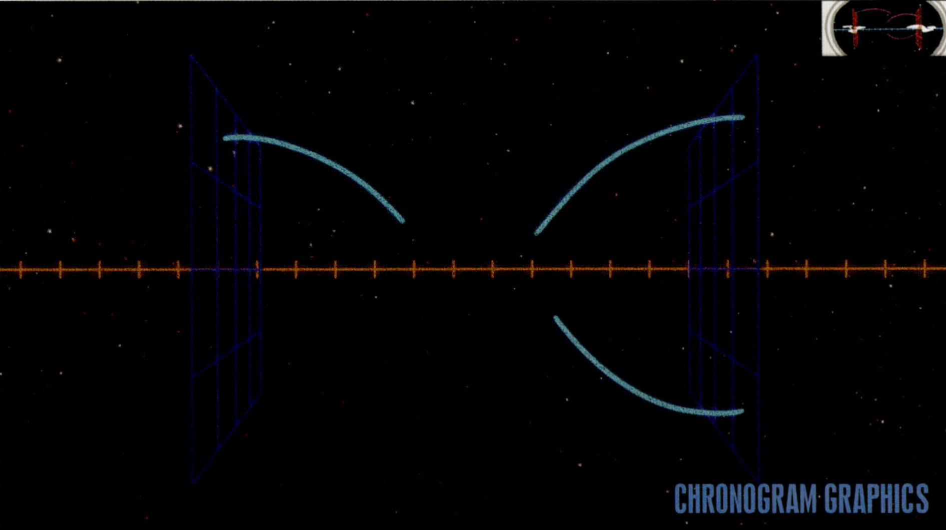
CHRONOGRAM GRAPHICS

We revisited our visual tropes from the movies again, but this time it was a movie that went off the rails a little more.

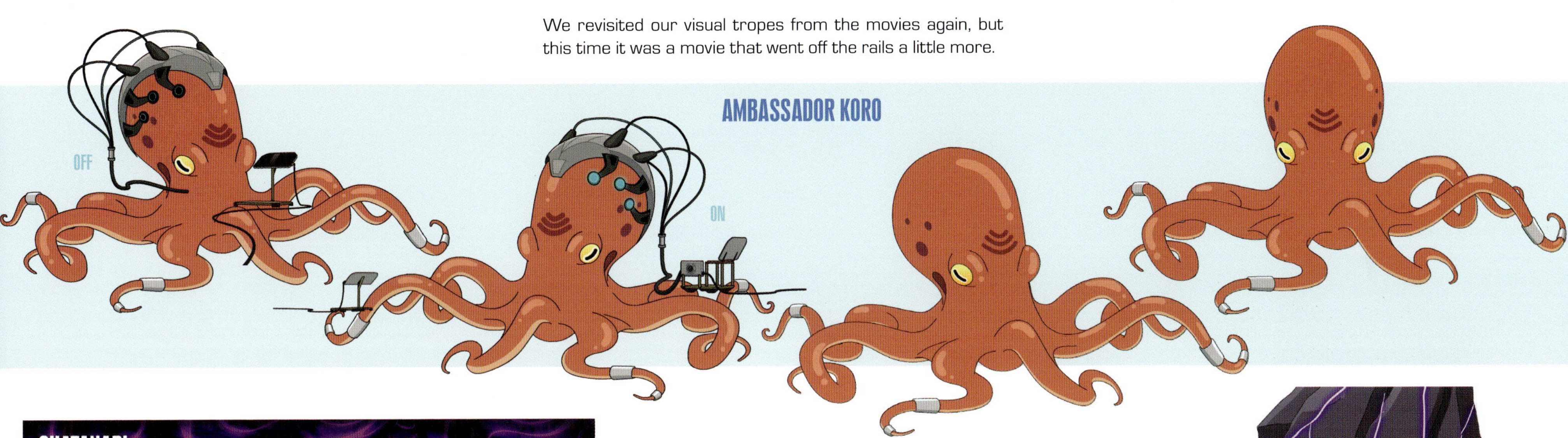

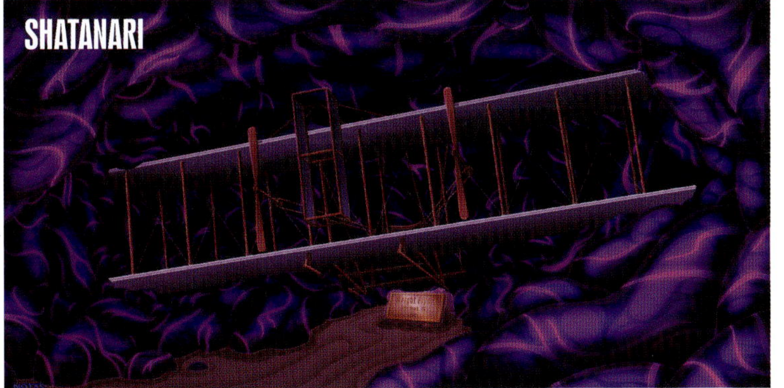

"This was a pretty tricky location. The design had a good start, but in order to make the place feel alive, we had to add a lot in comp to make the rocks feel translucent, almost like they were glowing heartbeats."

— Barry J. Kelly

"Ki-ty-ha was a character who was also a location, which was a really fun challenge for the character team. We received a rough idea of a triangular mountain, but then we took a crack at moving and rearranging a giant rock monster because he was a character at the end of the day, right? He had eyes and a mouth, and he spoke to Boimler, and Boimler kicked his way inside of Ki-ty-ha, which was very fun."

— Marisa Livingston

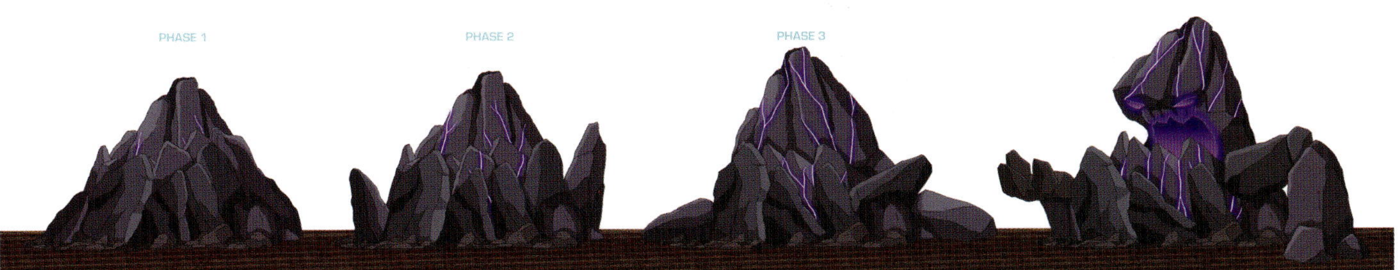

ROMULAN WARBIRD

TOP

BOTTON

3/4 VIEWS

FRONT

REAR

SIDE VIEW

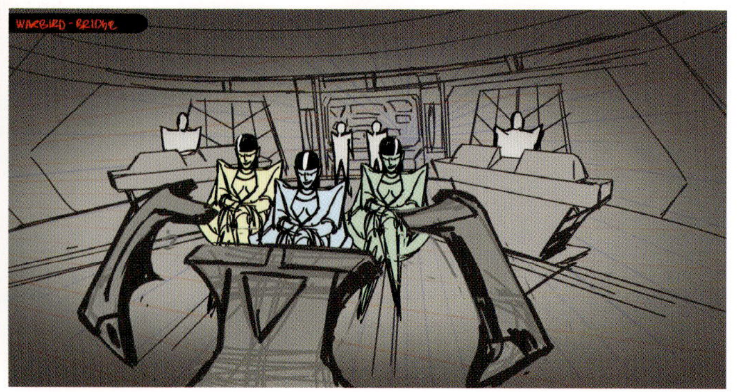

U.S.S. WAYFARER

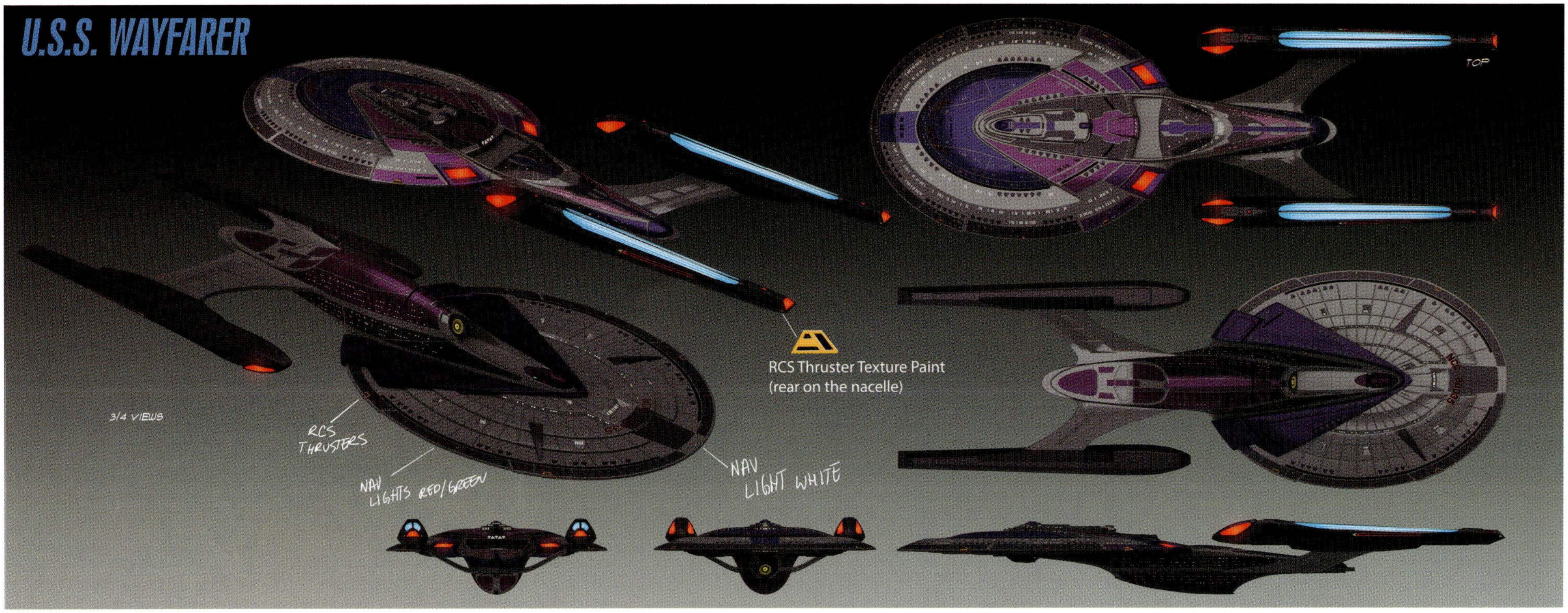

RCS Thruster Texture Paint
(rear on the nacelle)

3/4 VIEWS

RCS THRUSTERS

NAV LIGHTS RED/GREEN

NAV LIGHT WHITE

TOP

WAYFARER BRIDGE

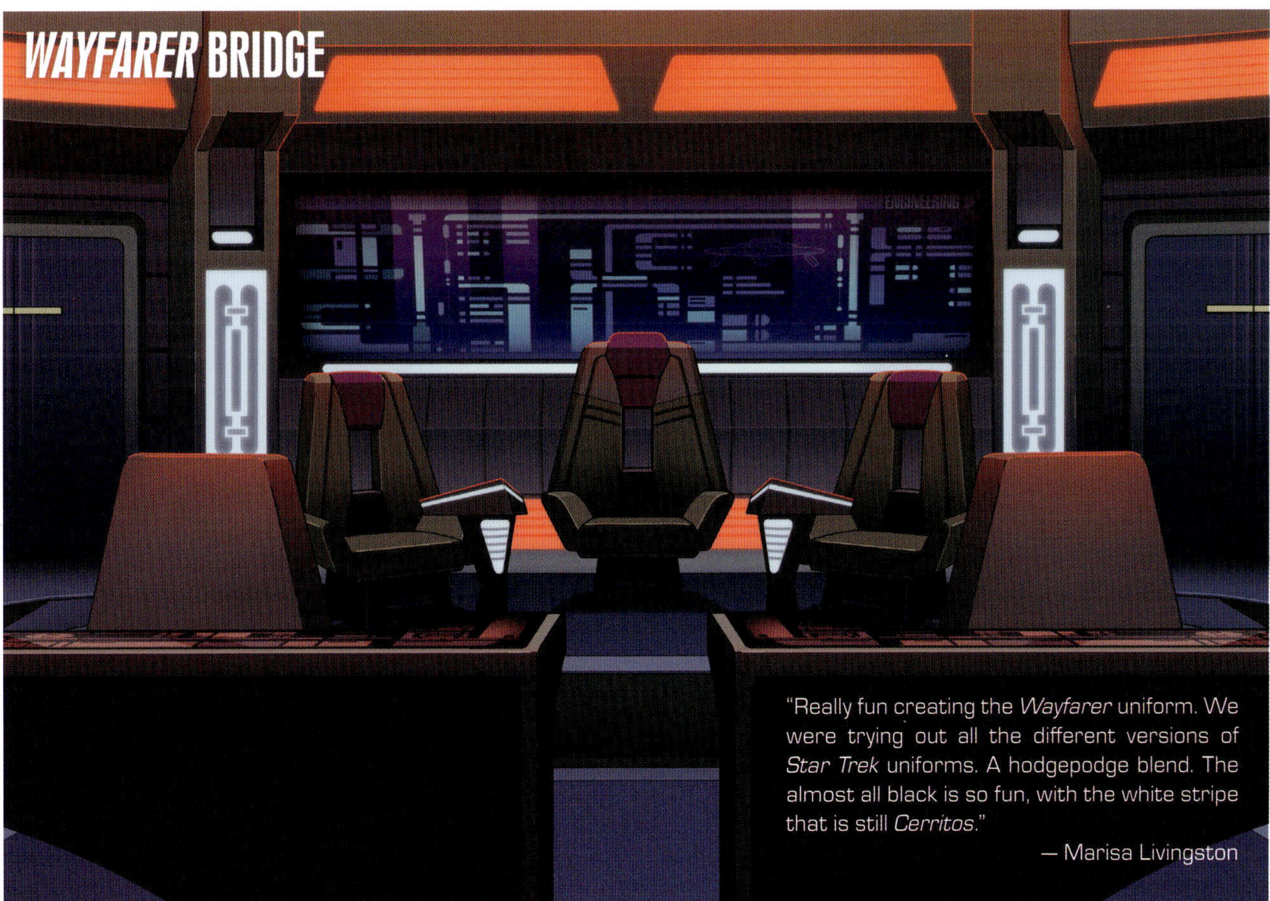

"Really fun creating the *Wayfarer* uniform. We were trying out all the different versions of *Star Trek* uniforms. A hodgepodge blend. The almost all black is so fun, with the white stripe that is still *Cerritos*."

— Marisa Livingston

WAYFARER SCIENTISTS

WAYFARER BRIDGE CREW

SYDNEY AQUARIUM

PUNKS

SYDNEY - 1982

STREET PUNKS

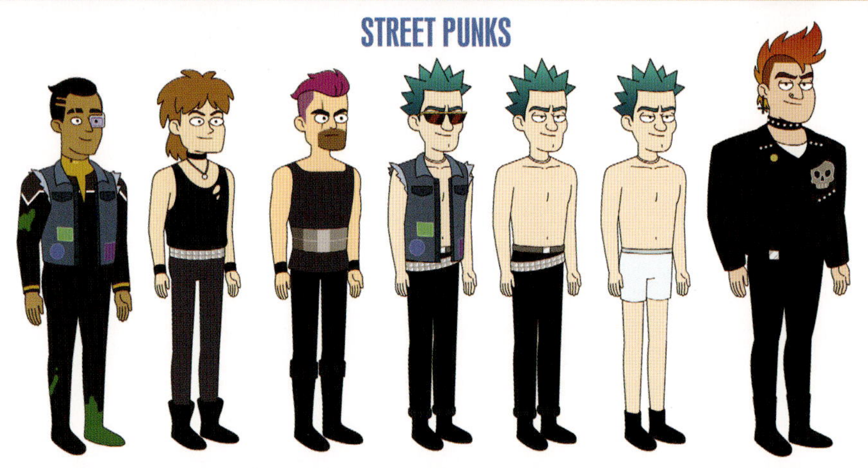

"We took liberty with Sydney. I tried to find an aquarium within view of the Sydney playhouse, but it did not exist. That playhouse is a good landmark, so the holodeck made a unique location for us!"

— Barry J. Kelly

SYDNEY, AUSTRALIA

IDAHO, U.S.A.

"Sulu's cameo brought a tear to my eye. The design team nailed him, and the animators found a great subtlety in his performance."

— Barry J. Kelly

"Translating a legacy character like Sulu was a huge consideration that we put a lot of time into. Robby Cook took the lead on this one, and I helped. We made him taller than Boimler because we decided it was Boimler who was imagining meeting Sulu. He was his hero! We made him cooler and more imposing by making him larger than Boimler. I'm not sure how much of that made it to animation, but for the design, that's what we were thinking."

— Marisa Livingston

SECTION 31 AGENT

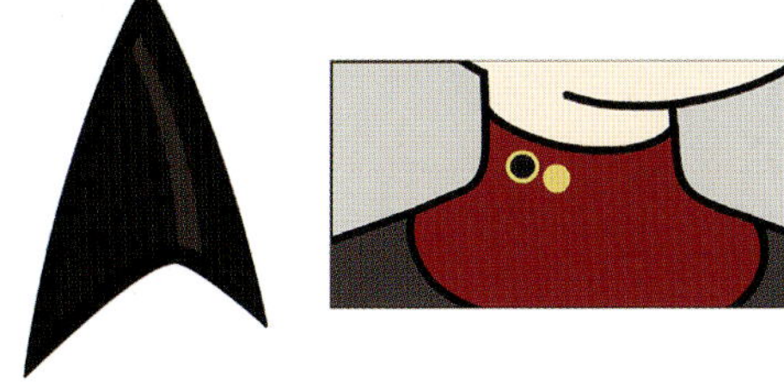

"This scene was a surprise for us. At least at first. It wasn't in the script when we got it, and then before we sent it to the network, Mike sent us a scene to tack on the end. We had no idea William lived for the first six weeks we were boarding this episode. Once we got the pages, our director, Mike Mullen, boarded it out quickly and made a memorable scene."

— Barry J. Kelly

LCARS S3E9

AIRDATE: 20221020
STARDATE: 58496.1

"Trusted Sources"

A visiting reporter on the *Cerritos* puts Captain Freeman on edge.

We needed an episode where Mariner appears to mess up, because she often does, and nobody believes her, which gives her a good reason to leave the *Cerritos* to join archeaologist Petra Aberdeen.

U.S.S. ALEDO

The real villain is the *Texas*-class ship. The design needed to feel nimble and fast, but something is off about them; a little too sinister, too pointy, no windows.

BREEN WARSHIP BRIDGE AND SOLDIER

"We designed the interior of the Breen ships based on cues from the exterior and the tech that they had."

— Nollan Obena

"Breen! I wanted these dudes to be scary as hell, an unstoppable force that's relentless. We wanted a tone of dread and foreboding on Brekka. Getting to use these aliens again was a perfect bad guy for this episode."

— Barry J. Kelly

BREEN SOLDIERS

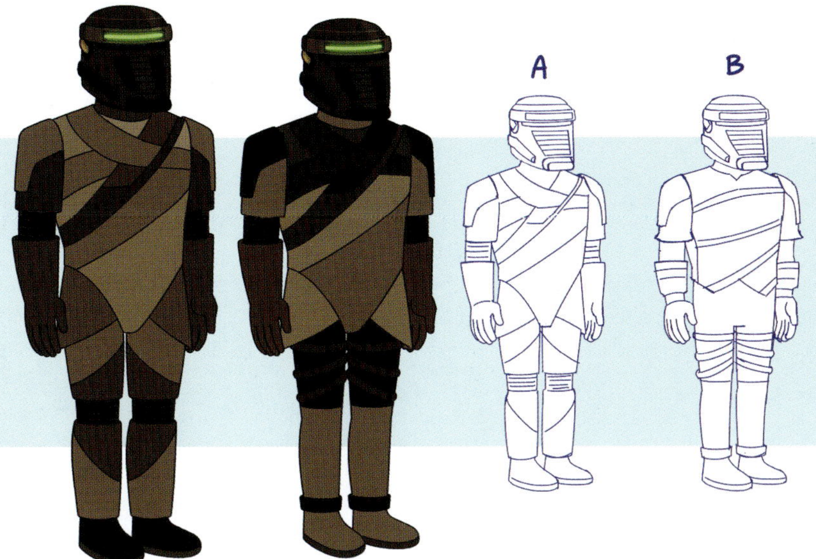

"The Breen ships were the same design, we just added a paintjob to make them unique to their *Lower Decks* appearance. That way you can distinguish between the Breen ships in DS9 and the faction in *Lower Decks*."

— Barry J. Kelly

BREEN WARSHIPS

BREKKA

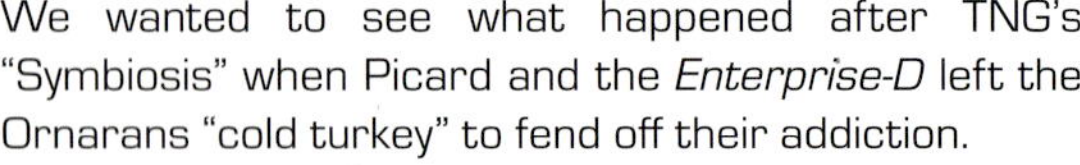

We wanted to see what happened after TNG's "Symbiosis" when Picard and the *Enterprise-D* left the Ornarans "cold turkey" to fend off their addiction.

"TNG: 'Symbiosis' made a great setup for a classic *Trek* story between two peoples from two nearby planets, but those planets were never seen on screen! So, we had to put on our 'TNG set design' hats and make two planets that feel like they could have fit into that TNG episode as classic matte paintings."

— Barry J. Kelly

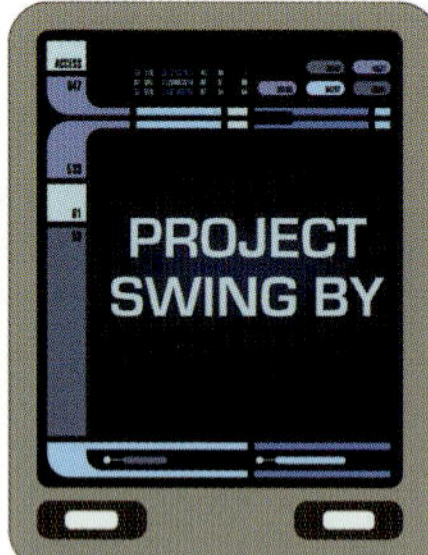

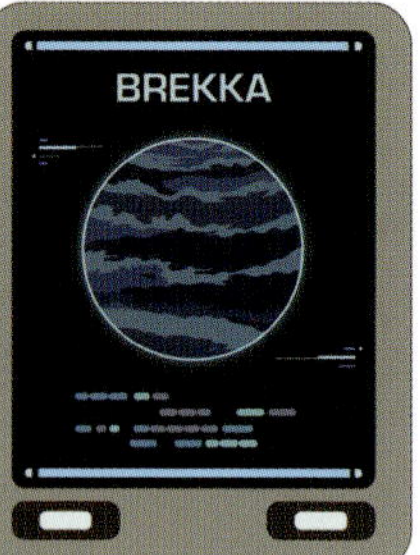

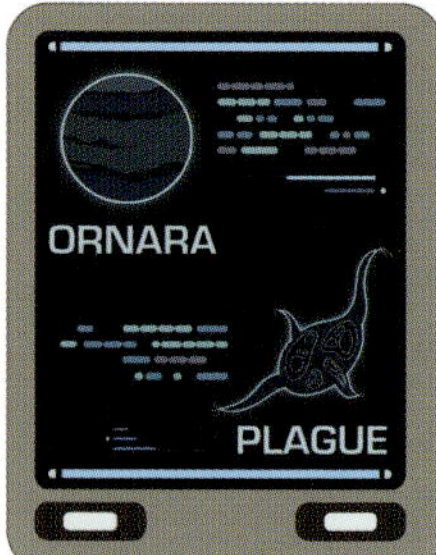

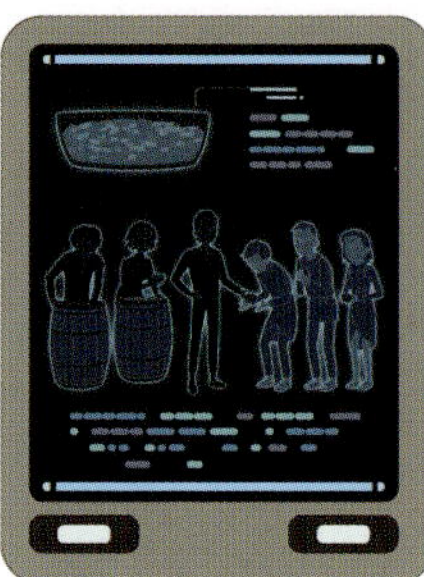

Meanwhile, the other planet, Brekka, was invaded by the undefeatable and cool-looking Breen.

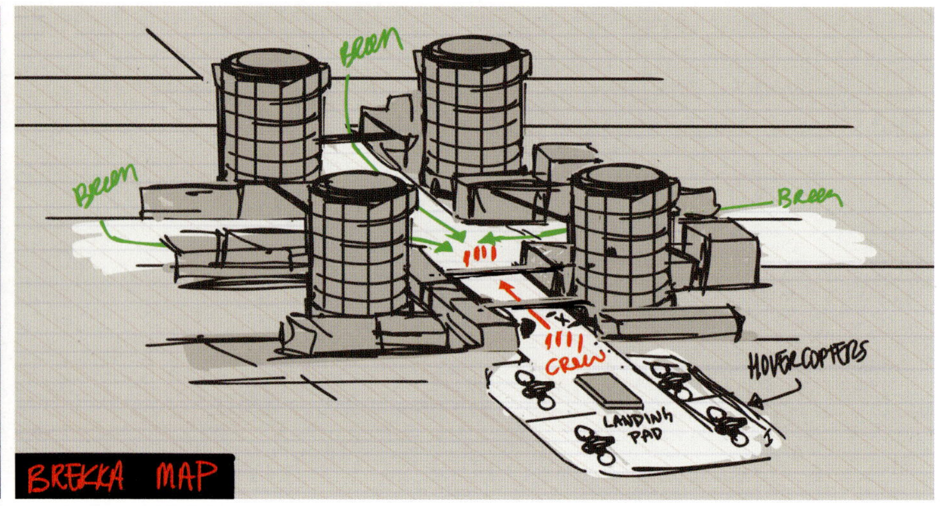

ORNARA

"This was my rough of the mural showing the progress of Ornara, a story in three parts. Fear and isolation, followed by chaos and madness, and finally enlightenment."

— Barry J. Kelly

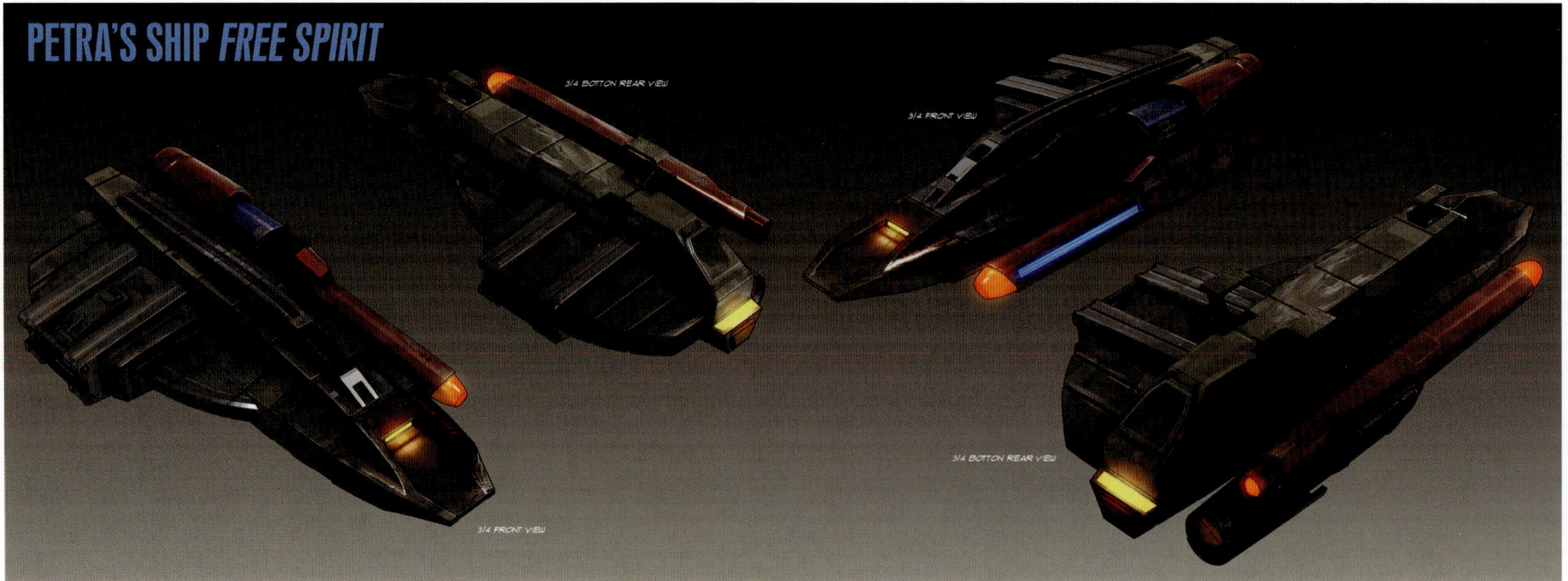

PETRA'S SHIP *FREE SPIRIT*
3/4 BOTTON REAR VIEW
3/4 FRONT VIEW
3/4 BOTTON REAR VIEW
3/4 FRONT VIEW

SIDE
TOP
SIDE
BOTTON
REAR
FRONT

U.S.S. ALEDO

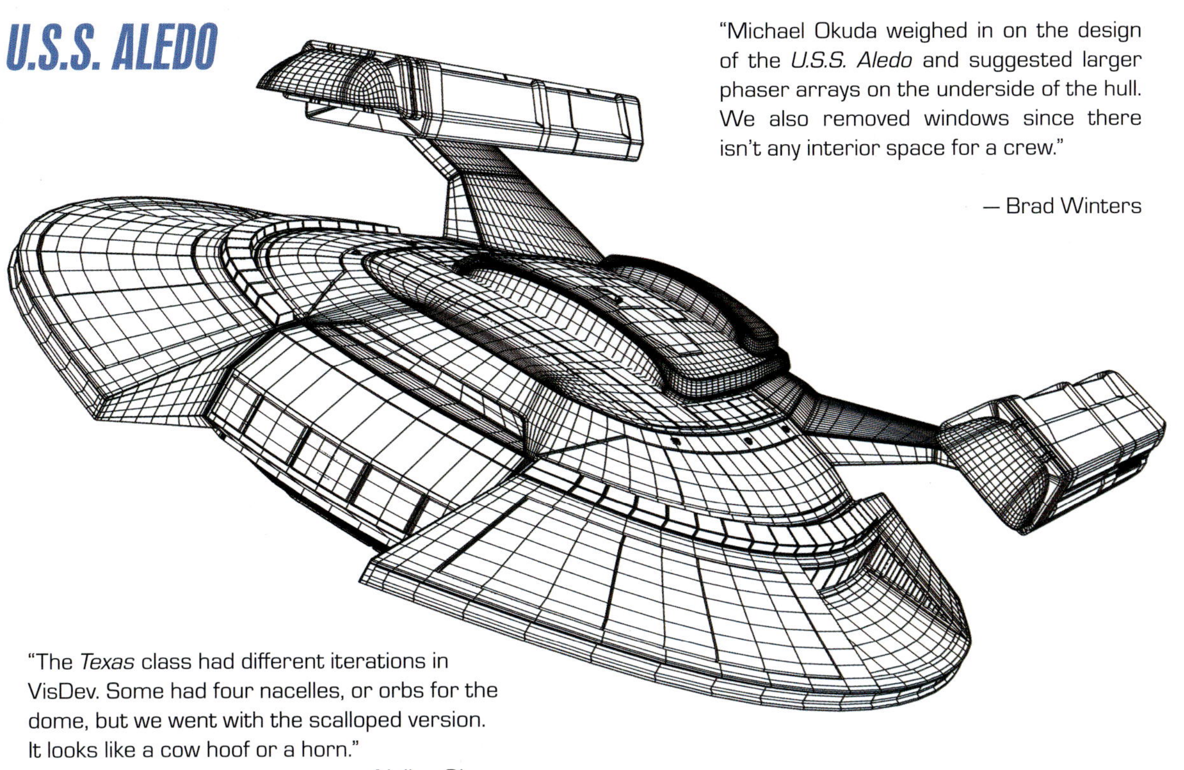

"Michael Okuda weighed in on the design of the *U.S.S. Aledo* and suggested larger phaser arrays on the underside of the hull. We also removed windows since there isn't any interior space for a crew."

— Brad Winters

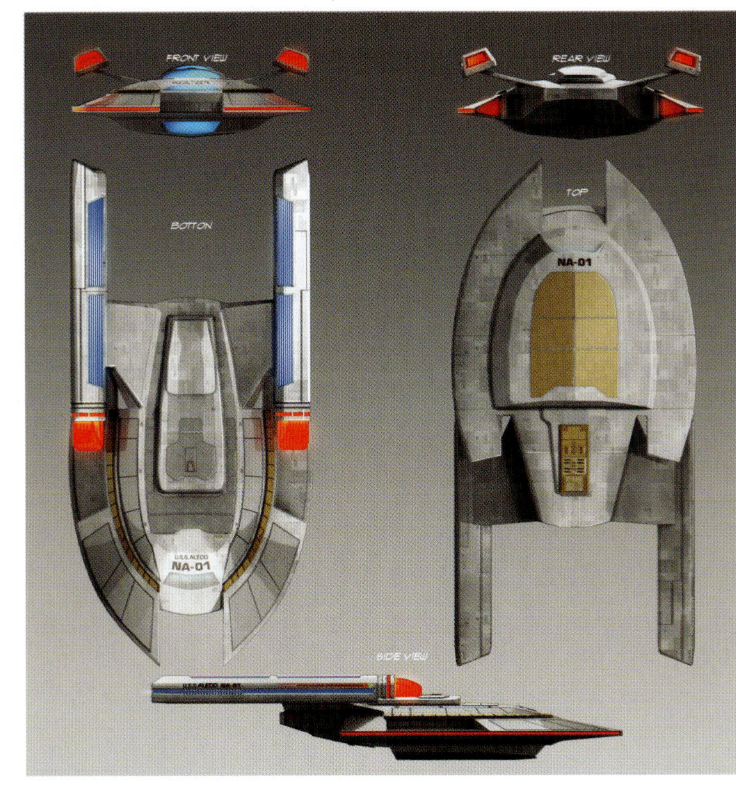

"The *Texas* class had different iterations in VisDev. Some had four nacelles, or orbs for the dome, but we went with the scalloped version. It looks like a cow hoof or a horn."

— Nollan Obena

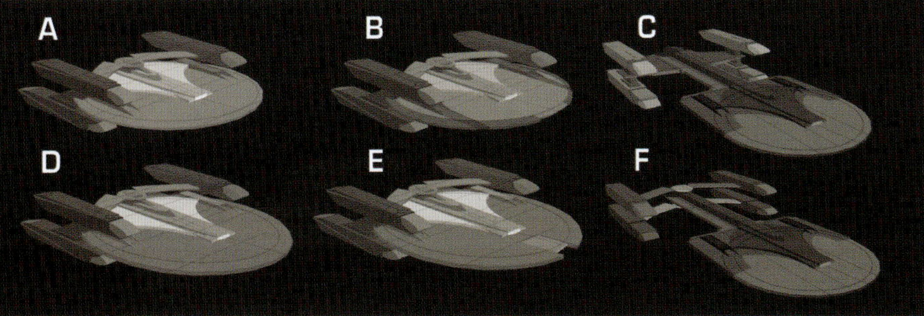

VICTORIA NUZE

"Victoria's badge is a reference to the reporters seen in *Star Trek Generations*."

— Brad Winters

"We figured Starbase 80 would have the dinkiest shuttles ever seen in TNG."

— Brad Winters

LCARS S3E10

AIRDATE: 20221027
STARDATE: 58499.2

"The Stars at Night"

In the season three finale, the *Cerritos* crew must prove their worth in a mission race.

This is an AI story that shows when you remove humans for AI jobs, it comes back to bite you in the ass.

STARFLEET COMMAND

"A classic Starfleet matte painting we had the chance to re-create."
— Barry J. Kelly

DOUGLAS STATION

U.S.S. VAN CITTERS

USS VAN CITTERS

TOP

3/4 VIEWS

"The *Van Citters*, a nod to our favorite *Star Trek* insider, uses the E model (*Sovereign* class), one of my favorite ships, no purple this time. Just the classic paintjob."

— Barry J. Kelly

STARFLEET COMMAND

1 2 3 4 5 6 7 8 9

ADMIRAL WONG

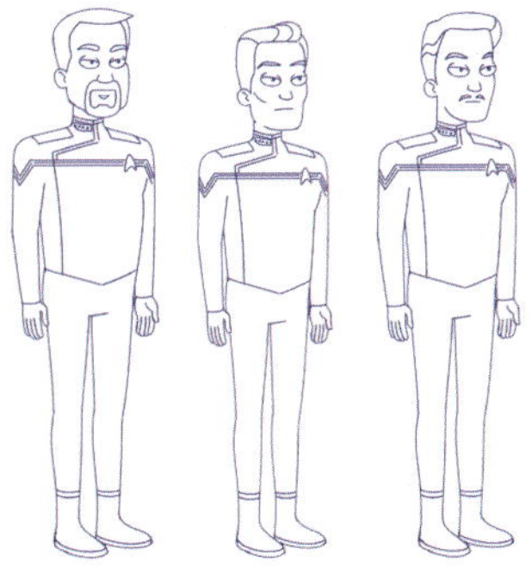

STARFLEET COMMAND WAR ROOM

ADMIRAL BUENAMIGO'S OFFICE

TEXAS-CLASS SHIPS

"The *Texas*-class ships get beat up across this episode, so we have to make states of the ship with progressive damage so the ships feel immersive with the action."

— Barry J. Kelly

ADMIRAL BUENAMIGO

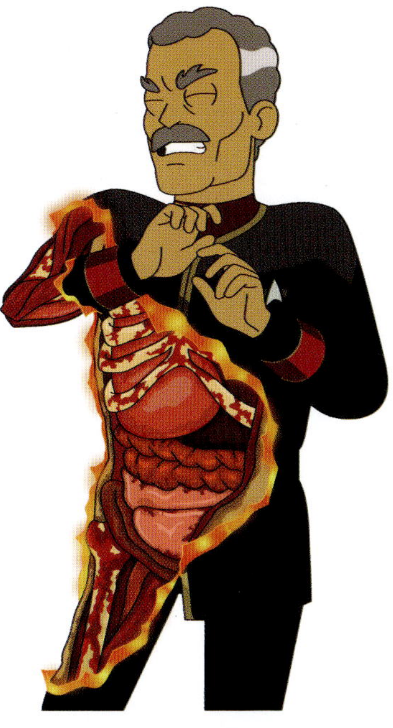

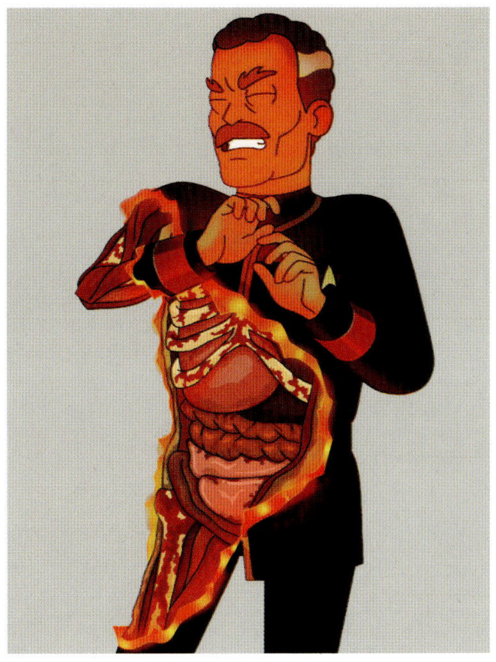

Through flashbacks, we finally see the explanation to Rutherford's implant, the AI behind the *Texas* class, and who was behind it all along.

"This overly brutal death is a visual callback to the over-the-top deaths of Riva's chorus in TNG: 'Loud as a Whisper.'"

— Brad Winters

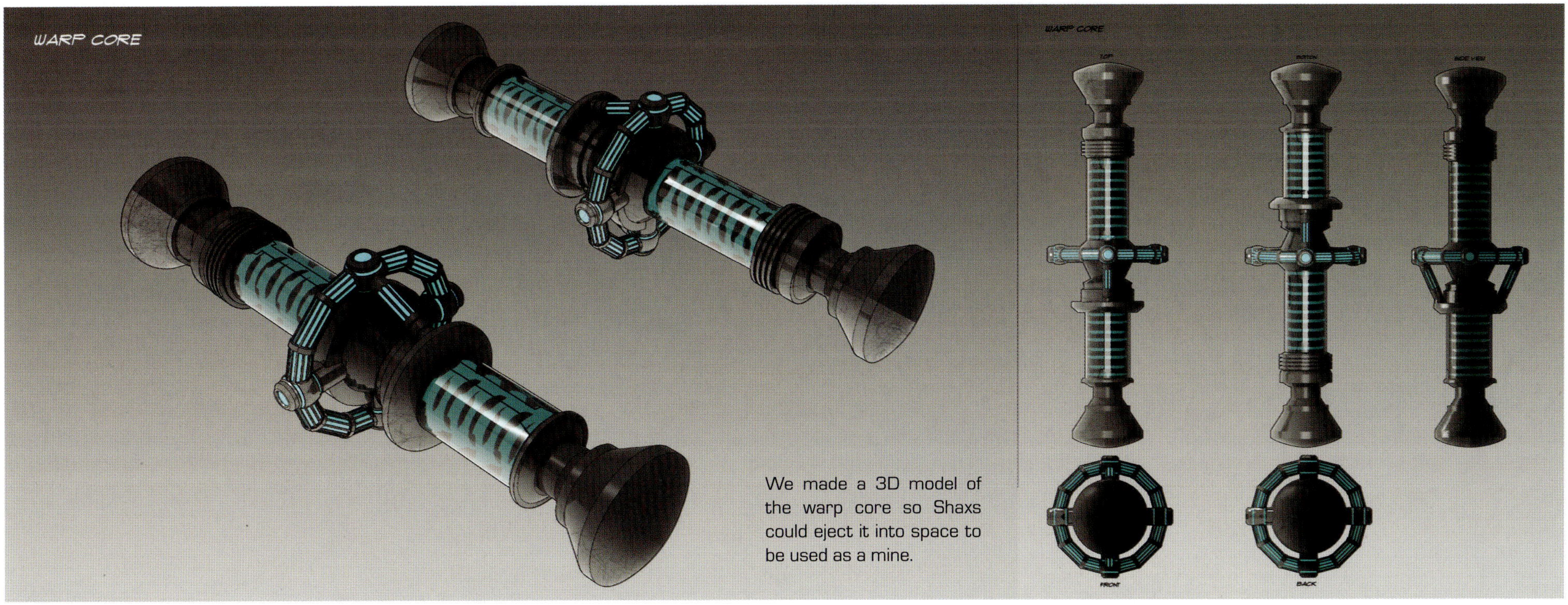

WARP CORE

WARP CORE

We made a 3D model of the warp core so Shaxs could eject it into space to be used as a mine.

U.S.S. ALHAMBRA BRIDGE CREW

U.S.S. OAKLAND BRIDGE CREW

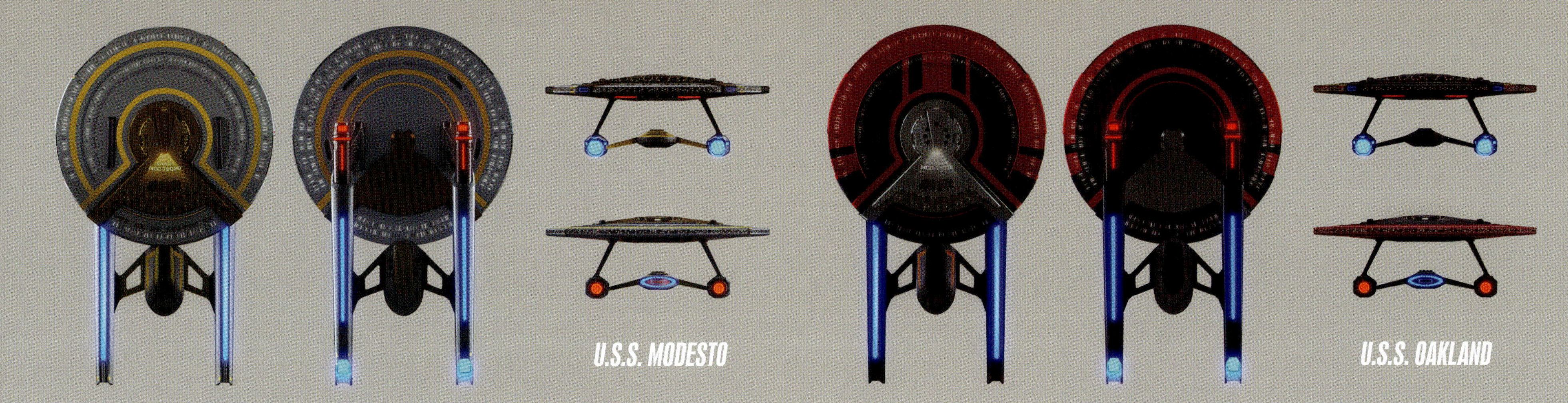

It's a story of everyone coming together, the whole *California*-class fleet, to defeat the unruly *Texas* class.

***U.S.S. MERCED* BRIDGE CREW**

***U.S.S. CARLSBAD* BRIDGE CREW**

***U.S.S. INGLEWOOD* BRIDGE CREW**

CHAPTER 07

LCARS 40274

02-654598

SEASON FOUR

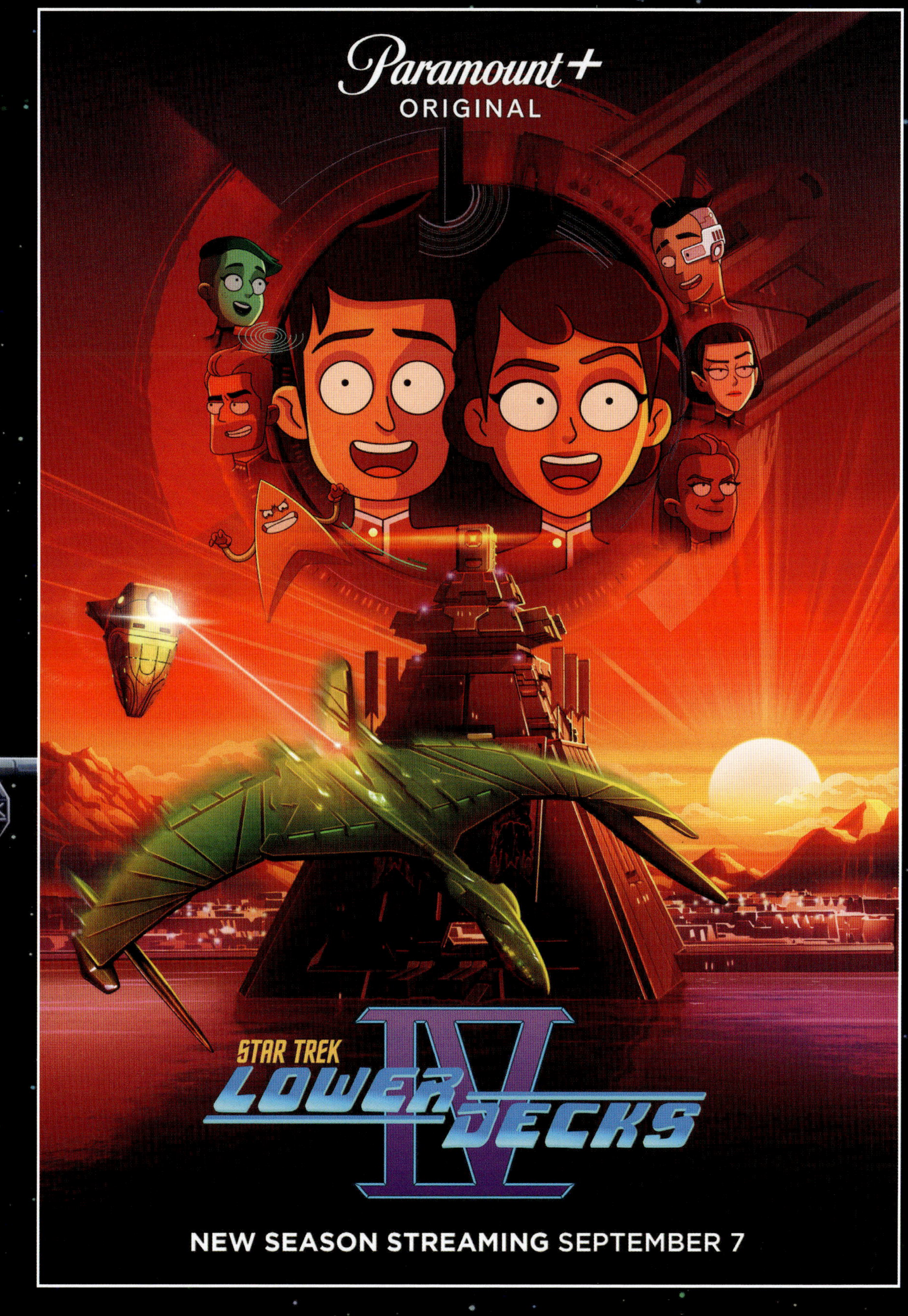
Paramount+
ORIGINAL
STAR TREK
LOWER DECKS
IV
NEW SEASON STREAMING SEPTEMBER 7

LCARS S4E1

AIRDATE: 20230907
STARDATE: 58724.3

"Twovix"

The *Cerritos* ensigns must assist a caretaker on the voyage of a historically significant starship.

This is a big VOY episode, which is another cast and crew favorite.

In the first episode of a new season, we reset the status quo. Everyone is back on the *Cerritos* working together, but at the end of the episode, surprise! Everyone gets promoted!

U.S.S. VOYAGER

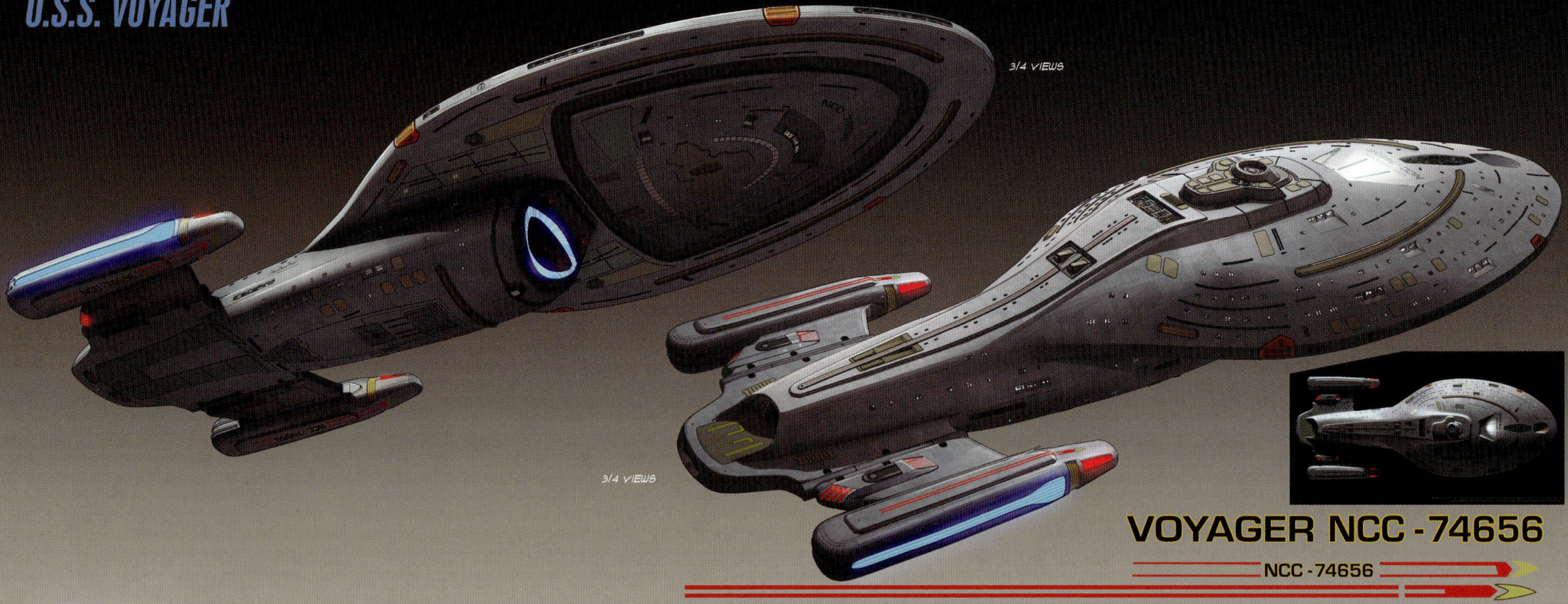

3/4 VIEWS

3/4 VIEWS

VOYAGER NCC-74656

NCC-74656

VOYAGER CREW MANNEQUINS

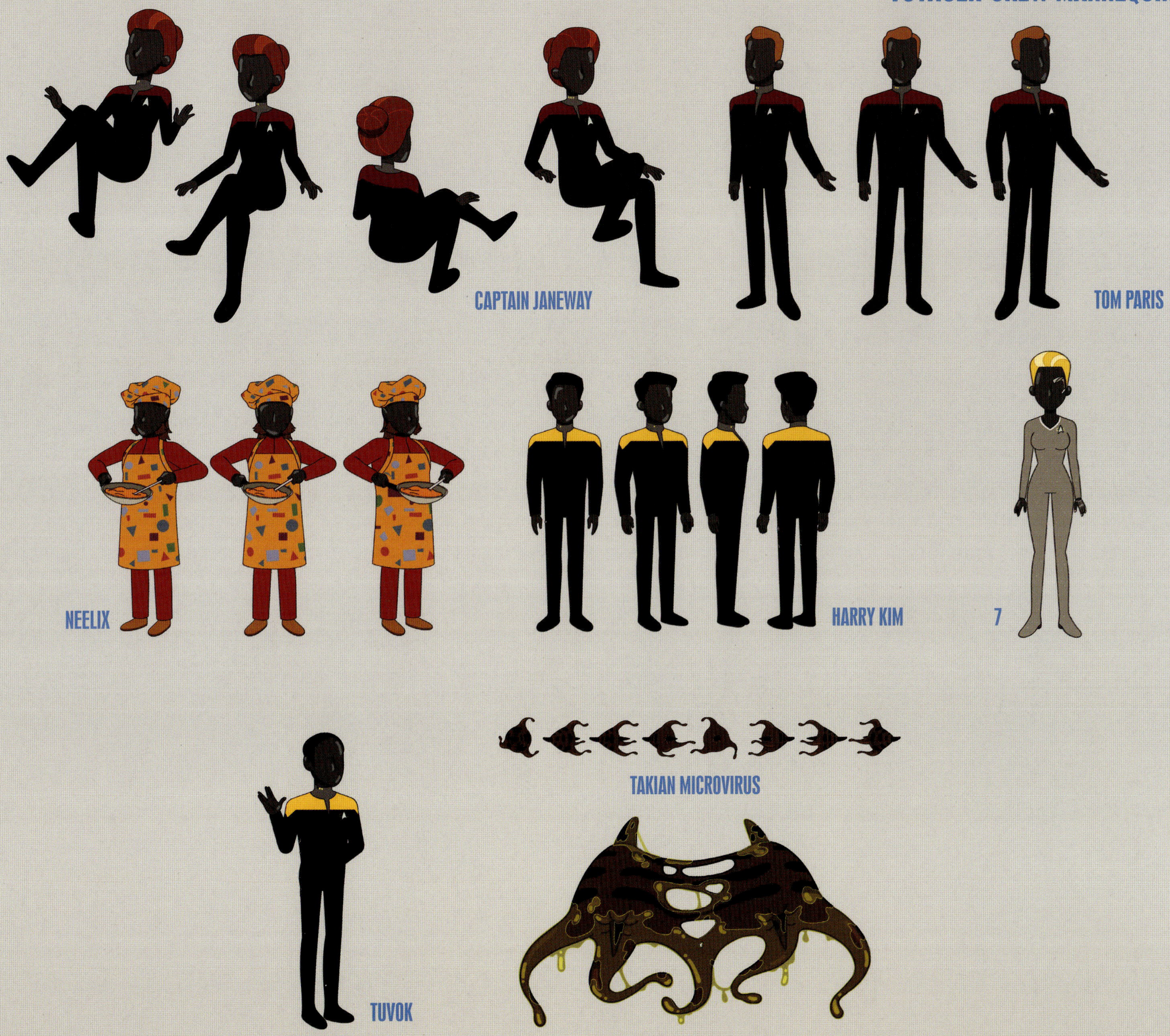

CAPTAIN JANEWAY

TOM PARIS

NEELIX

HARRY KIM

7

TUVOK

TAKIAN MICROVIRUS

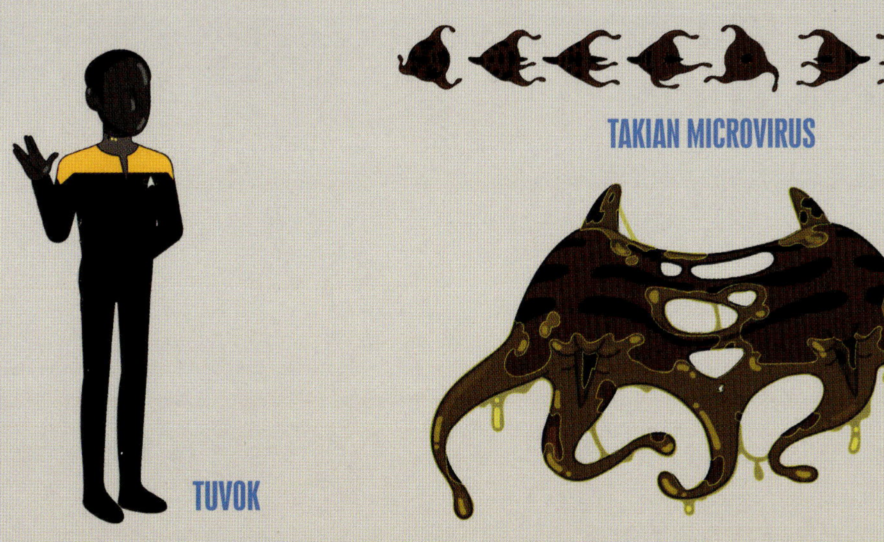

"I mistakenly thought this episode would be easy because we weren't designing anything from scratch. All we had to do was reference some screenshots from *Voyager* to understand what the rooms looked like. The problem was that it was often difficult to find screenshots that would give a wide enough view of a room to understand the dimensions, or the lighting would be dark and it would be hard to decipher what was going on in a particular area of a room."

— Denny Fincke

VOYAGER BORG CHAMBER

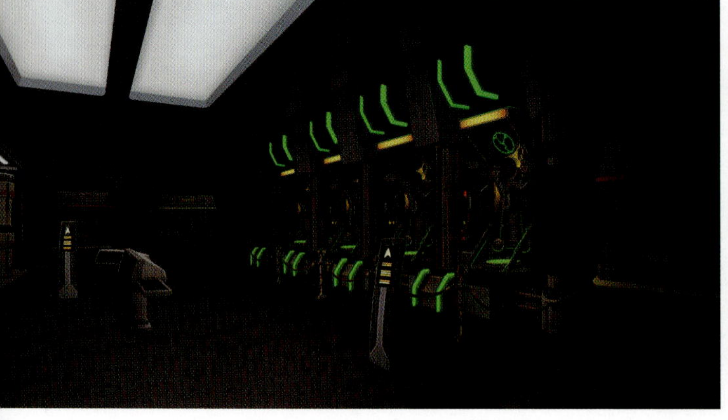

VOYAGER ENGINEERING

VOYAGER MESS HALL

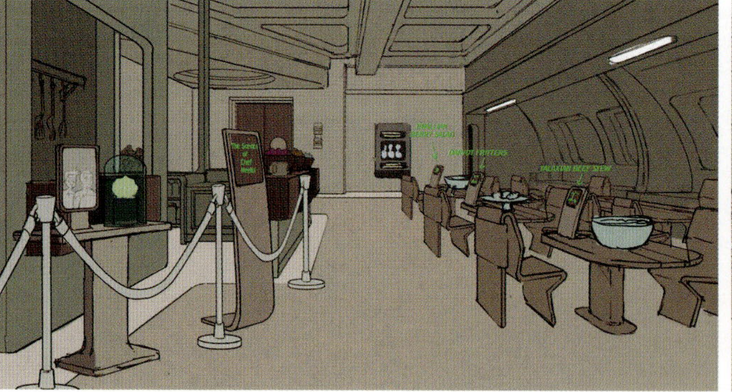

"There was an inherent pressure to accurately depict the details of the various rooms because we didn't want to disappoint the fans. I spent considerable time studying Neelix's cooking utensils in the mess hall to get them right. The geometry of the Borg regeneration alcoves was very complex and hard to understand."

— Denny Fincke

DR. CHAOTICA

BELJO TWEEKLE

MICHAEL SULLIVAN

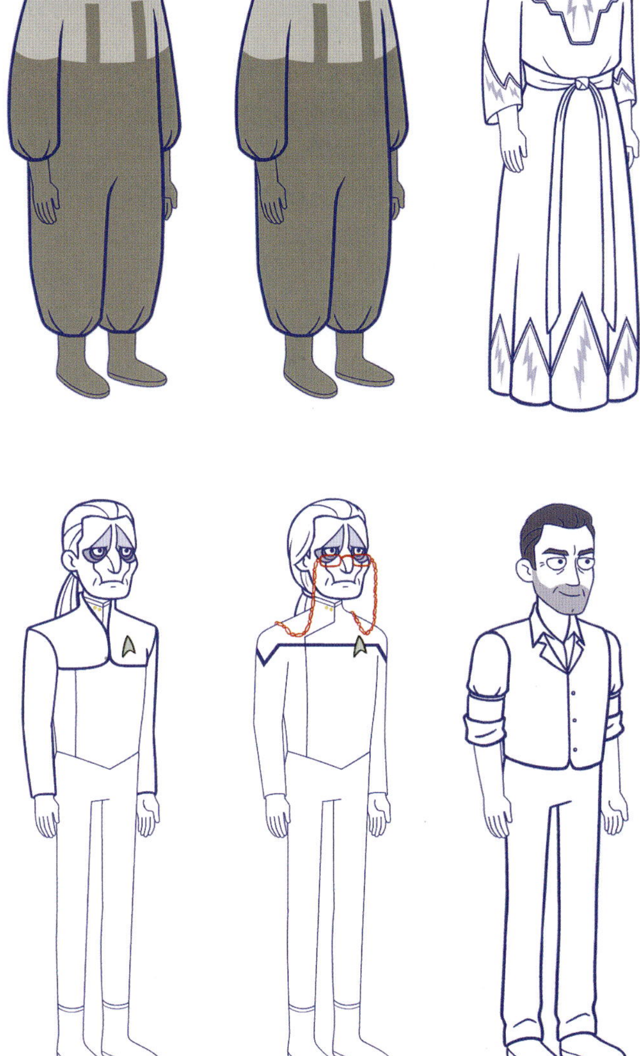

This was the first episode that we would air after *Strange New Worlds'* (SNW) "Those Old Scientists," so we threw in a quick mention.

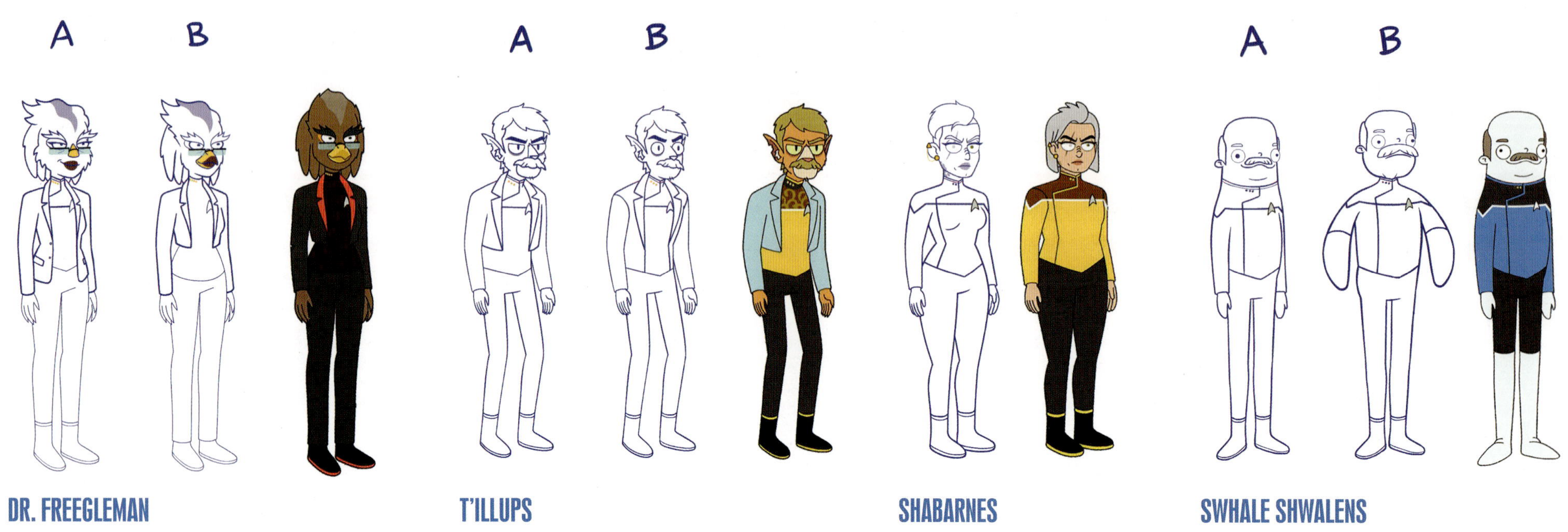
A
B
A
B
A
B
DR. FREEGLEMAN
T'ILLUPS
SHABARNES
SWHALE SHWALENS

TUVIX BLOB

A
B

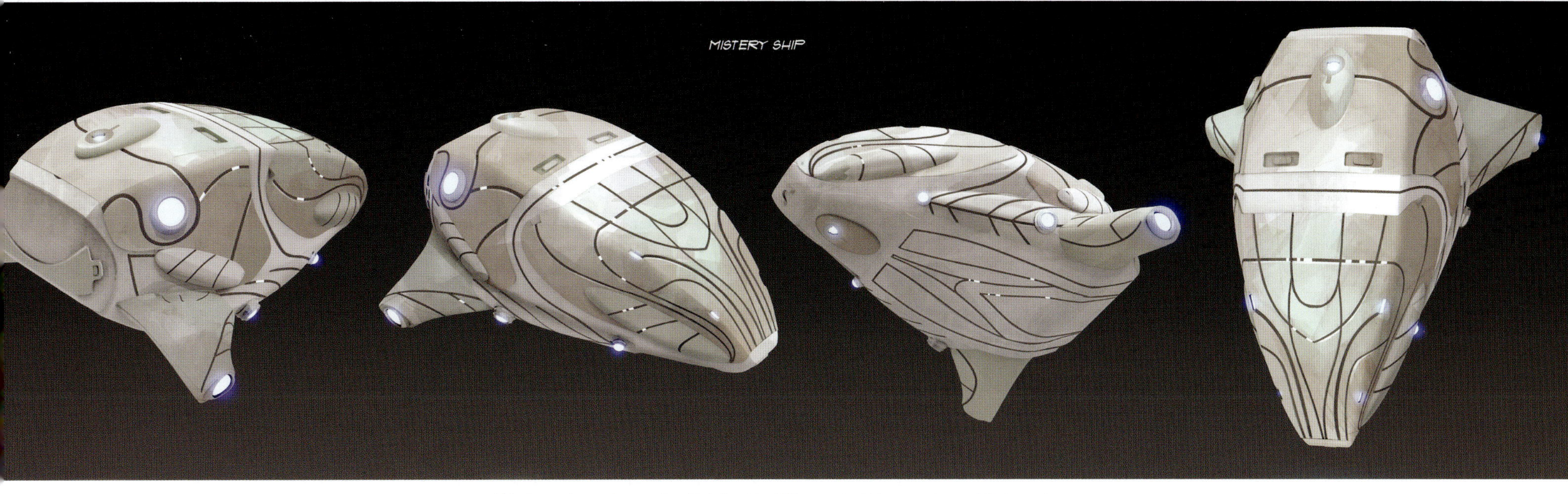

We introduce the main villain's ship. We wanted the mystery ship to not look like an identifiable alien ship we've seen in *Star Trek*.

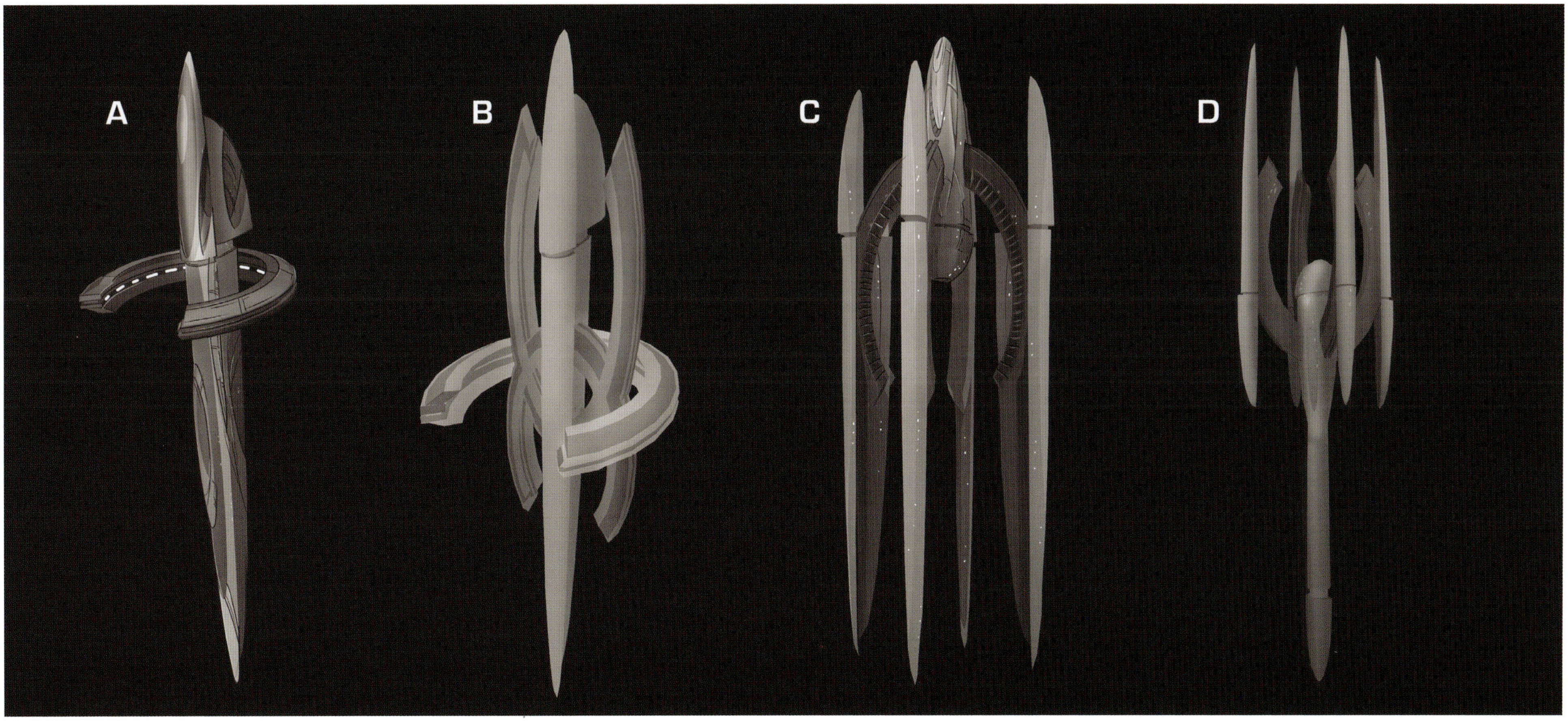

"The mystery-ship shape started out as an ocarina. We made it symmetrical and used the part where you blow as an intake, or propulsion thing. Then we wrapped some organic panels around it. It was one of our first ships that can go vertical to horizontal; we furnished the bridge with a floating chair so Locarno could always be upright. His cockpit was circular, so it was always within its axis."

— Nollan Obena

LCARS S4E2

AIRDATE: 20230907
STARDATE: UNKNOWN

"I Have No Bones Yet I Must Flee"

Mariner tries to get demoted, Rutherford tries to get promoted, Boimler makes a big move.

We wanted to show a big, TOS-like menagerie setup and an episode where we see Mariner fighting against being promoted and botching it again. It's worked before, but not on Ransom, which makes us like both of them more.

MENAGERIE

Narj, a treelike alien, was the first root-based life-form.

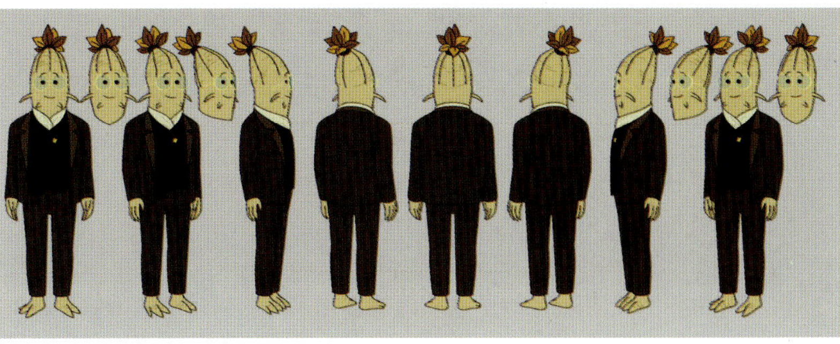

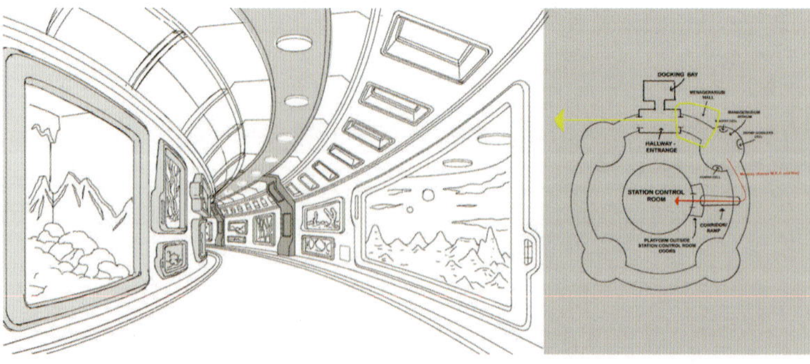

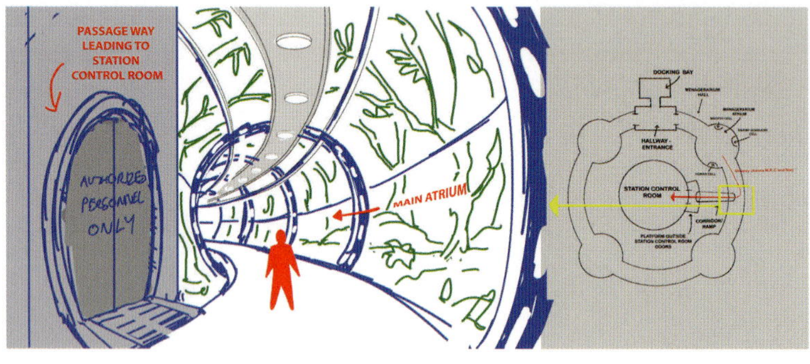

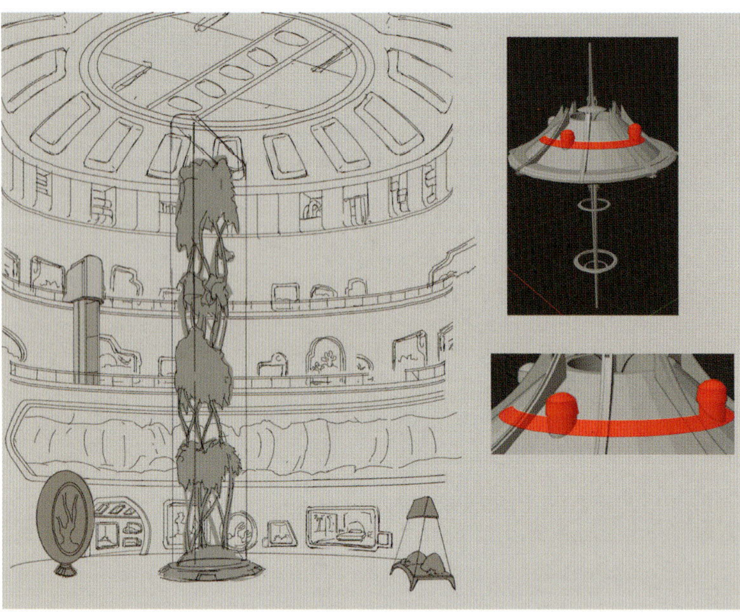

"The menagerie is another example of flipping a design to see what looks better."
— Nollan Obena

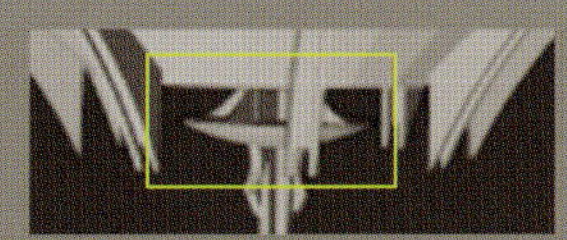

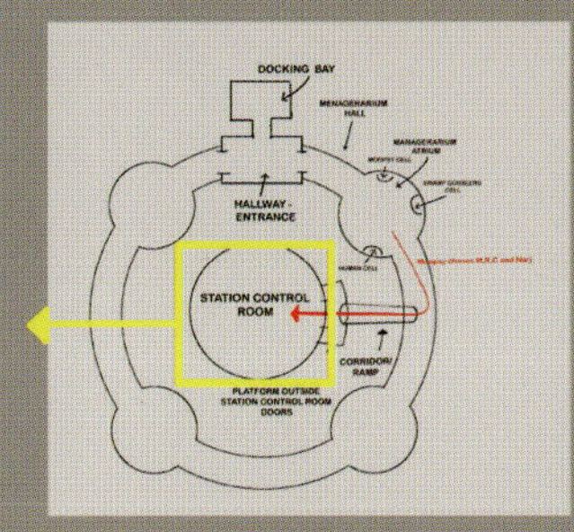

"The control room was tricky because it was a dark room, and we needed some light source to light the characters. When they turn on the light, the windows recede so we can see we're in space."

— Nollan Obena

The moopsy came about because we needed a threatening creature, something like the villain from *Deep Rising* and the bunny from *Monty Python and the Holy Grail*. We received a rough whiteboard drawing from Mike, but the artists came up with a cute design that moved like a baby seal, which was voiced by a kid. It's a really cute ridiculous villain to have in an episode.

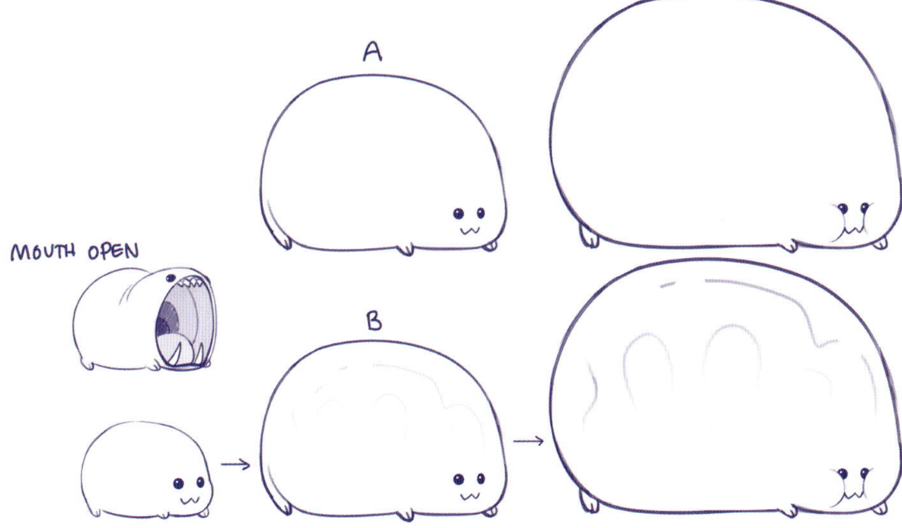

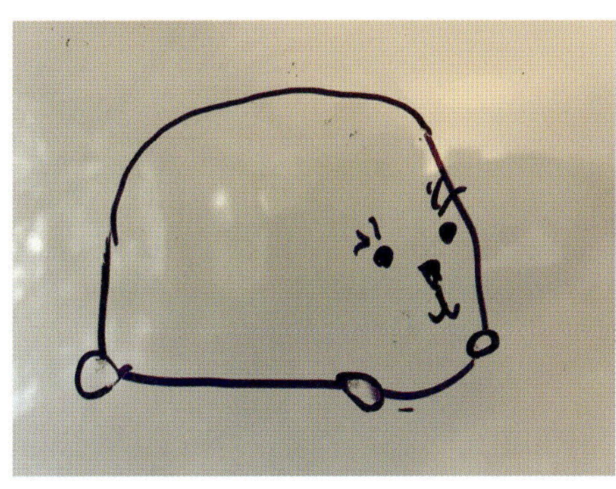

We updated the Tucker tubes that were seen in previous *Star Trek* series with a third tube, which replaced them as the "Billups tubes."

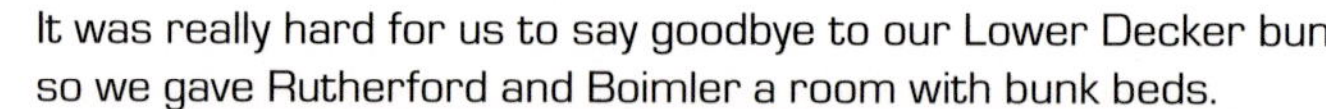
It was really hard for us to say goodbye to our Lower Decker bunks set, so we gave Rutherford and Boimler a room with bunk beds.

This was another episode where we had to create things that are not great on a starship, like living too close to a nacelle's red glow, or in between two holodecks.

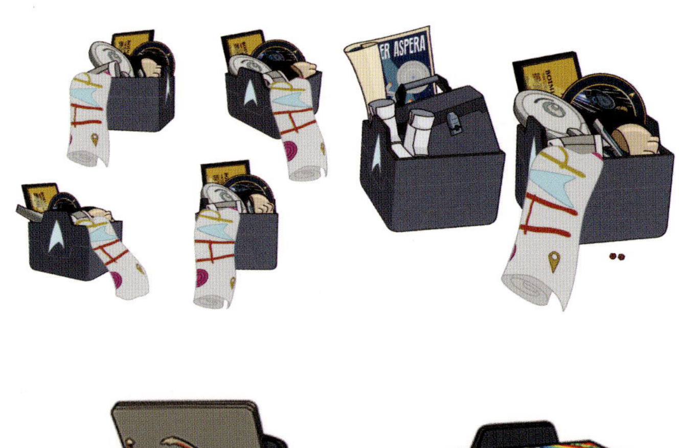

ROMULAN SHIP *KAVORE*

"This ship's design was based on Andrew Probert's original concept for the *D'deridex-class* warbird, combined with elements of the Romulan shuttle."

— Brad Winters

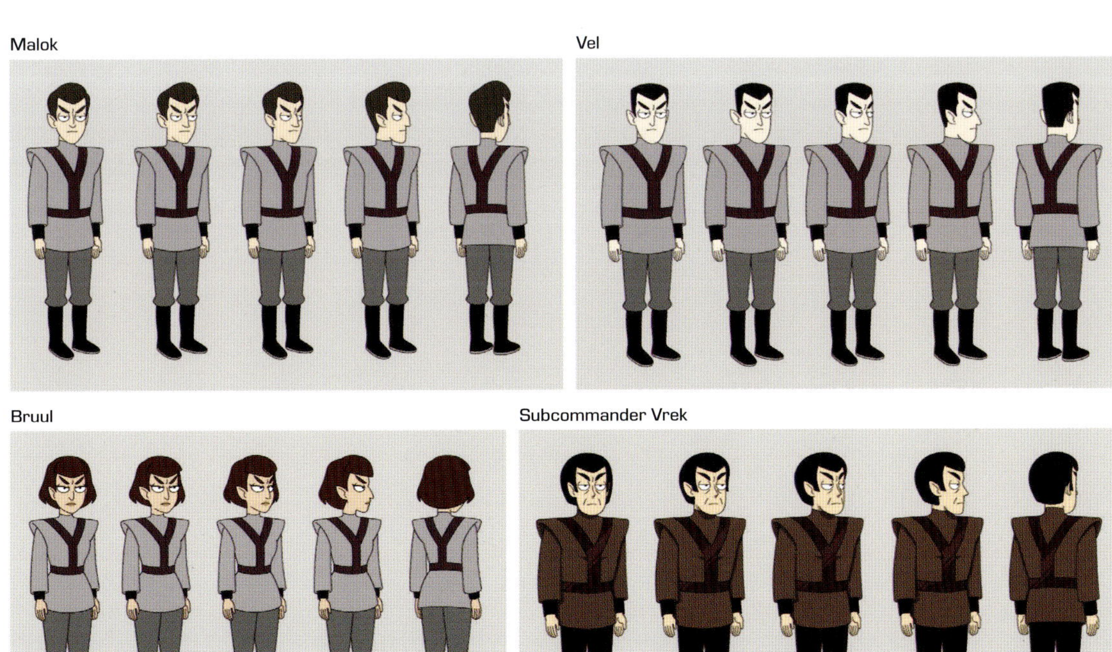

ROMULAN LOWER DECKERS

LCARS S4E3

AIRDATE: 20230914
STARDATE: 58759.1

"In the Cradle of Vexilon"

Boimler leads his first away mission on an alien megastructure.

It was a lot of fun getting to do something on a ring megastructure that went through a series of weather changes instantly.

"Not only are the designs different wherever Boimler is versus Freeman, but because there's destruction on the planet, we had to do different paint schemes for all the locations. But wherever we are, it's important that when we're outside, we see the ring curve up into the upper atmosphere."

— Nollan Obena

CORAZONIA SHUTTLES

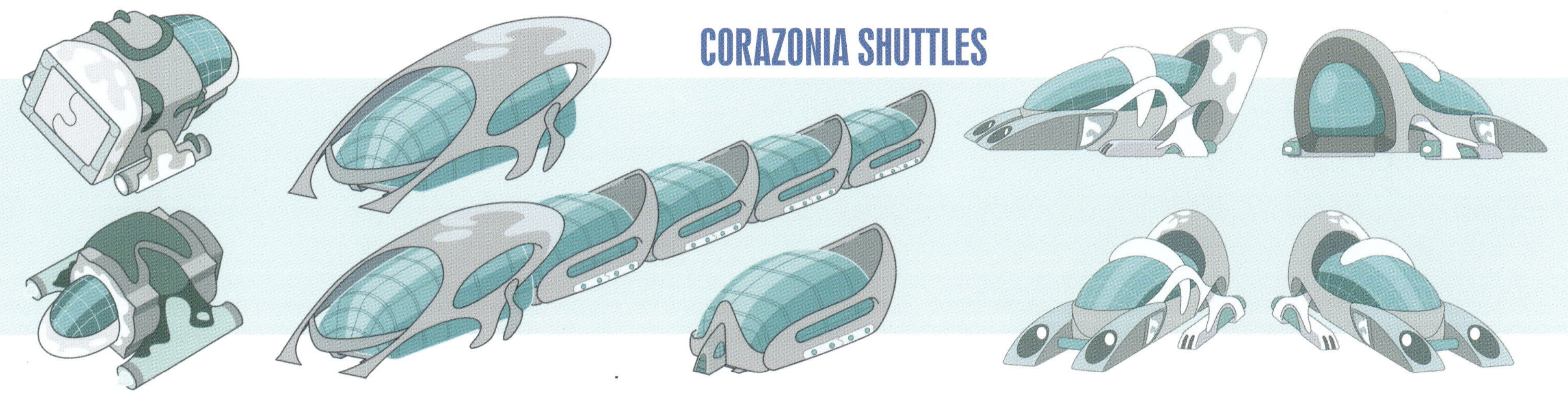

VEXILON TEMPLE

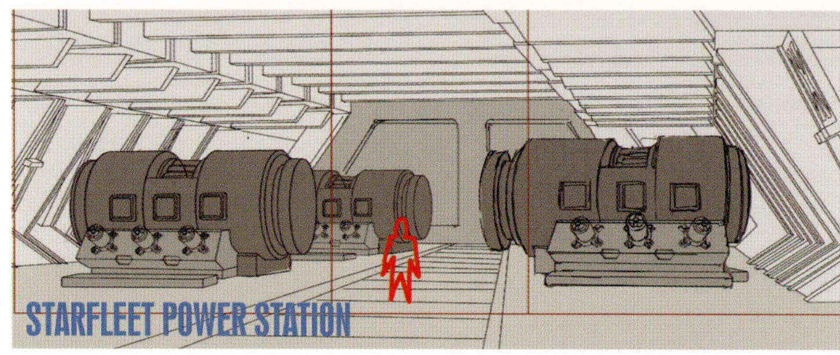

STARFLEET POWER STATION

This episode was exploring what it's like after you've been promoted. Boimler is challenged with his first leadership away mission and learns that you can't be pals with those you oversee. You have to command, rather than do it by committee or do it all on your own.

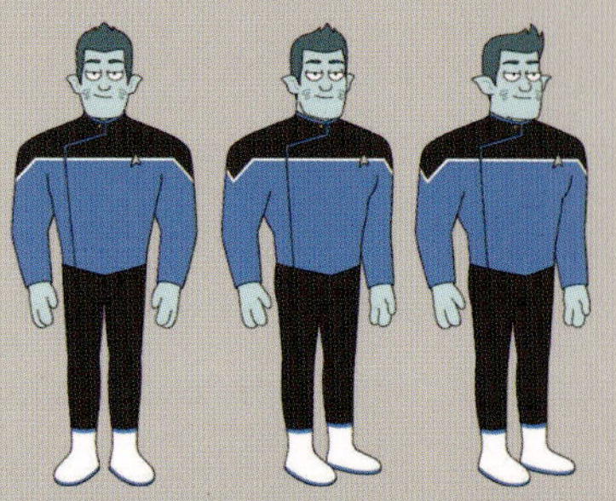

ENS. "BIG" MERP AND ENS. TAYLOR

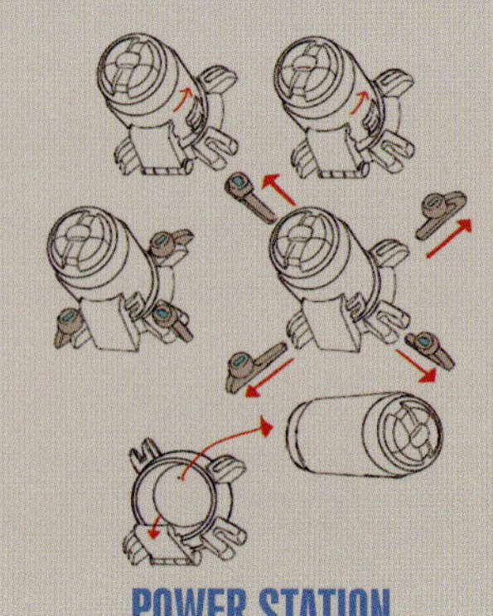

POWER STATION

LT. DIRK

ANOMALY STORAGE ROOM

We call back to the anomaly consolidation room from when the trio worked together in "The Spy Humongous" and show Rutherford getting trapped in the Wadi Chula game.

Meanwhile, Tendi, Mariner, and Rutherford are feeling like they're getting hazed on their new job by Lieutenant Dirk.

We meet Billups' ferret, Lancelot, for the first time in this episode.

LCARS S4E4

AIRDATE: 20230921
STARDATE: UNKNOWN

"Something Borrowed, Something Green"

Tendi is summoned back to Orion for a wedding.

In this episode we wanted to build out more of the Tendi family and Orion.

ORION SUPPLY SHIP

"I'm pretty sure this is the first time we went to the planet Orion, so it was a completely new territory for us to build and develop. We got to explore a matriarchal society. A fun female-character-laden episode."

— Marisa Livingston

TENDI ESTATE

"Orion is well manicured, like a museum, and we go into another area where the Tendis live that is an Italian-like villa with *Godfather*-type gangsters. When we go into the city, we go into more of a *Matrix*-looking neo-futurist city with a lot of neon and lava lamps."

— Nollan Obena

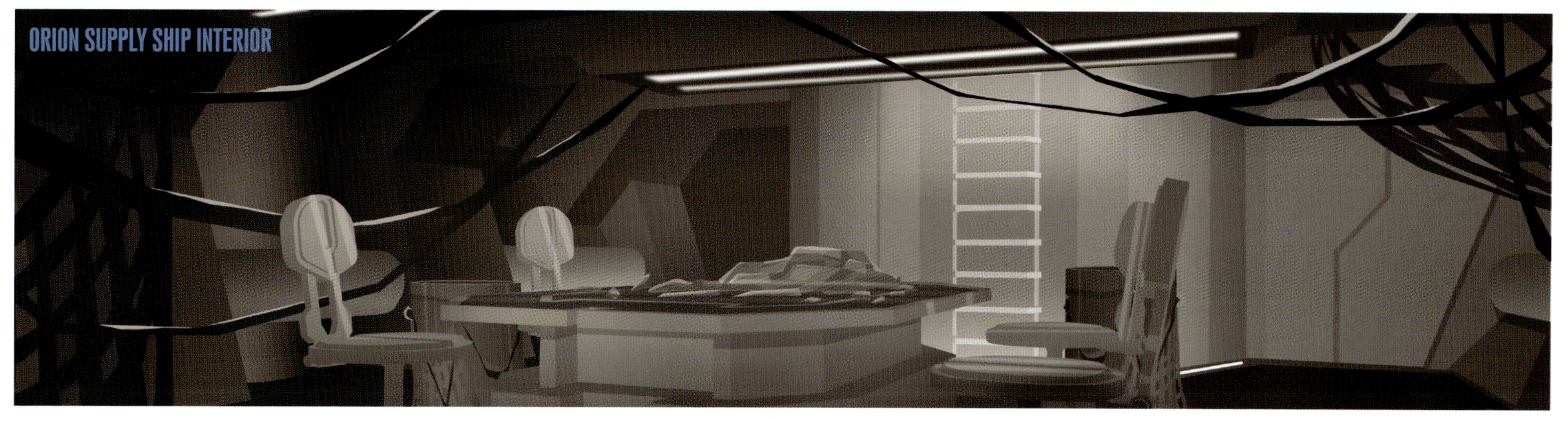

"It's so fun to just make a whole roster of powerful female characters for an episode."

— Marisa Livingston

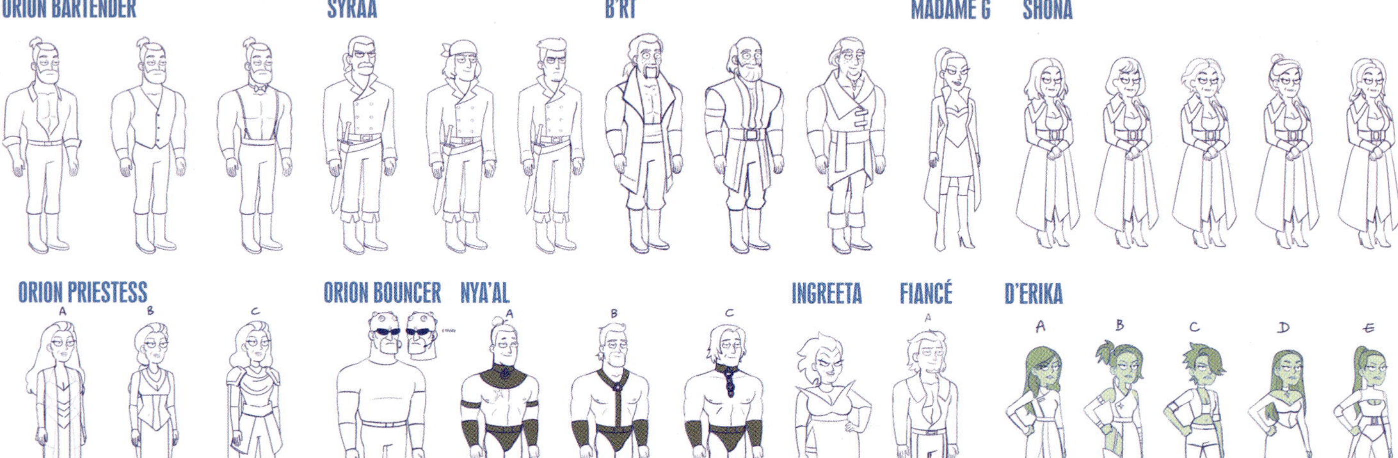

"We got to explore all kinds of outfits and design elements, like what a cool, futuristic spacefaring pirate society would look like and then also its seedy underbelly of nightclubs. There was so much room to grow on this episode, with no limitations other than the characters must be green."

— Marisa Livingston

INGREETA

NYA'AL

ORION BOUNCERS

ORION BARTENDER

"We were inspired by Divine for Ingreeta. She gives off badass drag-queen energy."

— Marisa Livingston

"Going into the underbelly of the city. It was cool seeing this elevator take us to this underworld where men dance inside these gold bird cages. Very opium-den looking."

— Nollan Obena

HOLODECK RIVERBOAT

Of course, we made "Twaining" a way to resolve conflicts on a starship. It's very TNG. It was also fun and silly to dress up a Coqquor in a wig as Mark Twain.

CAPTAIN COQQUOR

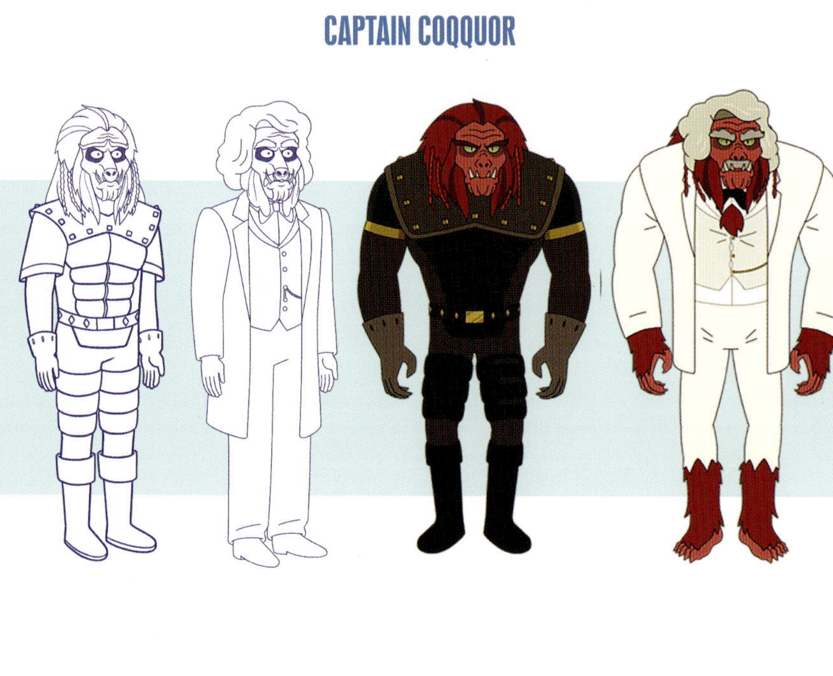

HOLODECK AUSTRIAN SALON

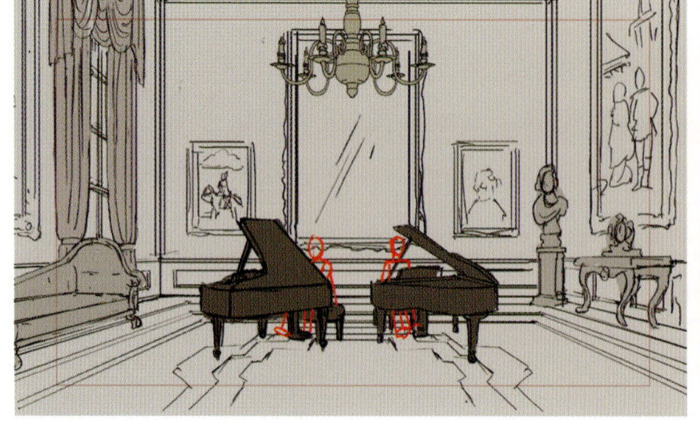

ORION SCRAPYARD

"For the Orion scrapyard, a lot of it was at night, but we had to transition to day because they had to end up at the wedding during the day. So we needed a transitional moment. We picked this one with a pan of the ship leaving. When we're at the shipyard it's still night, and we're cast into the shadows, but as the ship rises, we see the sun also starting to rise."

— Nollan Obena

We call back to the *Raven*-class ship when Tendi shows Mariner and T'Lyn where she and her sister used to play.

LCARS S4E5

AIRDATE: 20230928
STARDATE: UNKNOWN

"Empathalogical Fallacies"

A trio of Betazoids cause chaos on the *Cerritos*.

In this episode, we take a deep dive into the security of the *Cerritos*. It's not only about phasering people; it's also about emotional security.

CERRITOS **SECURITY TRAINING ROOM**

CERRITOS **SECURITY TRAINING ROOM ENTRYWAY**

BETAZOIDS

Dolorex 1A 1B 2A 2B — Cathiw 1A 1B 2A 2B — Katrot 1A 1B 2A 2B — Dolorex 1B 2B — Cathiw 1B 2B — Katrot 1A 2A

KATROT CATHIW DOLOREX

We subvert the trope of older Betazoid women and instead show that they're all badasses.

IT'S ROMULAN ALE O'CLOCK SOMEWHERE

This episode follows a T'Lyn story of her suppressing her emotions that are projecting onto the crew.

By the end of the episode, we learn more about T'Lyn and see her and Mariner become friends.

T'LYN'S QUARTERS

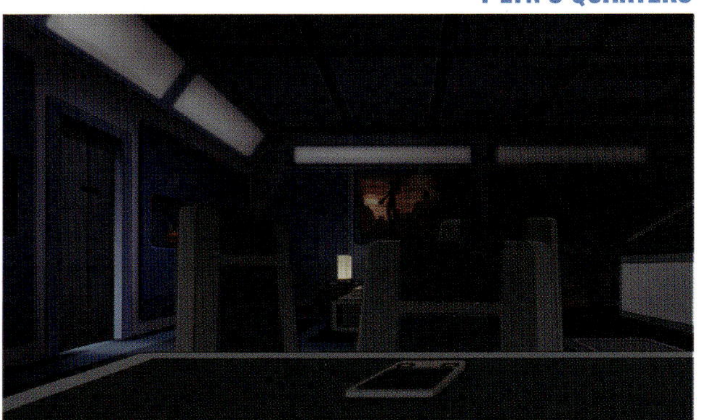

LCARS S4E6

AIRDATE: 20231005
STARDATE: 58901.5

"Parth Ferengi's Heart Place"

The *Cerritos* visits the Ferengi homeworld.

We decided to make Ferenginar a place that could join Starfleet and was beginning to make those steps.

We showed what life on Ferenginar could look like through various TV shows, commercials, restaurants, and a library that was also a bar.

FERENGINAR

"Even though the bulk of the buildings were domed, I tried to give each one a distinct look. The transit tubes connecting the buildings were a great mechanism to bring the composition together and move your eye through the image, from the foreground to the background and side to side."

— Denny Fincke

FERENGI PUBLIC LIBRARY/BAR

All You Can @#$%!
Uncle Quark's
Youth Casino
Slug-O Cola
Pour Homme
Sexeteria
Lodge
Slug Fest

BOOKS!
BOOKS!
BOOKS!
BOOKS!
BOOKS!
BOOKS!
BOOKS!
ISHKA
PUBLIC
LIBRARY

We were inspired by *Star Trek:* The Experience in Vegas when we designed "Quark's Federation Experience Bar and Grill."

We really wanted to do something with Chase Masterson as Leeta and build out something for her and Rom on Ferenginar, a place we had not seen much of before.

"The Dominion War Memorial looks somber and serious, but when you look closer it's receipts. It was supposed to be a normal kind of memorial with inscriptions on the tablets, but in post, we had them scroll up to look like a receipt."

— Nollan Obena

"We only had one painting and Quark's mom's house from which we had to extrapolate a lot of our design cues for Ferenginar."

— Nollan Obena

BOOKS
BOOKS
BOOKS
FERENGINAR HISTORIC
PUBLIC LIBRARY
BOOKS

BOOKS
BOOKS
BOOKS

LCARS S4E7

AIRDATE: 20231012
STARDATE: 58934.9

"A Few Badgeys More"

Three computerized villains return to cause problems for the *Cerritos* crew.

We wanted a big computer episode, with a prison break by AGIMUS and Peanut Hamper, and of course Badgey trying to kill the *Cerritos* crew.

BYNAR SHIP

"The first time we ever see a Bynar ship was in our show, which is two men's shavers put together."

— Nollan Obena

PLYMERIA

"Conquering a pre-warp society with an AGIMUS statue on the pyramid. How do we make it look like a dense city but they're easy to conquer? We made it look like an Iron Age/Bronze Age-ish city with waterfalls to make it look pretty."

— Nollan Obena

DAYSTROM ROBOTS

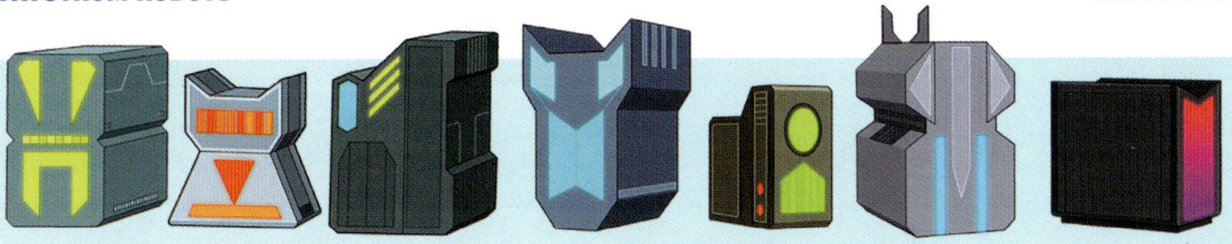

DAYSTROM GUARD

DAYSTROM THERAPIST

PEANUT HAMPER

DAYSTROM INSTITUTE

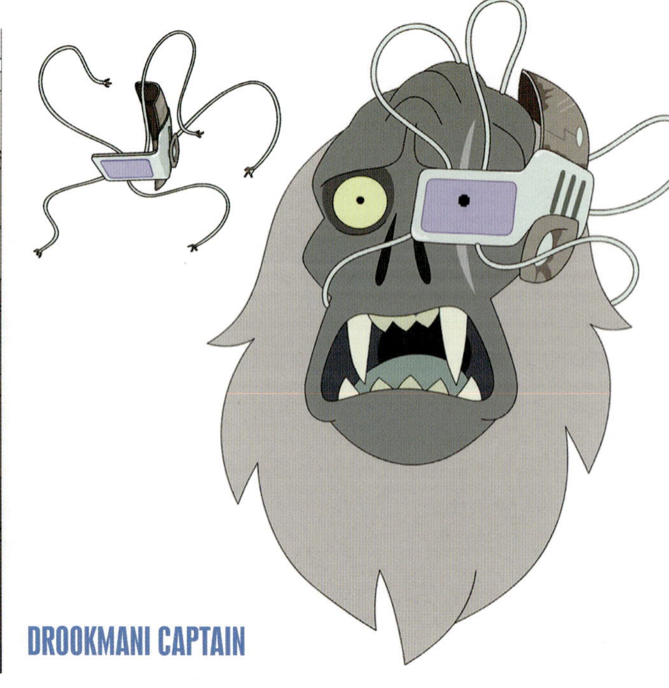

DROOKMANI CAPTAIN

DROOKMANI SHIP BRIDGE

BYNAR SHIP BRIDGE

DROOKMANI SHIP CREW

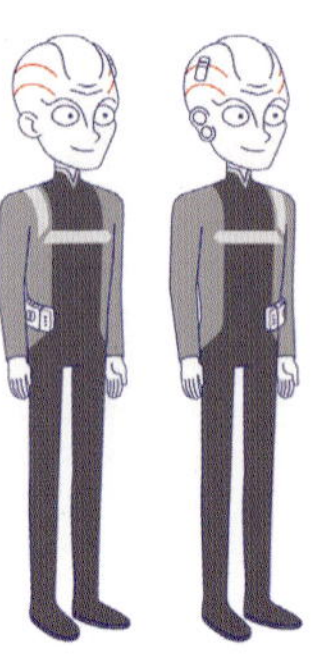

BYNAR SHIP CREW

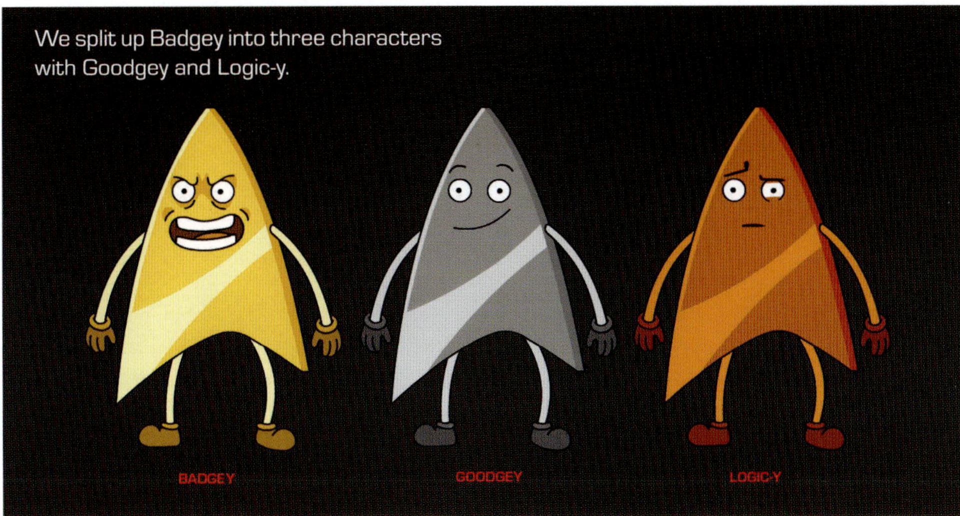

We split up Badgey into three characters with Goodgey and Logic-y.

"During boards we didn't quite know what it'd look like when Badgey took over all the ships. We did three different versions. We basically did bronze, silver, and gold metals. We did a lot of this in post because we couldn't visualize it in boards. We had all the colors and paint, but didn't know how to do it, so Scott Coleman was really helpful in doing all of this."

— Nollan Obena

Badgey's evolution into a god was inspired by Isaac Asimov's "The Last Question."

LCARS S4E8

AIRDATE: 20231019
STARDATE: UNKNOWN

"Caves"

The Lower Deckers go on a classic cave mission.

We revisited our pilot episode, "Second Contact," and saw a different view of Tendi's first day on the *Cerritos*.

We wanted to do an homage to the limitations of a live-action *Star Trek* series needing to redress the same physical set to look like a new location.

"This design was so gnarly. It was really hard for us to look at it."

— Marisa Livingston

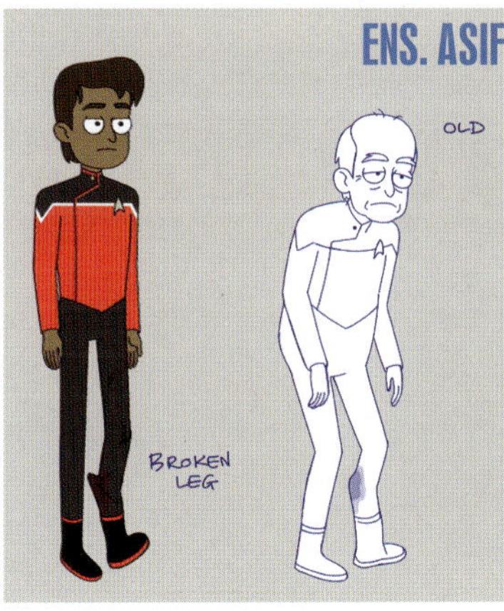

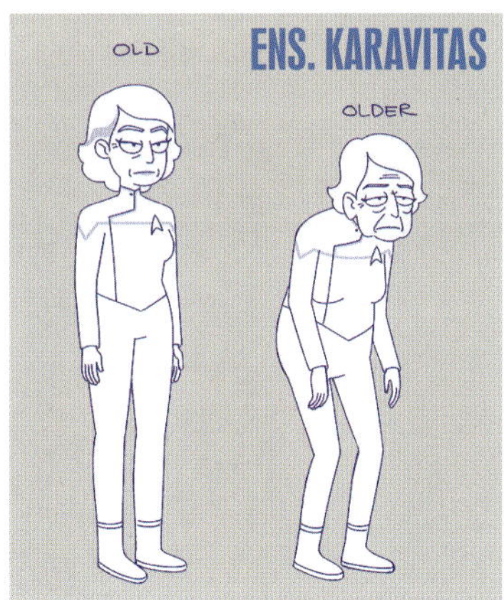

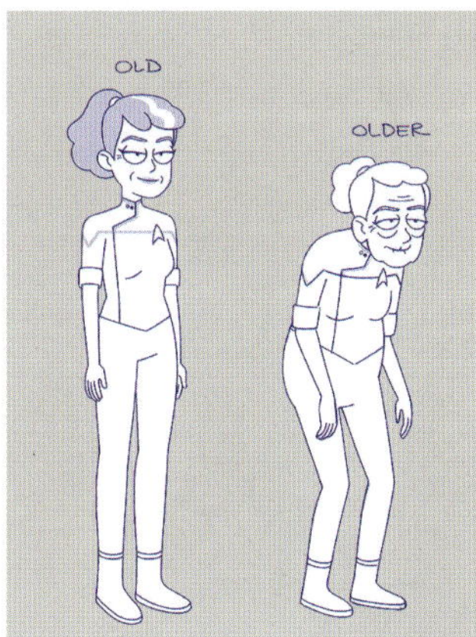

"This one was fun because it was basically referencing all the reuse sets in *Star Trek*. We were using one cave location but dressing it up throughout the episode."

— Nollan Obena

We added one noticeable natural rock feature that we'd see in every storyline to really suggest this is the same set.

LCARS S4E9

AIRDATE: 20231026
STARDATE: UNKNOWN

"The Inner Fight"

Captain Freeman assigns the Lower Deckers an overly safe mission to try and keep a self-destructive Mariner out of danger.

Throughout the season, Mariner has been trying to sabotage her promotion by making more and more dangerous and risky decisions. A menial mission to a space probe to keep her safe takes a turn when the Lower Deckers are attacked by a Klingon Bird of Prey and forced to transport onto Sherbal V.

It's a stormy volcanic planet with solidified lava bubbles. We made an environment shaped around raining glass.

NEW AXTON

We wanted New Axton to feel like it was a rustic *Star Trek V* outpost planet that doesn't fit in with the Federation vibe and feels out of place.

We call back to Balok's puppet from TOS: "The Corbomite Maneuver," animating the information broker similar to how the puppet moved in the original episode. However, we reveal through Rutherford's vision that the character in this episode was in fact alive, and not a dummy.

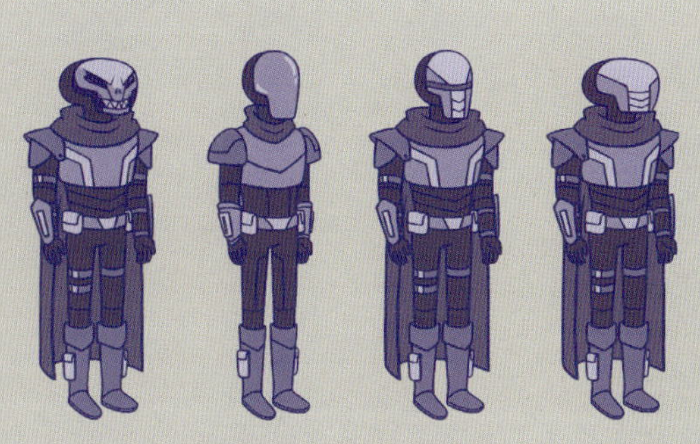

"The bounty hunter was supposed to be Migleemo, which is why the helmet is so big. But when we changed it to Billups, we kept the size of the helmet and added a skull face on it."

— Nollan Obena

"We designed a desert planet where all the bounty hunters hang out. We designed a ship specifically for Billups' bounty-hunter persona and had to make it look different, not Starfleet, from anything we've seen before. Took cues from an Apache helicopter."

— Nollan Obena

NICK LOCARNO'S HANGAR

We brought back Robert Duncan McNeill again to play his other *Star Trek* character, Nicholas "Nick" Locarno from TNG: "The First Duty," who ends up being behind the mystery ship of the season.

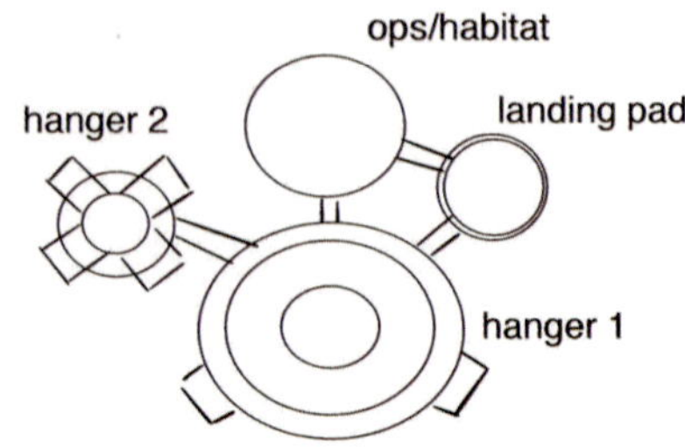

NICK LOCARNO

PERSIOFF IX

OUTPOST SCIENTISTS

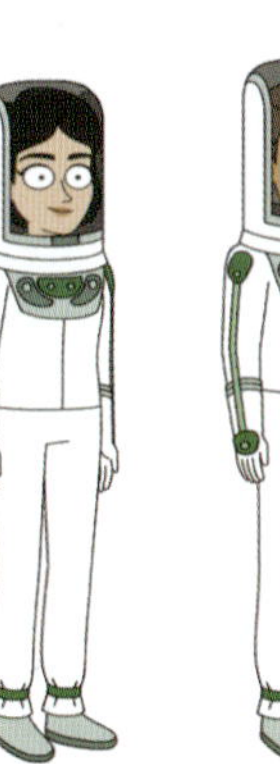

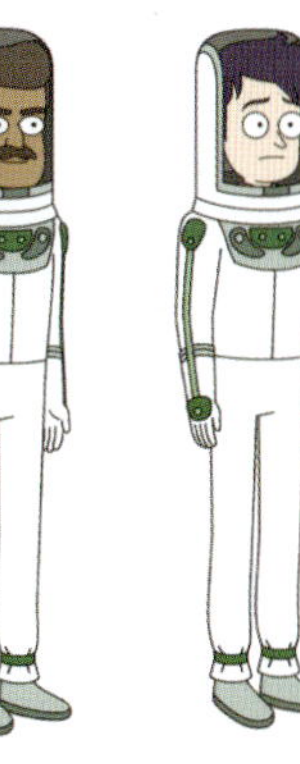

ORION CREW MEMBER

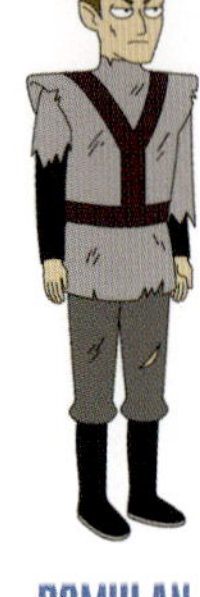

ROMULAN

CAPT. COSMIA

CAPT. GEM

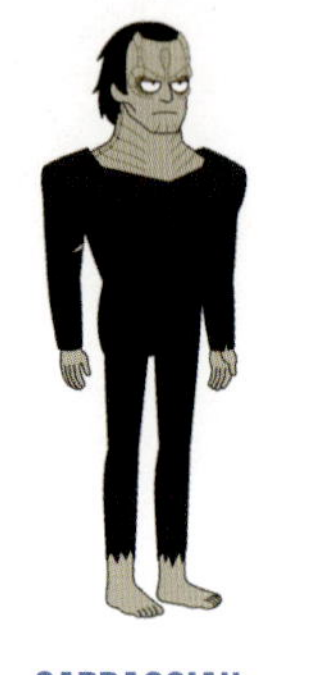

CARDASSIAN

SUBCOMMANDER VREK

MA'AH

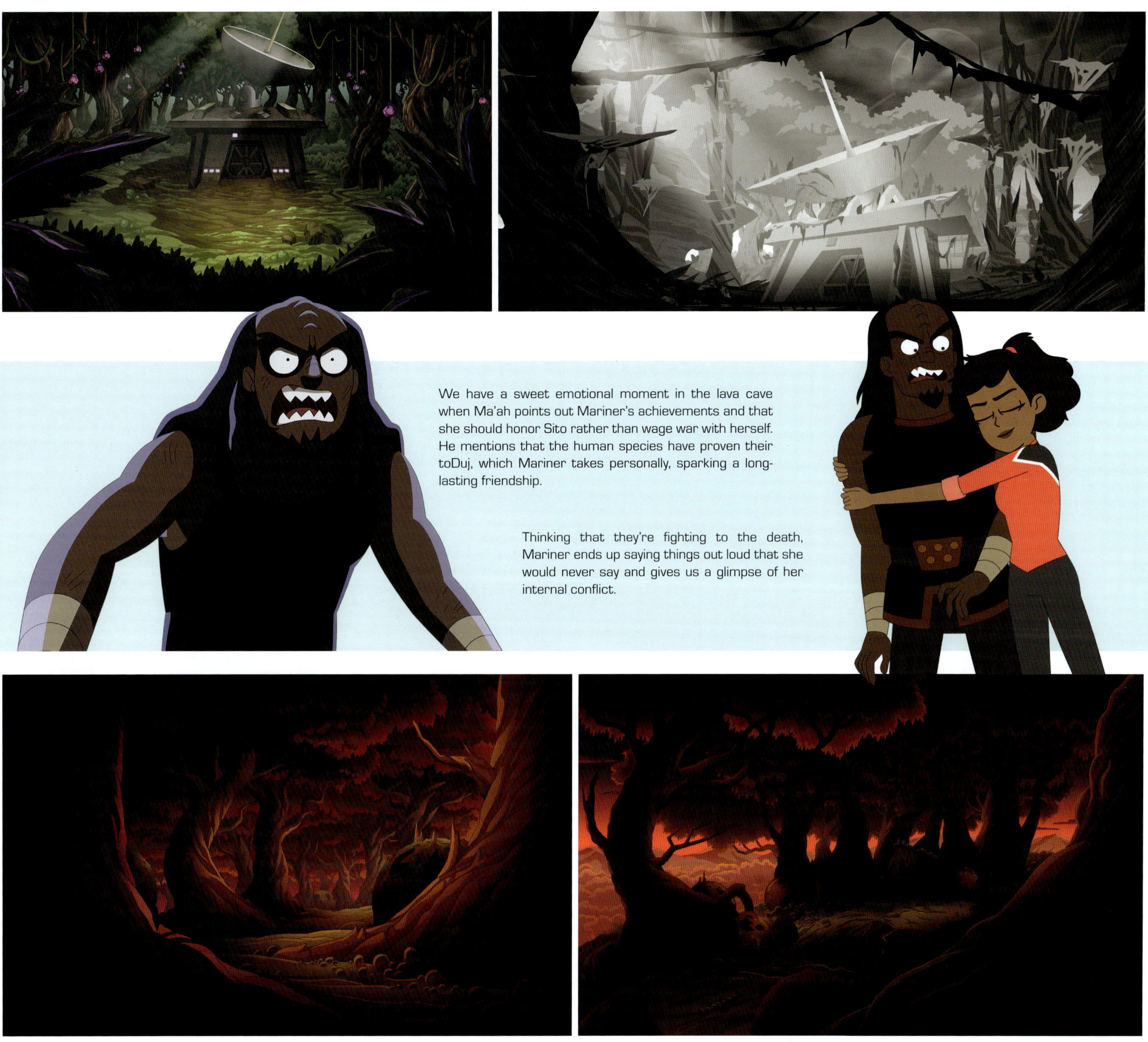

We have a sweet emotional moment in the lava cave when Ma'ah points out Mariner's achievements and that she should honor Sito rather than wage war with herself. He mentions that the human species have proven their toDuj, which Mariner takes personally, sparking a long-lasting friendship.

Thinking that they're fighting to the death, Mariner ends up saying things out loud that she would never say and gives us a glimpse of her internal conflict.

LCARS S4E10

AIRDATE: 20231102
STARDATE: UNKNOWN

"Old Friends, New Planets"

Mariner faces her past in the season four finale

At the end of the episode, we see Tendi fierce and determined as she leaves the *Cerritos* to go back to Orion. She has grown so much since season one.

DETRION SYSTEM ICE PLANET

U.S.S. PASSARO

We created a new ship under a new class for Mariner to steal. The *U.S.S. Passaro* is *Sabrerunner* class, which is a smaller version of the *Saber* class with *Steamrunner*-class aesthetics, and was named after a colleague and friend who helped us immensely throughout the seasons, Fabio Passaro.

STARFLEET ACADEMY

NICK LOCARNO JOSHUA ALBERT WESLEY CRUSHER SITO JAXA

In the cold open of this episode, we get a cool flashback to Starfleet Academy with the Nova Squadron from TNG: "The First Duty." We brought back Wil Wheaton and Shannon Fill in addition to Robert to play their roles from TNG. This is also the first time we see Josh Albert.

ORION BATTLESHIP

"Mike wanted an old relic, like an old warship, an Orion version of a battleship that was shaped like an arrowhead that could be tossed into a shield. It's similar to the medical ship, but not as organic. It's more abrasive because: 1) we need to throw it into a shield, and 2) it's older, so it needs to be clunkier. We only see it for a few seconds because we blow it up."

— Nollan Obena

D'ERIKA

D'ERIKA'S CHAMPION

On Orion, we see Tendi negotiate with her sister, D'Erika, and invoke barter by combat in an attempt to receive a battleship to save Mariner. She enlists Dr. Migleemo and instructs him to fluff his down, making him all puffed up, which is so cute.

ORION COMBAT ARENA

DR. MIGLEEMO

CAPTAIN'S YACHT

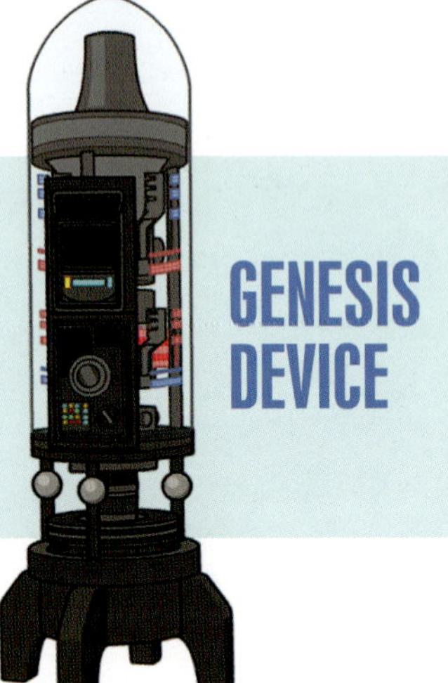
GENESIS
DEVICE

U.S.S. PASSARO

"The shield is made by Bynars, so we used a Bynar pattern from their design language."

— Nollan Obena

NOVA FLEET

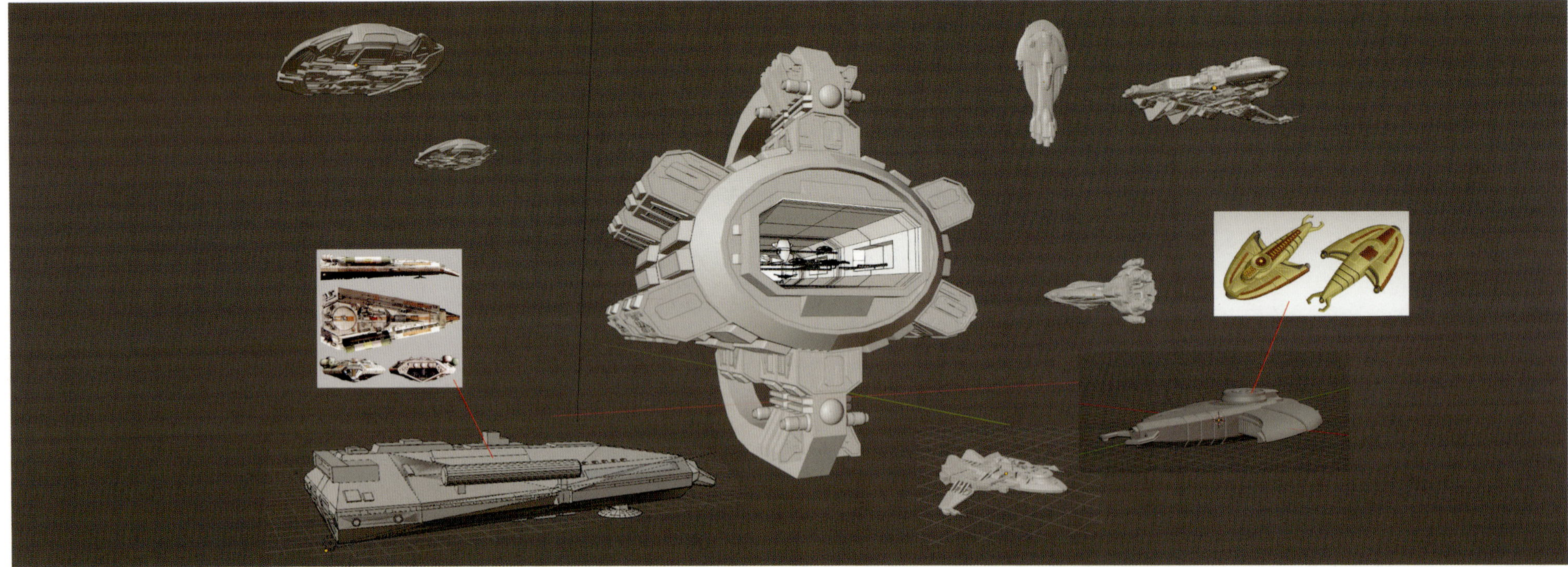

This episode is a big action *Wrath of Khan*–style movie where the legacy character thinks that he has it all figured out and can manipulate Mariner, but she never fires a shot. She outmaneuvers him, poking a hole in his siren song.

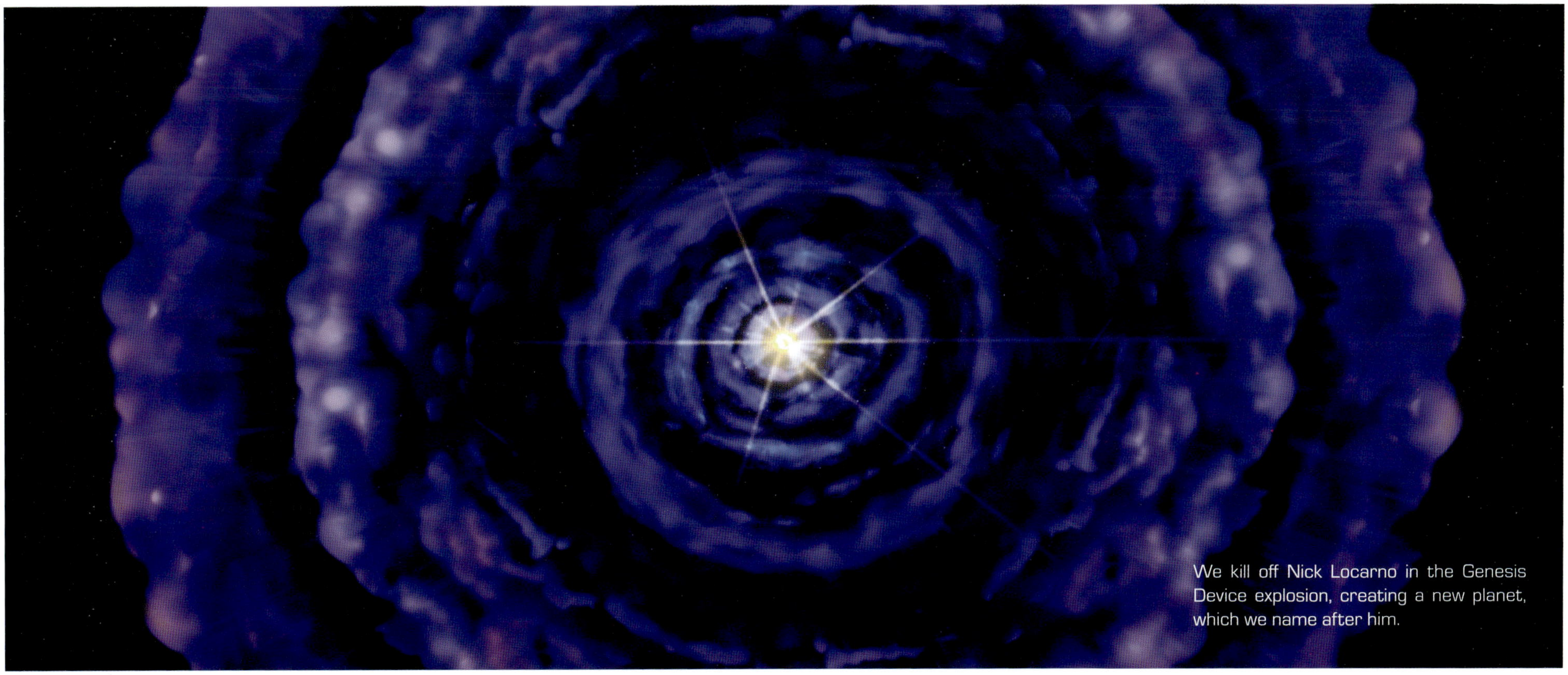

We kill off Nick Locarno in the Genesis Device explosion, creating a new planet, which we name after him.

CHAPTER 08 SEASON FIVE

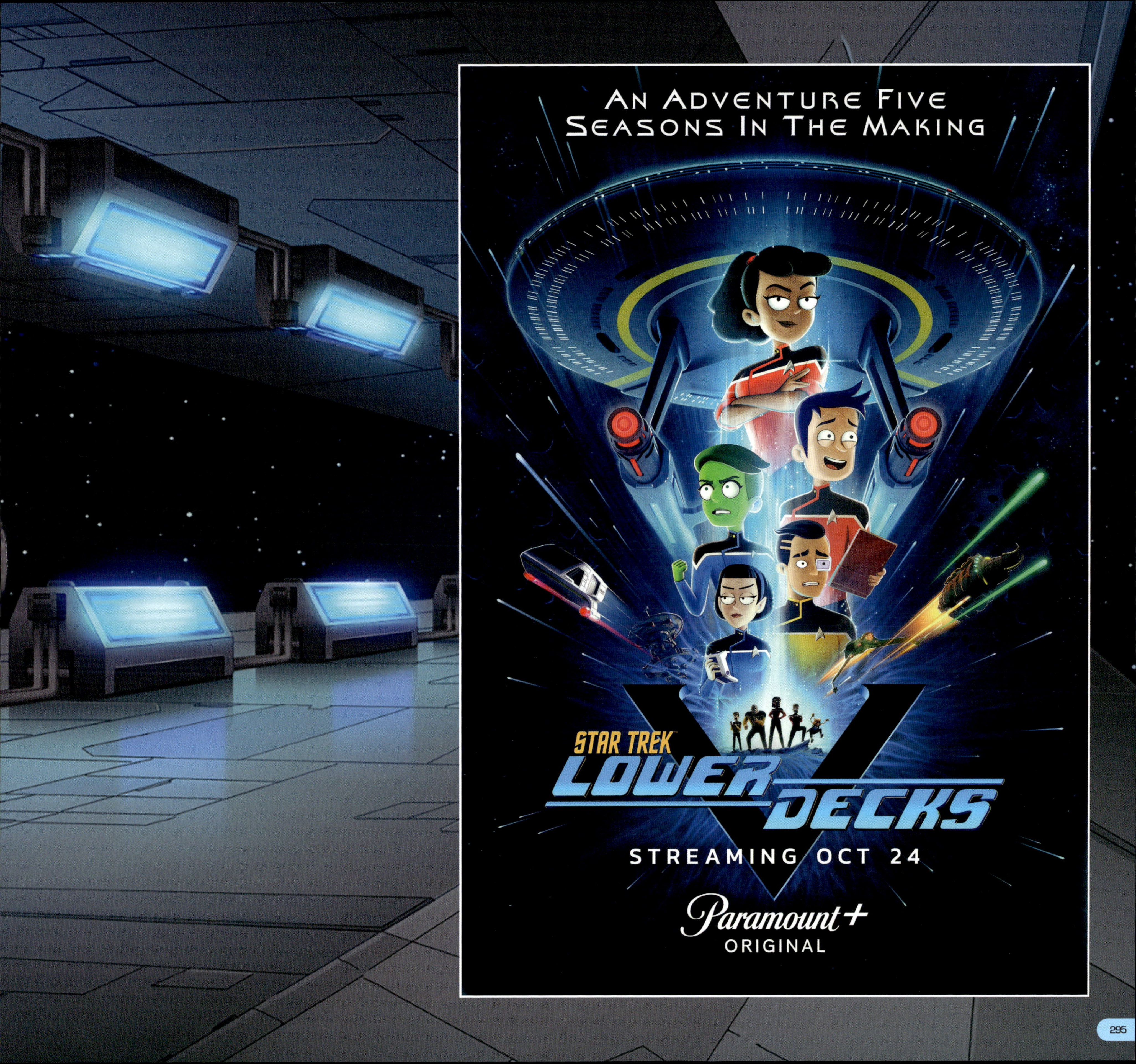

An Adventure Five
Seasons In The Making

Star Trek
Lower Decks

STREAMING OCT 24

Paramount+
ORIGINAL

LCARS S5E1

AIRDATE: 20241024
STARDATE: UNKNOWN

"Dos Cerritos"

A spatial anomaly forces the *Cerritos* crew to face their own faces. Tendi pirates.

This episode sets up the interdimensionality of the season with the quantum fissures.

ORION MEDICAL SHIP

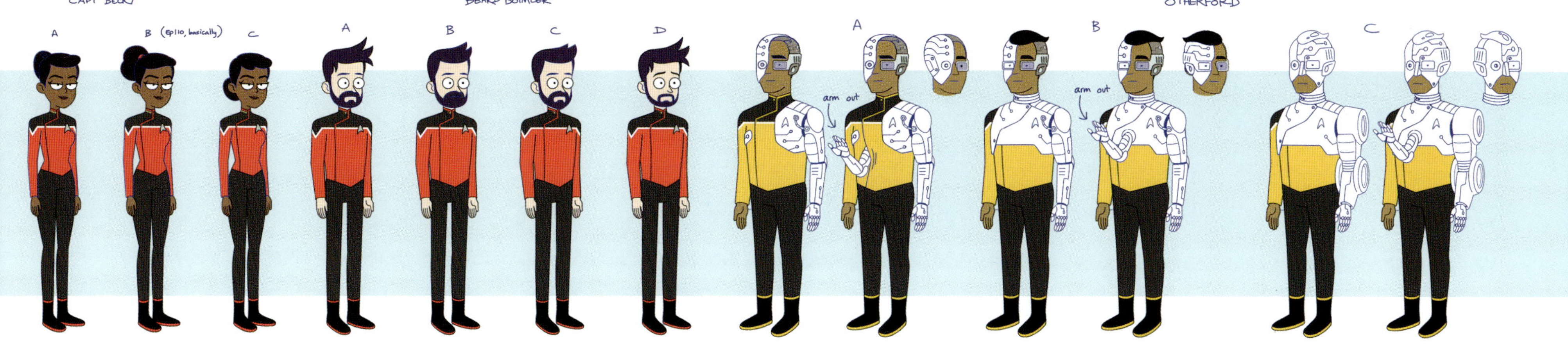

CAPT BECKY
A
B (Ep110, basically)
C
BEARD BOIMLER
A
B
C
D
OTHERFORD
A
arm out
B
arm out
C

ALT BILLUPS
A
B
C
D
ALT RANSOM
A
B
C
D

ALTERNATE COLOR CHANGE
ORTHOS VIEW

HALIIAN SHIP

We wanted to show where we left off with Tendi back with Orions pirating but also staying true to herself as a Starfleet officer.

SHIP GALLERY

SHIP GALLERY TREASURES

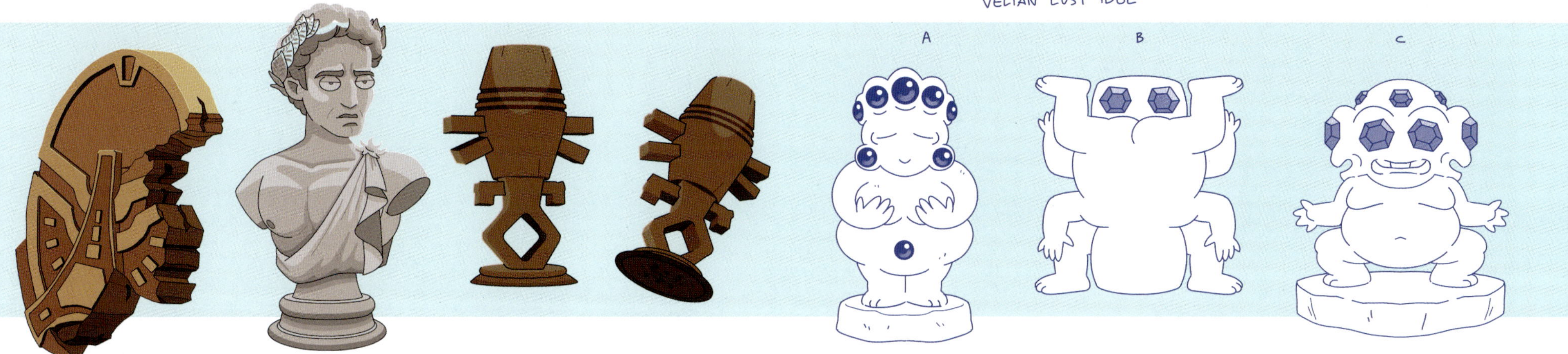

SECURITY GUARD

We bring back the species of Palor Toff from TNG: "The Most Toys."

ASMAN YORIF

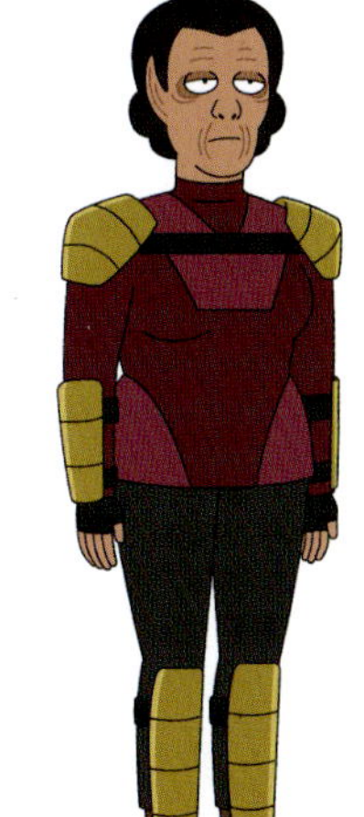

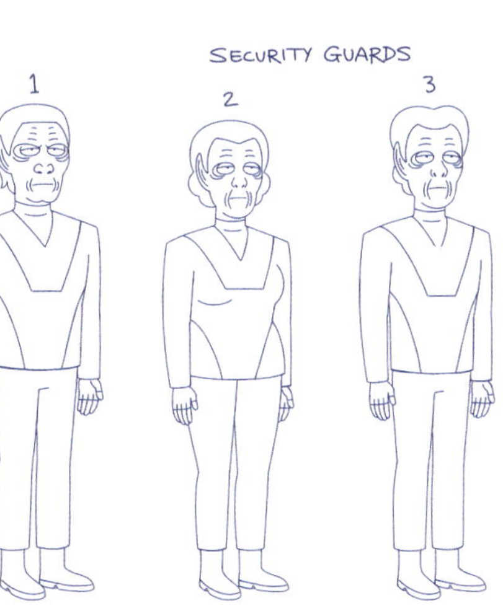

FROSTBITTEN BLADE

TENDI'S QUARTERS

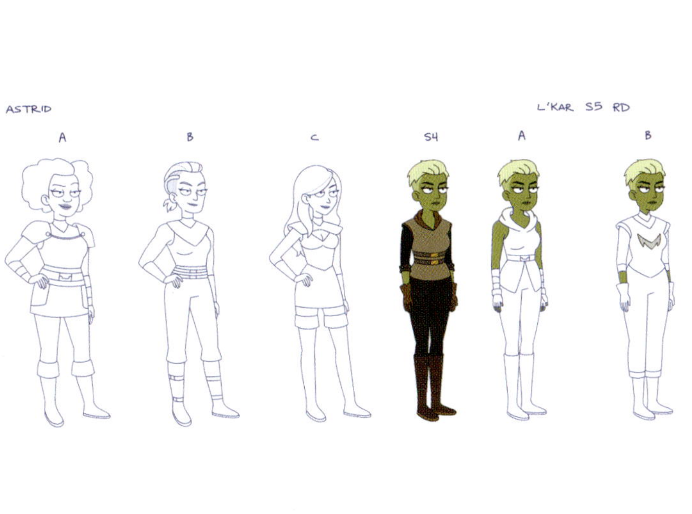
ASTRID
A
B
C
S4
L'KAR S5 RD
A
B

ASTRID
KITA
L'KAR

TENDI'S QUARTERS

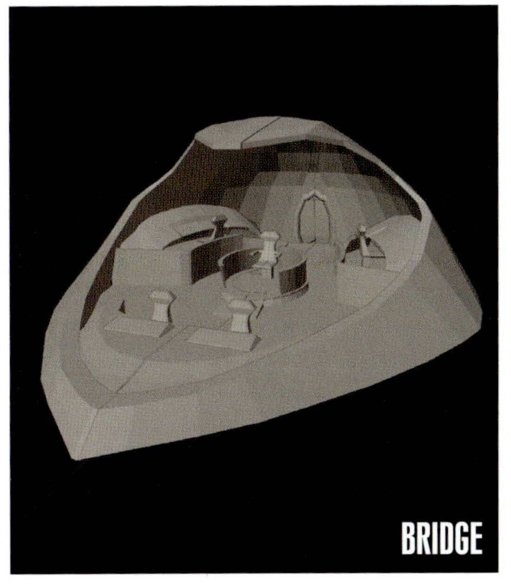
BRIDGE

CARGO HOLD

We bring back blue Orions from *Star Trek: The Animated Series* and create a distinguishable difference between the two Orion cultures, ultimately creating a war between them.

"Designing an old Orion medical ship was cool. The ship was made of see-through metal where you can see the pipes. Like the door, you can see the mechanisms of the door overlap each other. Everything had a window punched through it so we could see the design on the other side."

— Nollan Obena

BRIDGE

LCARS S5E2

AIRDATE: 20241024
STARDATE: 59376.9

"Shades of Green"

Tendi races to stop a conflict while Boimler and Mariner race to stop capitalists.

In the beginning of this episode we learn, with Tendi, that her sister is pregnant, but she's not supposed to know. Meanwhile, Boimler obsesses over his alternate self's success and confidence through the noticeably red PADD he stole.

TENDI'S SAILSHIP BRIDGE

We wanted to have a solar-sail ship race inspired by the Bajoran lightship in DS9: "Explorers."

ORION SAIL SHIPS

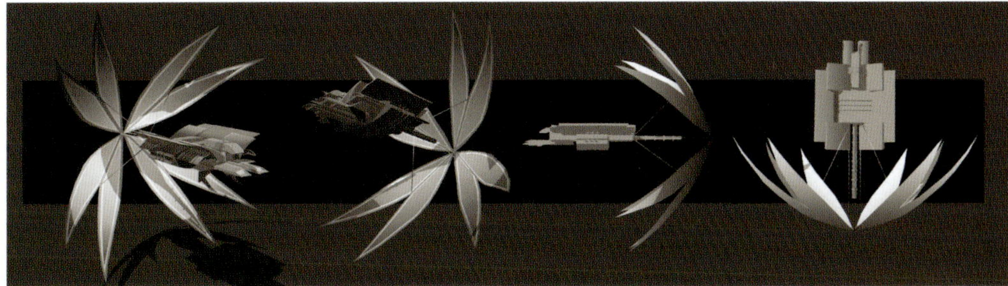

"For the Tendi sailer, we incorporated wood with the ornamental gold/copper metallic details that we saw in the medical ship."

— Nollan Obena

"For the blue Orion ships, we followed their existing design language. Since we reused the TAS ship, we did a version of that as their solar sail. The sails are gigantic elephant ears and are more square than Tendi's flowerlike sailer."

— Nollan Obena

"We put in some sails inspired by pontoons."

— Nollan Obena

"Then we made the blue's interior look like a laser tag room."

— Nollan Obena

TARGALUS IX

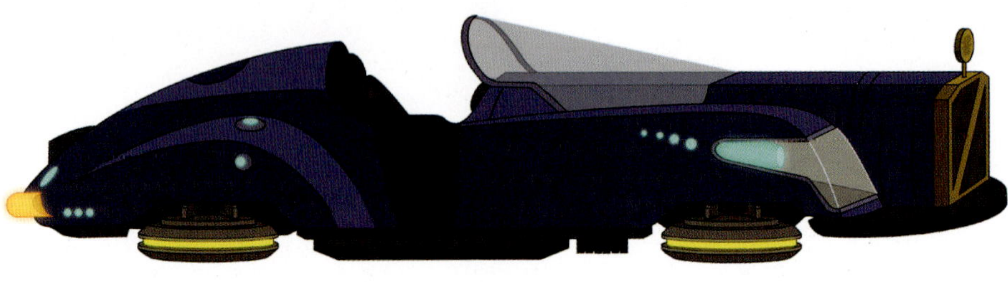

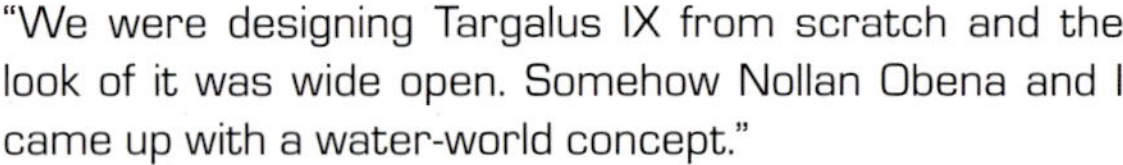

"We were designing Targalus IX from scratch and the look of it was wide open. Somehow Nollan Obena and I came up with a water-world concept."

— Denny Fincke

The *Cerritos* visits Targalus IX to help dismantle their capitalist system after they've acquired post-scarcity technology. We wanted to see what it would look like if wealth was obsolete and what challenges we could face with people resistant to change for the better.

TARGALANS

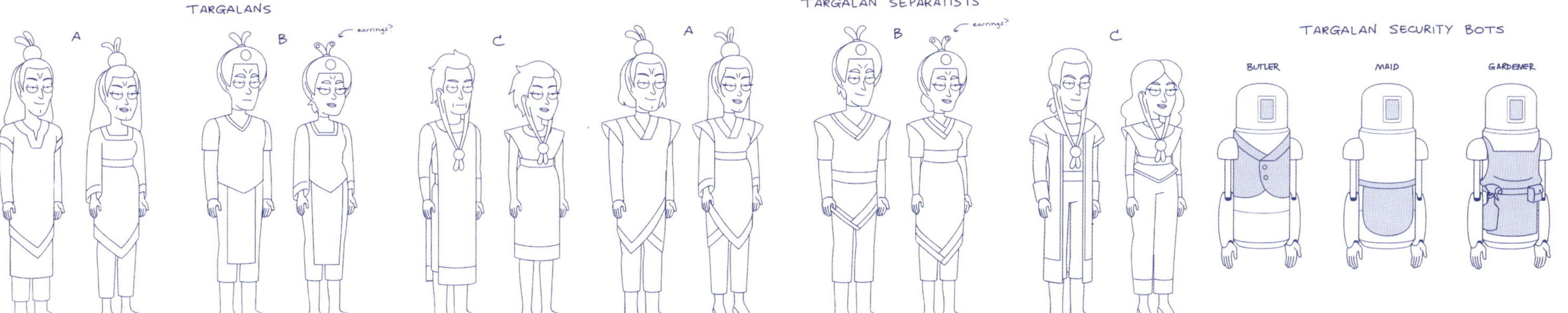

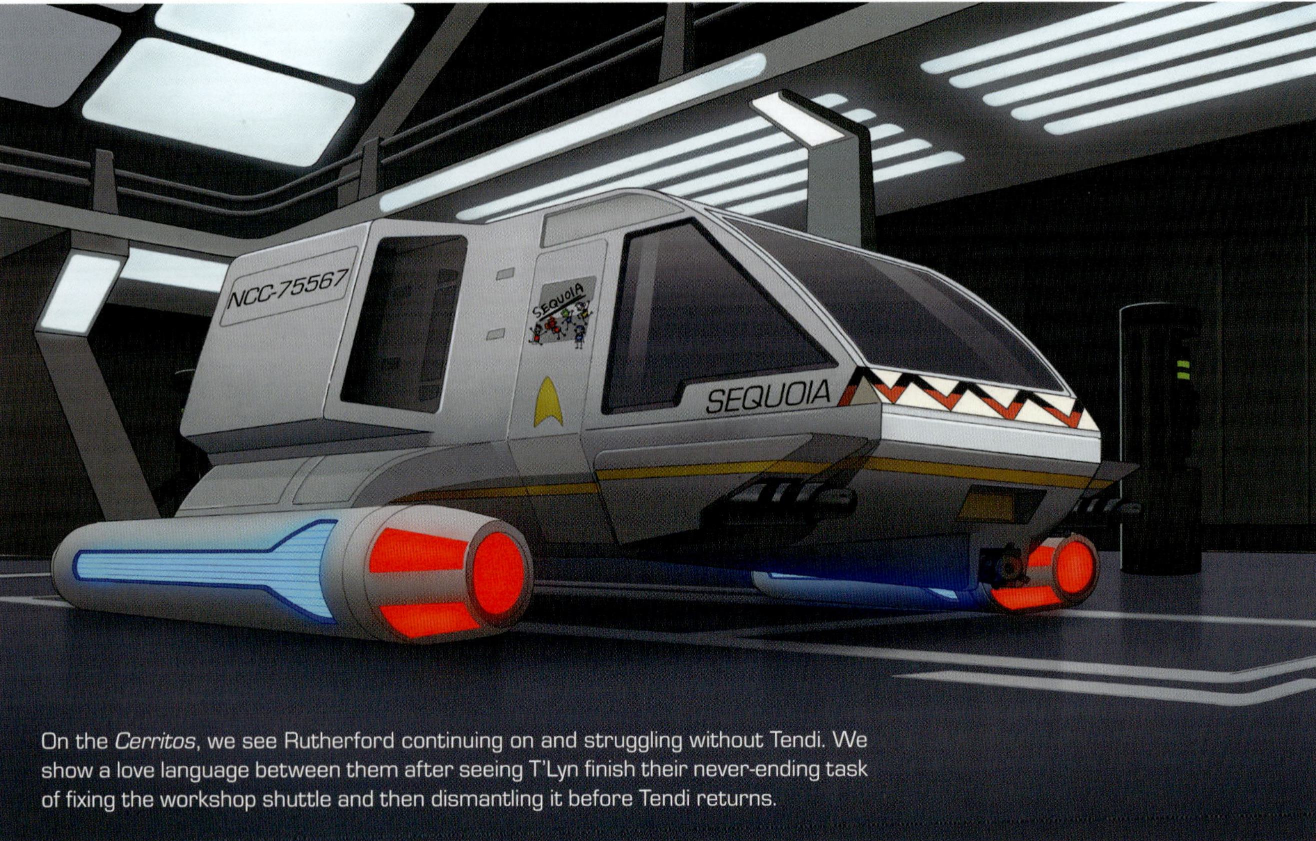

On the *Cerritos*, we see Rutherford continuing on and struggling without Tendi. We show a love language between them after seeing T'Lyn finish their never-ending task of fixing the workshop shuttle and then dismantling it before Tendi returns.

Boimler begins to grow a beard.

We introduce Ensigns Gorm and Mackler in this episode to start building out the new next generation.

ORION

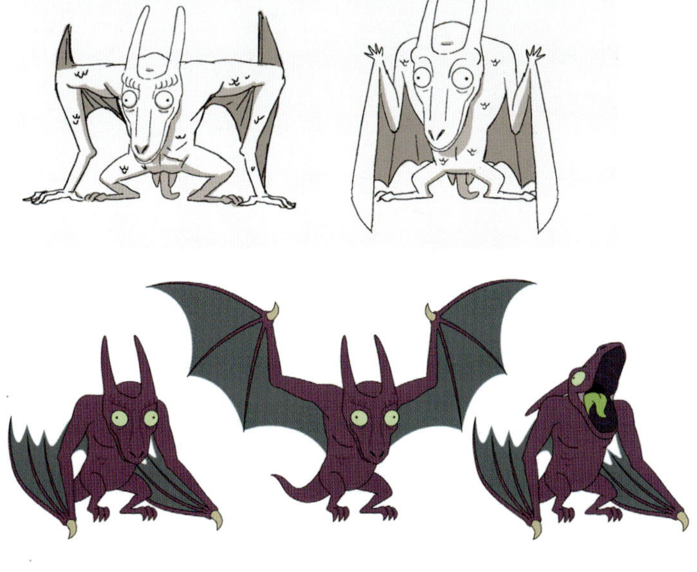
A
B

QUEEN SABOR
A
B
C
D

LCARS S5E3

AIRDATE: 20241031
STARDATE: 59393.7

"The Best Exotic Nanite Hotel"

The Lower Deckers hunt nanites on a resort...in space?!

This is a story inspired by *Heart of Darkness* by Joseph Conrad, with Boimler thinking he's a canary in a coal mine.

We wanted to create a beautiful resort hotel in space with multiple climates and attractions for all but remind everyone that this is still a hotel with waste bins and recycling bins out in the open.

"The domes are different environments. From the outside, we painted them different key colors, like if it was tropical, it'd be green, maybe some purple vegetation on another. Some cooler ones could be underwater or icy."

— Nollan Obena

THE COSMIC DUCHESS

THE COSMIC DUCHESS

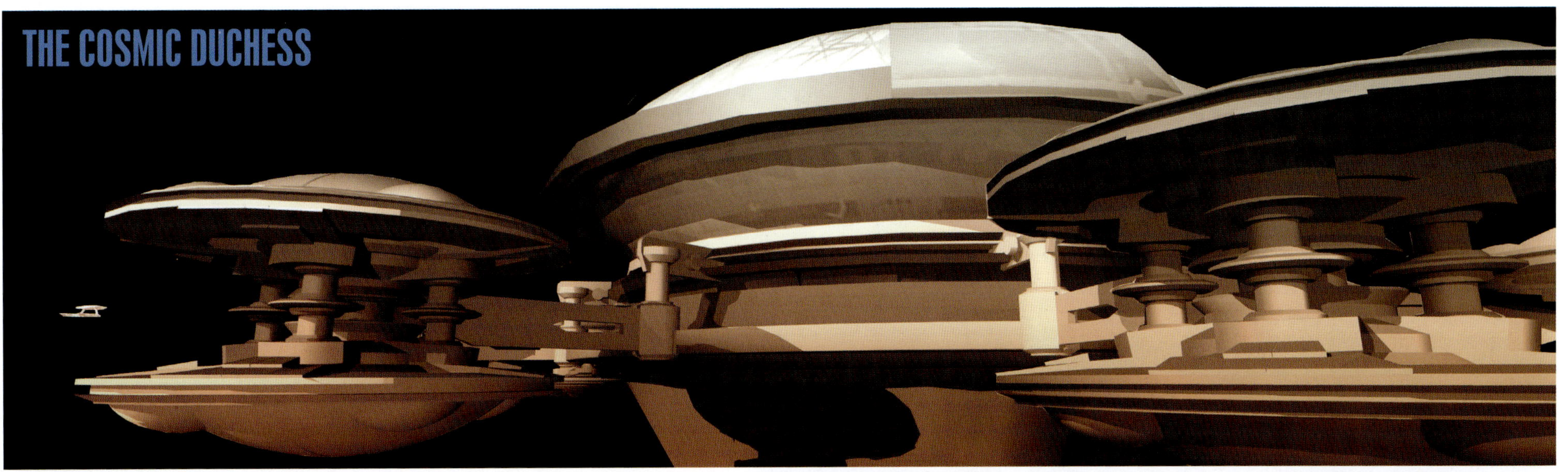

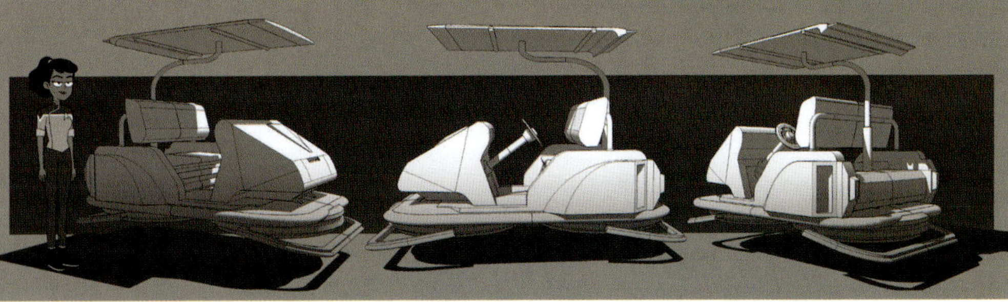

"The design of the Cosmic Duchess was originally upside down orbiting a moon. Then someone said, 'Why don't we put the moon in the center?' So, I flipped it, put the moon in the middle, scaled it up, and had the surrounding domes circulating the spire."

— Nollan Obena

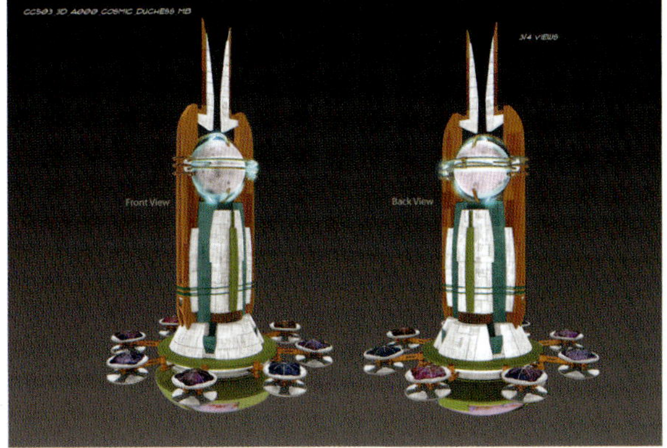

KROG

Krog's vibe tubes are referencing the instrument played in TNG: "We'll Always Have Paris"

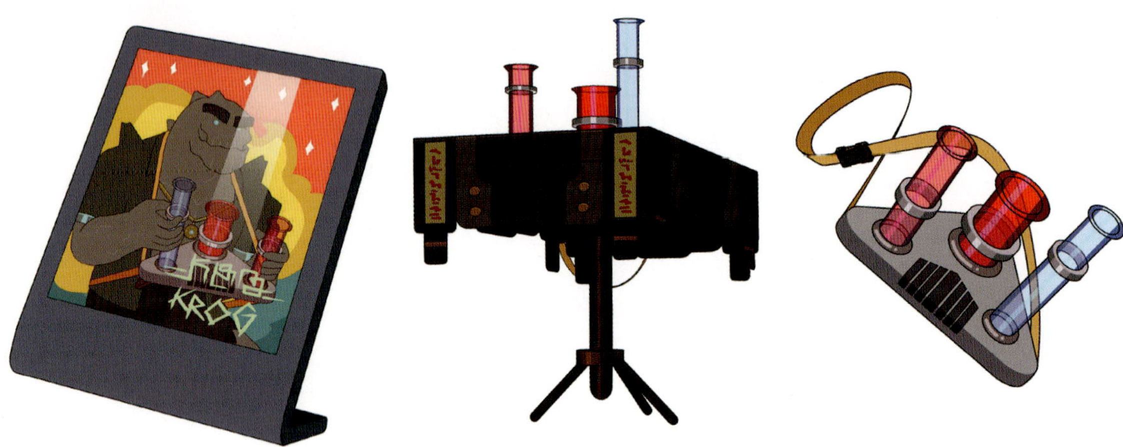

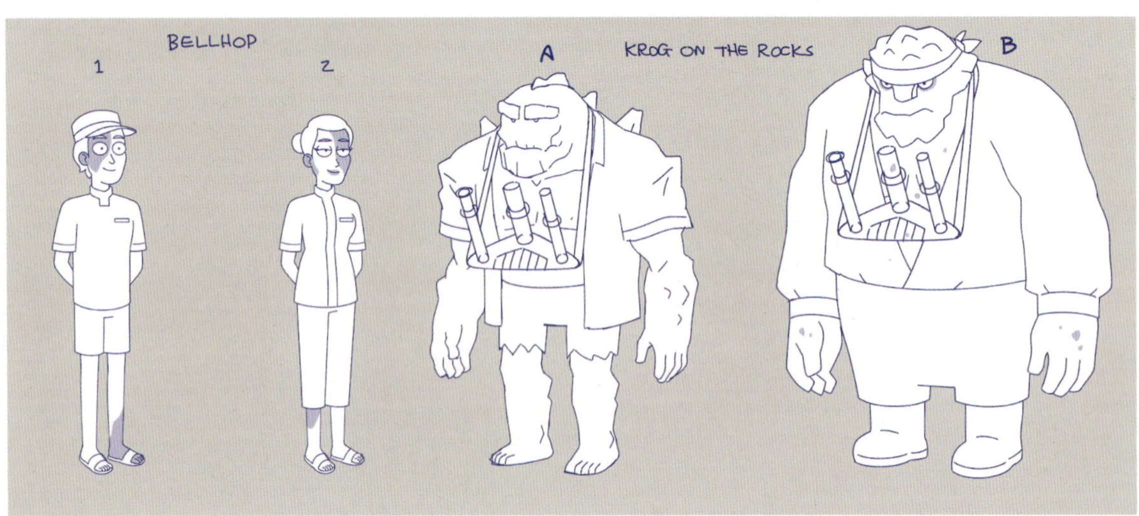

SC A075
THE
RISA BAR

CABANA BAR
Mike: let's just put the sign on the ground
TIKI BAR

CABANA BAR EMPLOYEES
GALLAMITES
KREETASSANS

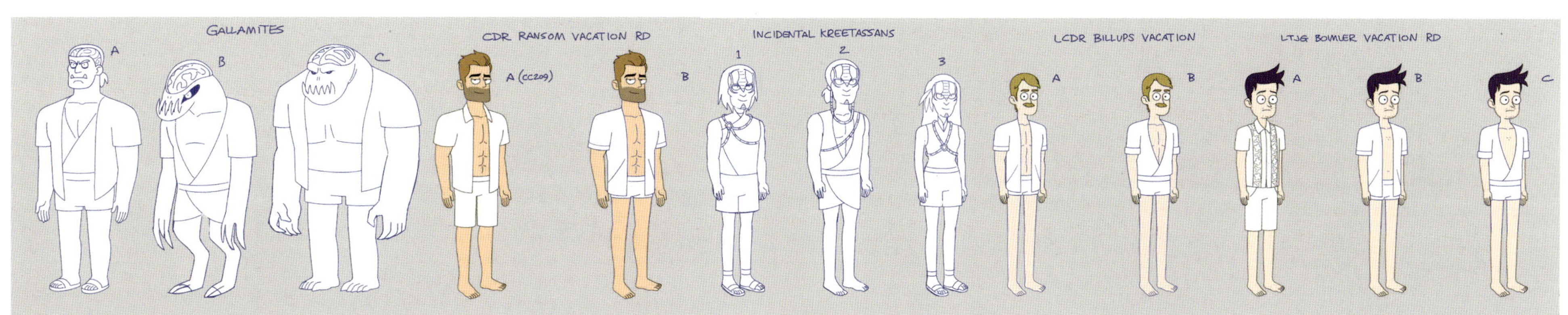
GALLAMITES
A
B
C
CDR RANSOM VACATION RD
A (CC209)
B
INCIDENTAL KREETASSANS
1
2
3
LCDR BILLUPS VACATION
A
B
LTJG BOIMLER VACATION RD
A
B
C

"In all the shots we have something organic and familiar in the environments, but also something sci-fi in the background. You can see hints of the honeycomb pattern we gave to the domes in the atmosphere of the environments."

— Nollan Obena

ADMIRAL MILIUS' QUARTERS

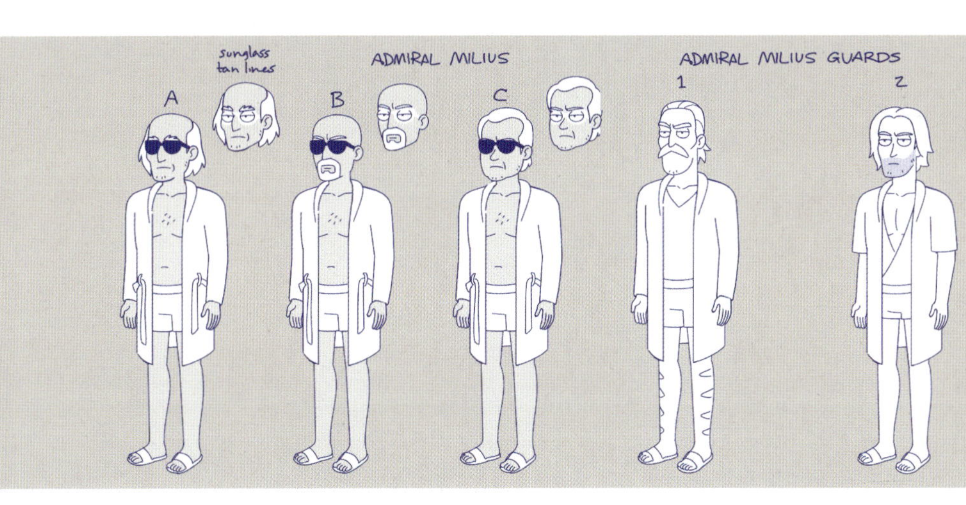

LCARS S5E4

AIRDATE: 20241107
STARDATE: UNKNOWN

"A Farewell to Farms"

Dr. Migleemo cooks up some hot dishes while Mariner prefers hers served cold.

We connect Mariner and Boimler with Ma'ah on a mission to chase down information about the quantum fissures. As a historical and cultural fan, Boimler of course geeks out over seeing the Warrior Pit and the Klingon Oversight Council.

This is another departure episode on Qo'noS. We wanted to expand on Ma'ah's story since "wej Duj" and "The Inner Fight" in previous seasons.

We now see Ma'ah with his brother Malor as bloodwine farmers, not warriors. What is life like for a Klingon if they are not warriors?

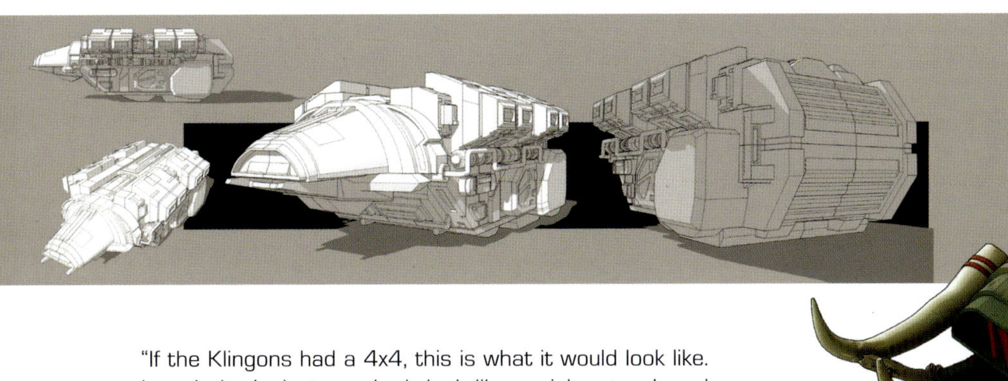

"If the Klingons had a 4x4, this is what it would look like. I made it clunky to make it look like a pickup truck and added the fog lights up above."

— Nollan Obena

QO'NOS

BARGH
K'ORIN
K'ELARRA
ENAJ

KLOWAHKA

"The Klowahka prison is like a bird cage. The species are foodies, so there are flying food trucks everywhere."

— Nollan Obena

LCARS S5E5

AIRDATE: 20241114
STARDATE: UNKNOWN

"Starbase 80?!"

Ransom uses too much disinfectant gel while Mariner gets paranoid about curses.

This episode takes place on Mariner and Freeman's most feared place: Starbase 80.

PROMENADE

OPERATIONS CENTER

KASSIA NOX

"After the main design language was established, how else can we make it terrible? Oh, let's just make the space brown, too. Let's make everything look terrible and depressing."

— Nollan Obena

One of our best new characters is Kassia Nox, who makes you understand why life on this station is not as bad as you think, and if you give everyone a chance they can be Starfleet material.

STARBASE 80 PHASER

STARBASE 80 PADD

PYRITHIAN BAT

BUGS

This was a fun clash with old and new *Star Trek*.

"Starbase 80 was probably my favorite. It was fun because it was going back into the TOS era and designing a starbase that basically hasn't progressed. Plus making everything dingy is pretty fun, too. We brought back the design language of TOS along with its lighting where there is an off-screen red light and an off-screen green light. And the super colorful pipes. That was always fun."

— Nollan Obena

But, like the *Cerritos*, don't discount Starbase 80. It might look bad, but it's actually better than you think.

We referenced the Tarchannen parasite from TNG: "Identity Crisis," which infected half of Dr. Harrison Horseberry before it was successfully removed.

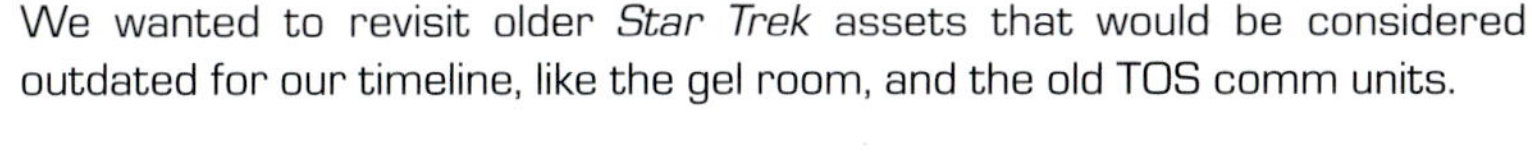
We wanted to revisit older *Star Trek* assets that would be considered outdated for our timeline, like the gel room, and the old TOS comm units.

N'OB'S
Lornak's
BAR

LCARS S5E6

AIRDATE: 20241121
STARDATE: 59482.3

"Of Gods and Angles"

Mariner teams up with a troubled ensign while the *Cerritos* hosts peace talks between civilizations.

This is a classic TNG episode referencing "Lonely Among Us" with two warring aliens on the same ship at the same time.

This was a true bottle episode, which takes place in familiar locations on the *Cerritos* with cubes and spheres as characters, thus allowing our design crew to catch up from an episode entirely on a new starbase.

ENS. OLLY

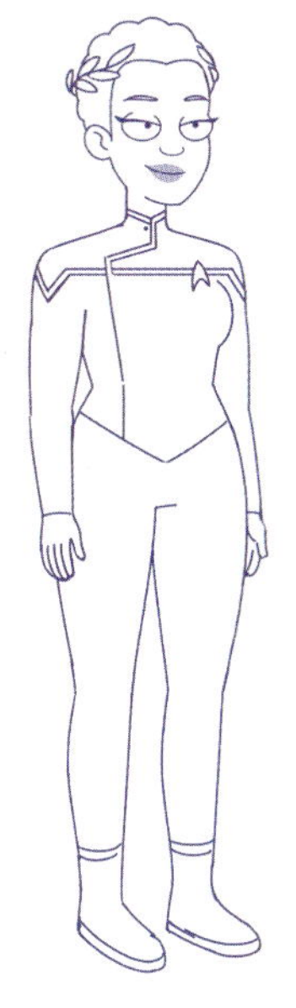

Ensign Olly is a callback to the TOS episode "Who Mourns for Adonais?" We wanted to show what it would be like to have Mariner working with an ensign seemingly similar to herself.

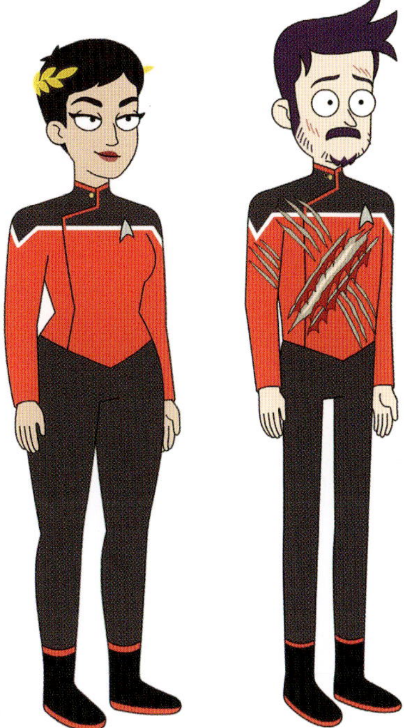

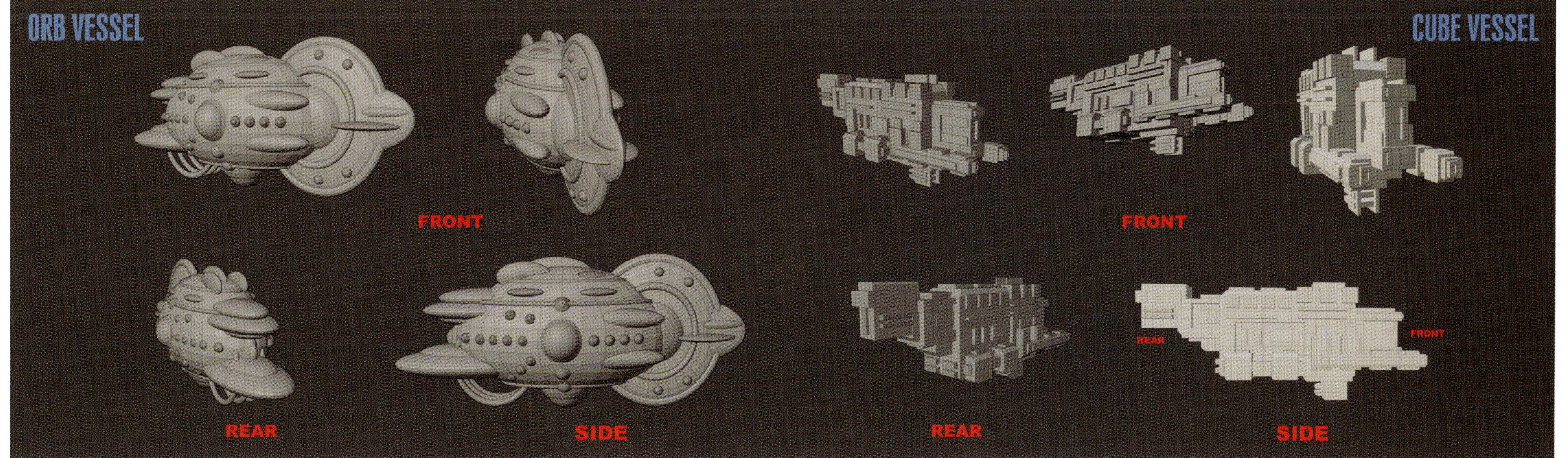

LCARS S5E7

AIRDATE: 20241128
STARDATE: 59499.6

"Fully Dilated"

It's a pre-warp-society undercover girls' trip!

This episode is a mixed reference to several episodes from *Star Trek: Enterprise* and TNG, including "Carbon Creek," "Who Watches the Watchers," "The Inner Light," and "Time's Arrow."

This is our third girls' trip episode, plus we added time dilation!

"We referenced the TNG 'Time's Arrow' episode. Mike wanted us to push it slightly further to suggest that this was an alien civilization and not simply a doppelgänger of an American town. Most of those modifications occurred later with the background design team finalizing the look of this episode."

— Denny Fincke

"The alien designs originally had tusks, but we had concerns about what the mouths would look like being animated. We tried placing them in different locations around the mouth, like on the jaws, but then we decided to go with ossicone-like antlers."

— Nollan Obena

"In this drawing, I referenced photos of the Lower East Side of New York City from the early 1900s for inspiration."

— Denny Fincke

We brought back Brent Spiner to play a purple-head version of Data.

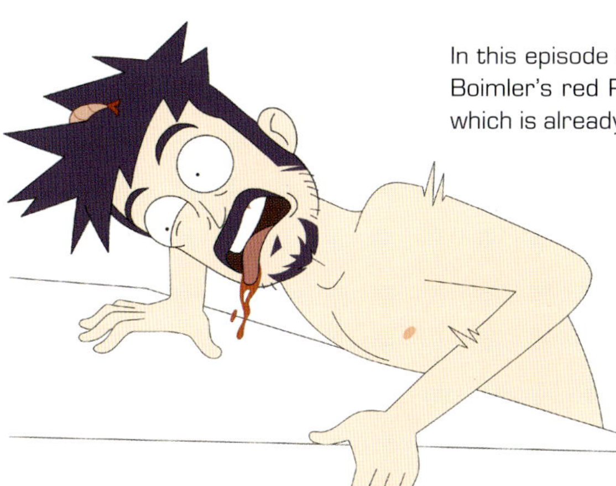

In this episode we see Rutherford is now following Boimler's red PADD, too, by growing out a beard, which is already more filled out.

We have a fun juxtaposition of the slow small-town life on Dilmer III and the frantic Rutherford and Boimler scenes as they try to get the transporter controls up and running again in a matter of seconds.

LCARS S5E8

AIRDATE: 20241205
STARDATE: UNKNOWN

"Upper Decks"

The Lower Deckers have a pumpkin-carving party while the bridge crew get the spotlight.

This was a true bottle episode, which took place in familiar locations on the *Cerritos*, thus allowing our crew to catch up from an episode that was mostly on a new planet.

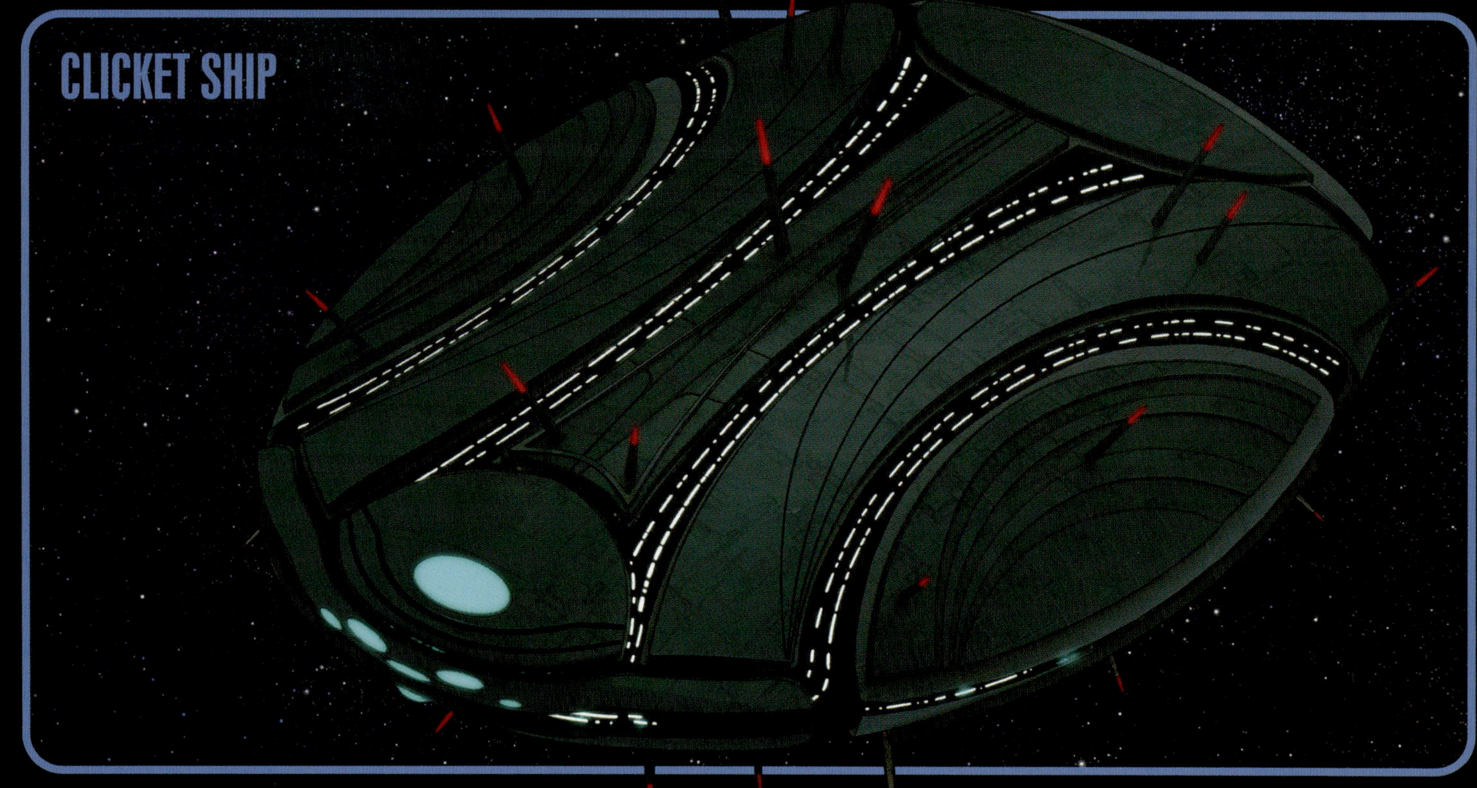

CLICKET SHIP

This is our inverse version of TNG's "Lower Decks" episode.

BUGHOON PLANET

CLICKET LEADER

PROFESSOR ZURKEL

We brought back the Clicket species, from season one's "Veritas," who hate being complimented.

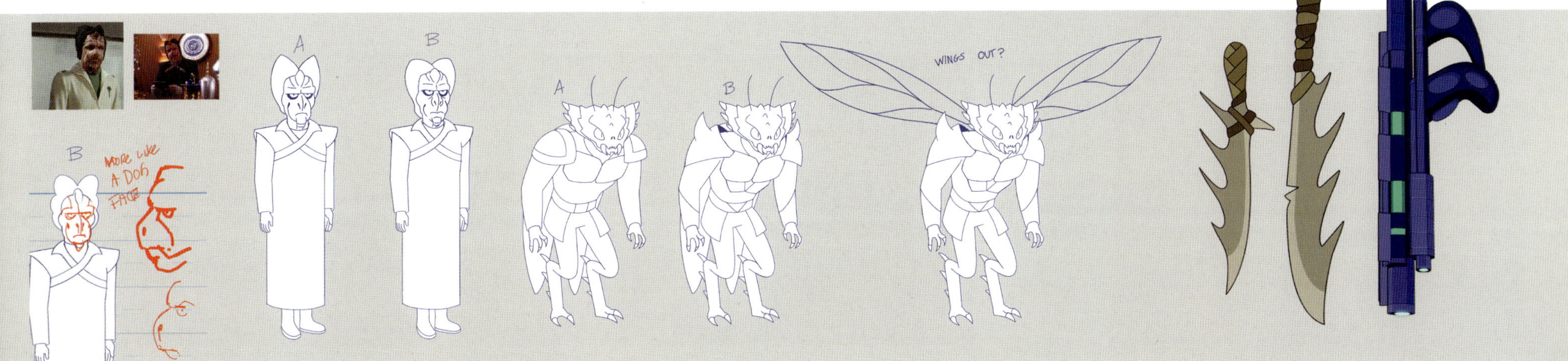

We wanted to show what it was like if the bridge crew were the main heroes of the show. What do their daily lives look like outside of the Lower Deckers story?

ENGINEERING GOLEM

ENS. MEREDITH

ADM. FREEMAN

ENS. BARNES

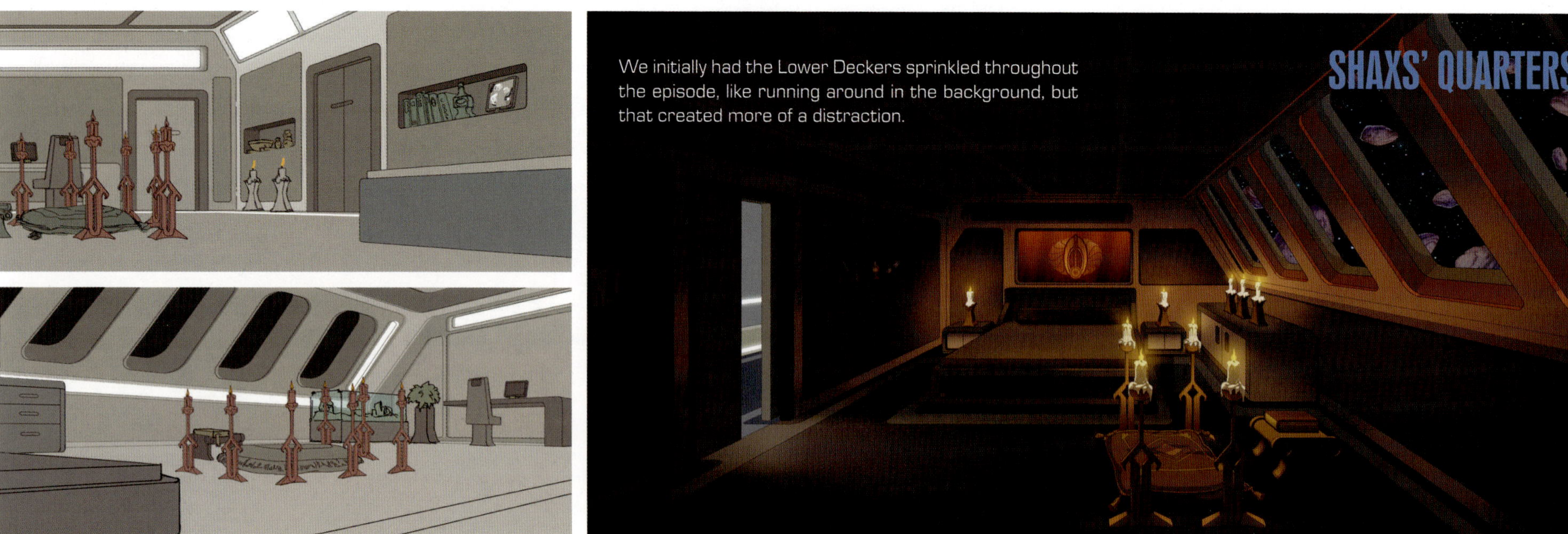

We initially had the Lower Deckers sprinkled throughout the episode, like running around in the background, but that created more of a distraction.

SHAXS' QUARTERS

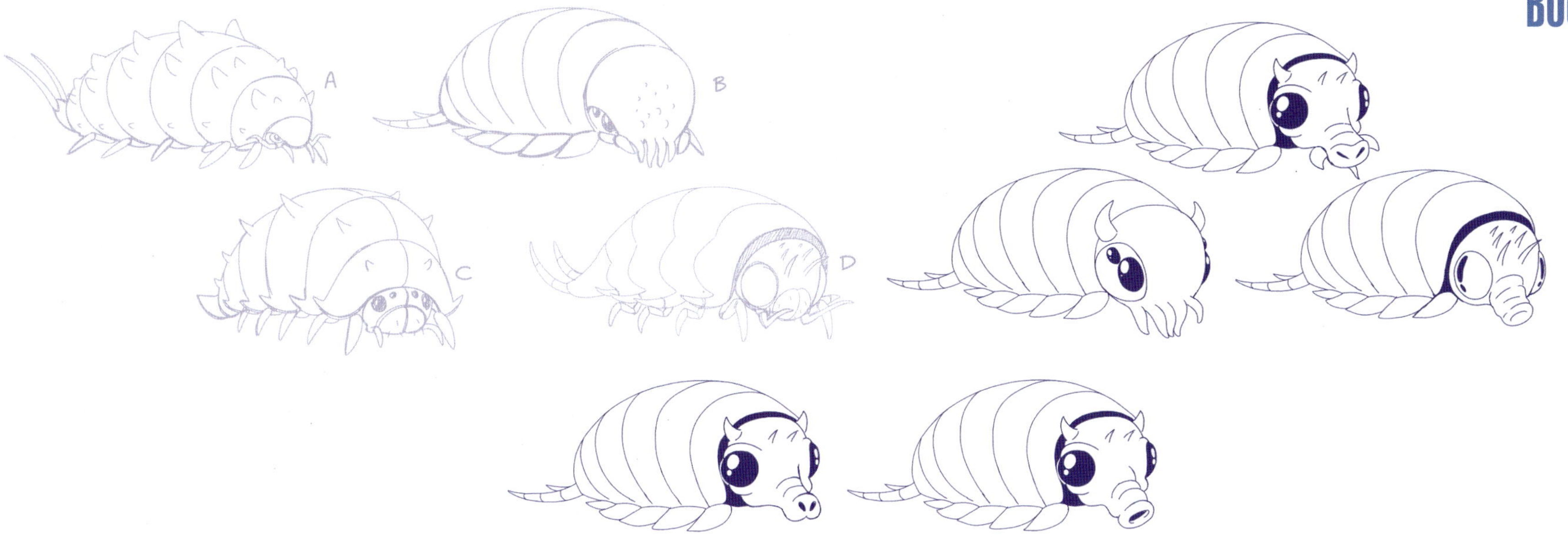

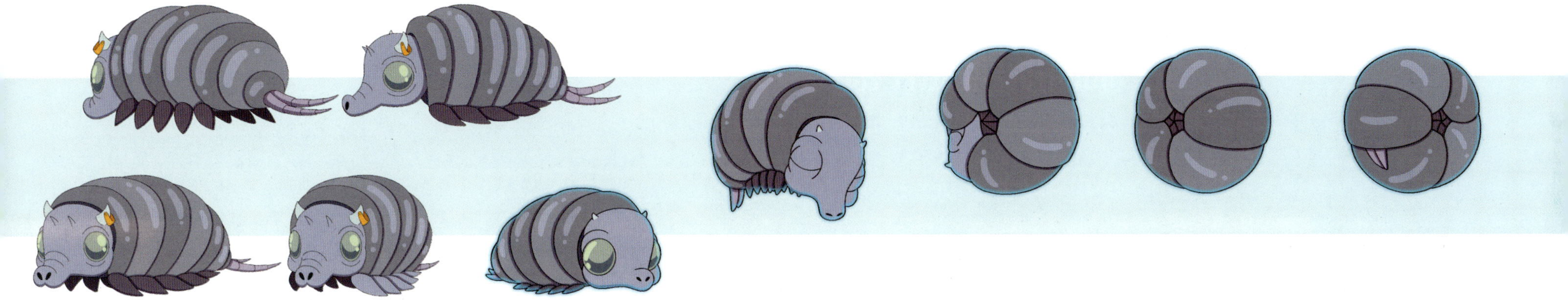

LCARS S5E9

AIRDATE: 20241212
STARDATE: UNKNOWN

"Fissure Quest"

Fissures must be closed before they get inflamed.

The point of this episode is that multiversal stories can be an effective storytelling tool. We see the relationship between Boimler and Mariner across different universes.

QUANTUM REALITY LCARS

U.S.S. ANAXIMANDER

This was a fun episode where we were able to bring back several legacy *Star Trek* actors to play their characters and live in the same timeline due to the multiverse.

ANAXIMANDER CREW

We brought back Jolene Blalock to play T'Pol, Alfre Woodard to play Lily Sloane, and Alexander Siddig to play an Emergency Medical Holographic Dr. Bashir, alongside Andrew Robinson, who played the romantic Elim Garak. Of course, Garrett Wang played all the Harry Kims aboard the *Anaximander*.

We revisit Khwopa and brought back the Khwopians from season two but altered the sweet aliens to be violent.

We designed several iterations of Harry Kim for the episode, and amongst the crew, we called one "Tall Socks Kim," but then later realized that we'd never have a chance to see his socks.

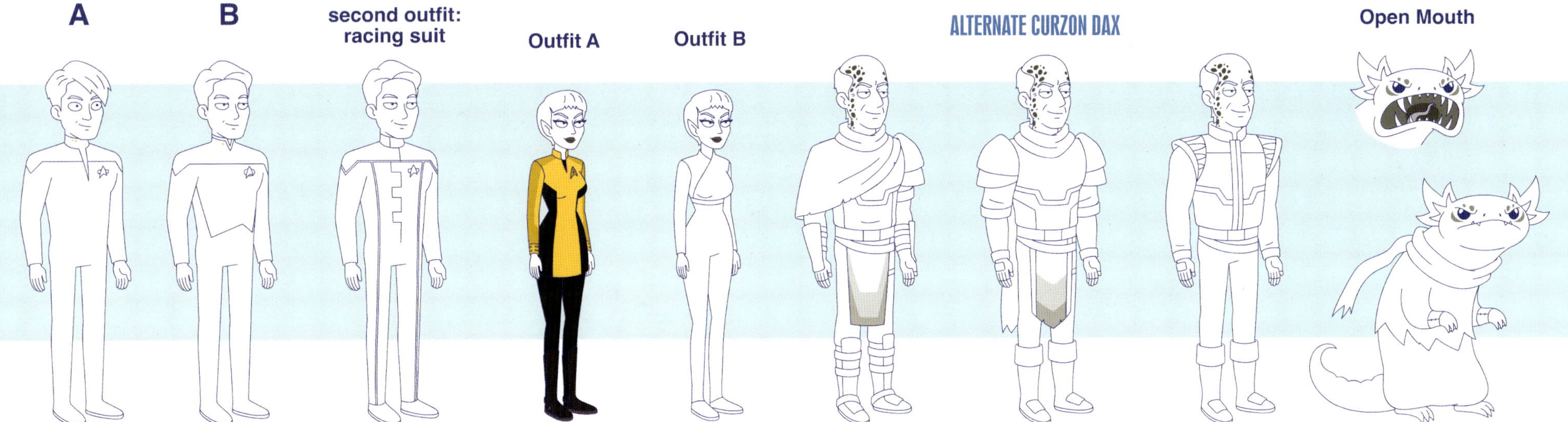

"The *Beagle's* backstory is a Vulcan and Earth combo ship, keeping in mind the Phoenix and Apollo 11. We like the '60s aesthetic, so we used the form of the NASA concept painting, but details are from the Phoenix and old ships, while adding a little Vulcan circle drive. One challenge we were facing was how do we get this ship to land? I needed to figure out what to do with the circular drive, so I broke it apart and made it make sense."

— Nollan Obena

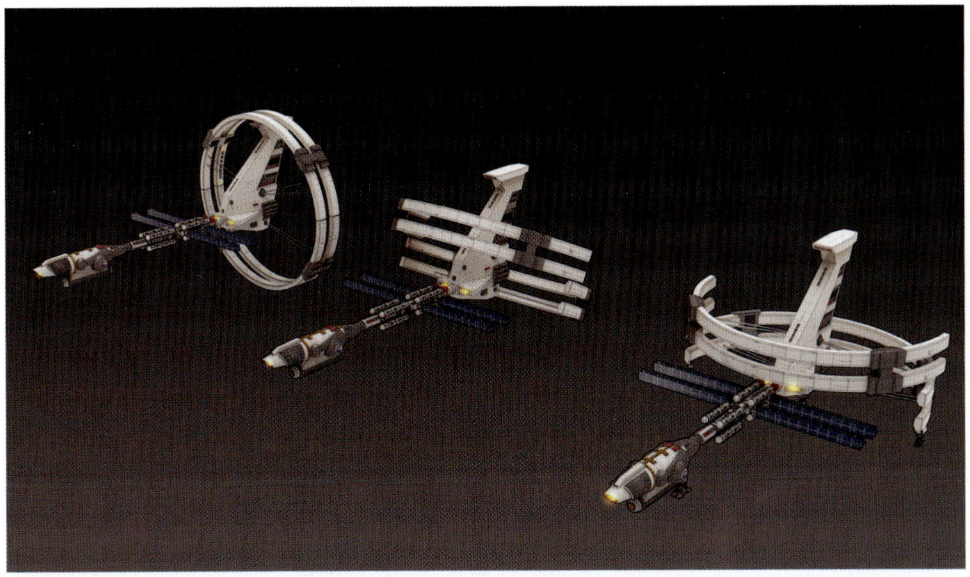

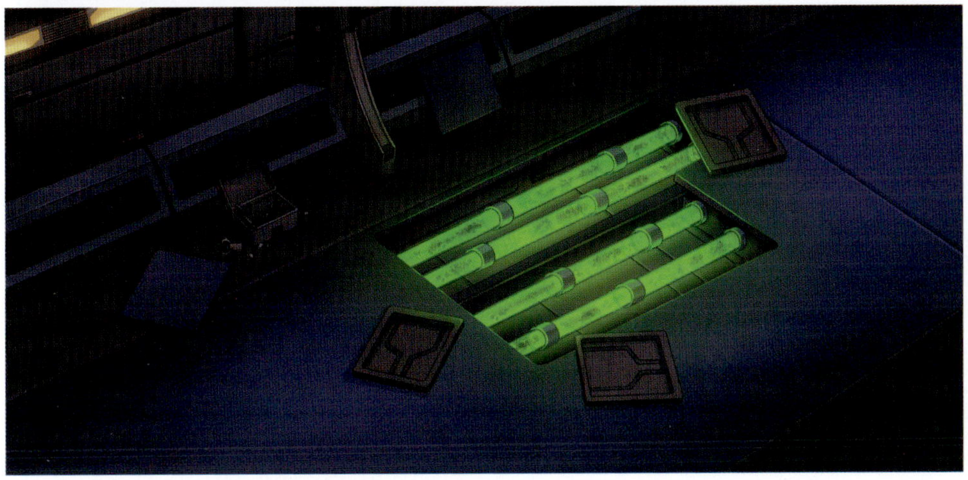

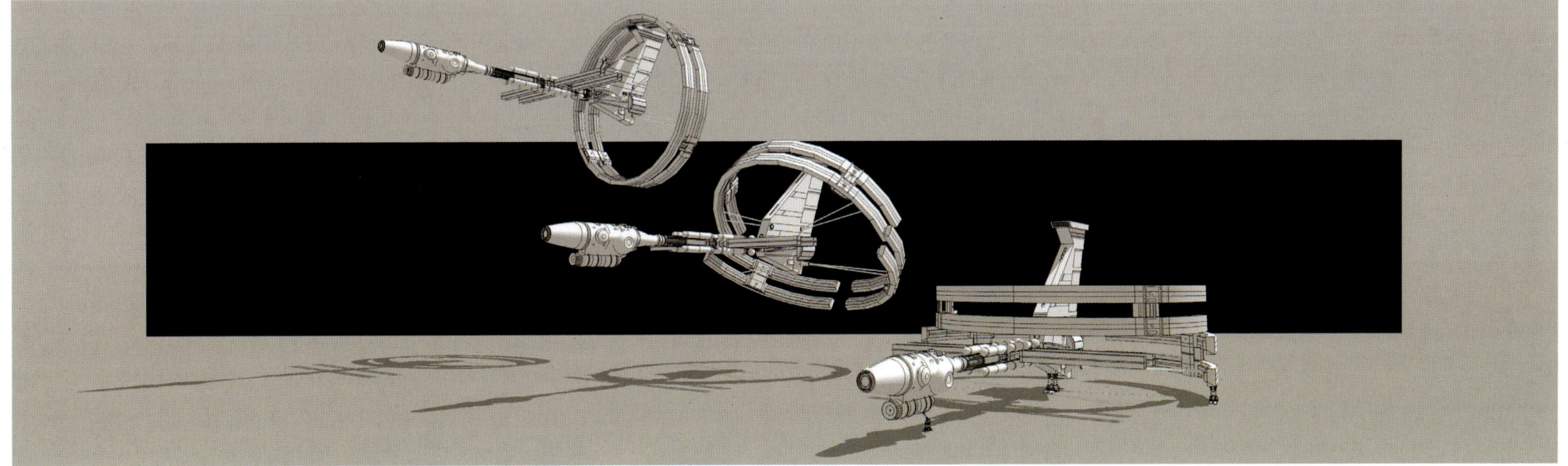

LCARS S5E10

AIRDATE: 20241219
STARDATE: UNKNOWN

"The New Next Generation"

Season finale where lots of wild stuff happens!

This season/series finale was another big ship-based ending where the *Cerritos* is turned into multiple options because of the quantum waves hitting them.

We knew when making this episode that it was going to be the end. So, we wanted to leave fans satisfied, but also open, for the characters to keep moving.

TERRAN *CERRITOS* BRIDGE

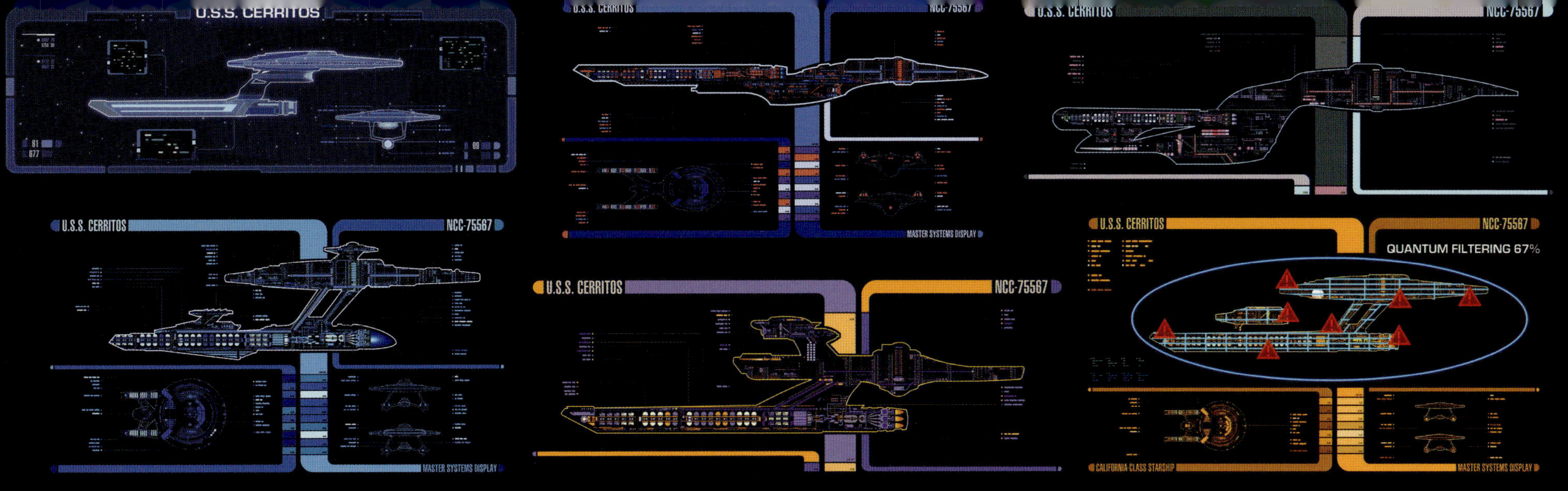

"Episode 510 was fun because we got to visit designs from *Discovery* and redesign the *Cerritos* several times."

— Nollan Obena

"While watching the animation, we realized that the single-nacelle *Cerritos* hits another field, so we needed to come up with something quick, like a color variation."

— Nollan Obena

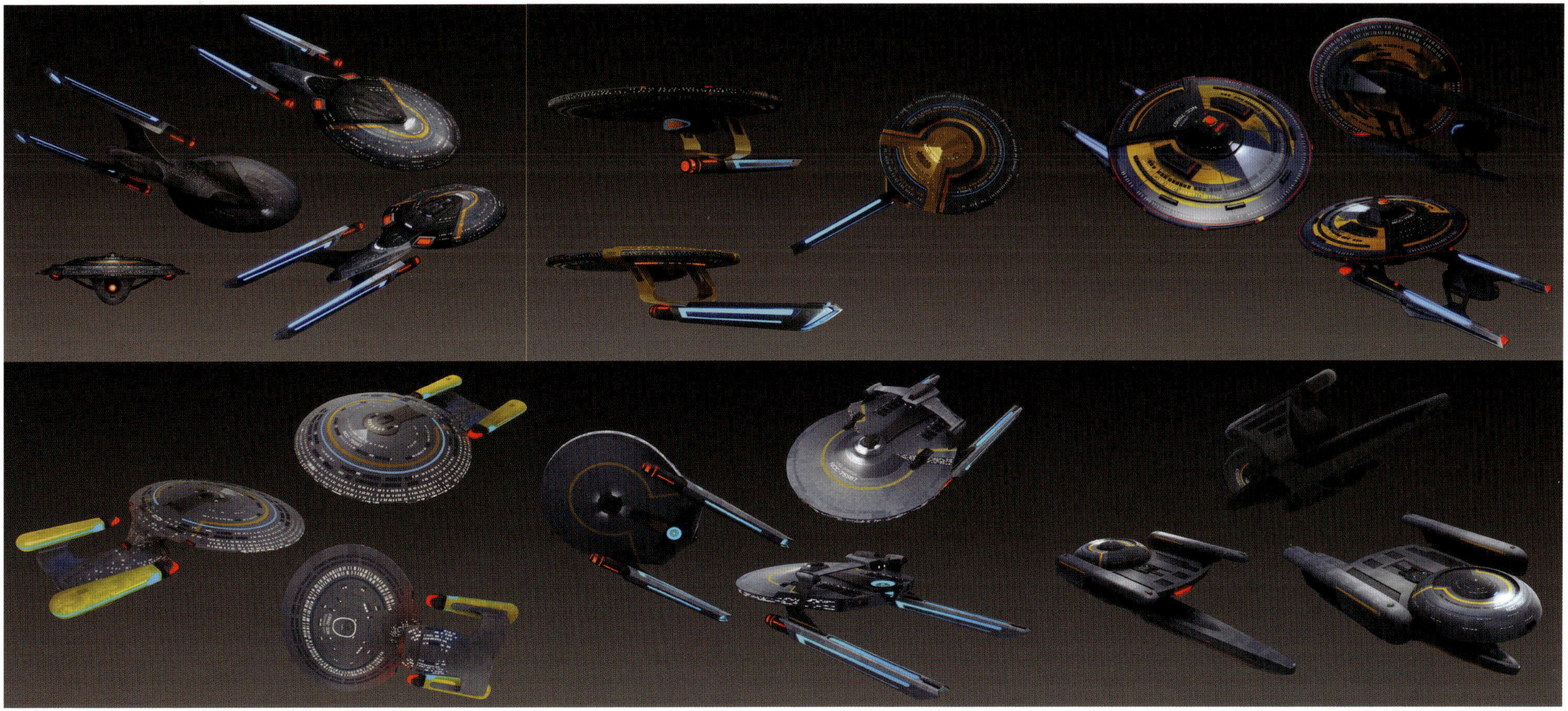

We brought back the Klingons with Ma'ah and Malor to help drive the episode story and show a cool space chase battle.

A

B

C

RELGA

Mariner gives a beautiful heart-filled speech on how the show wants you to feel about being a Lower Decker.

We have a new mission now with Ransom's ship and new ensigns with interesting things out there to still tell stories about. The Lower Deckers are always going to be Lower Deckers. The *Cerritos* is a Lower Decker. The *California* class is a Lower Decker. We see Captain Freeman moving to a new adventure while believing in Mariner and herself.

QUANTUM FISSURE

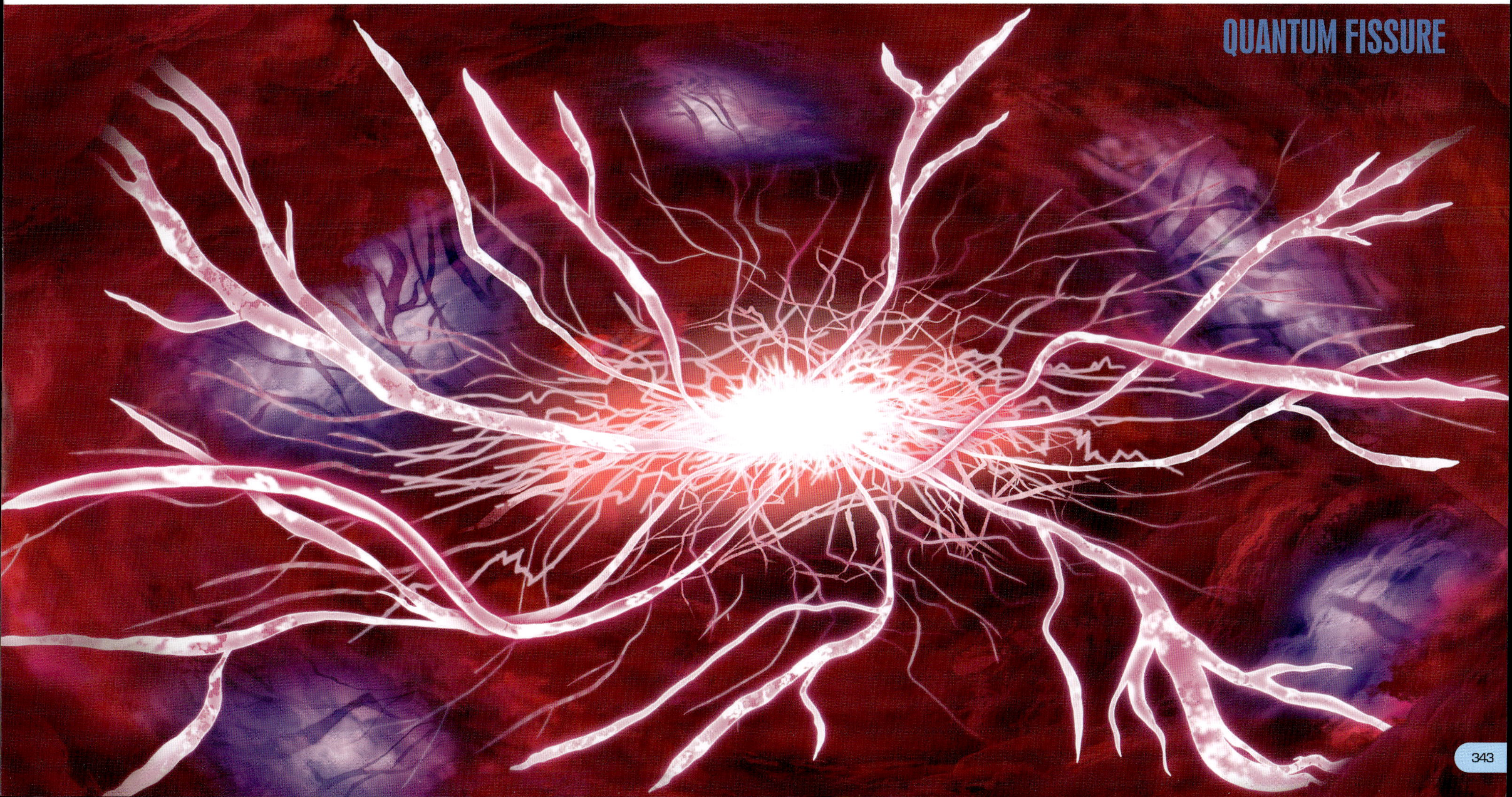

02-654598

LCARS 40274

We would like to thank the supremely talented artists who contributed to *The Art of Star Trek: Lower Decks* and helped make it such a beloved addition to the *Star Trek* universe.

Sherwin Abesamis
Manoela Veloso Argolo
Heather Arm
Kim Arndt
Grace Babineau
David Beall
Anthony M. Benedetto
Marcelo Bonifacio
Kyle Bowman
Kat Brechtel
Antonio Caggiano
Nikita Chan
Richard Chang
Breanna Cheek
Howard Chen
Jay T. Chen
Yudi Chen
Andy Chiang
Stacey Chomiak
Avery Christie
Ivy Chu
Liam Cobb
Keith Conroy
Robby Cook
Vincent Consenzo
Brandon Cuellar
Zan Czyzewski
Andrew DeLange
Anka Do
Francis Dooley
Miranda Dressler
Lais Tissiani Dutra
Erica Feld
Denny Fincke
Elizabeth Fuselier
Gerardo Garcia
Niko Guardia
Matthew Hernandez
Rebecca Hu
Julie Hyun
Hayley Kalberg
Reina Kanemitsu
Barry J. Kelly
Richard Kim
Sebastian Kings
Shay Klassen
Derek Kosol
Kevin Chiya Kuan
Laura Lalande
Matt Laskowski
Becky Lau
Khang Le
Juno Lee
Xiao Qi Lee
Claire Lenth
Melissa Levengood
Stephanie Liaw
Beatriz Lickfold
Felo Lira
Bijiao Liu
Lynn Liu
Marisa Livingston
Angela V Llerena
Michael Lockwood
Ivan Louey
Johnny Lu
Shay Luri
Miguel Macias
Michael Maglio
Ryan Magno
Dalia Mallet
Peter Markowski
Joseph Martinez
Audrey Masson
Kate Maxwell
Joey McCormick
Andrew McKeachie
Sophie McNalley
Eddy Andres Millan
Kenny Mok
Forrest Molloy
Mike Mullen
Philip Murphy
Kip Noschese
Eric Nyquist
Nollan Obena
Chinatsu Oyama
Elyssa Pahn
Olivia Pecini
Alexandre Pelletier
Mallory Pittman
Jennifer Poirier
Maribel Pozos
Pablo Rivera
James T. Robb
Sunny Shah
Kat Shea
Kirk Shinmoto
Kyle Shipman
Crystal Yoori Son
Amber Spillman
Bob Suarez
Antuanette Sun
Hui Sun
Mark Taihei
Sean Tourangeau
Amanda Turnage
Abby Jo Turner
Tuan Vo
Bobby Walker
Brandon Williams
Amanda Wong
Vicki Xu
Robert Zukiwsky
Jason Zurek